SAVAGES

Eenie, meenie, miny, moe.
Which DeAngelis has got to go?

Sheridan Anne
PSYCHOS: Depraved Sinners #1

Cover Design: Artscandare
Editing: Fox Proof Edits
Formatting: Sheridan Anne

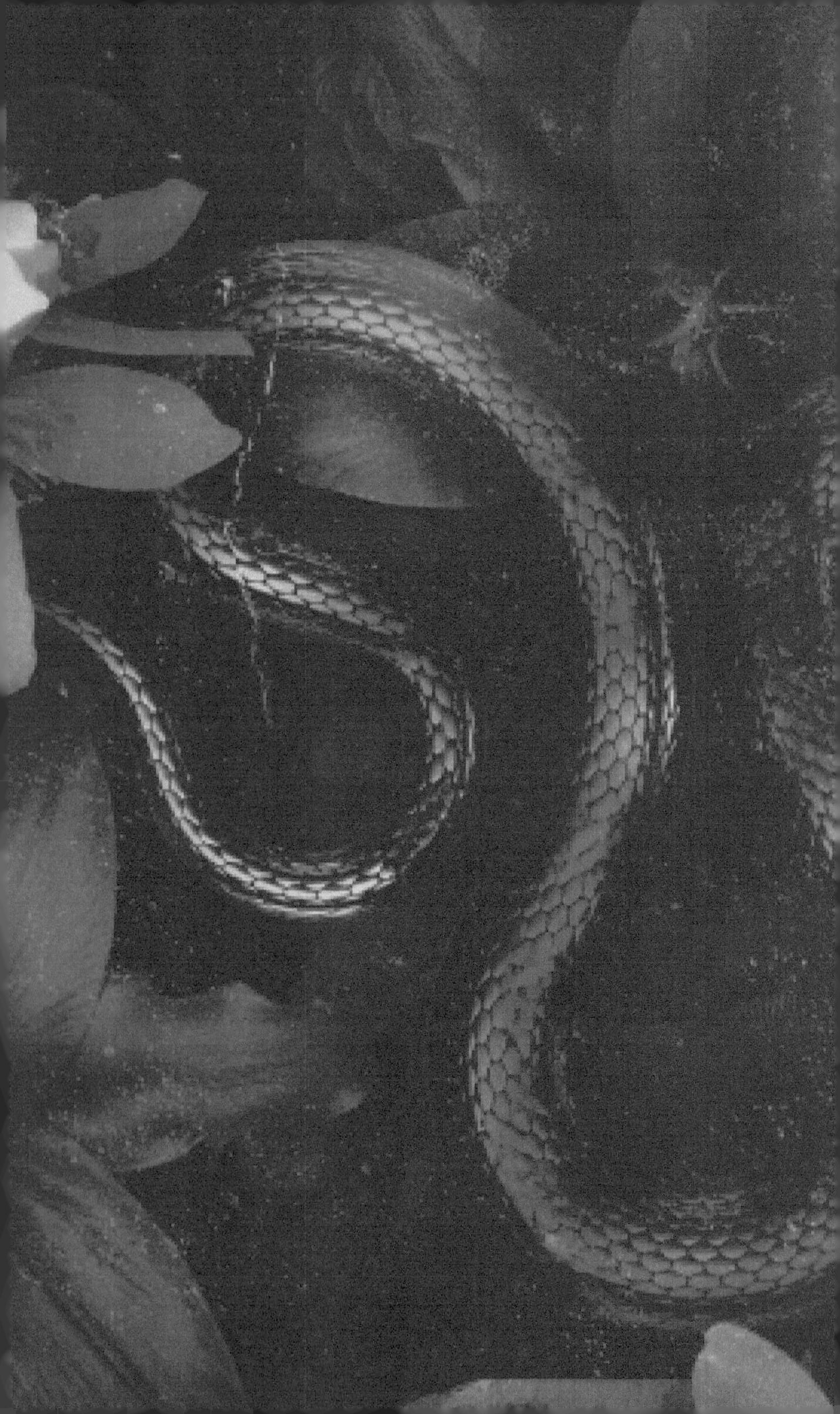

Because who doesn't want to get down and dirty with a few savages???

Also, here's a representation of the two stages of grief, following
THE ATHENS cliffhanger.

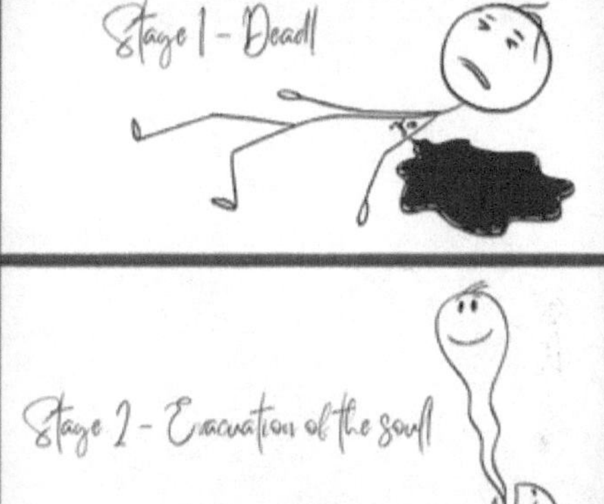
Stage 1 - Dead!
Stage 2 - Evacuation of the soul

CHAPTER ONE

LEVI

The sweet sound of bone crunching beneath my baseball bat does nothing to ease the fury rippling through my veins.

Someone knows where the fuck Shayne is, and I won't be leaving until I've cut out every last tongue that refuses to talk. Though I can't guarantee that my brothers or I won't end these bastards' miserable lives before we get around to finding out Shayne's location. What can I say? We're desperate, and you can't blame a desperate man for what he does with a weapon in his hand, especially when it comes to Shayne Mariano.

"I'm growing impatient," I rumble, my chest vibrating with anger as the sheer image of my father torturing Shayne makes my stomach churn with unease. God knows that girl has already suffered enough at our hands, she doesn't need my father's bullshit as well.

My stare pierces into the guard's dead eyes and there's no doubt that he's saying his final prayers. If this fucker doesn't start talking and tell me where the hell my girl is, he won't live to see another sunrise, let alone another fucking minute.

Who am I kidding? He could tell me everything I want to know and offer me a fucking door-to-door service to go and collect her and I still wouldn't let this asshole walk out of here alive. Even if he doesn't know a damn thing. That's just the price you pay for being one of my father's henchmen. This is the life you sign up for.

My father's guard spits a mouthful of blood at my feet and glares up at me through his thick row of dark lashes. "Go to hell."

Well, shit. Now he's gone and done it.

Rage pulses through me and I let out a roar as my bat swings toward his ribs with the kind of force that would have even my father worshiping at my feet. The bat crushes his ribs, and the satisfaction is barely enough to keep me breathing.

The guard cries out before quickly turning his pain into a low, furious growl, clenching his hands into tight fists. He sweats, his breath coming in short, sharp gasps as he clenches his jaw, trying not to scream as his bones shatter under my bat. I've got to give it to the guy, he's tough. He's putting in a good effort, but only a few short days ago, I looked him dead in the eye just moments before he shot taser prongs into Shayne's scarred, aching body, and dropped her to the ground in our fucking driveway. That image spurs me on.

Nobody takes from the DeAngelis brothers and gets away with it, especially not my father.

Watching him hold his tongue has irritation burning through my veins, and the helplessness begins to overwhelm me. It's been two days. Two long fucking days and every passing second is another second that we're letting her down.

My brothers fume silently behind me. They've tortured enough motherfuckers over the past forty-eight hours to know how this is going to end. One glance at Roman tells me that he's moments from stepping in and handling this himself, while a scathing look from Marcus warns me that he's about to break.

It's one thing to have one DeAngelis brother at breaking point, but to push all three of us to the edge and threaten to push us over, that means heads will roll, blood will be spilled, and patience will be tested—patience that not one of us possess.

The guard's head tilts up and he looks to the darkened ceiling, sucking short pants through his clenched jaw, and I don't doubt that his shattered ribs have punctured a lung. "Last warning before I cut out your tongue. Where the fuck is she?"

The guard roars, fighting against his binds, and as his eyes drop from the ceiling to meet mine once again, I know exactly how this is going to go. "Like I would ever tell you sick bastards."

I gently swing the bat in front of me, just enough to catch against his junk and watch the fear in his eyes as I lean into it, slowly crushing everything beneath it. "What a shame," I murmur, truly let down by his inability to make a good decision. "In another life, you would have made a good soldier for us. We would have even treated you well. A soldier who refuses to talk is an asset, but you're also a soldier who let his guard down enough to get captured, and that to us is nothing but a pain in the ass."

His breaths become more ragged and forced as his glare sharpens with hostility. "I will never work for you."

Marcus laughs and pushes off the bloodied counter, slowly striding toward our hostage as I ease off his balls and let the bat hang by my side. Marcus drops his gaze to the red scar across the top of his hand from where Shayne stabbed him and ultimately claimed his heart, and that one small gesture tells me that everything he does from this moment on is for her.

"Look at you, assuming you'll be able to make decisions like who you work for after this," Marcus mutters, walking around the guard until he's standing behind his chair, the harsh light gently rocking above them. "Let me be very clear. You will not be walking out of here alive. You will die here tonight, but it is your choice as to how that happens. It can be quick, or it can be the most brutal death any man could possibly experience. You know where he's keeping her. Just tell us what we need to know and we will be kind. Keep biting your tongue though, and Roman will tear out your throat with his bare hands."

Roman straightens beside me at the thought of brutally murdering this man.

"I ain't saying shit," the guard spits, flinching away from Marcus as he inches even closer.

"Such a fool," Marcus laughs. "Are you that terrified of our father, or do you foolishly believe that you owe him your loyalty?"

The guard clenches his jaw and studiously stares across the room, avoiding eye contact, and our answer is crystal clear. This man is a little bitch with no backbone and absolutely no sign of a set of balls. Fuck, Shayne has a bigger set of balls than this guy.

Roman inches closer, slipping his hand deep into his pocket and gripping the long, steep pin that I know he's hiding in there. He glances down at the pathetic excuse of a man with nothing but disgust. "You're an idiot to fear our father over us. You do not owe him your loyalty. After all, he knows you're here and he's left you to die. He's not coming to save you. Nothing will stand in our way of ending your life tonight, so be smart about this. Tell us what we need to know, and you will die quickly, otherwise, you will learn the hard way that all those stories, all those whispers you've always heard about us are true."

The guard swallows hard but his dickish, stubborn nature keeps his mouth shut.

Roman pulls the long metal pin from his pocket and I take a step to the side. "I'm going to ask you one more time," Roman warns, his tone thick with venom. "Where is Giovanni keeping Shayne Mariano?"

The guard raises his chin in defiance and a wicked grin stretches over his lips. "That mouth of yours sure would look good wrapped around my cock."

Ahhh, fuck. We're in for a long night.

Roman laughs and the sound sends a shiver down my spine. "If you wanted to suck my dick, all you needed to do was ask."

The guard tenses and Marcus leans over him, pressing his hands over the guy's wrists, keeping him still as Roman steps right in front of him. My jaw clenches, every moment of Roman's dramatics just adding another second before I can finally get to my girl.

The guard lowers his gaze, assuming that Roman is about to whip his cock out and force him to swallow it, but he would never. Roman has shoved his dick into the most questionable places over the years, but he'd never risk it getting bitten off like this. Though, if it sends a wave of panic soaring through the guard's veins, then I'm all for it. Besides, Roman wouldn't shit all over Shayne by giving this guy something that so clearly belongs to her, despite how much they both deny it. Roman has one hell of a serious hard-on for that girl, and that's only made clearer by the way he takes the guard's pointer finger and presses the tip of the pin just below his nail.

The guard frets, fighting around both Marcus and Roman's hold, but he's trapped, his broken ribs and punctured lung making his efforts laughable.

"Tell us where he's keeping her," I mutter, my voice dark and filled with a lethal promise to destroy him.

Roman waits a beat, but when he refuses to respond, he presses against the pin, piercing through the tip of his finger and pushing it deep below the surface. The pin scrapes along the bone and I watch with a sick satisfaction as I see it moving below the skin.

The guard roars, tears springing from his eyes, and Marcus laughs in his ear. But I can't tear my eyes away. My heart races, the sick sense of torture filling my veins with an addictive power. The pin plunges right down to the guard's knuckle and I smile, knowing the one quick move from Roman would have the pin tearing right through his flesh with his whole nail detaching and flying across the room. I bet he could even hit the far wall with that little bastard.

Fuck, that's gotta hurt. I've been on my big brother's bad side more times than I can count, but I've never pissed him off enough to try this shit on me. He wouldn't though. Blood is thicker than water, and no matter what, we have one another's backs.

The guard wails, growing weaker by the second, and Roman releases the pin, leaving it protruding from his finger. "What's it going to be?" he questions. "Still have tight lips or is that tongue of yours gonna loosen up?"

The guard glances away and Roman laughs before curling his fingers and gently flicking the end of the pin sending a searing wave of pain through the guy's finger. I can't help the smirk that stretches across my lips. Roman's always had a way with torture that Marcus and I simply don't possess. Marcus is wild and gets carried away. The second he sees just a little bit of blood splatter, there's no controlling him. He's gotta decorate the whole fucking room. Me? I like my kills simple. Straight to the point where I don't have to clean up afterward, though if the crime calls for a messy punishment, then I'm more than happy to play along.

Roman though, he likes his victims begging for mercy and believes that if they're not still cursing his name in hell and making the dead fear him, then he didn't do his job well enough.

Knowing the guy isn't about to talk, Roman digs into his pocket again and pulls out a second pin. I roll my eyes. If the first pin didn't get him talking, then the second pin isn't going to work. This one is purely for fun.

Roman steps right between the guy's knees and bends to meet him eye to eye before reaching to his belt buckle. Not a word is said as Roman strips the man of his belt and pulls his jeans down to his knees. He looks down at the small appendage flopped against his right thigh, and his face twists with disgust. Roman holds out the pin between them, giving the guard a close-up view of it, letting him see just how thick, long, and sharp it really is. "Have you ever played pin the tail on the donkey?" Roman muses as the guy's eyes go wide with crippling fear. "Our version is a little different. Just as fun though."

"It's okay," Marcus murmurs in his ear. "It's not like you're going to be able to use it after this anyway."

The guard whimpers, his brows creasing with fear as Roman reaches down and takes the guy's limp dick in his hand. I let out a sigh, never happier that Roman drew the short straw on this one. I can't say that I envy him right now, though knowing Roman, he's looking past the fact that he has another man's dick in his hand and is already getting off on the fear he's invoking.

What can I say? Roman might be the most cautious and put together of the three of us, but he's just as sick as Marcus.

The tip of the pin presses to the tip of his dick and Roman grins before slowly glancing up to meet the guard's eyes. He's sweating, knowing just what this means for him, not that it matters. The only way he'll be leaving this warehouse is in a body bag.

He shakes his head, pleading with my eldest brother to spare him the agony, but Roman isn't one to pick up subtle clues. "Please," he whimpers, tears brimming in his bloodshot eyes. "No. Please. No."

Roman arches a brow and as Marcus holds him down, he pushes the sharp tip of the pin into the small opening at the tip of his dick. The guard screams out, his blood-curdling tone echoing through the empty warehouse. "STOP. STOP. Please. I'll do anything."

Roman doesn't relent. He already knows what we want.

Marcus' hand goes under his throat as my fingers curl around the knife on the counter behind me, the baseball bat long forgotten. Marcus yanks his head back, meeting his terrified eyes as Roman pushes the pin deeper into his junk. "WHERE THE FUCK IS SHE?" Marcus roars.

The guard cries. "I … I don't know," he says, tears streaming down his face. "I only heard whispers."

Roman pushes deeper. "Tell me what I want to know, and I can make it all go away."

"A cabin," he rushes out, his breathing labored and strained.

Roman lowers his face, his jaw clenched in frustration. "Where?" he spits.

"I … I … I don't know. In the desert somewhere. They don't tell me anything," he sobs.

Then just like that, Roman tears the pin from his dick and the guy lets out a strained breath, but his relief is short-lived as I move into Roman's spot and slit his throat with one simple flick of my wrist. Roman drops the bloodied pin and reaches out, then just as Marcus promised, Roman pushes his hand through the opening of his wound and tears his throat out, ending the guard's miserable life.

"Well, fuck," Marcus spits, releasing the guy's head and stepping back only to wipe the blood from his hands onto the guy's shirt. "She's in the desert? How the hell are we supposed to find her out there?"

Roman shakes his head, dropping the guard's throat at his feet and shaking the remaining blood off his hand as though it disgusts him. "No fucking idea," he mutters, his jaw clenched, knowing that while we got the answers we were looking for, it's only left us ten steps back. "I wasn't even aware that Father had a cabin, but I'm not surprised. This is just the kind of shit he'd do to fuck with us."

Tossing the knife back onto the counter, I let out a frustrated breath. "If only she still had that fucking tracker…"

"Yeah," Marcus scoffs, stepping around the bound body and grabbing the front of my shirt. "Whose fault is that? If you two bastards hadn't put your fucking hands on my girl, we wouldn't be in this situation."

Guilt soars through my chest. He's right. Roman and I chose not to trust her when Marcus was lying in bed bleeding out from a gunshot wound and look where the fuck that got us. I now know better than to question Shayne's word, but it was a lesson we all learned in the worst possible way. She tells me she's moved past it, but even now, when I catch her off guard and move even an inch, the way she flinches kills me.

But after what I did, what Roman did, I'd give up everything I have just to make sure she's safe. Fuck, I would have done that anyway, but now, I owe her a lifetime of service. I would drop to my knees and give her the heart right out of my chest if she asked for it, even if her intention was to crush it.

"Lay off it," Roman demands, not in the mood to have this same conversation we've had a million times over the past few weeks, each time ending the exact same—Marcus wants to kill me, and fuck it, I almost let him. If it weren't for how badly I want to see Shayne soar, then I'm sure I would have allowed him to do his worst already.

Roman steps between me and Marcus and pushes him back. "We're both at fault for what happened to Shayne, but don't act like you didn't know about that fucking tracker. You know every scar on her body, you knew it was gone the moment you saw her. We should have fit her with a new one before we went to that tomb party. We all let her down. Now stop fucking moping about it and help me figure out a way to locate this goddamn cabin or I swear to God, Marc, I'll leave you on the ground right beside this motherfucker."

Marcus clenches his jaw, hating nothing more than having our big brother put him in his place, but Roman is right. These extra moments wasted getting pissy at each other and playing the blame game isn't getting us anywhere closer to Shayne, and in a world like this, every second counts.

CHAPTER TWO

The putrid tang of Felicity's decaying body rests in my nose and makes me gag. Though after two days of this, I figured I'd be used to it by now. Nope, what a load of bullshit that was. I will never be used to this. The heat swirling around the cells doesn't help either. It's like a sauna of rotting flesh and maggots in here.

The pools of blood kept this dingy cell damp for most of yesterday, inviting all the bugs until the harsh desert heat finally began drying things out, which included Felicity's blood all over my clothes and skin.

I've never felt so disgusted in my life, which surely makes me an awful person seeing as this poor woman beside me lost her life only a short forty-eight hours ago after pushing out a baby—Roman's baby at that. But on the other hand, it's decaying flesh, and it's the worst thing in the world.

Guilt soars through me at the thought. I shouldn't be focusing on the smell. I should be focused on getting out of here and keeping myself away from her body. I don't want to disrespect her in any way because when the boys eventually come for me, they're going to want to bury her properly, and I can only imagine the foul comments and snide remarks I'd receive from Roman if I were to harm her body in any way by trying to push her aside.

Fuck. What the hell is wrong with me?

She just died after being held hostage and giving birth in a cell. Her baby was stolen from my very arms just moments after promising her that I would keep him safe. I'm a walking fucking curse.

The thought of her stolen baby, Roman's precious newborn son, has my gaze shifting over her face for the millionth time. I've been in this cramped cell for two days now, and to be honest, there's really nothing else to look at down here, apart from the bitch who lives across the narrow, damp hallway.

My gaze rests on Felicity's face and it's clear to see why Roman was so in love with her. With a bit of color in her cheeks and clean, volumized hair, she would have been stunning. But the version of her that I met was a haunted ghost of the woman she used to be. What sucks is that after all this time, the boys thought she was dead, and they didn't even try to look for her. They could have saved her from this. They could have given her the world and Roman would have raised his baby and played happy little family.

They'll come for me. I can feel it in my bones, in my chest, they're going to come. They won't leave me here to rot. They're my only shot.

All I know is that when they come, I need to be ready because a move like this is going to ensure a war, a war much bigger than the bullshit family killing spree going on. The boys won't just roll over and accept it like they've trained to do with everything else in their lives. They'll seek vengeance and I'll be right there to watch it happen.

I need to be ready.

Taking a breath, I lean back against the dirty ground, closing my eyes to imagine that I'm somewhere else, that I'm not lying next to a decaying corpse, that whenever I move, bits of dried blood flakes don't pick up in the dust and coat my dirty skin.

My hands hover by my face and I clench my nonexistent abs before letting out a slow breath and rising into a sit-up. I lower myself back down and try to picture the boys' perfect faces, their wicked smirks when they're about to tear someone's flesh into bright red ribbons, their bodies, and the way they make me come alive under their skillful touch.

My stomach clenches, and just when I start to feel the familiar burn, an unwanted sound fills the underground cell. "What the fuck are you doing?"

My eyes snap open and I stare up at the dirty ceiling, knowing damn well that I would rather have heard Giovanni's voice than hers.

Ariana McFuckface … shit, I can't even remember her last name. How appalling of me. Have the boys even offered me one? Maybe she took on DeAngelis after marrying Giovanni. I wouldn't be surprised. She's always drooled over DeAngelis dick. Though, I can't say I blame her. It's not like I'm any different. Those DeAngelis boys really do know how to use their equipment, and damn, it's some mighty fine equipment they have.

I let out a heavy sigh and sit up, leaning back against my dirty hands as I glare across the cells to find Ariana's scrunched up face. "Working out," I throw back at her. "What does it look like I'm doing?"

She rolls her eyes, just as clearly frustrated by conversing with me as I am by her. "I know what a fucking workout is, dipshit. I meant why. What's the point? We're going to die down here. Your precious little boy toys aren't coming to save us, and you can hardly expect that Giovanni is going to keep paying these assholes to keep us here. He'll want them back to serve as his protection detail. They'll go at a moment's notice and leave us to starve."

I laugh, allowing a wicked smirk to cut across my face. "That's cute that you think the boys will save you too."

Her glare hardens and I let out a sigh, wanting this conversation over sooner rather than later. "I want to be ready. When the boys come, they'll come guns blazing, and if I need to do my part, then I want to be ready for it."

Ariana raises a brow and looks at me like a naive little child who thinks the world will be handed to her on a silver platter. "And if they don't come?"

I shrug my shoulders, knowing that's not the case. They'll come no matter what they have to risk. I have absolute faith in them despite our rocky and questionable past. "They will."

She rolls her eyes and mutters something under her breath. "For fuck's sake. Do you always shit rainbows and unicorns? You know life doesn't always work out how you think it will, right? Nothing is ever a guarantee in this life, and the quicker you learn that the better. Otherwise, you're leading yourself toward disappointment."

"Holy fuck," I grumble, lying back down to start another round of sit-ups, my determination knowing no bounds. "Have you always been a bitter asshole or has that just come with age?"

"I swear to God, Shayne. If I ever get out of here, I will strangle you."

"You're not," I mutter, feeling the burn deep in my stomach. "You're never getting out of here, and I'll personally make sure of it. When the boys come for me, and they will, we will happily walk away from you. You deserve so much worse than this after your bullshit stunt with Lucas Miller."

Ariana leans back against the wall and reaches for her toes, clearly cramping in her little cell just as I am, only she doesn't have to share hers with a corpse, though I guess that's on me. "Fuck me," she breathes. "You're such a fucking brat. I don't know what those boys see in you. You're a child with a chip on your shoulder. I'm a goddamn woman."

"Correction," I say through deep breaths, stopping at the top of my sit-up to meet her hard stare. "You're a desperate whore. There's a big difference."

She ignores my comment and holds my stare a minute longer. "Would you just … stop. You have these massive blinders on, like it's not possible for you to see through the boys' bullshit. They're not invincible, you know. They're just men, and one of these days, someone is going to get the better of them. Besides, if they were coming for you, then where the hell are they? It's been two days. They probably think you're dead," she says, her gaze flicking toward the dead body by my side, "just like they thought she was."

A shiver trails down my spine. It's completely possible they think I'm dead. That it was all in my head and they don't care for me as much as I hoped. That they have absolutely no intention of coming for me, or that I was just another one of the many girls on their list that have come and gone, whose name they can't remember, but the moment I start believing that is the moment I give up on any kind of future I have with them. They're coming for me. I know they will.

I shake my head, the words feeling alien on my tongue. "If something happens and they don't come, then … fuck, I don't know. I'll get out on my own. I'll figure out a way, but if that time comes, I will be ready, and when I do free myself from this fucked-up little cell, just know there is no way in hell I'll be taking you with me."

Ariana rolls her eyes. "Wow, what a shocker, but don't stress about it. I'd rather die down in this cell than owe you my life."

"Good, I'm glad we agree on that. Besides, I'm not one to carry around dead weight."

She raises a brow. "Excuse you?"

An unladylike scoff comes bounding out of my mouth. "You heard me. It's a fucking desert out there. You wouldn't get a hundred feet before collapsing in a dirty heap and crying about it. You'll walk your ass back here and hand yourself over. You don't have what it takes to see it through, which is probably why Roman never fought for you. You're weak, and a man like that needs a real woman by his side, not someone who will crumble and bitch out under the pressure."

Feeling way too proud of my jibe, I lower myself back down and continue my workout, thinking of nothing but my list of things I need to accomplish.

Get out of here.

Slit Giovanni's throat.

Save Roman's baby.

I repeat my list over and over as though my repetition can somehow make it all happen, and with each sit-up I do, I catch Ariana's curious eyes still on me.

"What?" I snap, needing a moment to rest and not liking the way she watches me. "I'm not some frightened little bitch anymore, so you can guarantee that I'm not about to crawl through Felicity's dried blood to fuck you through the bars. Besides, you're really not my type."

She lets out a frustrated groan, and I can only imagine what the other women locked up deeper in the cells must think of our fucked-up little relationship. "You really need to get over yourself. I didn't eat your pussy just so I could taste you. I did it to prove to the boys just how easily I could take their toys."

"No matter what your reasoning, you deserve a bullet through the head for that. Ever heard of this crazy concept called consent?"

Ariana's brows drop low. "I'm not a rapist."

"Aren't you?"

Ariana scoffs. "And to think I was about to tell you that I can finally see why the boys are so infatuated with you."

I narrow my stare, but she's got me hook, line, and sinker. "What the hell is that supposed to mean?"

She lets out a deep sigh and adjusts herself on her cell floor, the sheer layer of sweat coating her skin glistening in the harsh fluorescent light. Her gaze drops to Felicity, not wanting to meet my hard stare. "What you did for her," she starts. "I know I sure as hell wouldn't have risked my life to do that. You were out of the fucking cell. You could have run, but you chose to stay and help her. You're stronger than I gave you credit for. You surprised me, and again when refusing to let go of that baby. You would have given up your own life if it meant saving him."

I narrow my stare on her, not liking the sudden change in her tone. It's impossible to know if the words spewing from her mouth are honest or not, but either way, she is trying to soften me up, trying to get in my good graces in the hopes that maybe I might take pity on her and save her ass when I eventually get out of here.

"Any woman who would run instead of helping another like I did, in my eyes, isn't a woman at all," I tell her, unable to resist sparing a glance toward the woman I couldn't save. "Now cut the shit. I don't want to hear your stupid attempts to manipulate me. You're a liar, and no amount of buttering me up is going to save you. You could have a fucking crown on your head and the most prestigious title to your name, but after setting me up to take the fall with Lucas Miller, I still wouldn't save you."

She leans back against the hard stone wall, her curious gaze unwavering. "You're stronger than the other girls they've kept. Perhaps that's why you've made it this far."

I scoff. "I made it this far because I know how to run fast."

A grin pulls at the side of her lips, and I glance away, positive that she's finding amusement in her little bullshit game, laughing at my expense which only cements the fact that I will allow her to rot and starve in these cells right alongside Felicity. Though, Roman won't let that happen … the Felicity part, that is.

"They're going to make you their queen, aren't they?" she questions, drawing my attention back to her.

My brows crease as I watch her. "What's that even supposed to mean? Being their queen?"

She looks at me in that same 'you're a naive little brat who doesn't deserve what she's got' way before letting out a heavy sigh. "It means that once they overtake their father's reign, they will make sure that not only they worship you, but the whole fucking company does. You will be the center of everyone's world and in return, you will have the biggest target on your back."

I scoff, not at all impressed. "I've worn a target on my back since the second they brought me into this world."

Ariana laughs. "You think the target you've had now is bad, just you wait. Gia Moretti will want you dead. So will all of Giovanni's brothers and nephews. And while you're stupid enough to think Roman, Levi, and Marcus are invincible, they won't be able to save you from this, and they will have nobody but themselves to blame."

I swallow hard and glance away, not wanting her to see just how much her words have struck a deep fear within me. Every day with those boys is a game of survival, hell, look at me now. I'm rotting in their father's desert cells next to a dead woman. I won't survive a life worse than this. It's one thing finding the strength to kill my father, but living a life like this every single day is bound to take its toll.

"Were you con—" I cut myself off hearing the telltale sounds of someone storming through the front door above us. The heavy footsteps warn us that it's a man and my gaze instantly flicks toward Ariana to find her just as nervous as I feel.

She holds a finger up, warning me to keep my mouth shut as we strain to listen to the noises above, as there's only one reason someone would show up here. "Where is she?" the voice demands.

My back stiffens. There's something familiar about his tone, but I can't quite place it. Judging by the way Ariana's face turns a ghostly shade of white, she knows exactly who it is.

"Down there," one of our jailers responds.

My eyes remain locked on Ariana's as she watches me back, horror clear in her eyes as she begins to shake her head. "Is that Giovanni?" I question, my blood turning cold with every step the man takes leading him toward the basement door.

"No," she murmurs, her voice shaking with fear as we hear his hand on the doorknob, slowly twisting. Her eyes widen and as if snapping out of her terror-filled trance, she scrambles back in her cell. "Play dead," she whispers.

"What?" I rush out, certain that I didn't hear her correctly. Why the fuck would I play dead if someone is coming down here? How could I possibly protect myself like that?

"For fu—Just … for once in your miserable life just do what I'm asking. He's not here for you," she spits as the door begins to open and her eyes cut to the top of the stairs. "He wants me. Play. Dead."

His heavy boot hits the top step and fear rattles through my chest at seeing just how terrified she is of this man, and against my better judgment, I drop my body to the ground and hope to whoever exists above that this doesn't get me killed.

CHAPTER THREE

y body drops against Felicity's decaying corpse, my neck twisted at an awkward angle, and I do everything I can not to breathe her in. Her hair presses against my cheek and the strong scent of death plays havoc against my nose. Tears sting my eyes as my heart races with the unknown.

I don't like this one little bit.

The sound of heavy footsteps on the old, rickety stairs fills the cells, each step echoing through the basement with a haunting bang. I can't help the need to peer through my thick lashes, keeping an eye on Ariana. If she truly thought this guy was coming for her, then why the hell would she tell me to play dead? Is this her version of protecting me? But that can't be right. It was only a handful of weeks ago that she was telling Lucas Miller where to find me with explicit instructions that I wasn't to come out of it alive, and Lucas was more than willing to oblige. Shame he was a total idiot. If only she knew how to choose a killer with a brain, then perhaps I wouldn't be here right now.

Funny how life has its brutal little ways of turning my life to complete shit.

Ariana's face drains of all color and she looks up at the descending man as though the devil personally invited him. The stairs lead down past my cell so all I see are his obnoxious, expensive shoes and black suit pants, getting a little more leg with every step he walks down. Though by the time he reaches halfway, his hands are dangling by his side, and I find big, gold rings decorating his short, chunky fingers.

This dude is definitely Mafia. There's no doubt about it. He gives off Giovanni vibes, but … extra, as though he's trying to make up for something that he's lacking, and considering where he is, I can guarantee he's lacking a whole lot.

Ariana digs her feet into the ground and pushes back, getting further and further away, and within mere seconds, her back presses into the furthest corner of her cell. My heart races, violently hammering in my chest. Ariana has always been so put together, even when Marcus pinned her to her door with a knife through her hand, but this woman I see in the opposite cell is a complete stranger. It takes no brain at all to realize that she's been abused by this man before.

She looks back at me, and for the first time, I fear for her. The ghost in her eyes gives away her darkest secrets, and the subtle shake of her head and desperation in her features warns me that what's about to happen needs to stay within the confines of this cell.

After three more steps, the man hits the basement floor and I see him for what he is—a short, stumpy, egotistical asshole who thinks the world owes him pussy and respect, only they're the two things he can't get without throwing money at it.

He immediately begins scanning the cells and I close my eyes just enough to peer through my long lashes while keeping up the dead ruse. My body goes still, and I focus on taking shallow breaths and holding them as long as I can, determined not to allow my chest to rise and fall and get me in all kinds of trouble. It would be just my luck to get myself killed due to the fact that I need oxygen.

The man turns in the opposite direction of Ariana's cell and makes his way toward me, and as he comes closer and steps under the dangling fluorescent light, I'm struck with a familiar face ... only this one has slight changes.

A shorter, younger, and less handsome version of Giovanni stands before me, his gaze narrowed on my body as he tries to determine what the fuck went down in here.

This is clearly one of his four brothers, but it's impossible to tell which. I've never had the displeasure of meeting any of them, nor do I ever intend to. My guess is that they're just like Giovanni, only worse as they have something to prove to live up to the enormous shadow their eldest brother has cast over them.

He hovers close to the cell door, and I'm not lost on the knowledge that he would have a key somewhere buried in that expensive suit of his, though I'm not stupid enough to try and get it now. I'm too far from the cell door and would lose my element of surprise before I made it close enough to strangle him.

He watches me closely, clearly not entirely fooled by my state of deadness, but not sure enough to be certain. Maybe he thinks I'm just sleeping, too exhausted by hunger and the whole kidnapping experience to keep myself conscious.

He steps closer to the bars, his eyes narrowed and watching me far too closely. My pulse thunders and the sound is deafening in my ears, but I keep myself still. I've come too far to lose the game now. Besides, I want to see the day when Roman, Levi, and Marcus rule over this bastard and make his life a living hell.

"You," he spits, clearly not remembering my name, assuming he's even been told it before. But considering he's Giovanni's brother, I can only imagine what type of fun-filled conversations they've had about the princess locked up in the giant castle with her three devils keeping guard. Though one thing is for sure, in every story that has been told, Giovanni has underestimated me, and I can't wait for the day that comes back to haunt him.

Felicity's hair itches against my cheek as her rotten stench stings my nose but I keep myself grounded, focusing on the better moments as I watch this man stare back at me with his hand pressing against his junk, slowly rubbing.

A lump forms in my throat and I have to force myself not to gag. "I'm talking to you," he growls, pressing so close to the bars that his fat caves around them.

"She's dead," Ariana spits from her cell, her tone wild and shaking, making the younger version of Giovanni pause and look back. "Your brother strangled her two days ago."

His lips kick up into a wicked grin before his tongue rolls over his bottom lip. "There you are," he taunts, making it clear that she had been his target all along. "So impatient. Don't you worry, I'll make my way to you eventually."

"You're fucking sick, Phillip."

He just laughs as though it was his greatest compliment before turning his attention back on me. "Ever fucked a dead body, Ari? They don't scream. Don't move. They can't escape you and you're free to do whatever the fuck you want."

Fucking Ariana. Set me up to take the fall again.

"Fuck her all you want," Ariana says through gritted teeth, "though you and I both know your nephews will be coming for her, and if they find her tight little body defiled by your grubby hands and limp dick, they will personally see to it that they end your life, and you know how they get when they're emotional. They wouldn't be able to resist using those two precious daughters against you."

Phillip's eyes flash with indecision, knowing damn well that she's right. The boys will slaughter him just for thinking about defiling my dead body. His eyes brighten with a sick desperation as his hand digs into his pocket and pulls out an old, iron key. "They'll never know it was me."

"Look around you, asshole," Ariana laughs, indicating toward the four corners of the room and pointing out the four cameras that most likely don't work. "You really think Giovanni isn't watching his little toys? You know how he doesn't like to share. Despite how much he hates me, I'm still his wife, and she is his only weapon against his sons."

"Oh, really?" he laughs with a confidence that sends shivers over my skin. He glances back toward Ariana and shuffles himself across the dirty floor just in time to miss the way his sick tone has my hairs standing on edge, giving me away. "You may still be his wife, but he's more than happy to share."

My stare flicks back toward Ariana's, watching as horror settles over her face, realizing at the same time as I do that he's whoring out his wife for a quick buck. "He sold me?" she demands, sucking in a sharp breath filled with the worst kind of betrayal.

Phillip laughs as he drops his gaze over her body, but the way she quickly glances back at me with a knowing sadness deep in her eyes tells me that she had been expecting this, and honestly, I'm not surprised. She was forced by Giovanni's side for years. If anyone knows just how sick and twisted his mind is, it would be her.

"You're damn right, he did," he slurs, distracted by her body as he pulls off his suit jacket to reveal a sweat-soaked button-down shirt that rides up at the front, showing off his greasy, hairy stomach below. "Surely you didn't think he was just going to let you sit and rot here when he could be making money off your tight little cunt." He quickly glances back at me, too far away to see how my eyes are opened to narrow slits. "Shame the bitch is dead though. He would have made a nice profit off that one."

His chunky gold chain dangles around his neck and the matching bracelet clangs against the metal as he pushes the key into the lock. I shake my head, watching with tears filling my eyes, knowing without a doubt what's about to happen, but what can I do? I'm trapped in here and screaming at him only ensures that I'll be hurt too.

"If you fucking touch me ..." she says, trailing off, her threat clear as day.

Phillip laughs and releases his belt from his suit pants before sliding the door open with a loud BANG that makes me flinch. He stands imposingly at her cell door, his intentions crystal clear. "Don't act like you don't want it," he says. "You're a fucking whore for DeAngelis dick. From what I hear, you've been making your way around the family. Fucked a few of my brothers. My nephews. Even Antonio got up inside that dried up, used cunt of yours. It was only a matter of time before you came begging to me."

Ariana laughs despite the fear in her eyes, showing just how strong she can truly be. "You don't think us Mafia wives talk? You don't think your wife has told me all about your little ... shortcomings. We laugh about it all the time. So trust me, I would have never come begging for you, not when the only time your wife has ever come was when you were sleeping beside her."

Phillip storms into her cell, dropping down over her and slamming his hand to her mouth while I'm all too aware of the keys he's left dangling from the cell door. "If you know what's good for you, you'll shut the fuck up," he seethes through a clenched jaw, her words clearly ringing true to garner such a feisty response out of the joke of the century.

She glares up at him, buckling beneath him, trying to get his stench-filled body off her, but the wild, erratic movements only work against her. "Calm down," he taunts. "There will be plenty of time for that."

Ariana rages at him, her words muffled by his hand on her mouth, and though I know I should close my eyes, I can't seem to look away from the horrors unfolding before me. Phillip presses his weight over her, keeping her pinned as he brings up his other hand and forces her wrists together. Taking his belt, he binds her wrists before pulling up and dragging her across her dirty cell while she struggles against his violent hold.

He loops the belt around the metal bars, ensuring she can't get away, and tightens until her fingers turn a sickly shade of red before losing color all together. Phillip reaches for her dirty clothes and starts yanking her pants down her legs as she tries to kick at him and do what she can to save herself, but it's too late. I can't help her like this, and with her wrists bound and locked against the bar, I don't see how she could possibly help herself. This is going to happen and there's nothing that either of us can do about it but wait until the abuse is over.

Her pants fly across the dirty cell, and he tears her underwear from her body, leaving her more exposed and vulnerable. "Don't fucking touch me," she spits, horrified as he releases the button on his suit pants and pulls his dick free.

She kicks up, narrowly avoiding his junk as Phillip springs back to avoid crushing his balls, immediately slamming a foot against her ribs. Her cry echoes through the whole basement. The sound cripples me and a tear rolls down the side of my face, the dead body beneath me all but forgotten.

Phillip drops down, his knee slamming against her inner thigh with all his weight. "Try that shit again and I will slit your throat and then fuck you. Is that clear?"

Ariana whimpers, and even from across the basement with the shitty lighting, I can see the big tears fall from her eyes. My heart breaks and without a doubt, this horrendous torture is worse for me to take in than having to endure Lucas' torture. Hell, even Roman and Levi's.

The night in the old industrial area, I came close to this same shit with Draven Miller, but I knew that the boys were close by. Even back then, I knew they wouldn't allow him to hurt me, but Ariana has no one. No white knight to swoop in and save her. Hell, we've both been lucky that the bastards upstairs haven't already tried this shit on us.

Ariana turns her face toward me, meeting my haunted, broken stare as Phillip forces himself between her thighs. He spits on her, spreading his saliva between her legs so he can pretend that she truly wants it. His stare remains locked on her pussy and dread fills me as he takes hold of his dick and presses down over her.

Ariana's face breaks as he forces himself through her entrance, taking from her what wasn't his to take. He fucks her hard, no regard for her body in the slightest as he grows sweaty and fills the basement with loud grunts, but I keep my gaze locked on hers.

Silent messages pass between us, and though we can't stand one another, she knows that no matter what, in these dirty cells, we are one. I have her back, and though I threatened to leave her ass here, after this, I won't have the stomach to leave her behind, even after the hell she's rained down on me.

The abuse goes on and on and with his violent, hard thrusts, I don't doubt that she's in a world of pain. Shame crosses her features, and after a long moment, she turns her head in the opposite direction to endure the rest of the abuse in private.

Not wanting to make this any harder on her, I give her the privacy she needs and close my eyes as the tears continue to stream down my face.

Two hours pass before Phillip pulls himself off Ariana's broken and bleeding body, his limp dick hanging between his legs. He takes his time getting dressed as I struggle to swallow past the massive lump in my throat, but fuck, what I feel isn't even remotely important right now.

After turning her face toward her cell wall, that's exactly where it stayed. She didn't make a sound. Didn't cry. Didn't scream for him to get off her. Just endured her abuse in silence. Even now as he walks around her cell collecting his clothes, she just stares at the wall as though she fell into a trance to get through the trauma.

Phillip is drenched in sweat, and I don't doubt that Ariana would kill for a shower. I can't say that I have ever been in her position or know what it feels like to have your body violated in that way, but I'm more than familiar with being abused and tortured. While a hot shower won't wash away the memories, pain, or scars, it goes a long way in helping to remind me that I'm still alive.

The woman that I've come to know over the past few months would have made a snide comment about not feeling his small dick inside her. She would have made sure that if she were going down, Phillip would go down with her, but Ariana's silence speaks volumes. In the space of two hours, he's broken her.

Phillip steps into her side and releases the buckle on the belt, freeing her hands. Then the moment she can, she scrambles across the dirty floor, curling into a ball as far away as her cell will allow, all while Phillip watches her with a cocky smirk across his stupid face.

Fuck, I want to kill him more than I want to kill Giovanni.

Where the fuck are the boys? He's going to walk out of here as though he didn't just violate her in the worst way. He's going to get on with his life while leaving her in a constant state of panic, always fearing that he could return at any time. He's going to get away with it.

Anger burns through me as a soft whimper escapes my lips, but the sound of his belt buckle clanging against the metal bars masks my slip up. Phillip threads it back through his belt loops and keeps his stare on Ariana, wanting to see just how badly he broke her. But when he realizes that she won't be looking up anytime soon, he reaches for his suit jacket and pulls it on.

With his shoes fastened and his shirt tucked back in, it looks as though he's about to take his stupid, fucked-up pride and leave us in peace. Instead, he steps back into Ariana's cell and grips her arm.

She squeals as Phillip yanks her to her feet and my body flinches, ready to throw down if that's what I have to do, but any attempt would be wasted as long as I'm locked in this cell. He begins dragging her toward the door and her fighting spirit returns. "LET GO OF ME," she screams, his intentions crystal clear. "NO. NO. LET ME GO."

Her nails dig into his skin, and he pulls back, blowing out a pained breath through his clenched jaw. "BITCH," he roars, backhanding her across the face, the momentum sending her crumbling back to the ground. "You're a fool if you thought I would pay for just one night. You are mine now, Ariana. You will suck my dick every morning and I will fuck your ass every night. Now get the fuck up."

She stares up at him in horror as panic soars through me. "I've been waiting a long time for you, Ariana," he warns when she doesn't make a move to get up. "I'm going to make you regret the day you decided to be a little cock tease. From now on, you answer to me, and I swear to God, if you ever attempt to get away from me, I will destroy you. NOW MOVE."

Ariana swallows hard, and having no choice with absolutely no way out, she shakily gets to her feet. Leaving her pants and torn underwear behind, Phillip grabs her by the back of her neck and pushes her through the cell door.

He leads her toward the stairs, and as she spares one last pleading look toward me, he drags her up them one by one, letting her know the vile things he plans on doing to her.

CHAPTER FOUR

F our fucking days.

They're not coming.

My gaze drops to Felicity and it's clear how this is going to go. They abandoned her. They thought she was dead, and they left her to rot here as their father's personal heir maker, and that's exactly what's going to happen to me, besides the baby thing. After the shit I've been through, statistically falling pregnant would be some kind of cosmic joke.

I was an idiot to remove that tracking device in my arm, but to be fair, Roman and Levi were trying to torture me … well, there was really no trying about it. They did it and they sure as hell succeeded. If they were graded, they would've received top marks for every aspect. Creepy comments. Tick. Sharp knives. Tick. Letting me think that I might just survive only to pull the rug out from under me. Tick, tick, fucking tick. What can I say? Those boys excel at everything they do, and torture is one of their many talents.

All I know is, the second I get out of this mess and call out the boys for not saving me sooner, I'll be inserting that little tracking device right back into my arm. Fuck, I'll do the procedure myself if I have to. I'll even shove another one of those contraceptive rods back in as well. After all, now isn't exactly a great time to have a baby around. Hell, I had one in my arms for all of thirty seconds before I lost him. Not to mention, Dill and Doe didn't even have names until last week. What kind of shitty parenting is that?

The thought of Dill and Doe has my chest restricting. The last I saw of Dill he was fearlessly protecting me against Giovanni in the woods outside the mansion. That wolf deserves a medal … or at least the biggest steak I can find. Assuming he's okay, of course. That bullet tore out of that gun and Dill's devastating howl tore through the forest and broke me. I've never heard anything like it, but I have to believe that he is okay. I don't know where I'd be if Dill didn't make it.

Letting out a sigh, I find my gaze shifting back toward Ariana's cell, but more importantly, the key that still dangles from the lock. It's like some kind of cruel torture, dangling my freedom so close in front of my face, but just out of reach. I have bruised my arms and chest more than once over the past two days, trying to force myself through the bars just enough to grab hold of the stupid key. I've used my clothes as a lasso and attempted to scale the fucking bars to try and reach it with my legs. Typically, I'm not a desperate kind of girl, but fuck, I'll do anything it takes to get my hands on that key.

The boys aren't coming, and I'm done sitting around waiting for them to show up and save me. I should have been trying to save myself from the beginning, but a part of me still wants to blindly trust them, to believe they're doing everything they can to try and find me.

They wouldn't abandon me, not if they thought there was still hope, but I can't sit around and do nothing anymore. No one has come down to check on me since Phillip disappeared with Ariana. I haven't been fed. Haven't received water. I'm dirty as fuck and the heat is wearing me down, not to mention the decaying body beside me isn't looking so great.

Get out of here.

Slit Giovanni's throat.

Save Roman's baby.

Find Ariana.

End Phillip's miserable life.

Fuck, I'm going to be a busy girl once I finally break free of this hell. My list just keeps growing. I feel like Arya Stark repeating my list over and over again, but it seems to be the only thing that helps to pass the time.

My mind keeps taking me back to Ariana's face as Phillip dragged her out of here. I hate that woman, she's a real cold bitch, but what she did for me down here ... she saved me from that same fate. She made sure he didn't harm me, and while I don't understand her reasoning for wanting to protect me, I appreciate it all the same.

A loud grumble comes from upstairs just moments before the door swings open and I hear one of the guards on the stairs. Panic surges through me and I watch the stairs like a hawk, my heart thundering wildly in my chest. Without the boys by my side, that brave warrior I thought I could have been has quickly slipped away. I'm left with nothing but scars and memories to spur me on, and I just have to hope that's enough to keep me going.

Another guard steps out behind him and the two of them make their way down the stairs, heavily thumping against the rickety metal steps. The whole staircase shakes beneath their weight and I'm sure if they moved their asses any faster, the whole thing would crumble beneath them.

They hit the bottom step and the guy in front hooks his fingers around the railing to propel himself around the corner, directly facing me as the other does the same, sending an intense fear rattling through my chest.

My body tenses. There's at least another three women down here, but their attention is on me, and I don't fucking like it. I hate not knowing, but to be honest, if something is going to happen, I'm glad it's coming for me and not the other women who have been suffering down here for who knows how long. I don't know what they did to land themselves in Giovanni's desert prison, but I'm certain they don't deserve to be here, just as I don't. I haven't spoken to them, and they haven't attempted conversation with me either, but one look at them tells me they've already given up on any chance of survival.

Not me though.

The men stride toward me with scowls stretched across their faces. "Get up," the guy in front mutters, wiping his forearm over his sweat-soaked, dirty face, his lips curling into a sadistic grin. "It's your lucky day."

I don't dare move, knowing all too well that their version of 'my lucky day' is far from what I would consider lucky, and if anything, they're probably down here to fuck me while no one is around to hear me scream.

He stops at the door of my cell and his friend moves in beside him, his filthy gaze slowly scanning over my blood-stained body. "He told you to get up," he leers. "Don't make him ask again."

My gaze shifts back to the first guy and seeing the cocky confidence stretched over his face, I reluctantly pull myself to my feet, knowing that resisting is only going to make it worse for me. I hover by the back of my cell, keeping as far as I can from the men, but when a key clinks in the lock and the heavy door slides open with a metallic BANG, I realize I don't stand a chance.

Swallowing hard, I keep my stare sharp, watching their every little move as they advance into my cell. They storm toward me, and I back up until the hard surface of the stone wall slams against my back. "Don't touch me," I spit, yanking my arm away as the guards attempt to grab me.

The guard who spoke first laughs, the corner of his lips lifting in a sickening sneer. "Don't worry, princess. We're not here to fuck you if that's what you're worried about."

The other guard scoffs and looks down at my body in disgust. "Not that we would anyway. Look at you, covered in your own piss and that bitch's dried blood. Couldn't get me to touch you, not even if you paid me."

Relief swarms through me but it still doesn't explain what the fuck they're doing in here.

The first guard grips my elbow and yanks me toward him, but my lack of energy has me falling into him. He catches me in strong hands and forces me in front of him, gripping the top of my arms in a bruising hold. He shoves me forward and I try to resist, pulling back against him, too scared of what the outside of this cell could mean for me. "Where are you taking me?" I demand, my fingers gripping the metal bar of the cell.

"Time for a bath," he murmurs in my ear, the sick bastard getting off on my fear. His friend steps into my side and pries my fingers from the bar. I relentlessly try to hold on, but after a moment of struggle, he brings his knee up and slams it against my wrist. A wailing scream tears out of me as a dull throbbing shoots through my hand and I'm forced to release the bar.

The guard holding me doesn't miss his chance and pushes me out the door of the cell as his friend laughs and follows us through. He releases my arms and pushes me hard, sending me sprawling across the basement.

I face plant into the bars of Ariana's empty cell and barely catch myself before he's on me again. He grabs my waist and spins me around before slamming my back against the metal bar. "What do you want with me?" I spit, tasting blood in my mouth as my cheek aches from the face plant.

"You get to go home," he tells me, a wicked secret hidden deep within his eyes as his friend strides down the opposite end of the hall, his footfalls making a haunting echo through the remaining empty cells.

My brows furrow and I look back at him with a daunting confusion. "Home?" I question, not trusting him for a second, especially with that wicked gleam sparkling in his eyes.

He steps into me and I suck in a deep breath, preparing myself for the worst as my fingers knot around the closest bar, my knuckles turning white as I grip them with everything I've got. "That's right," he tells me, the venomous tone in his voice sending a wave of unease pulsing through my veins as a deafening motor drums to life. "You're going home. It might not be the home that you were hoping for, but I'm sure you'll be *very comfortable there.*"

I stare up at him, the ugly realization dawning on me. "He sold me."

"He sure fucking did," he booms, laughing with delight as the other guy returns with a thick, black fire hose that looks as though it could tear my skin right off my body. "And when your new owner gets here, you better look fucking perfect." He grips my chin, tearing it up to meet his dark stare. "You're going to smile. You're going to spread your fucking legs. And you're going to fucking love it. Got it, bitch? If you blow this and make me look like a fucking idiot in front of Giovanni, I will make you wish you were never born."

He releases my chin with a harsh shove and the back of my head rebounds off the metal bar. A pained grunt tears from my lips, but before I get the chance to truly process what this means, water shoots from the fire hose.

The freezing water blasts against my skin like a million knives tearing into my flesh and I scream out as the two of them laugh. My old, torn clothes work as a barrier between the freezing water and my scarred flesh, but it's not nearly enough to save me from the fierce agony that shoots through my body.

I turn, unable to handle the force of the cold water against my chest and allow my back to take the brunt of the pain. The hose travels up and down, and I flinch as they send the water shooting between my legs. They laugh, my misery their greatest pleasure.

Felicity's dried blood washes from my body as I drop to the ground, crying in pain as I fall onto my sore wrist, my skin turning an angry shade of red. They step in closer and grab my arm, flipping me over to make sure they get every little crevice of my body.

The water blasts against my face and my arms shoot up, desperately trying to protect myself as I listen to their howling laughs. The blasting water slams against my head, washing out the filth that's matted into my hair over the past few days, and it's the most horrendous thing I have ever endured. The pressure is insane, and it feels as though the water could literally fracture my skull.

Their relentless torture continues until the water rushing off me finally runs clear, but the water doesn't stop, it's simply redirected toward my cell where he hoses down Felicity's decaying body and clears away the blood staining the floor.

The guard who grabbed me steps in closer and curls his hand around my arm, yanking me to my feet. "Would you look at that," he mutters, his gaze dropping down my clean, wet body as I stand before him looking like a drowned rat. "You might have a little something to offer me after all."

Dread sinks into my chest as he laughs and reaches for his belt buckle. "It'd be a shame to let you go without test driving you first." A cocky grin stretches over his lips as he glances back over his shoulder at his colleague. "What do you think, Jase? Should we take her for a ride?"

The other guy laughs. "I don't see why not? After all, we've been stuck out here in the desert for weeks and I'll be damned if I don't get something out of it."

Hell to the motherfucking no. Not today, assholes.

My gaze sweeps around the cells as my heart thunders in my chest, but nothing scares me more than the soft jingle of his belt coming undone. I glance up at the top of the stairs as he grips onto my waist, his fingers digging into my raw skin. "Don't even think about running," he spits. "There's nowhere you can go where I won't find you."

My hand stretches out as he grabs the top of my soaking pants. "Now spread those fucking legs."

My fingers curl around the old iron key left in Ariana's cell door, and I yank it out just moments before swinging my arm in a shallow arc, remembering Marcus' finest lesson—when in doubt, *aim for an artery.* I stab the blunt tip of the old key right through the side of his neck, needing every bit of strength I have to pierce through his thick layer of skin.

The key sinks deep into his neck until it has nowhere else to go, and I clench my jaw as his eyes go wide, barely registering what the fuck just happened. A fierce battle cry tears out of me, and with every bit of determination I have, I rip the key out again, the metal prongs on the side tearing through his flesh like butter.

Blood spurts from his artery, splattering right across the dirty, wet cells, turning me a sickening shade of bright red. I can't help but think of Marcus. He lives for this kind of shit, and I know he'd be proud, but now is not the time to dwell.

Blood soaks me as he slams his hand against his neck, his face turning white. It happens so quickly that the guy with the hose barely has a second to look over his shoulder before his colleague is dropping to his knees.

"Fuck," I grunt, having to move fast as the other guy drops the fire hose and sprints toward me. I fall with the bleeding guy and hope he has some kind of weapon on him, but I get nowhere before the other man is on me, the pressure from the wild hose sending it flying around like a disaster waiting to happen.

He yanks me up, gripping my arm so tight that it cuts off my circulation. He spins me and slams my chest against the metal bars. "My, oh my. You are a feisty little thing, aren't you?" he purrs, leaning into me, letting me feel his excitement pressing up against my ass. "Giovanni isn't going to like—*oomph.*"

My ass slams back against his junk and he buckles, loosening his hold just enough for me to slip out of his grasp. "Fuck, you little bitch," he roars as I spin around and slam my knee up hard enough to crush his balls.

"That was for my fucking wrist, asshole," I spit as I dash back, skipping over his dead colleague and splashing my bare feet down into the pool of blood beneath him.

Every little nerve within me screams to head for the stairs and break free of this fucked-up little dungeon, but I can't get there without putting myself right in the line of fire, and I can't leave this dungeon until he stops breathing. It's a desert outside these walls, and I won't survive out there, not with him coming after me. So instead, I race in the opposite direction to where the wild hose is flying around the back of the cells.

The blasting water sprays around the cell, soaking everything in its path, its reckless pressure making it fly around like a blow-up air dancer outside a used-auto dealership. I race for it, momentarily putting me right in its path. The water blasts across my chest and I suck in a loud gasp, pushing through the stabbing pain as I dart out of its way.

My hands grip the nozzle and I put my weight over it to try and control its wild flailing before turning it on the fucker who sprayed me in the first place. He stands crouched by the stairs, gripping the railing to keep from falling as he groans in agony, his balls hopefully shredding inside his pants. His jaw clenches and he glares at me with a ferociousness that would have any woman trembling, but I've got the upper hand here and I will not back down, not now.

With his balls crushed, there's nowhere for him to go, and I don't miss my opportunity. Turning the violent spray on him, I push the little lever as far as it goes, upping the pressure and slamming it directly into his chest. The momentum pushes him back, whooshing him right off his feet until his back rams up against the metal bars.

His high-pitched scream tears through the basement, the sound absolutely sickening, but I don't dare relent as I struggle to hold onto the thick hose, the pressure threatening to lift me off my feet. Instead, I put everything I have into it as I move closer toward him, the water keeping him pinned to the bars.

His scream is blood curdling and guilt fires through me, but assholes like this don't deserve to live, especially if it's a me or him type situation. I have to end him.

Drawing on every last bit of my DeAngelis vibes, I raise the nozzle of the hose and watch as the spray of water slams over his face. He instantly starts choking on the water, blubbering, and trying to catch a breath around it, but I don't stop, knowing damn well that given the chance, he sure as fuck would have tried the same thing on me. Hell, if they didn't have orders from Giovanni to prepare me for a buyer, then I probably would have already suffered the same fate.

Holding the hose still burns my muscles, but I fight against it, my determination winning out as his blubbering and cries slowly begin to fade. His hands droop but just to be sure, I keep the hose aimed at his face a while longer. When I'm finally met with a loud silence, I remove the spray from the guard and watch as he drops to the ground beside his colleague.

The hose sags in my hands as I turn it off, and the loud motor finally falls silent. Fear pounds in my chest as I creep toward the two bodies, waiting for them to spring to life again. "Fucking hell," I breathe. Two bodies in less than two minutes. The boys will be proud, assuming I ever see them again to tell the story … and assuming they're still alive, but I have to believe they are. They're my only hope of survival.

Not knowing what's going on upstairs, or if there's even anybody up there, I pat my hands over the guards' bodies until I finally find what I'm looking for. My fingers curl around the handle of a knife, and I tear it from its holster before cringing. The blade slices through the drowned man's throat and blood spills like a waterfall over his chest, but I can't take the chance that he will survive this.

Then grabbing the blood-soaked key, I turn toward the other cells, determined to get us all out of here alive.

CHAPTER FIVE

The cell door squeals as I slide it open. "Come on," I rush out, staring at the woman who's been locked down here for what looks like months, her hair matted and clothes falling off her boney frame. "We have to get out of here. Hurry up."

She gapes at me, furiously shaking her head and she bounds to her feet and grips the metal door. She yanks on it hard until the heavy metal slams shut with a loud, echoing BANG. "Get out of here, girl," she spits, terror in her eyes. "Giovanni will have your head for this."

My brows crease as I stare back at her, trying to pull the door free again. "What the hell is wrong with you? We have to go now."

"NO," she roars at me, spittle hitting my face. "I'd rather die in this cell than be on the run from those bastards again. Do you have any idea what that was like? They leave me alone down here. Just GO. LEAVE ME BE."

Fucking hell.

My lips press into a hard line and for a brief moment, I consider knocking the woman out and dragging her by the hair, but what good would that do me? If there are more men upstairs, I'll be fucked and so would she. There's just no helping people who don't want to be helped.

The other two women though … I'd seen their bodies in the strained light, heard soft mumblings over the past few days, yet at some point, they'd slowly faded away, leaving this world without me even knowing.

Against my better judgment, I turn to the stairs and let out a heavy breath while clutching the knife tightly in my hand. I don't know what I'm about to find up there, but now is my only shot, assuming those cameras up in the corner of the cells actually work.

My knees shake and I take my first step up, fearing for absolutely everything. My sanity. My life. Hell, even the woman left down here behind me, though it didn't escape my notice that she never threw away the key dangling from the lock.

Reaching the top step, I pause as my hand curls around the door handle.

Here goes nothing. It's either die fighting, or be sold to some arrogant bastard who, no doubt, will make me beg for the sweet release of death.

Turning the handle, I push the door open just a sliver and am smacked in the face with a wave of cool air conditioning before I peer out the small gap. I hear soft murmuring coming from an adjoining room and footsteps in the opposite direction. There's a good chance that the murmuring is coming from a television, but there's no way to be sure.

Letting out a shaky breath, I go for it.

The door creaks as I push it open, instantly giving me away. My heart leaps into the back of my throat and I dart toward the sound of the maybe-television. "How'd that little bitch taste?" Comes a laugh from a man sitting in an old dirty recliner.

His head tilts up and he meets my terrified stare immediately. His eyes go wide but his reaction time is far too slow as I reach him only a second later. I push back on the recliner and the chair instantly falls back, the man struggling to get out of it as I slam my hand down over his mouth and dig the sharp blade of the knife deep into his throat.

I press down harder over his mouth as my eyes flick between him and the big entrance of the living room, certain that our struggle is going to alert anyone else in the old, dingy house.

Blood pours from his open throat and he quickly suffocates on his own blood, his body relaxing under my hold. I don't waste a second, gluing my back to the wall and creeping through the house, my heart hammering wildly in my chest while knowing the only reason I'm able to put these assholes to sleep is because I hold the element of surprise. Without that, I'm fucked.

"Yo, Ralph," a voice hollers from the opposite room. There's a short pause before a muttered curse flows through the air. "Ralph. Where the fuck are you at?"

The man pauses again before muttering to himself, clearly irritated with being ignored. "For fuck's sake," he says louder, dropping something on the counter with a loud clang before I hear him crossing through the kitchen.

The footfalls take him toward the living room where I'd just slaughtered his friend and my whole body tenses. "I'm fucking talking to—"

His words fall away before I hear an irritated, "fuck," breathed through the room.

My gaze shifts toward the front door. It would only take a second to pull it open and sprint out into the hot desert, but without food and water for the past four days, and this asshole racing after me, I'll only get so far before I'm dragged back with a vengeance.

I have to stay, and I have to make it count.

The man slowly makes his way around the house, and I hear his every step, taunting me like a sick promise to end my miserable life. "Where are you, pretty girl?" he questions, instantly knowing that it's me up here and not any of Giovanni's other prisoners. After all, no one has come down to check on us in days, he probably has no idea that the other two women are dead. Giovanni though … I get the distinct feeling that he would.

"Come out, come out wherever you are."

A shiver trails down my spine and I clutch the knife a little tighter, sliding myself along the wall to get a better vantage point of the house. Listening carefully, I track his movements through the property and take note of exactly where he is and what direction he's taking.

The footsteps fade away into the distance, and my heart pounds just a little harder, making my hands quiver at my sides.

Not wanting to stand here with a target painted on my back, I keep sliding across the wall, each sidestep taken with caution until I'm able to peer around the corner into the kitchen. As I do, I find a grinning man staring right back at me.

My eyes bug out of my head as a sharp squeal tears from the back of my throat. I take off like a fucking rocket, my feet pounding against the old floorboards as the man darts after me, his hand shooting out and capturing my hair into his fist. He yanks back and my body falls to the ground with a loud bang, the sound rocking right through the old home.

The man laughs as he circles me, his wicked gaze locked on mine. "What's the matter, pretty girl? I just wanted to talk."

Yeah right.

I scramble across the floor and the asshole jumps forward, his heavy boot slamming down over my long, wet hair and keeping me pinned. A loud wail tears out of me as I grip my trapped strands and desperately try to pull free.

The man laughs as tears well in my eyes. "You've been nothing but trouble since you got here," he spits, shifting his weight just enough to press his other foot down over my chest, giving him a bigger advantage than I ever should have allowed. One more shift of his weight and the fucker could crush me like a damn bug.

My hand clenches and before allowing myself a chance to think about what I'm doing, my hand flies up. The blade glistens in the hot afternoon sun streaming through the window just moments before it plunges deep into the back of his calf.

The man screams but I'm not nearly done as I pull down hard and slice the whole fucking muscle off the back of his leg as though I was carving a fucking Thanksgiving turkey. Blood spills all over me as the man stumbles back and falls to the ground, his face turning a sickly shade of white.

He howls in agony and the sound is like music to my ears. I get up off the ground, my knees shaking beneath me and as I turn to look at the man, I know just how effortlessly I could end his life. "Do it," he spits at me, the agony too much for him to bear. "FUCKING DO IT."

A grin tears across my face, and rather than putting him out of his misery, I simply turn and race for the door as his pained screams fill the space behind me. It won't be long and he'll be dead, but knowing that he'll go in pain makes something stir deep in my gut, something that makes me feel like a fucking queen.

The door slams behind me, but I'm not foolish enough to take my time. I run, slamming one foot down after another, the blistering afternoon sun bearing down on me. It takes only a minute before a light sweat coats my body and my mouth immediately goes dry, sucking in the hot desert air.

The blood coating my skin quickly dries, and as I come down from my high and think over everything I just did, a harsh panic tears through my chest. I'm a fucking killer, through and through. I was relentless and brutal, but what can I say? I was trained by the absolute best in the business. They'll be so proud to hear that I didn't just back down and accept what they wanted to do with me, but they're also moments that will live on in my head for a long time to come.

What I did here today cost me and has brought a darkness over my soul, but in the end, all that matters is that I'm free. At least for now. I'm stuck out in the desert and have no idea how far the nearest property is or how long it will be before I can get help. Hell, just because Giovanni's men couldn't kill me, doesn't mean that coyotes won't once the sun goes down.

All I see for miles is dirt and trees. No water. No pathways. No clear roads to walk along. I'm out here all alone with nowhere to run and absolutely nowhere to hide.

At least an hour passes before the afternoon sun is dropping lower in the sky, sending my shadow spiraling out before me, distorting my figure. I hear nothing but my feet dragging through the dirt and my rough panting as I try to swallow to keep my throat from completely drying out.

I glance back over my shoulder, and while it feels like I've been walking for a lifetime, I can still clearly see the house in the distance. The blood covering my body is well and truly dried, and although their version of a bath was one of the most horrendous things I've endured, it went a long way in making me feel clean. My hair is no longer matted and while my clothes are dirty again, they don't have that awful scent of decaying flesh.

My feet ache against the hard ground and I wish for the millionth time that I had worn shoes when I went bounding out of the DeAngelis mansion after Dill. It would have made my life a million times easier. Hell, if I had just allowed the wolf to take the freaking purple dick, I wouldn't be in this situation at all and Dill would be just fine … at least, I hope he is. I have to believe that he is, because the alternative … fuck, I can't go there.

A soft hum breaks the silence, and my head snaps up, my heart pounding erratically as I fear the worst. A black car speeds through the desert in the distance, kicking up dust beneath the tires and sending an overwhelming wave of panic through my veins. This property is the only property out here for miles. There's no way in hell that this car is just out here lost. This is one of Giovanni's men, or hell, it's Giovanni himself.

My feet come to an abrupt stop as I look around, desperate for some kind of escape, but where the hell can I go? If I can see the car, the occupants inside of it can sure as fuck see me too.

I didn't come this far just to be railroaded now.

Those guards said something about a buyer who was coming to get me ... fuck.

The car speeds through the desert at ridiculous speeds, and as it gets closer, I can make out the shape. It's not just some small-town car but a big SUV. The late sun hits the windshield and makes it impossible to see the people inside, but what's the point in looking? It probably has blacked out windows anyway.

With fear ruling my every move, I take off at a sprint in the opposite direction, away from both the car and the house, taking me deeper into the desert. I quickly drain what's left of my energy as the car continues hurtling toward me, my pathetic pained run laughable against a speed like that.

Time slows, and as I run, my throat becomes drier and my pace slower as though the universe is punishing me for loving my new life with three well-known serial killers. I pant, struggling with every step I take, and as tears form in my eyes, the black SUV flies around me, cutting me off and forcing me to an abrupt stop.

The tires screech as the driver hits the brakes, the heavy vehicle skidding along the dirt, struggling to find traction as dust flies up around it like a daunting storm cloud. The passenger side door flies open and a man storms toward me, my energy finally gives out and I drop to my knees.

CHAPTER SIX

Levi flies out of the passenger side door as Marcus hurtles after him, racing toward me as my dirty knees sink lower into the hard ground. Heavy sobs tear from the back of my throat seeing a big, black wolf bounding toward me, one wolf, not two. Once Levi reaches me, Roman jerks the SUV to a stop and bails from the driver's door.

Hot sobs tear from my throat as I bury my head in my hands, and just as I expect Levi to scoop me up, he continues around me, drawing his gun and holding his arm out straight. Doe's ferocious low growl fills the silence before two loud bullets ring out through the late afternoon.

Marcus hits the ground, his strong arms curling around my body and pulling me into his familiar chest. I peer out behind us, straining my neck to find a body sprawled over the ground at least half a mile back.

"Shit," I breathe, recognizing the guard I knocked out on my first day here, the guy I'd dropped down in the cells so I could get to Felicity. I figured Giovanni would have killed him after he let me get the best of him. I should have checked every room in the house before running out of there. Hell, the fucker was probably taking a shit while everything was going on and had absolutely no idea that every last man in the place had been brutally murdered.

Marcus' warmth surrounds me as he holds me to his chest and I turn into him, listening to the rapid beat of his heart as I try to calm myself. "You're safe, babe. We've got you. I'll never let you out of my sight again."

I close my eyes, sinking deeper into his hold as Levi and Roman hover around me, the comfort of their safety immediately taking the weight off my shoulders. Doe presses her side into me, her silent way of checking that I'm alright, and after a short breath, she takes off like a bullet toward the man behind me.

Breathing in Marcus' familiar scent, a tear falls down my cheek, mixing into the grime and dirt coating my skin. "You came," I breathe, still unable to believe the bullshit that went down inside that property. Hell, I was starting to believe that I was never going to see them again.

Roman reaches down and takes my hand from around Marcus' neck. "Damn fucking right, we did," he tells me. "I just wish we'd gotten to you sooner. The shit we had to do to find you…"

I nod, knowing all too well what kind of shit they would have done because it probably reflects the kind of shit I had to do too. "I thought," I start, having to stop and swallow past my dry throat. "I thought you weren't going to come."

Levi crouches down and takes my chin in his hands, forcing my exhausted stare to his. "I would have moved heaven and hell to get to you," he rumbles low, the agony in his voice telling me just how scared he's been over the last few days.

Holding his stare, I let him see the true horror living deep within my eyes. "I killed them all," I tell him, my voice cracking with a pained sob, knowing Marcus and Roman are listening intently. "I … the things …"

My words fall away but there's no need to say them, they understand more than anyone else what this little adventure has cost me.

"Shhhhh," Levi murmurs, trailing his fingers over the side of my face as we hear Doe's low growl in the distance. "It's over now. We've got you."

Those words dance in my mind like ice water on a hot summer's day, calming the terror pulsing through my veins. I allow them to truly sink in, to take away the fear and allow my heart to finally stop racing. I'm safe now. They've got me. They came for me and now we can go home.

Marcus' hands slip under my ass, lifting us both up from the dirty ground. Refusing to let me go, he strides back toward the big SUV with Roman and Levi at his sides. The knowledge of finally being able to get out of here, to be able to eat, drink, and sleep in peace settles over me like a warm blanket on a cold night. The idea of safety and comfort makes me feel like the weight of the world has finally been lifted.

Marcus climbs in the backseat of the SUV, keeping me in his lap as Levi and Roman get in. A bottle of water sails between the seats, and Marcus quickly grabs it before cracking the lid. He holds it up for me to take small sips, and just as Roman hits the gas, a loud gasp tears from the back of my throat. "DOE," I rush out, gaping as I stare through the window, desperately searching for the precious wolf who's become one of my closest friends.

Marcus trails his fingers over my cheek, wiping a stray tear I wasn't aware of. "She's fine. We're not leaving just yet."

My brows furrow and my heart kicks into gear realizing that Roman is heading right for the house. I shake my head, not wanting to witness the bloody massacre all over again. "No," I rush out, the fear clear in my eyes. "I don't want to go back there. Please, Roman. Please. Take me home. I can't. I can't go back in there."

He meets my terrified stare in the rearview mirror, and I see the regret in his eyes. "I'm sorry, Empress. We have to," he tells me. "It's been four fucking days and we don't have a goddamn clue where my father has disappeared. No one has heard from him, and that fucked-up cabin could hold the information we need. We can't leave. Not yet."

"You can stay in the car," Levi suggests. "No one is forcing you back in there."

I swallow hard as the SUV rolls to a stop next to the body of the man that was following me for the past few hours. Roman lowers his window, and when his hand falls out of the car, I hear Doe's low growl just outside. Just as I'm about to ask what the fuck is going on, a loud gunshot rings out and the need to question fades away. He was making sure the guard was well and truly dead, just as I should have done before walking out of there. Had the boys not come for me, that bastard would have got to me the second I decided to rest.

Roman hits the gas again sailing through the desert with dirt flying up in a thick cloud behind the car. I can't help but glance out the window and watch as Doe runs effortlessly beside us, her long strides matching our speed with ease, despite the heat and dry air. She's an absolute goddess, so sleek and dark as night with the ability to tear a man to shreds.

An image of Dill rushes through my mind, but I hold back any questions that I don't want the answers to right now. I'm not ready to hear that he's gone, not ready to feel that overwhelming grief when I'm already dealing with so much.

We reach the old house in no time and bile rises in my throat seeing the bloodied footprints leading out of the door. Roman brings the car to a stop and a shudder runs through me. "You're okay," Marcus reminds me, his soft fingers on my skin feeling like a million tiny knives.

Shaking my head, I try to focus on anything but the house. I can't go in there, but I can't be left out here alone. The fear of … fuck, the fear of everything. It's too much. I just need today to cry, to be overwhelmed and emotional. I need a good sleep and some food and after that, I'll come back. I'll learn how to put it all behind me and move on, but until then, I have every right to be a fucking mess.

Roman and Levi push their doors wide and make their way out of the SUV as I remain seated on Marcus' lap, the indecision clouding me, but as the boys start walking closer to the house and I feel the safety of their arms going with them, I reluctantly pull myself off Marcus' lap and push my way out of the SUV.

Doe waits for us on the small porch, her tongue hanging out of her mouth as she pants from the long run. Levi stops by her and uncaps the lid of a water bottle before glancing around. He finds a broken pot that looks as though it got into a fight with a gun and came off worse for it, though it's still deep enough to serve as a water bowl for now. He fills it as much as he can, and Doe dives straight in, her long tongue desperately scooping the cool water into her mouth and instantly making me jealous.

"Here," Levi mutters, seeing the look on my face and offering me what's left of the bottle. I take it graciously and lift it to my lips, the cool water instantly soaking down my sore, scratchy throat and making it a million times easier to breathe.

Not wanting to give it up, I hold onto the bottle like a security blanket as Marcus moves in behind me. The door has been left open and Roman pushes against it, letting it swing the rest of the way before peering in.

Dread fills me knowing what he must see inside, and I watch as his brows arch, intrigue settling over his handsome features. "What the ever-loving …"

I cringe as he trails off. It doesn't take a genius to know where he was going with that. I'm a fucking savage. Most people in my situation would have just stabbed the guy, but not me. I had to slice half his fucking leg off.

What the fuck is wrong with me?

Roman steps over the threshold and the rest of us trail in behind him. "Are you sure everyone is dead?" Levi questions as his gaze settles on the man slouched against the wall, sitting in a pool of his own blood as his calf muscle, perfectly sliced and diced, rests by his foot. "There were no other guards?"

I shake my head, unable to look away from the man. "I ... I thought I got them all, but then that guy outside..."

Levi nods as I trail off, understanding what wasn't spoken out loud—that I wasn't nearly as thorough as I should have been, and they need to be prepared that someone could jump out at any time to try and finish the job. Though the idea of that happening now that the boys are here doesn't scare me nearly as much as it had before.

Hands fall to my waist, and I feel Marcus moving in behind me as I glance over my shoulder at the calfless man on the ground. "Well fuck me in the ass and call me Fred," he beams, his fingers tightening on my waist with the utmost pride and respect. "Did you do this all by yourself?"

I swallow and glance back at him, trying to get a read on his face to make sure I'm not imagining things. "I, umm ... yeah."

"Fucking hell," he murmurs, shaking his head in astonishment. "Look at that splatter and positioning. It's like a fucking work of art. This is incredible. I couldn't have done it better myself." His gaze drops to meet my stare, his brow furrowing, and for just a brief moment, I could have sworn that a flicker of nervousness sweeps through his gaze. "Did you ..." he cringes, pausing for the quickest beat. "Did you want me to box up the calf? I can preserve it for you like a fucking trophy. I know that tongue in my room freaks you the fuck out, but this … fuck, babe. If you don't want it, I'll take it."

I arch a brow, the need to feel guilt over what I've done quickly fading away. "You know, the sincerity in your eyes sometimes makes me forget just how fucked up you really are," I tell him. "Have at the calf. It's all yours, but just so you know, that thing is not coming home with me in the car. You can strap it to the roof."

Marcus beams at me as though all his Christmases have come at once. "I'm going to etch your name into his skin and put it on display," he tells me as though it's the greatest honor. "Have I ever told you how fucking incredible you are? Every time you're thrown into some bullshit situation and I think you're about to break, you go and do something that blows me away. Holy fucking shit, babe. If you don't let me worship you for the rest of your goddamn life …"

"If you're done getting hard over the guy's leg," Roman mutters, done with his brother's overwhelming adoration. "We have a house to check."

Marcus rolls his eyes but nonetheless, takes my hand and leads me through the house. I watch the boys carefully, seeing how they silently take in each room, making sense of everything that went down just by looking at the mess I left behind. They don't ask questions, and I sure as hell don't offer any answers, but I don't need to.

They look behind every door, not leaving a single stone unturned while checking over every little detail that I missed. Phone numbers scrawled on torn paper, the amount of dishes in the sink, the trash sprawled throughout every single room. The disappointment torn across each of their faces tells me that they didn't find what they were looking for.

"Come on," Roman finally says. "Let's check out the basement and then we can get out of here. Shayne looks like she could use a decent meal, a shower, and her own fucking bed."

The boys nod and as Roman reaches for the small handle of the basement, my heart breaks recalling exactly what—*or who*—he would see down there.

Breaking free of Marcus' hold, I race toward Roman as the door swings open, my heart pounding wildly with desperation to save him from the horrors he'll find. "WAIT," I rush out, barging out in front of him and squeezing myself between him and the door, bracing my hands on either side as the overwhelming smell of her decaying body rushes through the open door.

Roman stares at me, reading my body language as though it was scrawled across my forehead in bright red marker. "What don't you want me to see?" he demands, his eyes narrowing to slits as that terrifying scar reminds me how careful I need to be when it comes to Felicity.

"Can you smell that?" Marcus murmurs, quickly glancing toward Levi as the three of them crowd around me, their interest piqued.

Levi nods and I glance up at him, my distraction only frustrating Roman more. "Shayne," he snaps. "Tell me what the fuck is going on. Now."

Fuck.

I let out a shaky breath, my heart falling right out of my chest and landing in a messy heap on my sleeve for the whole fucking world to see. I know he sees the pain and regret stretched over my face, and judging by the terror starting to form in his eyes, he knows exactly where this is going. "When I got here … she … I couldn't …"

"Who's she?" he growls, the sound vibrating right through his chest and sending a wave of unease sailing through my bones.

A heavy lump forms in my throat and devastation washes over me, but the longer I take to say it, the worse it's going to be, so I suck it up, knowing that he needs this so much more than I do. "Felicity," I finally say, my voice breaking with regret.

Roman doesn't even give me a chance to explain before he grabs hold of me and throws me back toward his brothers with a ruthless force that knocks me right off my feet. And just like that, he's gone, his footfalls echoing through the massive basement as he races toward the woman he loves.

The woman who will never be me.

CHAPTER SEVEN

ROMAN

Shayne's body flies from my hands. I'm distantly aware of my brothers catching her before she falls, and fuck, I know I pushed her way too hard, but the moment Felicity's sweet name came trembling from between her lips, all train of thought left me.

Nothing else matters except getting to her.

Taking two steps at a time, I race down into the basement that looks like a fucking whore house gone wrong. Cells line every fucking wall, half of them open, half of them with random women, their backs against the hard concrete, but the void of color in their cheeks tells me they're long gone.

Two guards lay at the bottom of the steps, one with a gaping hole in the side of his neck while the other has a slit throat, but the way the blood sits over his body makes it clear the fucker was already dead before she cut him.

Without skipping a beat, I launch myself over the side of the rusted railing, not wanting to waste precious moments scrambling over their bodies as I try to find my girl. The guards aren't important. We can circle back to that once I've got Felicity back in my arms.

My feet slam against the concrete ground and I barely notice the soft splash beneath them before glancing down to find the basement floor soaked with water, not even the desert heat doing enough to dry this out. I want to pause to ask what the fuck is going on, but there will be time to answer questions afterward.

I look over every fucking cell, desperate to see those rosy cheeks and that beautiful long blonde hair, but I find nothing, and the desperation quickly sets in as I hear my brothers and Shayne on the stairs. How the fuck could Shayne do this? She just left her behind to rot in a fucking cell. I know she was fighting for her life, but leaving her? I thought Shayne was better than that. I know we had a rocky start, but we moved past that. I thought we were cool now. I'll never let her live this down. Something else has to be going on. There has to be more to the story.

"FELICITY," I call, my panic starting to overwhelm me as I find myself spinning, looking back and forth, trying to get to her. There's a woman at the opposite end and she gapes at me in horror before hiding her face and scrambling back in her cell as though I'm here to rain hell over her, but to be completely honest, I couldn't give a shit about her. The cell is open so she's free to leave whenever the hell she wants.

I was so sure that Felicity was dead when her body gave out in my arms, but Marcus was right about her being his shooter. I just couldn't entertain the idea that the love of my life was still out there, fighting for hers in a world I was supposed to protect her from. She was so innocent, thrown into this bullshit just like Shayne was, only she wasn't as strong as Shayne. Felicity needed me; our baby needed me. The girl I once knew would have never shot my brother. Our father put her up to it; there is no other explanation.

But there's still time to turn this around. I'm here now, and I can bring her home, protect her, start over again in the hope that one day she'll forgive me for abandoning her here for so long.

I could have killed my brother when that accusation came flying out of Shayne's mouth at my dining table. How dare he try to fuck with her memory like that? But he kept at it, determined that it was her, and I was a fucking idiot for not believing him. I saw the signs and I ignored every last one of them. There is still time. If I'd only listened, if I'd given it the time of day, I could have saved her from this bullshit.

My father will pay for keeping her from me. I'll fucking destroy him for this.

My gaze skims over a cell that has signs of an attack, torn underwear, dried blood, and a pair of pants that are inside out. My mind takes me to the worst fucking place, and I find myself looking up at Shayne. There's something oddly familiar about those pants. They're not Shayne's though. She's still fully dressed in the clothes she was wearing the day she was taken.

Felicity. They must be hers.

"Where the fuck is she?" I roar, looking up and meeting Shayne's stare on the steps, hiding behind my brothers as though she's terrified that I'm about to take out my frustrations on her. I would never hurt her like that, not after the bullshit I've already put her though, but fuck, if one of my brothers wanted to try me right now, I'd be more than happy to take my guilt out on them.

Shayne nods toward the cell just down from me and points. "She's in there," she starts. "But—"

I break away, spinning on my heel and darting toward the cell to find a fucking mess. "FELICITY," I rush out, my brothers racing down the rest of the stairs.

"Roman, wait," I hear Shayne calling out, whatever she needs to say is not important right now, all that matters is getting to Felicity.

I reach her cell within two big strides and dive through the open door, my gaze shooting down to the body sprawled out on the floor, unable to understand what the fuck I'm looking at. This isn't my Felicity. This is ... this is nothing but a shell. Her stomach is swollen and her bright blonde hair dirty and matted. Those lips that would brush against mine are thin and gray, the color completely drained from her body. *Her stiff, decaying body.*

"Fuck," I hear Marcus moving in behind me, his hand falling to my shoulder and making me realize that I'm on my knees.

I reach out to her, gripping onto her perfect, delicate little hand unable to believe what I'm seeing. She can't be dead, not when I only just got her back. My hand clenches around hers, the red-hot anger burning through me. She looks as though she's been gone for at least a few days, and that realization has pure agony spearing through my chest.

My eyes sting, a feeling I've never experienced before, and I want nothing more than to sink my fingers into someone's chest and tear their heart right out of their body.

"FUCK," I roar, this feeling weighing down on me, something I haven't felt since that night my father stormed the castle and shot her through the chest. She was supposed to be gone then. I'd come to terms with it, but she's been alive this whole fucking time and I left her here to rot, left her in my father's grasps, too fucking overwhelmed by grief and anger to even question it.

I failed her. I let her down and I'll never fucking forgive myself.

A broken sigh sounds beside me, and I feel Shayne's presence like a fucking beacon calling to me. "How?" I breathe, the word getting stuck in my throat.

She moves in closer, and it somehow makes the pain just a little more tolerable. She drops to her knees, looking down at Felicity as though they were best friends. She reaches out and brushes the matted strands of hair off her face, revealing the sunken hollows of her cheeks, cheeks that were once full of life.

"Your father has kept her locked up this whole time," Shayne starts, lowering her voice to a whisper as she struggles to get the words out. "The night I got here was when it happened. She was all alone in here, already in labor. She was screaming. I'll never forget it. I was locked up across the basement, but I couldn't ignore it. They were just upstairs, acting as though nothing was happening and I …"

She trails off, realizing there are more important things she needs to share right now. "I knocked out one of the guards … the one you just shot outside, and I helped her. She was so scared. She didn't want to push because she knew what your father was going to do the second the baby was delivered."

Dread pulses through me and my chest sinks, fearing the worst. "My baby," I breathe, feeling it deep in my gut. He's gone. My father would have killed him in front of her eyes before killing her just to get his fucking rocks off.

"No," Shayne rushes out, taking my hand in hers and holding it so close to her chest that I feel the rapid beat of her heart beneath. "She gave birth to a beautiful little boy, Roman," she tells me, her eyes watering as she recalls the magical moment. "He was perfect, and fuck, he had a good set of lungs on him. Felicity," she continues, pausing for a moment to find herself. "She held him in her arms, and seeing the way she looked at her son, it was the most beautiful thing I have ever seen."

My heart constricts and the agony tearing through me is like never before. I've never been so fucking jealous. I would have loved to witness the birth of my son, to be here as he was brought into the world and see that unconditional love shining through Felicity's eyes as she looked down at him for the first time. "Stop dancing around it," I demand. "Give it to me straight. What the fuck happened?"

Shayne's brows furrow and I see the fear in her eyes, wanting to save me from whatever she's about to say, but she knows I need to hear it just as much as my brothers do. "A few minutes after your son was born, Felicity started to hemorrhage. There was just blood … everywhere. I couldn't stop it, couldn't control it. It just kept coming and I panicked. I couldn't help her. I swear, I was trying to save her, but there was just … nothing," she says with a heavy sob, squeezing my hand as though that's magically going to make the pain go away. "There was nothing I could do but watch her die while she held onto her son."

My gaze lingers on Felicity's body, and the longer I stare, the harder it gets. "Was she scared?" I question, at odds with my emotions, glad that she died from birthing complications rather than at my father's hand. "When she died. Was she scared?"

Shayne shakes her head. "I don't believe so," she murmurs. "She was concerned about the baby. That's all that mattered to her. She was terrified of what would happen to him growing up in this world, but I assured her that he would be safe with us. I … I can't exactly speak for her, but I think she was almost relieved to go, that it was finally over for her."

Shayne's words kill me more than she will ever know, the thought of Felicity enduring this hell for so long at my father's hands and not being here to save her. What would she have thought of me?

Levi moves in closer, standing directly behind Shayne, his hand dropping to her shoulder. "Where's the baby, Shayne?" he questions, asking the one question I'm too fucking scared to hear the answer to. "What happened to him?"

Shayne looks back at me, fresh tears forming in her eyes. "I tried to stop him," she says, choking on her sobs as they get stuck in her throat. "But your father … he … he …"

My eyes close as the overwhelming grief takes over me. She said earlier that he was fine, but I won't believe it until I hear exactly what happened. "Spit it out," I roar, the mix of frustration, guilt, fear, and devastation creating a vile mix.

"He was down here the whole time, watching her die and he just … he did nothing but watch," she cries, tears streaming down her blood-stained face. "I tried to run with the baby, but he blocked me in. I had nowhere to go and his hand … he overpowered me. He took the baby and promised that he would use him as a weapon against you. I swear," she adds, her violent sobs tearing at my already shattered heart. "I held onto him as long as I could. Your son … he's gone. Your father took him, and I don't know how to find him."

With that, I take one last lingering look at Felicity's body, taking in the face that I'll never see full of life ever again. I get to my feet and walk the fuck out.

CHAPTER EIGHT

Felicity's body rests in the back of the SUV, the smell singeing my nose just as it has done for the past four days, forcing me to relive every fucked-up little moment from my time down in Giovanni's basement. Roman couldn't bear to leave her behind, and I don't blame him. If I could have taken her with me when I first escaped, I would have. I would have done anything to try and make what happened down there okay.

Roman killed me today. Seeing the intense agony in his eyes was the hardest thing I've ever endured. I've never experienced someone else's raw grief like that, and being the one who had to break the news, the one who could have saved her, and the one who's personally responsible for letting their father take off with his newborn son … yeah, the weight I thought had lifted off my shoulder has crashed back over me with extra bricks added to the load.

He'll never forgive me for letting her die like that, and he sure as fuck won't forgive me for letting his son be taken. I was weak in those cells. I was desperate and I let him down. I let them all down.

Roman sits up front with Marcus while Levi sits in the back with me, his arm curled tightly around my body as my head rests against his big shoulder. Doe is on my other side, curled up in a ball as she rests quietly, her big head draped across my lap. The SUV is huge, but the backseat simply isn't enough space for Levi and me plus a ginormous wolf. She would have been more comfortable in the back, but with Felicity taking up residence in there, we didn't want to risk it.

My fingers thread into the fur on top of Doe's head and she gently stirs beneath me only to make a show of getting comfortable, silently pleading for me to scratch her head. My fingers move in and out in a gentle massage behind her ears, and a low groan travels through her chest. Pain tears at me knowing the grief she must be feeling at not having her brother here with us. The two of them were like peas in a pod, always together, causing havoc over the castle and doing everything in their power to make my life a living hell. It's as though they had some kind of competition between themselves to see who could get on my nerves the quickest, though Dill won that competition every single time. He had a gift for it, but there was no mistaking the kindness in his jet-black eyes.

I've been avoiding the question, not ready to hear all the gruesome details about Dill's downfall, but I owe it to him to hear it. He protected me with his life out there in the woods. The least I can do is hear about his final moments and pay him the respect he's owed. "Dill?" I question, my tone low and wavering. "What … how did he …"

A heavy sigh pulls from deep within me, and I let the rest of my question fade away, the words too hard to get out. Sensing Levi's gaze, I lift my head off his shoulder and meet his haunted stare. "He's okay," he murmurs.

My brows furrow and I glance back down at Doe. "He's okay?" I question, repeating his words back to him as I shake my head. "No. He was shot. I heard him howling. He couldn't have lived through that."

Marcus grunts from the front seat and glances back at me, his lips curved into an amused grin. "You really think Dill was going to let a single bullet take him down? That big bastard would have chewed that fucker up and spat it back out the other end. He's a warrior, Shayne. Just like you."

My heart flutters, its pace kicking up a gear as a fresh new hope surges through my veins. "He's okay?" I question again. "I figured that because he wasn't here …"

Levi's hand falls to my thigh, gently squeezing and forcing my gaze back to his. "He's alright," he murmurs. "My father is a lousy shot. The bullet tore through his midsection and fucked with some of his internal organs, but we got him to the animal clinic just in time. He's at home recovering, and trust me when I tell you, he's pissed that he didn't get to come. It would have been too much strain on his body."

Relief overwhelms my system, and hot tears well in my eyes as the raging grief I've held down for the incredible wolf begins washing away. "I thought we'd lost him," I whisper, my voice breaking as losing Dill, on top of everything else, was just the bullshit cherry on top of this shitstorm cake.

"Don't get me wrong," Levi says. "Dill isn't completely out of the woods yet. He had a big surgery to repair the internal damage. He's on all sorts of pain medication and probably won't be able to take a proper dump for a while. He's a grouchy asshole, but he'll pull through. He always does."

My fingers knot tighter into Doe's fur, and I find myself leaning over her, curling my other arm around her strong body and holding her tight. "Did you hear that?" I whisper, my tone hitching up with hope while feeling like an idiot for talking to the wolf as though she can understand my every word. "Dill is going to be okay."

Doe raises her head just enough to rub her face past mine, and a wave of warmth washes through me at her understanding and affection. She doesn't linger or even meet my eye before dropping back into my lap and putting an abrupt end to our short conversation. But what can I say? Doe is a woman of few words, and I shouldn't expect anything else.

Letting out a sigh, I straighten in my seat and let my head fall back, allowing my eyes to flutter closed. It's been a hellish few days, and I should really use these next few hours to get some sleep, but the moment my eyelids close and block out the car around me, the haunting images of delivering Roman's baby boy materialize in my mind.

My eyes spring open as the slightest gasp escapes me. I can't help but glance up only to find Roman's lethal stare meeting mine through the rearview mirror. I immediately look away, unable to handle the weight of his disapproval.

"What's wrong?" Levi questions, glancing down at me through narrowed eyes.

Pain rests heavily in my chest as I stare out the side window, watching the endless expanse of desert. My shoulders droop and helplessness comes over me. "Can't sleep," I tell him. "Every time I close my eyes, I see it. It's like a fucked-up movie playing on repeat in my head and I can't make it stop."

I see him nodding out of my peripheral as he reaches out and takes my hand in his. "Would it help to know that at some point, each of us have been held captive?" he questions. "You're not alone in this, Shayne. Each of those terrible things you witnessed or had to do, we've done them too. We know how it feels, what you're going through, and what it's like fearing that you might never live to see another sunrise."

My head whips toward him before quickly glancing into the front seats. Neither Marcus or Roman turn back, but I sense them listening. "You've been taken?"

Levi nods and I feel him holding onto my hand just a little bit tighter. "I was sixteen. I'd just slaughtered the nephew of one of the world's richest men and he didn't appreciate it much."

"No shit," I mutter, turning my gaze toward the front seat to find Marcus twisting in his seat to watch me without having to strain his neck. "What about you?"

"Twenty-two," he tells me, his lips twisting into an amused smirk. "Fucked the wrong man's wife."

A smile pulls at the corners of my mouth and something lightens in my chest, as though whatever is keeping me bound so tight is starting to fray and ease. "Why am I not surprised?"

Marcus' dark, obsidian eyes glisten with laughter. "It wasn't the best experience of my life, and if she wasn't so good in bed, I would have been really fucking pissed."

"I bet you never saw her again."

Marcus laughs as the dusty desert track slowly turns into an old, broken-down road that looks as though it hasn't been tended to in years. "On the contrary," he tells me. "Just out of spite of that old fucker, I screwed her brains out for another three months. I would have kept going, but the asshole found the wrong end of some loser's gun. It wasn't much fun after that."

I shake my head before cutting my gaze across to Roman, though the hard set of his jaw and his whitening knuckles on the steering wheel suggests that asking about his time held captive isn't something he's willing to talk about.

"Look," Marcus says, the contrast in his tone from just a moment ago sending a wave of unease through me. "I know you probably don't want to talk about this and that it's going to stir up some old wounds, but we need to revisit your tracking device. You have a target on your back, and now that you've escaped our father's clutches, he's going to be pissed. I won't risk you being taken again and us not knowing how to get to you. Four days is unacceptable."

"I know," I murmur. "You can put it back in."

"Wait," he says, his brows furrowing as he pauses, almost as though he's repeating my words over in his head. "You agree with me?

After what happened with Roman and Levi and you tearing it out, I was ready for a whole fucking argument."

"How could I not agree with you? If I had that stupid thing in my arm, you guys would have caught up to us the moment we got here..." I imagine what would have been different had they tracked me to the cabin right away. The boys could have found us here, gotten help for Felicity before it was too late, saved Ariana from being abused and sold. Roman would still have his girl and his baby in his arms right now if it weren't for my reckless mistakes. When I see Roman's eyes in the rearview again, it's clear that he knows exactly what I'm thinking. He's probably thought the same things since finding Felicity dead. It's all my fault. Breaking away, I glance down at my hands. "What I went through there ... I can't risk that happening again. I won't."

Marcus' eyes gleam with relief, and it makes me realize just how worried he's been about the topic, though I don't know why. Had I disagreed, I'm sure they would have found another way to get a tracker on me. "What about contraceptives?" Levi questions. "Will you allow us to insert a fresh one? I know you felt railroaded with the last one, and I don't want you to feel as though we're taking away your choice. It's your body, I want you to do what you're comfortable with, but I also think it's a smart decision to ensure you're protected against any unplanned pregnancies, at least ... until you're ready."

Biting down on my lip, my gaze falls to the angry red scar on my arm as I let out a heavy sigh. An unplanned pregnancy really would fuck with my vibe right now. There's too much going on in my life to have to worry about that. The responsible thing to do would be to protect myself. "Okay," I finally say, glancing back up at him. "But I won't have any of you digging into my skin. I want a doctor. A real doctor," I quickly add. "Not some asshole who's on your father's payroll and who will get killed at the end of the appointment."

Levi meets Roman's heavy stare through the rearview mirror, and after a painful silence, he finally nods. "Fine," Roman says. "But one of us will be present during your appointment."

I arch a brow, irritation bubbling to the surface. "Are you kidding me?" I scoff. "After all this time, you don't trust me to sit through one measly doctor appointment and keep my mouth shut?"

His dark stare keeps me hostage, and the longer he holds it, the faster my heart beats. "It's not you I don't trust," he finally spits.

Ahhhh, the doctor. I guess that makes sense.

Unable to handle his intensity, I let out a breath and drop my gaze back to the wolf in my lap when Levi's thumb rubs over the back of my knuckles. "This appointment," he starts. "Did you want me to book you for a thorough examination?"

"Examination?"

His jaw clenches and anger pulses through his heavy stare. "I saw that cell, Shayne. The blood on the ground, the torn underwear. I know what happened to you and I don't want you feeling ashamed or scared. I don't expect you to talk about it or even acknowledge what happened in there, but I think it's a good idea to get yourself checked over."

His words swirl around my mind as my chest grows heavier. I should have cut him off the second I realized what he was talking about, but the moment the words 'torn underwear' came out of his mouth, guilt came slamming down over my shoulders, and along with it, a shitload of indecision.

What happened to Ariana in the cell with the boys' uncle is her business, and I sure as fuck feel as though she'd hate me for telling everyone, but how could I not? Knowing where she is right now, she's probably been abused a million times over the past couple of days.

"That cell," I say, the betrayal of what I'm about to do heavily weighing on me. "It wasn't mine. It was Ariana's."

Roman flinches in the front seat, his eyes shifting to the rearview mirror as Marcus' head whips around to look at me again. Levi's hand clenches in mine. "What did you just say?"

"It was Ariana's," I repeat. "She was already there when I was locked up. It looked like she'd been there at least a few days. We didn't really talk about it, but my guess is that she was captured after our little showdown at your father's property."

"The guards raped her?" Roman questions, his tone low and filled with venom, and while the four of us hate her for what she did to me, there's no denying the years of history between Ariana and Roman. Despite cutting her off and throwing her to the wolves, news like this is still hard to hear.

Shaking my head, I swallow over the lump in my throat, trying to find the strength to say the words out loud. After what Ariana went through in that cell, the least she deserves is for me to be able to get the words out without falling apart. "Your uncle. Phillip. Your father sold her to him. He came down, abused her for two hours, and then dragged her away."

"Fuck," Marcus spits, turning back in his seat to look out his window as the wild, overwhelming emotions force their way through his body.

Roman's chest rises and falls with rapid movements, and I can't help but notice the sharp cut of his jaw as he clenches his teeth, fury rippling through his dark eyes. Not wanting to direct anything to Roman, I turn my attention to the younger DeAngelis sitting right by my side. "I know you guys don't owe her anything after what she did, and trust me, I know how ridiculous it is of me to even consider this after everything she put me through, but she had my back down in those cells. When Phillip came in, she told me to play dead. He wanted to take me first and then take her home for seconds, but she drew his attention back on her. She saved me from suffering the same way she did, and the whole time she kept her mouth shut, protecting me while he defiled her. The things …" I shake my head, the haunting images flying through my head too much to handle. "I just laid there and played dead then watched in silence while he dragged her away. And I'm sorry, I know you're not forgiving men, and going back on your word to disown her isn't your style, but after what she did for me … in the very least your uncle deserves to lose his life."

Marcus rubs his hand over his face as he glances toward Roman. "If Phillip knew where to find that cabin and had made a deal with our father, there's a good chance that he knows something that we don't."

Roman shakes his head, reading into whatever Marcus is trying to get at. "He won't lead us to him. Phillip is too careful. He covers his tracks."

"Either way, Shayne is right. We can't leave Ariana there to be abused day in and day out."

"Are you forgetting that she almost had Shayne slaughtered in a fucking bathtub?" Roman questions, his tone louder and full of a conflicted fury.

"Fuck no, I haven't," Marcus fires back. "Ariana needs to be punished for what she did, and she will be, but not like this and not by Phillip's hand. The ball is in Shayne's court, and she can decide how she wants to execute this one. So don't go fooling yourself by acting as though you're okay with this. We know where you draw your lines, brother. This will eat at you for the rest of your life."

Roman lets out a heavy sigh and quickly meets my hard stare before turning his attention back to the deserted road. "Then I guess it's time we pay our uncle a visit."

CHAPTER NINE

Hot clouds of steam fill the bathroom as I pull my stained tank over my head. My reflection is foggy in the mirror, but not even that will mask the nasty scars and dirt marring my skin. I don't bother looking for long. I know what I will find, and it's not something I need to dwell on right now.

After peeling my blood-stained pants from my legs, I scoop up my discarded tank and toss every bit of clothing I wore in the cell into the trash. Fuck, if I had the energy right now, those clothes would be burning in the bathtub, but the trash can will have to do for now.

Striding across the bathroom, I step directly into the hot flow of water. It singes my body and I suck in a loud breath through my teeth, quickly jumping away and slamming my back against the cold tiles. I slowly inch forward, taking my time as I stick my foot into the hot stream and watch as it slowly washes away the dried blood and grime coating my skin.

Getting used to the heat, I watch as the water turns my skin a soft shade of pink, and only after spending twenty minutes staring at the plain white tiles of the shower wall do I grab the body wash and scrub every crevice and inch of my skin. I wash myself over and over again, knowing that no amount of body wash will make me feel clean.

My head tips back under the water and I rinse it with shampoo, feeling my long locks of hair falling right down to my ass, the water making it appear so much longer. After spending ten minutes sailing a razor over all the important parts and making me feel somewhat like myself, my back falls against the cool shower tiles again.

I slide down the wall until my ass hits the floor and my knees come up against my chest. Curling my arms around my legs, I drop my head against my knees and close my eyes as the water crashes down over me like a waterfall.

It was a five-hour drive back to the DeAngelis mansion, and though this home comes fully equipped with everything a girl could ever need, it doesn't feel like home to me. A part of me had hoped to hide within the walls of the boys' gothic castle, and though that place holds horrendous memories of its own, it also offers me the illusion of safety.

A part of me is convinced that I'll be safe here, that Giovanni won't be stupid enough to come here again, but I'm starting to learn that my basic instincts can't be trusted. I've turned down a million wrong paths since being dragged into this unforgiving world, and I'm barely finding my feet. I've never experienced unpredictability on this scale before.

Shit, a girl can't even chase a dildo wielding wolf through the woods without getting kidnapped. Though to be fair, in the movies, girls are always getting kidnapped in the woods when they foolishly decide to go out alone. I guess the joke is on me.

"What are you doing?" A familiar voice asks.

My head snaps up and I'm immediately hit with the hot spray directly in my face. I pull back enough to avoid it and find Levi hovering in the doorway, his shoulder pressed against the frame and his thick, muscled arms crossed over his chest. "Trying to convince myself that I don't really need to sleep."

"I can get you something for that," he offers. "You'll be out in two seconds."

I shake my head, the idea bouncing around in my mind like a sick tease, offering me the world but coming with far too many consequences. "No," I finally say. "I don't want to risk not being able to wake myself if the dreams come."

"Fair enough," he murmurs. "What do you need?"

Looking up through my lashes, I shrug my shoulders. "I just need to breathe. I need to go twenty minutes without remembering one of the sick, vile things I had to do. I just … I need a break from it all. I need to forget."

Levi pushes off the door frame as his hand flies back over his head and grips the top of his shirt. He shrugs out of it, putting those gorgeous tattoos on display as he strides toward the shower. He tosses his shirt carelessly onto the basin and steps right into the spray of water, his black jeans riding low on his defined hips.

"Consider it done," he murmurs just as he reaches down and grabs me under my arms. He tears me up off the shower floor, and the momentum of his movements has my body slamming up against his. My arms fly around his neck as my back presses against the cool shower wall.

A gasp tears from my throat as my legs instinctively wrap around his waist, the fly of his jeans pressing up against my clit and sending a wave of hot electricity pulsing right through my core. His hips rock and I feel him hardening through his soaked jeans, always so ready to give me what I need.

My eyes close as a low moan travels up my throat and I do nothing but allow myself to feel. He moves slowly, grinding against my pussy as his warm lips press down against my neck, his tongue brushing over my sensitive, bruised skin.

Every haunting thought fades from my head, just as he knew it would, and all that's left is my need to be with him, to feel him inside me, stretching me and making me feel alive. I tilt my head, allowing him more access as he holds onto me with one hand, his other brushing down my side before trailing back up and cupping my tit. His finger circles my nipple and it hardens beneath his teasing touch like an invitation that he doesn't dare skip out on.

He pinches my nipple just as his fly rubs past my clit and my body jolts, a gasp sailing from between my lips as the electricity intensifies. "Fuck, Levi," I breathe, damn sure that if our bodies weren't glued together, I'd already have his velvety cock in my hands, working him like I know he needs.

His lips grow more intense on my neck, and I grab his face, desperate to taste his kiss. He gives me exactly what I need, not relenting for a damn second as his tongue dives into my mouth, his bruising kiss setting my body alight.

His hand roams over my body, leaving a trail of desperation in its wake, and as it continues down, I groan into his mouth, the anticipation almost too much. He pulls back just an inch, allowing enough space for his hand to slip between our bodies, and without skipping a beat, the pad of his thumb strokes over my clit. "Oh, fuck," I gasp against his lips, my legs tightening around him. "Again."

Not one to disappoint, his thumb hits my clit, and instead of stroking right over it, he rubs lazy circles and my whole body sags in instant satisfaction, my eyes closing as I do nothing but feel.

As he worships my clit with the sweetest devotion, his fingers fall further. They find my entrance and push up into me, curving just right to hit that delicious spot deep inside. "Holy shit, Levi. Yes," I moan, my nails digging into his shoulder.

He pulls back from my lips and I immediately miss their touch, but as he takes my thigh and unwinds it from his waist, he drops to his knees, and I realize that his lips could be much better suited somewhere else.

His big hands slide up my legs and grip onto my thighs just under my ass before effortlessly lifting me. I grip onto his shoulders as he spreads my thighs and seats me on his shoulders, my pussy directly in line with his mouth, and damn it, he wastes no time.

His skilled tongue flicks over my clit and I cry out, my loud, gasping groan filled with the best kind of satisfaction. Just when I think it can't get any better, his lips close over my cunt, and he works me in that delicious way that only Levi DeAngelis can.

Sucking. Nipping. Teasing. Taunting.

"Oh, fuck!"

With his dark, heated eyes on me, he reaches down and I become mesmerized, watching as he undoes his jeans and pulls his thick cock from its confines. Its angry veins call to me like a damn siren, daring me to lose my mind and do all sorts of wicked things. I'm way too far to even consider reaching for it, but as his hand curls around his long shaft, I realize that sometimes watching the show can be so much better.

Levi's eyes bore into mine as he works his cock up and down, making me bite down on my lip in hunger. My back presses harder against the wall, and he reaches up with his other hand, gripping my tit and giving it a firm squeeze as he works my pussy.

His tongue flicks over my clit and I cry out knowing that I won't be leaving this shower until he's fucked me within an inch of my life.

My body burns for it, the desperation pulsing through me like never before. "Oh God, Levi. Yes, don't fucking stop. Right there," I cry, my pants becoming wild and frantic as he fucks me with his tongue, his slow torturous pace on his cock making everything clench deep within me, imagining that same, intense pace pushing deep inside my cunt.

My head tilts back against the tiles and I close my eyes, intent to feel every intense second, and damn it, it's more than anything I could have asked for. Everything tightens deep in my core, and I suck in a breath knowing it won't be long, but as his tongue and lips continue working me with that incredible, raw skill, my orgasm creeps up faster than I could have imagined.

It builds and builds and I'm forced to tangle my fingers into his hair just to hold on. My fingers pull into a fist, and I grip onto him tightly as my orgasm reaches its climax and I explode on his tongue. "Oh, FUCK," I cry, my voice echoing through the big bathroom, the sound of the shower barely drowning it out.

My pussy convulses, my whole body shaking and clenching as he sets every nerve alight, the mind-blowing sensation rocking through my body and making me feel like a damn goddess, even more so as I feel his hungry smile against my throbbing cunt.

I've barely come down from my high before Levi is pulling me off his shoulders and curling his arm around my waist. He stands and I feel his rock-hard cock pressing against my stomach making my mouth water. I can't help but curl my hand around his impressive size, and as I do, his fingers knot into the back of my hair and tear my head back.

His hungry stare bores into mine. "I'm going to fuck your tight little cunt," he warns me. "You're going to scream for me, baby. Is that understood?"

Holy fuck.

Yes, sir.

His lips crush down over mine and I taste my arousal on his tongue as his arm tightens around my waist. Levi lifts me and my legs curl around him, holding on tight before he steps out of the shower. Not having enough hands to shut off the water, we leave it running and I make a mental note to come back later and turn it off, though I can't guarantee that I'll be in any state to walk after he's through with me.

With water rushing off us, he walks straight out into my bedroom and adjusts his hold on my waist, gripping me tightly. He throws me down on my bed, but with one hand on my thigh, I'm left spread wide with my tits gently bouncing from my crash landing.

"Fucking gorgeous," he mutters, almost sounding as though he's in pain simply from not already being buried deep inside me. His heavy, heated gaze sweeps over my body and lingers on my pussy, adoration and desire pulsing wickedly in his eyes. Marcus has always been the one to fuck me in any which way, but when Levi does it, he needs to be at a vantage point, always with the best view to watch as his cock slams deep inside me, only to re-emerge coated with my arousal. What can I say? He's a visual kind of guy, and I'm not gonna lie, I love it when he watches. It's one thing to taste me as he gets me off but getting to see it is the cherry on top of the fuck fest cake.

Without warning, he takes my hips and flips me over, pushing my knees up under me and forcing my chest down into my comforter so that my ass is flying high and proud. His low, hungry growl tears through the room and I can't help but spread my knees further apart, wanting him to see everything I have on offer. "Fucking hell," he mutters darkly, his tone warning me that I'm going to be feeling him deep inside me for days to come.

A shiver travels down my spine as he steps in close behind me and trails his fingers over the high curve of my ass. A breathy moan escapes me as I impatiently look back over my shoulder, watching him intently. I gently sway my hips from side to side, tempting and inviting him to hurry the fuck up, but a man like Levi DeAngelis can't be coaxed. He'll fuck me on his time, in his way, and I'll be left with no damn choice but to love it.

His fingers trail over my cunt and a jolt of electricity fires through me. "So fucking wet," he murmurs with pride as his fingers mix with my arousal. His other hand cups my ass cheek and his fingers slowly push inside me and curve around, massaging my walls as he goes. My pussy clenches with anticipation and his low laugh fills the room. "So impatient."

I push back against him, forcing his fingers deeper inside my cunt and this new angle has a groan rumbling through my chest. "You like that, baby?" he mutters, the wicked tone in his voice filled with a deep hunger as I feel the tip of his cock gently pressing against my clit.

"Hooooly fuck, yes," I tell him, the anticipation building like never before.

His hand on my ass cheek pushes down to meet his other, and I gasp as he pushes his thumb inside me, stretching my pussy that little bit further. Before I can get used to the feel of so many fingers, he draws his coated thumb back and trails it higher before applying the type of pressure that has my eyes rolling in the back of my head. He pushes deeper and I press back into him again, needing so much more.

I keep my eyes locked on him, watching the way he takes me in, moving his fingers deep inside me as his thumb teases my ass. His desire only pulses that much stronger, and as the anticipation gets too much for him, he draws his fingers out of me and I prepare myself for him to do his worst.

Levi glances up and meets my hooded stare, and I watch as he brings his glistening fingers to his mouth and sucks them dry. He puts on a show licking his fingers, and just as he lines his thick cock up with my entrance, the word "Mine," tears from his lips.

His fingers grip onto my hips, and not a second later, he buries his cock deep inside me, stretching me wide. I cry out, the raw groan like music to my ears. "Fuck, yes. Again."

Levi pauses, his balls pressed right up against my clit as an intense growl rumbles in his chest. His eyes roll to the back of his head, and I push my ass back, taking all I can get. He slowly draws back, the anticipation building so much more, then without warning, slams back into me again, his tip hitting me in all the right places.

Levi picks up his pace and fucks me like a true fucking gentleman should—raw, hard, and fast. And just as he wanted, a crazed scream tears from my lips, his name quickly followed with breathy, gasped pants. My pussy clenches around him, squeezing him tight, and his fingers digging into my hips tells me just how much he likes it.

He pushes deeper and presses against my back, forcing my ass higher, and God damnnnnn. Any fucking day. Yes, Daddy.

He slams into me over and over and as that familiar tightening grows deep inside, I slip my hand beneath me and press my fingers to my clit. Rubbing tight little circles, my pussy clenches as my ass tightens around his thumb, the anticipation quickly taking over. "Holy fucking hell," I mutter into the comforter, my words muffled by the expensive goose down blanket.

Levi fucks me harder, his pace picking up as my fingers work tirelessly against my clit. He spanks me hard, the sound rocking through my bedroom as everything clenches within me, tearing a loud groan from both of us. My ass stings in the most delicious way, and before I even get a chance to warn him, my orgasm tears through me like lightning.

My pussy convulses and I turn into a quivering wreck. Sucking in a sharp breath, I clench my eyes as my fingers fist into the comforter. "Oh, fuuuuck," I groan just as Levi comes with me, his hot seed shooting into me as his thumb pauses on my ass, slowly pushing deeper.

My orgasm pulses through me, and as Levi keeps moving, allowing me to ride out my high, it only grows more intense. I cry out, the overpowering adrenaline proving too much for me to handle. My body finally releases me from its hold, allowing me a chance to catch my breath. As I come down from my high, Levi gently pulls out of me, and I collapse, curling into an exhausted ball and looking up at this incredible beast of a man.

He looks down at me, adoration in his warm eyes as I feel his seed slowly leaking out of me and smooshing between my legs, but hell, I'm not about to get up and leave, not when Levi's looking at me like this.

He bends down and scoops me into his capable, inked arms, holding me tight to his chest as he walks around the edge of the bed. He drops down, sitting up against the headboard of the bed and holds me on his lap, not giving a flying fuck that I'm making all sorts of a mess on his lap.

My head rests against his chest and I listen to the rhythmic beat of his heart as his hand curls up around me, holding me still. "Sleep now," he tells me, more than coming through on his challenge to make me forget. "I'm not going anywhere. I'll hold you all night long if you need me to."

And without another word, the safety of his strong arms comes over me and I fall into a long, dreamless sleep, the monsters and demons of my mind finally put to rest.

CHAPTER TEN

The late afternoon sun shines through my bedroom window, and I squint into the bright light, finding Levi's arms still tightly wrapped around me despite being asleep for a lifetime. It must be somewhere around five in the afternoon, meaning I've been out for at least twenty hours.

"I thought you were never going to wake," Levi murmurs into the silence, placing his phone down on the bed and pulling me into his chest. "How are you feeling?"

I shrug my shoulders, not really sure how to answer that. "Fine, I guess," I say, giving him a generic answer that gives away absolutely nothing, but to be honest, I have no idea how I feel. Sure, my life is still just as fucked up as it's always been. There's no denying that, but today is a new day and a chance to put it all behind me. Today is my first shot at moving on, and I want to make it count.

Pulling out of Levi's arms, I scoot to the edge of the bed and get up on shaky legs before rushing into the bathroom and dropping my ass onto the toilet. Twenty hours is far too long for me to go without peeing, and with Levi's manhood still spread far and wide between my legs, I'm overdue for a cleanup.

After getting myself cleaned up, I step back out into the massive bedroom that has somehow become my own. I walk across the plush carpet and step into the walk-in closet, finding brand new black lingerie dangling from a satin hanger. After ripping off the expensive tags, I watch myself through the floor-to-ceiling mirror as I slip the black lace over my body. It fits me perfectly, and damn, I'm not going to lie, it's one of the sexiest pieces of lingerie I've ever worn.

Scanning over the racks of clothes that once belonged to Ariana, I find a black, silk robe and pull it off its hanger before squishing it between my hands. It's the softest silk gown I've ever touched. I can only imagine how much this thing cost, but either way, I will be living in it from this point on, unless one of those demanding DeAngelis brothers tell me otherwise.

Slipping my arms through the wide armholes, I trudge back out into the main bedroom. "Where are you going?" Levi asks as I make my way toward the door. "I wasn't nearly ready to let you go yet. It's been four fucking days, babe. There's a lot of missed time to make up for."

Everything clenches deep within me, and I feel the dull, sensual ache between my legs, reminding me exactly where he's been. I bite down on my lip, his offer to spend the day fucking me more than enticing, but if I don't eat something in the next three seconds, I think I might die.

Glancing over my shoulder, I give him a sultry smile, watching the way his eyes become hooded and flame with desire. I pause by the door and allow my heated gaze to travel up and down his strong body, his tattoos, dark eyes, and sculpted perfection making my mouth water. "I'm going to need a bit of energy if I have any hope of keeping up with you for the rest of the day," I tell him. "Do you need anything while I'm downstairs?"

Levi's eyes glisten with silent laughter as he shakes his head. "Nah, babe. Just make it quick. We can't risk you running into Marcus. That fucker will sink his claws in and whisk you away with some bullshit promise about blowing your mind with some kind of fucked-up kink."

Heat throbs below the surface and I clench my thighs again, imagining all the wicked things Marcus could do to me, though when it comes to Marcus, there is no guessing. I doubt even he knows how he's going to fuck me before it happens. He's a spur of the moment kind of guy and I love that about him. "In that case, maybe I should run into him," I tease, though truth be told, I'm more than considering leaving Levi up here high and dry while I ride his brother like a fucking cowgirl downstairs.

Levi's hand slips down under the blanket and I see the way he grabs his cock, giving it a hard squeeze to try and gain what little control he can. "If I have to come down there and find you, there will be trouble. Is that understood?"

A sparkle hits my eyes, and I hold back a grin as I lower my chin and look up at him through my thick row of lashes. Innocence washes over my features as I watch him through big, wide eyes, knowing just how much my little act affects him. After all, a man like Levi loves nothing more than taking a woman's purity and claiming it as his own. I'd bet Levi was the dude in high school going around collecting girls' virginities like he collects murder trophies. The silk robe slips off my shoulder, exposing my creamy skin below. His eyes quickly glaze over it, and as his tongue rolls over his bottom lip, he squeezes his cock just a little harder. I let those two teasing words fall from between my lips. "Yes, Daddy."

Levi's eyes widen and I bolt from the room as a throaty laugh tears from my chest. Fuck, he's going to make me come through on that. I always suspected that he had a bit of a daddy kink but seeing the way his eyes lit up like fireworks only proves my theory.

I race down the hallway, my silk gown flowing out behind me when I hear his deep tone booming through the hallway. "You don't know what kind of beast you've just unleashed, Shayne Mariano," he roars. I reach the top of the stairs and clutch the railing as I glance back, finding him hovering in the middle of the walkway down by my room. His eyes sparkle in amusement but there's something so much deeper there, something so raw that it makes my pussy clench with undeniable need. "There ain't nowhere you can run from me."

My bottom lip catches between my teeth and I wink back at him just moments before a wide, cheesy grin cuts across my face. "Watch me."

I fly down the stairs, feeling as though I just got away with murder, though I'm not fooled. I'm not as clever as I pretend to be. If Levi wanted to catch me and put this new daddy kink into practice, he would have, but he'd prefer to see me fed and healthy over everything else, even if it means getting around with a wicked case of blue balls for a few hours.

My feet hit the bottom step just as Marcus walks through to the dining room and pauses in the entryway, waiting for me to catch up. "Hey," he says, his eyes quickly skimming over my body and blazing with need as he takes in the black lingerie barely covered by the silk gown. His arm falls over my shoulder and he pulls me in close to his chest, pressing a kiss to my forehead as his hand sails low and rests over my ass. "You good?"

"Just hungry," I say, looking around the massive dining room and finding Dill and Doe resting in the corner of the room, both of them laying in doggy beds. While Doe looks her perfect normal self, Dill looks far from it. His tongue hangs out of his mouth as he lays on his back, his bandages on display for the world to see. His eyes are closed, and his violent snoring tells me just how out he really is. Dill never lets his guard down, even while sleeping. He's the perfect example of sleeping with one eye open, but right now, an elephant could come in here and shit all over the room and he'd just keep snoring with his tongue draped halfway across his face.

I hate seeing him like this, but I'm glad his pain medication seems to be doing the trick.

Walking deeper into the room, I find myself absolutely hating it. I'd gotten used to the boys' castle but being in Giovanni's home still feels wrong. Though, I can hardly expect the boys to rule over an empire from the confines of their prison castle a million miles away. This is where they need to be, where *we* need to be.

Marcus' hand sweeps over the silk gown, trailing over the subtle curves of my body. "Me too, babe," he says, his voice dropping low with his double meaning.

I gently push against his chest, a grin pulling at my lips. "Stop," I laugh, knowing all too well that while I have a million monsters inside my head and I'm still trying to put the past few days behind me, there's no denying that the boys are making me feel alive for the first time in days. They have a way of making me forget, making me live for the moment and plastering unexpected smiles across my face. Roman definitely doesn't count in that … most of the time. The chip on his shoulder keeps him from living life to its fullest, but I don't blame him. The shit he's had to endure is like nothing I could ever imagine, and something tells me that I'm only aware of the smallest portion of it.

"Not possible," he says, watching as I stride across the room, dropping down into the seat at the head of the table, the seat that used to belong to Giovanni. I pick at a bowl of grapes and lean back in my chair, kicking my feet up on the very edge of the table and allowing the silk to slip open, revealing more of my thigh than I would have ever been comfortable with before meeting the boys.

Marcus' gaze lingers on my thigh but seeing the savage way I inhale the grapes, he pulls back on his wicked thoughts and starts loading up a plate of food. "How are you feeling?" he questions, placing the plate down in front of me. "You were asleep for a while."

I shrug my shoulders. "I don't know," I tell him. "I haven't really had a chance to think about it, and honestly, I don't want to. I'm just … I'm angry, and every time the slightest memory flashes inside my head, I'm left with this overwhelming need to viciously slaughter your father like a fucking wild animal."

He presses a hand down on my shoulder and I wait for him to tell me to breathe, to be patient and let the boys handle it, but that's not even close to what comes pouring out of his mouth. "Good," he tells me, his obsidian eyes darkening with venom. "Hold onto that feeling. Let it burn deep inside you like a fucking inferno and build up like cancer growing inside of you. You will get what's owed to you. I promise you, babe. You will get your chance with him, and when you do, I want you to bring up those flames and extinguish them against him. It's going to be a fucking bloody masterpiece. Brutal and vicious, and you're going to look like a fucking avenging angel doing it. Vengeance will be yours."

I swallow hard, his determination and excitement at the very thought of me getting my hands on their father making something burn deep within me, and not the kind of burning that Giovanni's wicked games invoke in me, a very different kind of burn that has me ready to throw Marcus down on the table and fuck him until I scream. "What about you guys?" I ask, keeping my filthy mind on track. "You've all been tortured at your father's hands for years, and I know you would give me anything I wanted, but you guys deserve to be the ones to tear his flesh from his body."

"Don't be fooled, my sweet girl. Just because we will allow you to end him in the most priceless way imaginable, doesn't mean that he will be given to you in one piece. We will get our own. We have years of bullshit to make up for. You'll be lucky if you get to play with him long before he finally gives out."

That familiar burn intensifies, and as I remember Levi ready and waiting for me upstairs, that need pulses erratically through me. I wonder if they'd be down for a three-way.

My eyes blaze with excitement as I take a cherry off my plate and pop it into my mouth. My fingers trail up the side of Marcus' leg as I close my mouth over the cherry and tear the stem from between my lips. Marcus watches me with desire, and I slowly spread my legs, letting my other hand fall to my thigh.

Marcus pulls my chair back from the table and positions me so that I face him directly. He stands over me and grips my chin, forcing my heated stare to his dark eyes, and while he doesn't say a damn word, the desire is clear in his eyes, along with a million other silent thoughts passing between us, most of them thoughts that I'm not ready to hear just yet.

Marcus begins to lean down, and I tilt my chin up higher, ready to capture his lips in mine when I hear the front door slam before the sound of heavy boots thumping through the foyer.

My back stiffens and it's like having a bucket of ice water tipped over my head. "Don't move," Marcus murmurs, straightening and gliding across the dining room to discreetly peer out into the foyer. Nerves crash through my body. The only time we ever had to deal with intruders at the prison castle was when Giovanni showed up, or bitches stormed my room with a gun. I'm sure had the home not been locked up like Fort Knox, there would have been more enemies barging through the doors, but here in Giovanni's mansion, his doors are open, and anyone could walk through at any moment. The thought makes it difficult to sleep at night, especially with Giovanni on the rampage, determined to get his home and empire back under his hold.

Marcus pauses a moment, his hand falling to the small of his back where he pulls a gun from the waistband of his pants. My breath catches in my throat, and while I know Marcus could take down an intruder in a matter of seconds, I still hate the thought of him putting himself in danger, especially when his brothers aren't at his back. Though I don't doubt the sound of the front door slamming has Levi slowly creeping toward the top of the stairs.

Marcus slips through the opening, and just as I expect to hear a gunshot ring loudly through the foyer, Marcus lets out an irritated sigh. "Fuck's sake," he mutters before calling back through to the dining room. "It's just Roman."

I let out a relieved breath as Roman's loud stomping continues through the mansion and toward the dining room. "Where the fuck have you been?" I hear Marcus' low murmurs as he berates his brother for disappearing on us. "Shayne is in there shitting herself because she thinks someone was trying to break in."

Roman doesn't respond as he flies through the entrance of the dining room and storms right over to the open bar. He pours himself a glass of whiskey and throws it back before immediately pouring another. Marcus stops in the doorway and watches him with a frown as a heaviness comes down over my shoulders.

Roman's eyes are hard, and the sharp set of his jaw has me pushing up out of my chair. I cross the room and sense him watching me from the corner of his eye. He pours another drink before pulling the cap off a bottle of vodka and pouring one for me. He silently slides it across the bar, putting it right in front of me as I step in beside him.

"What's going on?" I question as Marcus remains by the door, silently listening.

Roman indicates the shot of vodka as he throws back another glass of whiskey. Realizing that I won't get any answers until I give him what he wants, I pick up the small glass and revel in the burn as the vodka makes its way down my throat.

Slamming the glass back down on the bar, I release it before reaching up and taking his chin. I force his stare to mine, knowing that I'm probably the last person he wants to see after I allowed his father to walk out with his newborn baby. "What is it?"

Roman's lips press into a hard line as he reaches up and grips my hand, releasing it from his chin. He doesn't let go and holds onto my hand as though it's his only lifeline. His dark gaze meets mine and there's something so devastating about it. It's filled with pain and grief, and it's almost impossible to hold his stare for a second longer.

Roman lets out a breath, and as his shoulders sink, the words come falling from his lips. "I buried Felicity."

Pain shoots through my chest and I'm completely lost for words, so instead of struggling to say the right thing, I step into him and wrap my arms around his strong body, holding him tight. Roman sinks into me and curls his arms around me as I distantly notice Marcus slipping out of the dining room to give Roman some privacy, despite the pain he must be feeling in his own heart. Marcus was close with Felicity, but his emotions have been a mess after she stormed into my bedroom and shot him. We've all been a mess since then.

"I'm sorry," I tell him, absolutely shattered by the idea of Roman standing out in some field or on a beach all alone, digging a hole for the mother of his child, the woman who holds such a high place in his heart. "We could have helped you. You didn't need to do that alone."

"I did," he tells me, his hand winding up into the back of my hair as his arm tightens around my waist and lifts me up off the ground. He pushes me back onto the bar and steps between my legs as I keep holding onto him. He braces himself against the bar and hangs his head so that his forehead presses against my shoulder. "I let her down. I let my father fool me, and because of that, she suffered in a fucking cell while growing my baby in her womb. She needed me more than ever and I let her down."

My fingers knot into his hair as Felicity's innocent face settles into my head and I find myself holding onto him tighter. Felicity wasn't built for this world. I only knew her for those few short minutes before her death, but even that was enough to show me who she was. She would have been the quiet girl at school, blushing when the popular guy paid her a little attention. This world would have eaten her up and spit her out the other end.

"We all let her down, Roman," I tell him, holding back the tears that well in my eyes, hating seeing Roman so crushed. I've never seen him hurting like this, and something tells me that opening up and showing his vulnerabilities isn't something he does often. Hell, for so long, I thought these guys weren't capable of feeling these normal human emotions, but every day they prove to me that they're more human than anyone I've ever met. "She wasn't scared of death," I continue, noticing the dirt under his nails from his long morning of digging her grave. "She was just glad that it was over and she didn't have to live with this fear anymore. She loved you, and she was so lucky to have had that reciprocated."

Roman scoffs and raises his head, his dead eyes lingering on mine. "To love me and my brothers means to live in fear and being loved in return means certain death. Is that something that you want? Because that's how it's going to end. You're going to be just like her."

I shake my head, knowing it's his fear and grief talking, though on some level, I think it might be true. "That won't happen to me," I tell him, my confidence in the brothers knowing no bounds. "You and your brothers won't allow it. You're going to take down your father and finally put an end to this. We're going to find your son and you'll get to live a million more years, ruling over this world and raising your son to be a proud, honest man, just like you and your brothers. Felicity may be gone, just like so many other innocent lives that have been lost in this war, but you have an opportunity to rise up. This is your game now, and your father is nothing but a pawn that you get to play. Enjoy it, Roman. Take revenge and make him pay for it all."

A flicker of fire burns deep in his eyes and he reaches around me, grabbing the bottle of whiskey off the bar before taking a step back, not once taking his eyes off mine. He holds my stare for a long moment as he brings the bottle of whiskey to his lips, and after throwing it back, the fire burns a little bit brighter. Roman moves into me again and curls his hand around the back of my neck before pulling me in. I smell him all around me, his addictive scent like a shot right to the heart as he holds me tight, then just when I think it's all over, he presses a firm, lingering kiss to my temple.

My eyes flutter closed, soaking in his touch, and then all too soon, he pulls away from me and strides out of the dining room without another damn word.

CHAPTER ELEVEN

The doctor packs up her tools as I glance down at my scarred arm, looking over my latest bandage, though at least this one is self-inflicted. "Thank you," I say again as she pushes back from her chair, studiously ignoring Marcus' hard stare from across the room.

"Of course," she says, side eyeing him with tight lips before pulling out a piece of paper and sliding it across the table toward me. "And remember, if you need anything … and I mean *anything*, you call me, okay?"

I give her a fake smile while inwardly laughing at the thought of me getting my hands on a cell phone to be able to call her in the first place, but truth be told, I'm perfectly fine in this fucked-up world and I think she can see that. She's a smart woman and I've appreciated her visit, but just one look at me and she can see the hell I've been through over the past few months. There's no denying that she knows who Marcus is; the whole world does. I just have to hope that she's smart enough to keep her mouth shut about today's appointment. If she knows what's good for her, she will, and I don't mean that as a threat. I truly hope she doesn't try anything stupid like swooping in to save me. I don't need a hero, not anymore. I am my own hero.

I get up to walk her out and she reaches down, placing a hand on my shoulder. "Careful," she says. "Take it slowly. Your arm may be numb for a little while longer, but the anesthetic will start to wear off and you might experience some discomfort. It shouldn't hang around for too long."

Nodding my head, I give her a genuine smile. I like this doctor. She was very thorough with me and actually seems to care. She didn't care for Marcus' grumpy ass attitude across the room, and she gave out just as much lip as he did in her endeavor to care for me. She did a quick pregnancy test to cover all bases before shoving this thing in my arm, and as we waited for the results, she looked over some of my still healing wounds, though there wasn't much she could do for them.

I don't know what it is about a pregnancy test that makes the worst kind of anxiety pulse through my veins, but it was the longest three minutes of my whole time being here so far, and that's saying a lot. I'm all for women having babies, good for them. I hope their little bundle of joy makes them the happiest motherfuckers around town, but that shit ain't for me, at least, not yet, and certainly not while I'm still navigating my way around this world. This life isn't safe for a baby, and Roman's new son is proof of that. Hell, we can barely keep track of that one. Having another would be a foolish move.

With some more care instructions and some medication to help with my healing wounds, the doctor walks out and I stand with Marcus as she makes her way down the grand entrance of the DeAngelis mansion. "Please don't hurt this one," I mutter, hoping to God that she can't hear my voice trailing across the wind. "I like her."

Marcus narrows his eyes and I know that one comment from me will keep her safe whether he likes it or not. His lips press into a tight line. "She's way too confident," he murmurs.

"I know," I laugh, slipping my arm through his and dropping my head to his shoulder. "That's what I like about her. Do you have any idea how refreshing it is to watch other people converse with you three when they're not afraid of you? It's the most amusing thing I've ever seen."

He shakes his head. "That only goes to prove just how stupid she is."

I roll my eyes as she gets into her car and makes a hasty escape. I'm sure she's not blind to the fact that her life was in immediate danger had she pushed the limits just a little too far. I bet she's sitting in that car with shaky hands on the steering wheel and sweat pooling under her ass. "She's not stupid," I tell him, pulling back on his arm as she disappears down the long drive. "She just cares, and what more could you ask for from your doctor?"

We step back inside the big mansion and find Roman and Levi pushing their way through to the internal garage. My brows furrow and I follow them in. "Going somewhere?" I ask, watching as they empty the back of a few SUVs, clearing them out.

"Heading back to the castle to get our shit," Levi says, glancing up at me. "You coming, or do you want to chill out here?"

I scoff, staring at him as though he just grew another head. "You're fucking kidding me, right? You want to leave me here alone so I can get kidnapped again? I mean, sure. I didn't think we'd be putting this new tracker into action quite so soon, but if you're sure."

Levi pauses, glancing up at me again before the corner of his mouth pulls into a wicked smirk. "That was pretty stupid, huh?"

I laugh and roll my eyes as Marcus strides past me to help the guys unload. "Probably your stupidest comment yet," I agree. "Give me ten minutes and I'll be ready to go."

Levi gets back to work without another word, and I slip back into the main part of the mansion and make my way up to my room to get dressed. I can only imagine the type of shit the boys need to collect from their old prison. They made quite the collection of weapons over the ten years they were locked up there, not to mention the fact that Levi doesn't have a drum kit here. How the hell is he supposed to give me wild drum fuckery without one of those?

After dressing in a matching crop and tights, I pull my hair into a high bun on top of my head and slip my feet into a pair of white sneakers. The comfort of this outfit is beyond anything I've ever known, and damn it, it looks cute too. I look like I'm ready to throw down at the gym and start counting calories and macros ... whatever the fuck they are, but in reality, I'm probably just going to stand back out of the way, having absolutely no idea how to handle the type of weapons they're wanting to collect.

Grabbing my pillow off my bed and a soft blanket out of my closet, I make my way back downstairs. It's a good few hours back to the castle, and after spending the night with Marcus and getting absolutely no sleep, a good nap would do me good.

I step through to the garage right as Marcus steps away from the cars to come and find me, my timing impeccable. "You riding with me?"

Glancing over his shoulder, I take in Roman as he pulls open his driver's side door and climbs into one of the three black SUVs lining the garage. "Depends," I mutter. "Do you plan on chit-chatting and listening to screeching music the whole way?"

Marcus scoffs, a grin stretching across his face. "How else do you intend to travel? That's the only way."

I look at him in horror. I can't think of anything worse, at least, just for today. A bit of silence will do me good, even if it means riding with the broodiest asshole in town. As much as I love Marcus' random chatter, and even if he promised to keep it to a minimum, he wouldn't be able to make any guarantees. He simply can't help himself. Roman though, despite his glares, fuming, and brooding, I can guarantee complete and utter silence. There's just no comparison.

Levi was out of the running before there was even a question. I can only imagine the loud bullshit that would come tearing through his speakers for the next few hours, and I simply can't stomach it today. The only way I'll listen to that is if it's a set of drums directly in front of me and I can feel the vibrations slamming against my chest as he looks at me with a promise to fuck me just as hard as he hits his drums, and damn it, he always comes through.

My gaze sweeps back to Roman and as he tosses something onto his passenger seat, my decision is made. "Ooooh, he's got snacks."

Traipsing past Marcus who looks at me like I just kicked his puppy, I slip straight into the backseat of Roman's SUV and place my pillow down on the leather seat, more than ready to get comfortable for the long ride. Roman stiffens as his head whips around into the backseat. His dark eyes are wide, and I don't think I've ever seen him look so horrified. "No," he says, gaping at me, the confusion marring his face like nothing I've ever seen, and damn it, I think I like bringing this reaction out of him. "Out. There's no fucking way. Ride with one of my brothers."

Giving him an innocent smile, I press my head down against my pillow and lay my blanket over myself, making a show of getting comfortable. "Too late now, I'm already here," I tell him before indicating toward his snacks with a raised, curious brow. "Got any candy up there?"

Roman turns back in his seat and blows out his cheeks, silently fuming as I pull my blanket right up to cover the wide shit-eating grin that tears across my face. A moment passes and I listen to the soft thuds of the boys closing their doors, and not a moment later, Roman tosses a packet of Reese's peanut butter cups into the back and hits the gas, sailing out of the garage with his brothers following suit.

After napping the majority of the way, Roman wakes me as we make our way down the long driveway of the massive castle. Pushing myself up from my pillow and sitting back in the center seat, I rub at my eyes and stare out through the windshield. "I've never gotten past how stunning this place is," I murmur on a yawn, unable to take my eyes off the castle that changed my life, though I'm still undecided if that change was for the better.

"After ten years of imprisonment, the novelty of it kinda wears off," he tells me.

I drop my tone, the heaviness of his words sinking into my chest. "I can only imagine."

All three of the SUVs are backed into the garage and I don't even want to know what type of things the guys are going to load the cars with. If it were up to me, I'd be getting back the clothes and sentimental shit that I've accumulated over the years, but the boys are a different breed.

They get busy, not wasting a damn second as they load up the first SUV and it becomes startlingly clear just how many of these trips we're going to have to make. Hell, the boys should have brought a fucking truck for this shit, though that would only draw the wrong kind of attention, and after the close call with the FBI at the tomb party, I bet they're looking for absolutely anything they can get their hands on to make a clean arrest.

Not wanting to handle all the weapons and feeling as though I'm only getting in the way, I head into the castle and make my way straight to the bathroom. It was a long trip, what's a girl to do?

After finishing up and splashing water over my face, I make my way around the castle, moving from room to room and scooping up anything I think the boys might want to keep. I'm all too aware of their mother laying up in the tallest room of the castle, Snow White style, and I don't doubt that the boys will eventually make arrangements to get her so they can bury her properly, but until then, I sure as fuck won't be going up there, especially by myself.

I place bags upon bags at the internal entrance of the garage and hate the way my stomach clenches as I collect all of Marcus' special trophies, knowing just how attached he is to this shit. I'm sure Levi and Roman will be doing the very same with their own trophies, but unlike Marcus, they haven't proudly shown theirs off, and I have no idea where they actually keep them.

I haul the last of it back to the garage and pass Levi in the den, pulling one of his many drum kits to pieces when a hand clamps down over my mouth and I'm dragged backward into a dark corner, my back pressed firmly up against a wide chest.

Terror rips through me and just as I go to slam my elbow back into my attacker's stomach the way the boys have trained me, a familiar, hushed, "Shhhhh," falls around me. I twist my head back to find Roman standing at my back and he cautiously releases his hand from my mouth as he holds up a finger, warning me to stay silent.

My brows furrow and I stare at him in confusion. Without missing a beat, he slips his arm around my waist and silently repositions me enough for us to both peer around the corner.

My heart leaps out of my chest, and as I suck in a gasp, Roman's hand slams down over my mouth, muffling the soft sound as we watch in silence while a man slips in through the dining room, peering his head around a corner in an attempt to keep himself hidden.

I recognize him instantly, and just seeing his face sends a wave of furious rage coursing through my veins as the need to pummel his ass slams into my chest. Judging by the look on Roman's face, he has absolutely no idea who the fuck this man is and that only pisses me off more. I look up at him and catch his eye, but not wanting to make a sound and give our location away, I'm at a loss.

My hand slips back and skims over the front of Roman's jeans. He flinches as my fingers brush past his junk, and he shoots a glare at me, assuming I'm trying to get down and dirty in the worst possible way. Ignoring his sharp glare, I continue feeling around before slipping my fingers into his pocket and letting out a silent breath of relief as my fingers curl around his phone.

Pulling it out, I waste no time opening up a new text message and quickly typing as Roman watches our new intruder over my shoulder. Finishing my explanation, I hold the phone up to Roman at an angle where he can read my message while also keeping an eye on the man slowly slipping out of the dining hall.

That's James. The fucker who kidnapped Jasmine. I recognize him from the tomb party.

Anger burns in Roman's eyes as a dark shadow cuts across my vision, and I find Marcus silently stalking the asshole through the castle. He catches my stare, and I don't miss the way his gaze sweeps over me, checking that I'm alright with Roman before continuing his stalking with a sick smirk twisting over his delicious lips. It's as though all his Christmases have come at once. There's nothing the DeAngelis brothers like more than stalking a victim on their own turf where they control the game. Trust me, I'd know.

Roman shifts us in our position, having the best vantage spot to watch James from all angles but as he moves toward the den, fear rattles through me.

"Levi?" I murmur, my voice so low that I doubt Roman even hears me, but the thought of Levi carelessly pulling his drum kit into pieces without knowing what's going on out here terrifies me and has a fat lump forming in my throat.

"Levi is a big boy," Roman tells me, silently moving us across the room as James disappears into the darkened den. "He can handle himself."

That's proven a moment later as we slip inside the den to find absolutely no sign of Levi, though only a moment ago he was sprawled out on the ground pulling the drum kit to pieces. I don't see him anywhere, but he's not the only person I can't see.

We hide in the shadow of the big party room, and while I hate being in this particular room, I suck it up. Now is not the time to get caught up in the terrors of my time here. My sharp gaze scans the room, searching for James. The hairs rising on the back of my neck tell me he's in here, though I come up blank until Roman takes my chin and turns me toward the corner of the room.

James stands in the shadows, his skillful gaze sailing around the room, though judging by the way he's still searching, he has absolutely no idea where any of us are, and I don't doubt that in a moment, he'll move onto the next room, searching until he gets what he wants.

But what is that? Why the fuck is he here? Did he find out about Jasmine? That I was the one who took her? Does he know that we brought her back here? Is he here looking for her or is he here to punish me? Who fucking knows. Perhaps this is completely unrelated and he has business with the boys that they don't know about.

A sickening shiver trails down my spine, and I know without a doubt that this is about me.

He's slowly slinking through the room, none the wiser about the three DeAngelis devils slowly stalking him. It's like a twisted game of cat and mouse, only James thinks he's the cat. He's never been so wrong.

If only there were a way to keep him from walking out of the den. There are too many passageways that lead out from here. If he were to walk out the back entrance, we wouldn't be able to follow him without being caught. We'd lose him first, and that's a risky game, one that I'm not willing to play, especially now that we have him in our sights.

If he thinks he's the cat, then why not give him a chance to flex?

The idea filters through my mind, but I know exactly what the boys would think about it, and as the phone silently vibrates in my hand and I glance down, that point is only proven.

Marcus - Don't even think about it.

My gaze shoots up and I find Marcus stepping out of the shadows just enough for me to find him, his fuming expression warning me that I'll be punished for what I'm about to do.

Roman's hold tightens on my body, keeping me close as he reads the message over my shoulder, trying to figure out what the hell Marcus could mean. But my mind is set, and without a hint of warning, I push out of his arms and drag my feet as I make my way across the room.

I keep my head down, but I feel the exact moment that James gets me in his sights. His wicked stare is like two laser beams pinning the back of my head, watching my every step like a lion playing with his meal, and despite just how dangerous this man is, I know that I have never been safer in my life.

Pushing my way in behind the fully stocked bar, I turn my back and reach up to grab a glass tumbler before placing it down on the bar as though I don't have a care in the world. It's well after midday now, and it's more than acceptable to pour myself a stiff drink.

Grabbing the bottle of vodka and the orange juice from the row of bar fridges below, I get to work pouring my drink, and all too soon, his game of cat and mouse begins.

Hiding the grin that stretches across my face, I watch out of the corner of my eye as James slowly stalks me, moving across the room in a way that he thinks he'll be able to get the jump on me, completely unaware of the fact that I'm drawing him out and that he's the one currently being stalked.

Turning around, I push the bottle of vodka back onto its high shelf and as I do, I catch Levi across the room. He doesn't look happy about the situation, but it's a little too late to change the plan. He watches me with a hard stare, his eyes focused heavily on mine, but I know he's also watching James slowly moving toward me. Levi won't let anything happen to me.

Holding his stare a moment longer, I wait, knowing James won't be able to resist jumping at me now that my back is turned. That's just what men like him do. They attack women when they're most vulnerable and not in a position to fight back, just as he did to Jasmine. He kidnapped her for weeks and she endured the worst kind of abuse at his hands, and because of that, he will not walk out of this castle alive. This sorry fucker has got another thing coming.

Levi nods and just as he mouths the word, "now," I spin around, and drop down low, narrowly avoiding James' arms as they swing toward me. Without skipping a beat, I kick my heel out with a powerful strike to his balls just as the boys taught me, only the momentum from his missed swing has him falling forward and my heel connecting with his guts instead.

It doesn't quite have the effect that I was hoping for, but it's enough to bring him down with a pained groan, if only for the quick second I need to get the upper hand.

The unexpected blow has him winded, and I take my chance, stepping into him and grabbing his head. Without a second of hesitation, I slam my knee up as hard as I can, crushing his skull into it. It kills my knee, and I know that I'll pay for it later, but damn it, the way his nose shatters under my knee is worth every second of pain.

Blood spurts like a tap as he roars in agony, only just realizing what a horrible mistake he's made by stepping into this castle. Obviously, he doesn't know who he's dealing with here. If he did, the mere thought of breaking into this property would have him crippled with fear.

Giving him a hard shove, James falls right to the ground. I step into him, my white sneaker pressing against his junk as he stares up at me with heavy regret in his eyes.

The boys peel out of the shadowed corners of the room, surrounding us from all angles, and as a wicked grin stretches across my face, I allow the power to sweep through my bones. "And so, we meet again."

CHAPTER TWELVE

Marcus glares at me across the open space of their underground playground as James hangs from chains behind us. I can't help but return his stare and arch my brow in irritation. "Seriously?" I snap. "Get the fuck over it. This is my game. He's here because I brought Jasmine here, so it's only fair that I get to handle it my way."

Marcus' eyes narrow and Levi takes a step back, wanting nothing to do with it as Roman leans against a table, looking bored. "I told you no," Marcus says.

"I heard your 'no' loud and clear and decided that you can go and fuck yourself with a machete," I say, looking up at him with big, round, innocent eyes, reminding him that while I am sugary sweet, I'm also as sour as they come. I'm not one he wants to cross when I'm fifty shades of pissed off. "I'm your equal, remember. Or have you forgotten? I'm not your little bitch to push around, not anymore."

Marcus scoffs and runs his hands through his hair as his frustration gets the best of him. He turns his back as anger crashes through him like a tsunami, then after a slow deep breath, he turns and steps into me, gripping my chin and forcing my stare to his. "You think that is what this is about? That I just want to flex my control over you? That I want to whip out my fucking dick and watch the way you drop to your knees like a good little girl that knows her place?" he spits, his dark eyes blazing with fury. "Fucking hell, Shayne. Don't you think I've learned anything over the past few months? I didn't want you putting yourself in that position because every fucking time you step out of our grasps, I'm terrified that I'm going to fucking lose you. I don't want you to do it because I don't want you to get hurt. I'm not trying to control you, babe. I want to fucking live for you."

I suck in a breath as he tears away from me, his emotions too much for him to bear let alone take in myself. Stepping straight back into him, I take his hands before they start tearing out his hair and thread his fingers through mine. "I'm fine," I murmur. "I knew what I was doing, and I knew that with you and your brothers in the room, I was safe. You wouldn't have let anything happen to me, and Roman sure as fuck wouldn't have allowed me to slip out of his hold if he didn't approve."

"Because Roman is a fucking idiot," Marcus scoffs before dropping his gaze over my body and pulling his hand from mine. His fingertips brush along the many scars marring my flesh. "Yeah," he mutters. "You're real fucking safe with us."

Anger blasts through me and I grip his chin in a bruising hold that he seems to revel in, loving any form of punishment any way he can get it. "Don't you dare," I spit at him, hating how he doubts himself. "Every single one of these scars were out of your control, and you've done everything you can to get vengeance for every fucking one of them. Now cut your bullshit and man the fuck up. I did what I did, and now it's time to see it through."

His eyes blaze as I hear Levi choke on his own fucking spit and smother a laugh. I don't doubt that these boys have never been spoken to like that in their lives, apart from the horrendous way their father has always treated them, but that doesn't count. They simply don't allow people to get away with this shit, and the fact that I can, fills my veins with a venomous type of power, one that no woman should be entitled to.

Marcus holds my stare for a moment longer, a challenge clear in his eyes, but I know he sees the one reflected in mine, and really, he's not mad at me. Sure, he's got his feathers ruffled, but he's really mad at himself. He hates how much he cares for me. Hates that the idea of me getting hurt makes him lose his mind. But what he hates most is the feeling of powerlessness, the feeling of not being able to turn it off, of not being able to push me away like he's always been taught. His heart won't allow him to.

"This conversation isn't over," he tells me.

My lips pull into a smirk as I push up onto my tippy toes and brush my lips over his, earning myself a roll of Roman's dark eyes. "It's more than over," I tell him. "Now let's go have some fun. Don't you think we deserve it?"

His eyes soften as the excitement begins to build deep within him. "Alright, let's go."

Hook. Line. And freaking sinker.

Roman pushes off the table as Marcus steps out of my personal space and turns toward the dangling man behind us. "You know what you're doing?" Levi questions, stepping in beside me as we make our way toward the grunting man.

I shake my head, my lips twisting with unease. "No," I tell them truthfully, the fact that I'm way out of my league is messing with my head. "I figured we were just going to … kill him."

"We will," Roman says, his piercing eyes focused heavily on James as his nose continues to drip from its recent break. "But first he needs to answer some questions."

My brows furrow. Questions? What kind of questions could they possibly ask him? We already know everything there is to know. He wanted Jasmine and has clearly tracked her movement back here and wants revenge for it.

We step up in front of him and the guy spits a mouthful of blood at me as he pulls against the heavy chains keeping him bound. My lips twist in disgust as his spit drops with a wet splash at my feet, and damn it, the fury that ripples through Marcus is almost comical.

I expect Marcus to take the lead, but Roman steps up, moves out in front of us and puts himself at James' side so as to not block our view. "What are you doing in our home?" Roman asks him, his deadly warning to not fuck with us sending chills down my spine.

James pulls against his chains, knowing damn well how this is going to end. He raises his head with a sickening smirk on his lips as he looks directly in my eyes. "I came for the bitch," he spits, choosing to go out in typical douchebag style. "She took what was mine."

Roman fixes him with a hard stare. "Come on, now. You know the rules. If you lose your bitch, that's on you. Mine isn't for sale."

Fury tears through James and he pulls hard on the chains, tearing at his skin until it bleeds. "I didn't fucking lose her. That bitch stole her."

"That *bitch*," Roman says, spitting the word. "Saved her in that fucking tomb when you left her to die. So as far as I'm concerned, you forfeited. Your little piece of ass was open for the taking, and you better fucking believe that we took her."

James laughs. "You think I give a shit about her?" he spits. "No. I want what I'm owed."

"Oh, you don't need to worry about that. You will have plenty of time with her, though I can't guarantee that you're going to enjoy it," Roman teases, slicing his devilish gaze back to me, his eyes sparkling with the endless things I could do to him. Only, something in James' words feels like lead spreading through my veins.

"Owed?" I question. "No one owes you shit. I saved her and that's the end of it."

James scoffs, yanking against his chains and splitting his skin. "Not according to Daddy DeAngelis," he says as though that's supposed to scare me. "I paid a pretty penny for you, and I won't stop until I get what's mine."

I laugh, understanding dawning on me as the boys watch on through narrowed, confused eyes. "You're the buyer those guards were preparing me for?" I ask with amusement, my lips twisting into a wicked grin. "I should have just stayed put. I could have killed you back then and had a nice ride for the journey home."

Marcus steps forward, his dark gaze sweeping to me. "What the fuck are you talking about?"

"Your father sold Ariana," I remind them. "It's only natural for him to have done the same with me. And apparently this asshole was his new buyer they were preparing me for. Though, I'm a bit disappointed. I would have preferred a guy with a bigger dick."

"Release me," James roars. "I'll show you just how fucking big my dick really is. What I did to Jasmine would be like child's play compared to how I'll destroy you."

Roman laughs, slipping his hands into his pockets as Levi crosses his big arms over his chest, his eyes narrowed on James. "How did you know where to find us?" he questions, the little pieces of the puzzle simply not fitting together. Something is missing, a key piece of information and the boys won't stop until they get what they want.

James scoffs. "Followed her foul stench."

Roman's fist promptly lunges out, cracking against James' cheek and splitting his skin with the forceful impact. Marcus laughs as my eyes go wide, watching the way James' body flies back; only the way he hangs from the chains in the ceiling has him coming straight back for more.

Roman reaches up and grips the chains at his wrist, pulling him into his face. "You were asked a question," he spits, absolutely hating having to deal with rich bastards who think they're above the law. "How did you find us?"

It's one thing having to deal with men like Roman and his brothers, men who are mentally deranged after a lifetime of abuse, men who are just as wicked as they are, but then there are men like James who are doing it all for show. They want to appear bad, broken, and psychotic. They want to be the big bad wolf, when in reality, they're little Miss Piggies who'll shit their pants at the first sign of real danger. Hell, I bet he felt like the fucking man when he was beating on Jasmine, raping her day and night, but I wonder just how big he feels now.

The two men hold each other's stares, but it won't take long before James caves. I've been on the receiving end of one of Roman's stares and it's brutal. Hell, he didn't even give me the full effect. He held back just to spare me. I think it's got something to do with that scar. It makes him look as though he'll tear your face right off your body with nothing but his teeth. Though, I wouldn't dare put the idea in his head because he seems like the kind of savage who'd follow through.

They hold each other's stare for a moment longer before James breaks under the pressure and is forced to glance away, but as a grin rips across his face, it's clear that he thinks he has one last card to play. "Your father," he spits. "Giovanni gave you up like a fucking dried out whore."

Levi snickers beside me as Roman just shakes his head. "Fucking hell," he says. "Even in hiding he still finds time to fuck with losers like you."

"What the fuck is that supposed to mean?"

Roman laughs. "If my father sent you here, then he sent you here to die. He was through with you and whatever … business arrangement you had."

James shakes his head, a smug look crossing his lips. "You've got no fucking clue, do you?"

Roman steps in close, his gaze shifting up and down before coming back to James, his stare like two deadly lasers penetrating deep inside his victim. "I couldn't give a shit what kind of deal you have with my father, because when your head is rolling around in that wheelbarrow over there," Roman says, pointing toward the very wheelbarrow the boys will use to discard his body, "your deal will be null and void. But there's no need to worry, he'll be joining you in hell the second his bitch ass steps out of hiding. Then the two of you can fuck around in hell and make all the goddamn deals you want."

"Fuck you," James roars, spitting a mouthful of blood all over Roman's face.

I suck in a breath, my back stiffening as I watch the show and I find myself gripping Levi's arm, certain that Roman is about to lose his shit and end this in one foul swoop, but to my surprise, he calmly takes a step back and wipes a hand down his face. "I really wish you hadn't done that," Roman says. "You see, we promised Shayne that she would get to end your life for Jasmine's sake, but now, I fear that you're going to force me to break my promise. You're lucky that I'm a man of my word, because I can guarantee that anything she has in mind is going to be a breath of fresh air compared to what I would have done to you."

I laugh, that sick little devil rearing its ugly head inside of me. "I don't know about that," I mutter, my plan making me all giddy, though I know it shouldn't. I should be fearing for my soul, but my excitement is too much. After what he did to Jasmine, he deserves the very worst, and I am going to take great pleasure in getting to be the one who gets to do it.

At that, Roman turns back to me. "Are you ready?"

I hesitate a moment, not wanting to seem too eager, after all, I'm supposed to be the innocent one of the group. What would they think of me if they knew just how sinister, sick, and twisted my thoughts have been? "You don't want to find out what this deal was first?" I ask, certain that selling me to him wasn't the deal they're referring to.

Roman shakes his head and the giddiness burns like an inferno inside me. He pulls his shirt over his head, exposing his sculpted torso below and my mouth waters as my thighs clench. He's fucking gorgeous. "No point," he murmurs, completely oblivious to the turmoil he's rained down over my body and mind. "Whatever deal they had won't matter after this. Though, he's obviously the guy my father was nervous about us meeting during the tomb party. So at least some questions have been answered."

"Okay," I say slowly. "So ..."

"So, the floor is all yours," Marcus says. "If you need help with anything, just let us know. Bare hands, tools, teeth ... whatever you want, but you better make me proud. I didn't come all the way down here for a simple bullet between the eyes."

I meet Marcus' flirty stare as a wicked grin stretches across my face. "Where are these tools you speak of?"

Marcus laughs before sweeping his hand toward the side of the room in a grand gesture. "Right this way, if you will."

He leads the way and I follow along with shaky hands. What I'm about to do is a big step. There's a huge difference between shooting my father and killing the man who held me hostage. This right here is cold-blooded revenge murder, but after the shit I've already done, what does one more kill really matter? If I get caught, I'm already doing maximum time. I might as well make it count and take as many assholes off the street in the process.

Marcus shows off the wide array of tools and I look over them with curious glances, trying to picture the outcome of each one. There's a power drill, a saw, all kinds of hammers. It's as though the boys stepped inside a hardware store and just said, 'we'll take one of everything' and walked out again.

My gaze skims over everything until I finally find what I'm looking for and smile at the fucker. Walking toward it, I curl my fingers around the handle and pick it up. It's much heavier than I thought, but I can manage. It's not like I'm going to need it for long.

"Fuck me," Marcus breathes in adoration, taking in the chainsaw in my hand. "You're my fucking queen. Have I ever told you that?"

I grin back at him and raise my brows. "And here I thought you were mad at me."

"Screw that, all I want to do is fuck you now."

"Well, you might just get your chance," I tell him, glancing back at James and then down at my chainsaw in thought. "You don't happen to have a splash mask, do you?" I question, waving my hand in front of my face, disgusted with the thought that I won't just be in the splash zone, I'll take the brunt of it. "Raincoat, perhaps?"

Marcus laughs. "Sorry, babe. You're on your own with this one," he tells me, pressing a gentle hand to the small of my back and leading me toward the boys.

"Well, fuck," Levi says, glancing at Roman as he takes in the chainsaw. "We underestimated you."

"People usually do," I tell him before stepping forward and having to put the chainsaw down in front of James as the weight of the stupid thing has my arm screaming for sweet release.

James looks at the chainsaw in horror, his breath coming in fast, sharp gasps as he shakes his head, yanking hard against the chains and making the sound echo through the massive underground playground. "No," he spits, giving me exactly what I want. "What the fuck is wrong with you? Are you fucked in the head? You won't get away with this you fucking psychotic bitch."

I hold up my hand and indicate for him to be quiet. "Hush now," I warn him, wishing there was some way that I could reach Jasmine to show her this precious moment, though that will never happen. She's long gone, safe with her family and trying to put the horrible things this man did behind her. "You are vile, are you aware of this?" I ask. "It would be my absolute pleasure to rid this world of you."

"Fuck you," he spits.

"Look, I hadn't planned on ramming anything up your ass. That wasn't in today's schedule," I tell him as I step toward him and tear his shirt down the center, letting it hang open. "But if you insist, I'd be more than happy to oblige."

Horror washes over his face and I'm not surprised by his fear of being fucked in the ass. Guys like that usually are. The idea of throwing a woman down and raping her repeatedly is cool, but the second his asshole is involved, he goes running like a fucking bitch. It irritates me. People who can't take what they dish out are the weakest type of humans. He's just lucky that I have absolutely no intention of messing around with his asshole. I couldn't think of anything worse. Besides, just because I plan to murder him, doesn't mean that I should be lowering my standards and beliefs.

Hearing Marcus and Levi's amused snickers behind me, I can't help the wide smile spreading across my face. I must look like a crazed lunatic. But hey, when in Rome, right? He hurt Jasmine in the most brutal and degrading kind of way, and for that, I will make sure that his final few moments on this big green earth are spent in the most horrifying kind of fear. Hell, who knows how many other women he's hurt.

Bending down, I reach for the chainsaw and look around it. I can't say that I've ever used one of these before, and to be honest, I'm kind of scared of it. I mean, I don't want to lose a finger, but I also don't want to appear like an amateur in front of this guy. I want him to fear me. I want him to start praying to whatever god he believes in. I want to see him piss his pants as he meets my eyes.

Levi clears his throat. "Do you need a hand with that?"

I shake my head, determined to figure it out. "I got this," I declare with the utmost confidence.

Roman mutters under his breath and that one little sound sends a wave of doubt through my mind that grows on me like cancer.

That asshole. Why does he always have to ruin a good thing?

Feeling around the chainsaw, I search for some kind of on button, but after going over it twice, all I find is this weird little plastic thing hanging out the side. Am I supposed to pull it? I shoot a glance toward Marcus and he subtly nods, reading my thoughts, and without a second of hesitation, I curl my fingers around the little plastic holder and pull it with everything I have.

A long rope comes out of the chainsaw and my arm aches from the movement, but not a damn thing happens. "What the hell?" I mutter, giving it another go while Roman watches me with a smirk.

My arm begins to burn and Levi eventually steps forward. "Move over," he tells me before picking up the chainsaw, curling his fingers around the plastic handle for the pull start motor. He tears it back with skilled precision, his muscles bulging and putting on the best kind of show as the motor immediately responds. But I don't doubt it, those fingers get my motor going too.

Levi hands me the chainsaw and gives me a brief explanation of what I need to do, and I give it a test, pulling back on the lever and watching how the blade spins. A sharp, barking laugh tears out of me as my eyes go wide. "Holy shit," I roar, glancing back at Marcus. "Did you see that?"

"Sure did, baby," he says, cheering me on.

Turning back toward James, I look up at him with a wide smile, letting him see the twisted, dark animal that lives deep inside of me. "Sorry about that," I say in a sickening sweet tone, filled with the most deceiving kind of innocence. "I'm a chainsaw virgin, but I think I've worked out all the kinks. I'm ready to go."

He glares at me, his jaw clenched tight, but I see the overwhelming fear in his eyes. I doubt he knows what I plan to do, but where a chainsaw is involved, it could never be good.

The motor rumbles through the boys' playground and bounces off every wall, and as I lift it a little higher, gripping the heavy machine tightly, my arms shake with its vibrations. A ferociousness comes over me as I step in nice and close to meet James' terrified stare. "This is for every woman you have ever hurt. Every woman whose innocence you stole, whose dignity you dragged through the mud. This is their vengeance, their time to fucking shine."

And with that, I pull the lever back, watching as the sharp jagged blade spins with an impossible speed. James' screams tear through the playground, the haunting sound like music to my ears, and without another second of hesitation, I press the jagged blade to his waist and tear straight through his flesh.

Blood spurts like a powerful hose, drenching me from head to toe, but I keep at it, ripping through his hip and crunching through his spine. The motor shakes and my arms feel the burn, but I won't dare stop, my determination like none other.

His lower half dangles and as I tear through the final bits of flesh, it drops like a sack of shit as his wrists keep his top half hanging from the chains. I don't even recall the moment he died. Was it when I first got him with the chainsaw or when I severed his spine? Perhaps it was the quick blood loss that did it. I have no idea.

Dropping the chainsaw with a heavy thump, the motor cuts out and I'm met with absolute silence behind me. Are they shocked by what I just did? Horrified? Turned on? I don't think I even care.

I feel a wave of darkness consuming my soul, and I know without a doubt that what I just did has cost me dearly, but I can't find it within myself to care. Those women deserved to have that monster put down like the fucking animal he was. Jasmine deserved it.

My hands wipe over my face, getting rid of the blood that soaks my skin, but all that does is smear it more. I feel like I've been struck by lightning and it's left me with invincible power pulsing through my veins.

Time slows and I can feel my heart thumping loudly in my ears as I turn to face the brothers. Roman watches me through a shocked stare and I briefly make out the shape of his mouth moving in the words "Holy shit." Concern flickers through Levi's gaze as he gapes at me in wonder, but Marcus … fuck, he looks as though he's just watched an angel descend from the heavens.

He walks into me and takes my shaky hand in his before he drops to his knees, James' blood splashing up around him. Marcus holds my stare, his big, dark eyes capturing mine with the kind of intensity that makes my heart pound a million times faster. "Shayne Mariano," he breathes, almost as though the words are hard to say. "I am so fucking in love with you."

CHAPTER THIRTEEN

Marcus' whispered words hit me like a million tiny knives stabbing into my skin and forcing their way into my bloodstream. I drop down onto his lap, my knees falling on either side of his strong thighs as his arms enclose around me. "You mean that?" I question, terrified of learning that this is some sick joke that gets him off, but then, I'm also terrified of what it would mean if every single word he speaks is as real as it gets.

Marcus nods slowly, his eyes not leaving mine for even a second. "I am in complete awe of your beauty, your strength, and your no bullshit determination. The way you've come into my world, grabbed it by the fucking horns, and stepped up to the challenge. Fuck, Shayne, you have captured me in a way that no other has ever done, and I promise you, from now until my dying days, that I will serve you with every fucking beat of my dead heart."

My jaw drops, a soft gasp tearing from the back of my throat. "Those are some fighting words right there, Marcus DeAngelis," I warn him, every single person in this room knowing all too well the consequences that a claim like that could have.

"I don't fucking care," he tells me, his arms tightening as he pulls me in even closer before lowering us both to the blood-soaked ground, his lips brushing over mine. "To hell with it all. You're my fucking world now."

His lips crush down over mine and I capture them with the same ferocity and desperation that pulses out of him. His tongue sweeps into my mouth, both of us fighting for domination as we become crazed with need and a mess of tangled limbs.

My hair soaks into the pool of blood beneath me as Marcus pulls back and sits up on me, straddling my waist with his strong thighs. His hungry stare looms over me, scouring every inch of my body, and when his bloodied fingers tangle into the front of my destroyed white tank and tears the fabric apart, a needy groan slips from deep in my throat.

Fucking hell. I need him.

Reaching up, I grip his belt and hastily undo it, and the clanging of the metal buckle echoes through the wide-open space. I get his fly undone when his patience to have me wears thin. He climbs off me and rids himself of his pants in seconds, and before I can even take him in, my destroyed sweats are flying across the room.

Marcus reaches down for me and I grip his hand. He yanks me up with a strong, powerful pull that sends me soaring right up out of the pool of blood and into his arms. He catches me with ease, and I feel his straining cock pressing tight against my clit.

Groans pull from deep within me as he turns and walks us toward the tool bench across the room, and I'm distantly aware that we're now alone down here. I don't know when Levi and Roman walked away, but I'm thankful they're giving us this moment.

Marcus swings one arm across the surface of the tool bench, scattering hammers and screwdrivers before dropping me to the table. Marcus' hungry kiss comes back to my lips as he steps between my knees and spreads my legs wide.

Reaching down between us, I grip his engorged cock and feel that velvety skin beneath my palm. My hand moves up and down, squeezing his tip as my thumb works right over its head. Marcus groans into my mouth and barely a moment passes before I feel his fingers pushing between my folds to tease my clit. He rubs tight circles with his thumb as his fingers dive a little deeper and push up into my cunt, curling just enough to hit that spot that has my eyes rolling to the back of my head.

I pull away from his kiss as I suck in a loud gasp, tipping my head back in pure ecstasy. His kiss falls to my throat, and I don't miss the way his lips linger on my skin, feeling the heavy thumping of my pulse beneath the surface. His teeth gently skim over my throat before I feel his addictive tongue working its way up to my ear, sending a wave of tingles through my body. I don't know what it is about that spot below my ear, but both Levi and Marcus have noticed just how crazy it makes me.

I work his cock as my lips fall to his shoulder and bite down as my eyes roll in my head. He groans, loving the pain, and I know if he had his way, he'd have me biting down harder, but I won't inflict that kind of pain on him. Stabbing a blade through his hand was enough for me, and from here on out, the only pain I'll give him will end with him coming all over me.

"Fuck, Marc," I pant as he works my cunt, his skilled fingers massaging deep inside of me. "I need you inside me. I need you to fuck me."

A deep growl rumbles through his chest as he tears his fingers out and grips my thighs. He pulls me hard, and I slide to the edge of the table as a loud squeak tears out of my throat. Marcus lines himself up perfectly, and as I catch myself against his strong chest, his cock plunges deep inside of me.

My arms fly around his neck as my nails dig into the tight muscles of his back. "Holy shit," I breathe, feeling him stretch me wide as he grips my thighs with a bruising hold.

He pauses as we both need a moment to adjust, our wicked pants sounding through the deadly playground. He slowly draws back and we both glance down, watching the way his thick, long cock slips back, coated with my arousal. Tingles spread over my body. There's simply nothing better than this.

I bite down on my lip before glancing up and meeting his heated stare.

Fuck, he's hungry for me.

The corner of his lips pull into a wicked smirk, and he holds my stare as he pushes back inside of me. I suck in a gasp as the butterflies explode deep in my stomach. Holy fuck. Whatever the hell this guy has that makes me feel like this needs to be bottled and sold for millions.

Marcus grips my chin and holds my stare, both of us panting heavily as he fucks me, stretching my walls like never before. "You're mine," he rumbles, the words speaking right to my heart. "When I fuck you, you're mine."

I nod. "Yours."

His pace quickens and my pants and gasps match his thrusts, the intensity of his heated stare almost too much for me to take.

His fingers grip me tighter and I throw my head back. I've not been one to tell a man that I love him, but damn it, if he fucks me any harder the words might just come screaming out.

He gives me what I want, thrusting deep inside of me over and over again until the familiar, delicious fire burns inside of me, growing stronger by the second like a rapid inferno desperate to explode. But I hold onto it, not nearly ready for this to be over.

Marcus drops his gaze, breaking our heated stare so he can watch the way he fucks me, just like Levi does, and damn it, I fucking love it. I feel so exposed, and it makes me feel like the most sensual woman who ever walked the planet. He grips my thighs and rocks his hips, going as far back as he can without fully falling out of me, only to slam back in, his body rolling, clenching, and flinching with each movement.

"Marc," I gasp, my nails digging in as the inferno deep inside of me builds higher. I reach down between us, feeling where we connect, feeling my arousal on his hard shaft and letting it mix onto my fingers. I can't resist touching myself, rubbing quick, tight circles over my clit, and the moment I do, my body flinches and jolts, the power bubbling up inside of me too much to bear.

"That's right, baby. Keep touching yourself," he rumbles, his voice deep and strained as he's pushed closer and closer to the edge, my pussy just moments from tearing him apart.

Fuck, there's nothing better than knowing I have the power to make these incredible DeAngelis brothers come undone.

"More," I pant with desperation. He gives me exactly what I'm asking for, his free hand twisting around me and knotting into my hair. He rips my head back and crushes his lips to my throat, his tongue roaming over my sensitive skin as his other hand cups my tit and gives it a firm squeeze before he rolls my pert nipple between his fingers. "Oh, fuck."

My fingers work my clit as he works my cunt and every damn other inch of my body, fucking me hard and fast with the type of intensity that could drive a woman insane. No wonder bitches be throwing themselves at these men.

I take him harder, letting him pull me off the table just a little bit further until I'm barely holding on. My body is forced back to keep myself up, and the new angle sends him soaring so much deeper. His responding growl is all I need to warn me that this new position has him by the balls and it won't be long until he gives himself to me.

My pussy clenches around him and we both groan as my fingers circle my clit. "Come for me," Marcus demands, his jaw clenching as his fingers tighten on my body.

"Oh fuck," I pant as I come hard. "I'm already there!"

My world explodes around me as my orgasm completely takes over, pulsing through my body like liquid gold. My head tips back as my pussy turns into a quivering mess, convulsing and squeezing Marcus' thick cock as he keeps moving inside of me.

"Holy fuck," Marcus spits through his clenched teeth. "You're so goddamn tight when you squeeze me like that."

I try to respond, try to tell him just how good it is for me, but my orgasm completely cripples me, and I'm lost for words. Its power leaves me defenseless and shattered in the best possible way. "Ah, fuck," Marc growls as he shoots his load deep inside my cunt, his cum streaming out of him in hot quick bursts.

He doesn't dare stop, letting me ride out my high as I struggle to catch my breath. He pinches my nipple, and the intensity sends a jolt of electricity shooting straight to my core, making me flinch with overwhelming pleasure. "Oh God, Marc. Yes."

His thumb and forefinger gently rub my nipple, keeping my body alive as he slows his movements, his stiff cock moving like a gentle wave washing back and forth.

I finally let go, my orgasm releasing me from its tight bonds, and I let out a deep breath, holding onto Marcus with everything I have as he meets my sated stare. "You and me, baby. We're going to make this world our bitch."

A grin kicks up the corner of my mouth and I believe it with every fiber of my being. Especially with his brothers at our side. We will be unstoppable.

Marcus scoops his arm around me and keeps himself buried deep inside my cunt as he lifts me off the table and walks us across the playground until we're moving into a massive bathroom. It's not as fancy as the bathrooms in the main part of the castle, but it's still better than anything I could have afforded.

The shower is huge, but something tells me it was made this way with the specific purpose of washing blood away after a particularly messy murder spree, and seeing as though blood is dripping from my hair and coating my body, it's kinda perfect for what I need.

Marc steps into the shower, cranking the taps as he goes and letting the freezing water stream down over us. A piercing squeal tears from the back of my throat as the water drenches us, immediately washing the blood off my body.

I feel him growing hard inside me, but I pull away, the blood starting to bug me. He reluctantly pulls out of me and sets me on my feet, but he doesn't dare step away, determined to keep his hands on my body as the water runs a deep shade of red.

After washing my hair and scrubbing James' blood from my body, Marcus meets my stare. "I don't know how the fuck I'm going to share you with my brothers now that I know how I feel about you."

"Brothers?" I question. "Since when did Roman become a part of this little arrangement? Pretty sure you only have to fight Levi for my attention."

Marcus scoffs, his fingers brushing over my body and skimming over the curve of my breast, stopping to tease my nipple, and getting a rise out of the way it hardens beneath his touch. "It's inevitable. You're into Roman, and that's cool, but you should know the way he looks at you … baby, he never looked at Felicity like that. He's just fucked up right now. He's angry and he'll never fucking admit it, but it's there. You've fucked with all of our heads."

My brow arches and I shake my head. "You don't think you've done the same to me, oh creepy one?" I murmur, reaching down between us and stroking my fingers over his cock, loving the way it reacts to my touch. "You've destroyed me for any other man, so I swear to God, Marc. If you three fuckheads die in this war and leave me, I'll be really fucking pissed."

His arm curls around my body and pulls me in tight, crushing my chest against his. "Is that your way of saying you love me too?"

A grin pulls at the corners of my lips as I jump up into his arms, wrapping my legs around his waist. He slams my back up against the cold tiles of the shower and reaches down between us, the back of his hand skimming over my sensitive clit and making me flinch. He takes his cock and effortlessly slides back inside me.

A deep, guttural groan tears from me as I pull him in and brush my lips over his. "What does it say about me if I were to admit I'd fallen in love with a savage like you?"

Marcus' lips pull into a wicked grin against mine. "It'd say that you're no longer visiting the dark side, Shayne, you fucking own it."

And with that, he fucks me all over again, making sure that with every damn thrust, I know that I'm his queen.

CHAPTER FOURTEEN

Levi's drums sound from the other room, and I roll my eyes as my ass drops onto the big couch. It was a long drive back to the DeAngelis mansion, and while Marcus and Roman had plans to head back to the castle for a second load, Levi couldn't wait to set up his drums. His fingers have been itching for it since we first ran Giovanni out of here.

Not being a great passenger and needing some down time, I opted to stay here with Levi and the wolves, knowing that I'll be safe to finally spend some time by myself and just chill. It's been way too long since I've been able to just do me.

A full bowl of popcorn and one of every soda in the house is lined up on the couch beside me. If I'm doing this, then I'm going to do it right.

Grabbing the remote, I turn on the TV and immediately boost

the volume up to drown out the sound of Levi's drumming. Don't get me wrong, that forceful, intense drumming is the sound of my soul, but not on my movie night. I won't be able to chill with that sound vibrating through the walls and reminding me just how good it can really be.

After crossing my legs under me and spreading a blanket over my body, I grab the bowl of popcorn and rest it in my lap. The first perfectly buttered piece sinks into my mouth as I flip through every last channel that Giovanni is paying for. I search through every streaming app until I finally find what I'm looking for—serial killer documentaries.

Now this is my jam.

I've watched these my whole life. Whenever my dad was out spending his night getting drunk and abusing the poor wait staff, I would watch documentaries until I heard his key forcing its way into the lock. Ten out of ten times he was drunk, and it'd take at least five minutes for him to get the front door open, giving me enough time to race to my bedroom and lock myself in there for the night. Most of the time, he was still passed out when I had to leave for school in the morning.

It was a perfect little system ... until it wasn't.

These documentaries, as fucked up as they are, remind me of my youth, the good times sitting on my couch all by myself. As bad as it sounds, being ten years old, home and alone with no food were the best nights of my childhood. It only went downhill from there. Not to mention, there's nothing better than a fucked-up story. While these stories are dark and twisted in every way, they reminded me that life could have been worse. I was just a kid, sitting at home with a lock on the back of my bedroom door, while the victims in these documentaries were coming face to face with pure evil.

I find one about The Midnight Butcher and it stirs something within me. I hit play and make myself comfortable, popping another piece of popcorn into my mouth. The Midnight Butcher's photo comes on the screen, and I recall a news story only a year or two ago about the guy. From memory, he lives in this state and was a real problem for a while, but the state is pretty fucking big, and from his victims' locations, he wasn't someone I had to worry about.

It's way after nightfall. It's been a long-ass day and I find myself smirking as the documentary goes on. This guy seems like a bit of an amateur. His kills are a little sloppy and wild. Roman would be disappointed and Marcus would just be embarrassed. Though it's not like I'm one to judge. My kills have been a complete mess. Hell, today's chainsaw experiment was a complete disaster, though I got the job done and managed to get a confession of love at the same time. I guess it was technically a success.

Shit, am I no better than the guys in these documentaries?

The glow of the TV lights up the room, and just as I watch an actor portraying the Butcher, stalking his latest victim, the couch dips beside me and the bowl of popcorn flies from my lap. "FUCK," I screech as Doe plonks down on the couch beside me, her big head dropping into my lap where the popcorn once was.

My hand presses to my chest, feeling the rapid beat of my heart beneath as Dill comes hobbling into the room, a slight limp in his step. "Hey, buddy," I say, watching as he makes his way to the spilled popcorn and starts cleaning up my mess.

My heart sinks watching him. He's doing a million times better, but he's still in so much pain. He definitely isn't the same wolf I've come to know. My hand falls to Doe's head and I scratch her behind the ears as Dill makes himself comfortable on the carpet, right under me, making sure that if I were to get up for a pee break, I'd trip over his humongous body.

Now that he's not on the strong painkillers and he's a lot more mobile, he's been following me everywhere I go. He's just as protective over me as I am of him, and I know it kills him that he's not back at full strength. He's not been able to run or chow down his food like he normally does, and while he'll never express it, I know he's still in so much pain. It kills me seeing him like this, but it won't be long until he's back to chatting up all those wolfy bitches he finds out in the wild. I bet this big bastard is a bit of a stud in the wolf world, and I can picture Doe so clearly, rolling her eyes in embarrassment at her big brother. Though, do we actually know that they're siblings? Or is that something I've made up in my mind?

The documentary goes on as Doe sleeps in my lap. I get lost in the story, judging his every move, knowing the boys could have done so much better. They stalked me like fucking professionals through my apartment, and then again through the maze garden back at the castle.

Good times!

I hear the door of the internal garage and a smile settles over my lips realizing that Marcus and Roman are back. I can't help but think of what Marcus said to me in the shower about Roman. I'm not blind, I know Roman feels something for me, but there's no way what he feels for me comes even close to the intense relationship he shared with Felicity. Hell, they even had a child together, and he was ready to give her his name.

Marcus comes striding through to the massive theater room with Roman hot on his heels. I'm not surprised to see Levi following them in a moment after. Marcus drops his ass onto the armrest of my couch and picks up a stray piece of popcorn as he watches the documentary with furrowed brows.

Levi looks around the room at the mess I made when the wolves came in. "What the fuck happened here?" he asks, walking around the couch and leaning against the backrest behind my head.

"Ask these big assholes," I mutter, indicating to the giant wolves.

I hear the soft fizz coming from Roman's beer as he cracks the lid while Marcus continues staring at the screen, watching a reenactment of the Butcher's final murder. "What the fuck are you watching?" he questions, his lips pulling up in disgust, seeing the shitty documentary special effects and movie editing. I can only imagine the thoughts rushing through his head, complete and utter judgment.

"It's a serial killer documentary. Some guy they referred to as The Midnight Butcher," I explain as another photo of the guy appears on the screen.

Marcus' eyes widen in surprise as Levi laughs behind me. "No fucking way," he says. "That's Jake."

My eyes bug out of my head and I whip around to face Levi.

"What do you mean *that's Jake?* Do you know this guy?"

"Yeah, of course I do," he tells me, taking a beer from Roman. "We're all tight around here. He's not a bad guy, just misunderstood. You met him at the party we had at the castle. He was watching you all night."

My eyes get impossibly wider. "WHAT?" I screech, waking Doe. "You invited this guy to your party?"

Marcus shrugs his shoulders, his lips pressed into a hard line. "Why not? We invited heaps of our friends," he says in a dull tone, something else clearly on his mind. "We had to reel him in a bit. He was watching you a little too hard. If we hadn't stepped in, he would have made a name for himself all over again."

I shake my head, still unable to believe it. "No, that's not right," I say, specifically remembering the part of the documentary that said the FBI caught the dude and locked him up. "He was arrested two years ago."

"Yeah," Roman laughs. "Just like we were arrested last month. The FBI likes to talk themselves up when it counts, but I bet you don't hear the stories of how they let their targets slip right through their fingers."

"No shit," I breathe, refusing to acknowledge Marcus' comments about what Jake wanted to do to me during the party. I've already got the attention of three crazed psychopathic serial killers; I don't need any more to watch out for. Besides, there's no guarantee that the next one is going to fall for my charm like these guys have.

Marcus lets out a frustrated sigh and fumes at the TV. "How

the hell did Jake get a documentary? I mean … where the fuck is my documentary? I've made much more exciting kills than that guy. These are all the same. They're boring. Now me? I'm a fucking star. I deserve to be on that screen, plus have you ever seen me on camera? I'm photogenic as fuck. That'd be the best goddamn documentary anyone had ever seen."

A smirk settles across my face, and just as I go to suggest he pay a producer a little visit, Doe's ears stand high under my hand. I glance down at her as a low growl rumbles through her chest. She shakes off my hand and sits up as Dill makes a similar sound deep in his chest.

A silence sounds through the theater room as Marcus takes the remote out of my hand and shuts off the TV, all three of the boys listening intently. "What is it?" I question, my heart kicking into gear. We've already dealt with one intruder at the castle today, I don't think I can handle another. I need at least a week before I get to call on that darkness inside my soul again.

"Shhhhh," Roman says, holding up a hand and looking to his brothers. "You hear that?"

I strain to listen as Doe growls again, the rumble making the hairs on the back of my neck stand tall. I hear nothing, but after a short pause, the familiar sound of tires on the driveway breaks through the silence. "Someone's here," I gasp, my eyes going wide.

Levi nods and reaches over the couch, taking my hand and forcing me to my feet as the four of us make our way out of the theater room. The wolves race in front of us, Dill doing his best to keep up with Doe. "I can only make out one car," Levi says, glancing over his shoulder at

Roman who nods.

We make our way out to the big foyer when the boys discreetly move in front of the window overlooking the front yard. "Black town car," Marcus says, standing exactly in the space I'd been in only a week ago when we'd run Giovanni out of here.

"Could be anyone," Roman says, moving in beside me and pressing a gun into my hand. I take it greedily, but just like every other time I've held a gun in my hand, I feel uncomfortable and laughably under prepared despite the few lessons the guys have given me.

I move in beside Marcus and watch the black car coming down the drive. He positions himself in front of me, being his overprotective self. I can't say that I hate it. After the week I've had, a little protection detail won't go astray.

The car pulls to a stop in front of the big obnoxious water fountain, and the boys wait impatiently, watching as the car door swings open and an expensive set of shoes hits the driveway. The thought trickles through my mind that any threat wouldn't be stopping in the middle of the drive like this, they'd be hidden away and sneaking onto the property, most likely through the woods out back, the very woods where I was taken by Giovanni. But then again, the majority of this dark world has no idea that Giovanni has been chased out of town. They assume he's still here sitting up on his throne and shitting all over the people he claims to rule, and while this visitor may not be an enemy of Giovanni's, it's very possible that they have a vendetta against his three devilish sons.

A suited man finally appears at the bottom of the drive and

Marcus blows out a breath of relief as I notice how similar he looks to Giovanni. "It's Louis," Marcus says, glancing over at Roman and Levi who are busy preparing themselves for some kind of shootout.

The boys instantly relax, shoving guns into the waistband of their pants as I glance up at Marcus. "Which one is Louis again?"

"My father's youngest brother, Ronaldo's father."

My brows arch, fear pounding in my chest. "Ronaldo," I repeat. "The one who Victor killed in retaliation for his son's murder?" I question, remembering the exact moment Levi shot Antonio's tongue off and Marcus requested we bring it home in a doggy box for his vast trophy collection. Ronaldo, the boys' cousin, was set up to take the fall and Antonio's father was quick to retaliate by taking Ronaldo's life, effectively setting off a carefully planned out war.

Marcus nods and I let out a shaky breath, glancing back at Roman. "What does he want?"

Roman's dark, broody eyes are narrowed, deep in thought as he slowly shakes his head. "I've got no fucking idea," he says as their uncle makes his way up the grand stairs. "But we're about to find out."

The boys form a wide semi-circle around the front door, covering all their bases as I keep myself carefully placed behind Marcus' shoulder, protected at all costs.

The door slowly opens and fear pounds through my chest. Louis is a senior member of the DeAngelis family; I don't doubt that he knows how to protect himself. The boys would have learned everything they know from men like Louis. I refuse to go into this unprotected, even if the likelihood of this turning into something bigger is near zero.

Louis pushes past the door and comes to an immediate stop, seeing the most brutal of his nephews waiting to greet him. "Uncle," Roman says, taking point. "Is there something we can do for you?"

Louis takes a moment to compose himself, definitely not having expected to see the three infamous killers hovering by the door as a welcome party. He raises his chin, wanting to take control of the conversation as he glances between his nephews, but he should know better than that. He lost any form of control he may have had over this family the moment the brothers stepped into the prime position. "Where is your father?" he demands. "I need to meet with him about an urgent matter."

Roman takes a step forward and his impressive height towers over his uncle, even from across the foyer. "My father is … unavailable."

Louis pauses, a flicker of nervousness glistening in his eyes. "What have you done?" he says, immediately catching on as he takes a discreet step back toward the door, more than ready to haul ass if he needs to. It's not odd for the boys to have been here. They were invited regularly for meetings and dinners, but having them here without warning definitely isn't the norm, and he's right to be nervous.

"My father was getting a little too comfortable in his role, don't you think?" Roman questions, the tone of his voice sending a shiver trailing down my spine.

"I'm not here for your games," Louis says. "Where's your father?"

"That's just the thing," Levi says. "Nobody knows. We ran him out of here over a week ago, and since then, he's been nothing but a ghost."

"Ran him out of here?" Louis repeats with a heavy suspicion in his tone, silently putting all the pieces of the puzzle together, but judging by the confusion flashing in his dark eyes, he's putting them together wrong. "Tell me now, did you kill my brother?"

"If only," Roman breathes. "Bastard got away before we got a chance, but don't be fooled, we will end his life the second his miserable ass steps out of hiding."

Louis raises a brow, clearly deep in thought. There's no question about it, he's tossing up his loyalties, trying to figure out which path will get him killed quickest and which will save him. He should know better than that, in this world, there are no guarantees. "Okay," he says slowly, his gaze flicking between the three of them, making sure no one makes any sudden movements. "Let me ask you this. Did you three have anything to do with my son's death?"

Roman shakes his head. "I believe you've shown up on the wrong brother's doorstep if you've come searching for answers."

"What is that supposed to mean?" Louis roars. "What do you know of this?"

Marcus lets out a heavy breath, a smirk resting over his lips as he takes a step toward his uncle. "Tsk, tsk," he starts. "Did your big brother not inform you of what happened to your only son, his youngest nephew?"

Louis snaps his glare to Marcus, and for a moment, I fear for his safety, but he's not stupid enough to make a move like that with his current company. "What do you know, boy?" he spits. "I want answers now. I will not grovel or beg for the likes of you three. Tell me what you know, now."

Roman pulls the gun from his waistband and steps into his uncle, pressing the barrel to his temple and hastily shutting him up. "I wonder if you would grovel and beg now?" Roman mutters. "What about when our father finally takes his last breath and we rule over this family? Would you grovel then?"

Louis glares at Roman, and I don't doubt that this is his first time in this position, though it would definitely be a first time facing off against a man as unpredictable as Roman. "There ain't no killing your father. He's a slippery motherfucker, always has been. You may have run him off for now and are up here in his home playing happy family, but he will prevail. That bastard always does. Do not fool yourself, boy. He will come back with a vengeance."

"I assume that means your loyalties lie with him."

"My loyalties lie with the head of this family, and until you can bring me proof of death, that position will remain your father's. Now tell me what you know of my son's death."

Roman slowly pulls back on the safety, releasing it with a soft click that sounds louder than a gunshot in this room. "And what if I told you that my father has known who killed your son since the moment it happened? Hell, he knew it was happening before Ronaldo did, yet he did nothing to prevent it when one word from him could have ended the whole thing. What would you say then?"

Louis' eyes flash with a heated anger that sends waves of guilt soaring through me. This is all on our shoulders. We started this war, we killed Antonio to use as bait, and in return, he lost his only son and is left without answers. But that's just the world these boys live in, and Louis is more than aware of that. If he wanted to protect his son from the dangers of Mafia life, he should have kept himself away just as Giovanni's other brother, Joseph, does. Though, from what the boys have told me, Louis is a dangerous man. For the most part, he's cool, calm, and collected, but if you push him enough, he'll burn the whole family to the ground.

"You're a liar, Roman DeAngelis. You always have been. You forget that I have known you since you were born into this family," Louis says, his eyes sharp and filled with venom. The way Roman is skirting around his son's death clearly has his feathers ruffled the wrong way. "You claim to be a man of your word, yet I haven't heard a snippet of truth being told since I walked through that door. You are not fit to rule in your father's place. You play games and enjoy destruction. Now, tell me what I've come all this way to know."

Roman stands in silence for a long moment, the tension growing thicker by the second as Louis attempts to hold some kind of dominance over Roman, though it's not possible. Roman was born for this and watching him now, it's as clear as day. "I'll tell you what you wish to know, once you tell me what I need to know."

Louis' brows furrow and he pulls back, watching Roman with uncertainty. "There is nothing that I know that could possibly benefit you."

"When was the last time you spoke to my father?"

Louis shakes his head, deep in thought. "I don't know, weeks ago. We spoke briefly at the last business dinner. I told him he was a fool for allowing you three a week of freedom. He should have kept you locked up in that big castle. How is this important?"

Roman clenches his jaw. "My father killed my fiancé and took my newborn son," he spits, that word fiancé killing something deep inside of me. "If you know where he would go, then you need to tell me right now."

Louis shakes his head. "You're a smart man, Roman. I see how you watch everyone, learn of their relationships so that you can exploit them later. You know just as well as I do that I don't know the answer to that question. You want to find your father and your son, then you need to speak with Victor. Wait too long, and you know the likelihood of finding that baby alive just as well as I do."

Roman narrows his eyes, holding Louis' stare a moment longer, the anger burning brightly within him as the fear of what could happen to his child haunts his every thought. "You want to learn what happened to your son, then I suggest you take the same course of action and seek out Victor."

Louis glances toward me and Marcus before flicking his gaze in the opposite direction to Levi. He meets Roman in the middle. "Why on earth would I need to speak to Victor? What does he have to do with this?"

"You search for answers on your son's death, so perhaps start with the man who killed him."

Louis' face falls and he shakes his head. "What are you saying? Victor killed my only son? No, he wouldn't do that. You're lying."

"Suit yourself," Roman tells him. "I've told you what you've come to know. If you choose not to believe me, then that is your own problem. Victor killed Ronaldo in retaliation, and your precious son slaughtered Antonio when he caught him balls deep inside his wife."

Louis clenches his jaw and takes a step back, rage burning through his eyes, though the rage is not focused on his nephews. I have no doubt that he will be going after Victor. He meets Roman's stare again before giving him a sharp nod. "I will see myself out."

Silence consumes us, and not a moment later, Louis is gone and flying down the grand steps.

The heavy thud of the door sounds through the foyer, and the second we're alone, Roman breaks, the fears for his lost son playing on his mind, getting worse with every passing second. "FUCK," he roars, dropping the gun and diving for the massive crystal vase across the foyer. He grabs it and throws it hard, letting it smash into a million shattered pieces against the expensive marble floor.

Crystal shards spread far and wide as Roman's hands fly to his head. His fingers dig in and I can only imagine what kind of bullshit is going through his head right now. He paces the foyer for a short moment before Levi steps toward him. "Roman …" he starts, ready to help him in any way he needs, but without a backward glance, Roman takes off deeper into the mansion, his pain tearing my heart in two.

CHAPTER FIFTEEN

My fist slams into Levi's chest with a heavy punch that sends a wave of pain searing up my arm. "Fuck," I grunt, shaking out my hand as Levi just stands there, completely unaffected by my hit.

He looks down at me with wide eyes as though only just realizing I tried to take his ass out. "Shit, little one. Are you alright?" he questions, taking my hand and looking it over to make sure I haven't done any damage.

I roll my eyes and let out a frustrated sigh. "This training session is a bust," I tell him. "Roman is passed out drunk, Marcus is too distracted doing who the hell knows what, and you're too lost inside your freaking head to pay attention. What's going on?"

His lips pull into a crooked grin that makes something swell inside my chest. "Did that bastard really tell you that he was in love with you?"

My brows furrow as I look up at him. "You were there. You heard him say it."

Deciding my hand is fine, he tugs against it and draws me into his chest. "I know, but did he mean it? There's a big fucking difference between getting hot and talking shit while watching your woman chainsaw some asshole in half and sincerely telling her that she's the one. Which one was it?"

Tilting my head up, I grin back at him, my eyes glistening with mischief. "My, oh my, Levi DeAngelis. You sound jealous."

His eyes sparkle right back at me, and I get just a moment's notice before his foot sweeps out behind me and pushes me back, sending me sprawling straight onto my back. He comes down with me, his arms caging around my body and taking the brunt of our fall. "Baby, I don't get jealous."

I laugh and push on his shoulder, forcing him to roll, though I have absolutely no strength to make him actually do it. I'm just lucky that he takes pity on me and allows me to play my game. He rolls, bringing me with him, not stopping until I'm straddled over his hips and can feel his erection through his workout shorts pressing up against my core and making my mouth water. "You don't get jealous, huh?" I muse. "What if I told you that he made me promise that I was only his? That this pussy was exclusively his?" I question, rocking my hips over his and feeling his cock flinch.

Levi grabs the front of my workout crop and pulls me down to him, catching me around the waist. "I'd say you're a tease playing a dirty game," he warns me, fire burning in his obsidian eyes. "That fucker wouldn't dare take you away from me, not if he values his life."

"You're right," I mutter, my lips brushing against his. "He does value his life, but that doesn't mean that he didn't at least try."

Levi shakes his head and lets out a frustrated breath before his eyes soften. "Give it to me straight, Shayne. Did he mean it?"

I nod, the memory of Marcus' raw honesty playing over in my head. "He meant it."

"Fuck, and here I thought that I'd be the first."

My brow arches high and I press up against his chest, needing to see his eyes clearly. "What are you saying?" I breathe, my heart kicking into gear and beating a shitload faster than what it had during that whole training session.

Levi sits up and takes me with him, holding me tight as he gets comfortable and leans back onto his hands, keeping his dark eyes locked on mine. "I don't know if you noticed this, babe, but I've been fucking crazy about you since you tried to throw yourself off the roof of the castle, then demanded I fuck you right then and there."

My pussy clenches at the sheer memory of that night, hanging off the side of the roof while this beast of a man slammed into me from behind. It was a fucking crazy night and one of my absolute favorites since being here ... you know, apart from the part where Giovanni showed up, put shock collars around his sons' necks and ordered me to choose which one of them should die.

"What can I say?" I question with a flirty smirk. "I like to live on the wild side. It's not my fault you guys are searching for a batshit crazy girl to match your insane psychological issues."

His lips press into a hard line, feigning irritation, but the small tick in the corner of his mouth gives him away. He fucking loves my smart mouth and he knows it. Hell, they all do. His arm curls around my waist and pulls me in before his lips crush down on mine. He kisses me deeply, his tongue sweeping into mine with a fierce determination, and I can't help but feel as though he's trying to make me forget that anybody else has been there. "You're trouble," he tells me as he pulls back just an inch, leaving barely a breath between us.

"You love it when I'm trouble," I murmur. "If I were boring, you would have fucked me off a long time ago. You, Levi DeAngelis, love a girl who challenges you. You love it when I push your buttons and snap back at you with a feisty attitude. It makes you want to spank my ass, and I don't think you've met a girl who makes you feel that way in a very long time."

He nods, his eyes softening as his fingers brush down the side of my face, pushing my hair back behind my ear. "You're right," he tells me. "Most girls are terrified of us. They shit their pants at just the sound of our name on somebody else's lips. That makes it very hard to get close to anyone, but you stuck with it. I'm standoffish at the best of times, but you persisted. You broke down my walls and pushed your little bratty way in, even after the hell I put you through when Marc got shot. You should have turned me away, you should have punished me for that, but you let me back in. I don't deserve you, Shayne."

I shrug my shoulders. "That first time you came into my cell and told me to get dressed for dinner, I knew I was going to have you. I wanted to break you. You were so tough and so sure of yourself that I wanted to make you second guess. I wanted to make you hate yourself for hurting me, and I think in doing that, I made you care, but I made me care too, and I never expected that I would feel something so deep for you. You're making me love you and a part of me hates that. You three kidnapped me, you hurt me in the most brutal ways and turned me into this stone-cold killer, you made me a stranger to the girl I used to be, and yet I keep coming back for more. Is there something wrong with me?"

A smirk cuts across his warm lips and I know exactly what's going to come out of his mouth before he even says it. "Fuck yeah, babe. You're more fucked in the head than we are."

I roll my eyes and shove his shoulder, making him fall back and catch himself on his hand. "You're an asshole."

"And you're a brat," he fires back. "But I wouldn't have it any other way. I don't know when, and I sure as fuck don't know how, but you made me fall in love with you, Shayne, and it honestly scares the shit out of me because I'm still waiting for you to realize that we're no good for you. You're going to get up and leave at some point, and it's going to fucking kill me."

My hand falls to his chest, and I feel the rapid beat of his heart beneath, knowing that it has absolutely everything to do with me. Meeting his eyes, I stare deep into them, tearing back the layers of my walls and letting him see the true, vulnerable me who lives inside. "That's not going to happen," I whisper, feeling his fingers tighten on my waist. "You and Marcus, hell maybe even Roman too … you've all opened my eyes to this insane, dark world that scares the shit out of me. It's raw and terrifying, but I want to be here because being here means that I get to have you, and I wouldn't trade that for anything. I'd rather die than have to live another day without you all," I tell him. "Sitting down in that cell in the desert, I started thinking that maybe I was never going to see you again and the very thought of it broke me. I know you didn't intend on this happening, and I sure as hell didn't either, but you've forced your way in, despite this crazy, intense world, and made me fall for you, and I'm never going to give you back. Your heart is mine whether you like it or not. No refunds. No exchange. It's a done deal."

"Are you sure about that?" he questions. "Because if you're just fucking with me to get me back for kidnapping and torturing you, I'm going to be fucking pissed and every cell inside me is going to tell me to fuck you up but I'm not going to be able to do it."

I lean in and press the softest kiss to his delicious lips. "You can't fake something like this," I whisper. "I know you feel it just like I do."

A soft smile pulls at his lips as he curls his arm around my waist, dropping me back to the hard floor of the training room once again. "Like I said," he murmurs, his dark, intense eyes boring into mine. "You're going to be trouble."

"Damn straight, I am," I grin. "But trouble is fun, and you're a sucker for a good time."

"I'm a fucking sucker for you."

His lips crush down on mine, completely devouring me and leaving no room for argument. Our tongues battle for dominance, and despite knowing that his stubborn nature will force him to keep going until he wins, I don't possibly give in, not yet at least.

His hand slides up my torso and slips under the fabric of my crop before pulling it over my head, forcing our kiss to break apart. "Jesus," I pant, trying to catch my breath. "What the hell are we going to tell the grandchildren when they ask how we met?"

Levi laughs, his breath brushing over my lips. "We tell them the truth."

"Oh yeah?" I laugh as his lips drop back to my neck. "And what's that?"

"That I have a weakness for women in chains and lingerie and you like to make deals with devils and the two just sorta … meshed together, and the rest was history."

"Really?" I question. "And here I thought it had something to do with a broody asshole who kidnapped me right out of my apartment, though I could be thinking of the million other men who have kidnapped me over the past few months. It's a little hard to keep track."

His hand skims up my body until his fingers are lightly curled around my throat. He gives a gentle squeeze as his lips pull into a wicked smirk. "Don't you dare confuse our first night together with those amateur attempts by other men. That night is special to me."

"Oh, I bet it is," I tease, remembering that night perfectly, and more specifically how this asshole had hidden in my closet, watching me get myself off … well, *attempt* to get myself off, seeing as though Tarzan decided to burst into flames and tried to torch my coochie. I lift up just enough to brush my lips over his, more than aware of how my movement has his fingers tightening around my throat. "Tell me, which part of it specifically got you hard? Watching me get myself off while you spied on me through my closet door, or stalking me through the halls?"

A low growl sounds through his throat as he grinds his hardening cock against my core, my questions making his eyes sparkle like some kind of devil. "You know what really gets me hard?" he questions, releasing my throat and skipping his fingers right down my body until he's cupping my pussy. "Watching your tight cunt squeezing my cock like it will never let it go."

A thrill pulses through me and I capture his lips again in mine. "Really?" I breathe. "I can't say that I know what you're talking about. You'll have to show me what you mean."

Hunger tears through his gaze, and within seconds, he's on his feet with his strong fingers curled around my ankle. He gives me a hard tug and I slide across the training room floor like a hockey puck on ice.

Levi spins me, whipping me around until I face the mirrored wall at the back of the room. He drops down behind me and spreads my legs wide, watching me through the big mirror as my pussy clenches in anticipation.

He reaches behind himself, and in the next moment, I see a sharp blade glistening in the light of the room. His eyes bore into mine through the mirror, and the longer he holds my stare, the more fidgety I become. Fuck, he's going to make me come before he's even touched me.

His arms curl around me and he grips onto the tight fabric of my workout tights before effortlessly tearing straight through them with the blade. The material falls from my legs, and he doesn't hesitate to do the same to my black, lace underwear. I'm not going to lie, I'm a little disappointed that he didn't just tear them off with his teeth. Beggars can't be choosers though.

Wanting me to have an unobstructed view of my pussy through the mirror, he lifts me just slightly and yanks the torn material out from under my ass. The moment it's gone, I see her—my pussy, glistening with my arousal in all her naked, bare glory.

I clench, and damn it, the grin that pulls at his lips is enough to cripple me. "See how fucking stunning you are?" he tells me, flipping the blade over in his hand, letting the sharp tip dig into his palm as he presses the curved handle to my collarbone.

My eyes zero in on his movements, breathing heavily as he trails the smooth handle across my body. It slips down between my tits going just slow enough to drive me wild with need. My pussy throbs and pulses with anticipation, and if he doesn't cut the shit and touch me soon, I'll have to do it myself.

Levi tsks me, shaking his head as he captures my stare through the mirror. "Patience," he warns, slowly trailing the knife down past my ribs, making me suck in a gasp as the subtle touch sends a wave of goosebumps over my skin.

I watch him closely, completely mesmerized with his every move as he goes further and further south, until finally, the smooth, cold handle brushes over my exposed clit. My body jolts and I gasp, not having expected to feel quite so sensitive.

He goes again, this time a little firmer as he rubs the slick handle in tight circles. "Oh, fuck," I breathe, reaching up behind me and curling my hand around the back of his neck. What is it about watching that makes it so much more intense?

He dips the handle lower, mixing with my arousal and I hold my breath in anticipation, watching as he slowly pushes the handle deep inside my core. My fingers knot into the back of his hair, squeezing tight as my pussy contracts, feeling the coolness of the handle as it rubs against my walls.

Levi slowly draws it back out of me and the handle glistens with my arousal. "This," he murmurs, dropping his lips to my neck while still watching me through the mirror, "is what I see."

My breath comes faster, my need for more burning so hot inside of me that I can't pull myself together long enough to form any type of response, so instead, I just watch, the hunger in my eyes telling him exactly what he needs to know.

"See the way your cunt squeezes around it?" he murmurs, his breath brushing across my skin like a gentle caress as he pushes the handle back inside and curls his other arm around me, capturing my clit between his fingers. I gasp, my body jolting and clenching. "The way you try to hold it there as though you can't bear the thought of me pulling it out? The way your body reacts to my every touch? That's what gets me hard."

A soft groan tears from deep in my chest and I watch him push deep inside of me again, his hand smearing with blood from the tip of the blade, but in all seriousness, he probably has absolutely no idea …

or even gives a shit.

Intense pleasure fills my every cell, rushing through me like a wave of satisfaction. I can't help but reach up and skim my fingers over my breasts, tilting my head back onto his shoulder, not once removing my gaze from my reflection.

I've never seen myself like this, so spread wide and open while being touched. I look like a crazed vixen and I fucking love every damn second of it. My body jolts and wriggles under his skillful touch as my groans, moans, and cries get louder and more intense.

I grip my tit, pinching down on my nipple as he fucks me just a little faster, his thrusts becoming wilder and more determined, watching as I come undone beneath him. My body spasms and the familiar burn deep inside of me takes control and spreads through my veins like wildfire. "OH FUCK," I cry, my orgasm tearing through me.

My pussy convulses, my walls squeezing around the handle as Levi's fingers continue working my clit. I'm in a world of fucking pleasure, and I don't know how to handle it. My body completely comes apart, every inch of me burning with the most intense satisfaction.

My orgasm gets more intense by the second, and I gasp out when Levi tears his hand away from my clit. He presses in behind my back and snakes his arm around my waist, lifting me up.

He slides in beneath me, keeping my legs spread, and as my pussy throbs and pulses, he tears the handle out of me, tosses it aside, and slams me down over his bulging cock. "Awwwwwww, fuck," I groan, the orgasm too much, too intense.

My fingers thread between his on my hips as he slams up into me, fucking me with everything that he's got, groaning with the way my pussy clenches and spasms around him. My orgasm refuses to ease, the intensity forcing tears to my eyes. "FUCK. YES. YES," I cry, fisting my hands around his and squeezing tight.

He watches me through the mirror, his gaze locked on the way his cock moves in and out of me, and damn it, I've never seen anything so erotic in my life.

His cock looks like a fucking monster from this position, and I can't tear my eyes off it, watching as it comes out coated in my arousal. It even feels like a fucking monster. His jaw clenches and the concentration on his face tells me that he's close, determined to come with me before my orgasm begins to ease, and damn it, that's exactly what he does.

I watch as he slams up into me one more time, coming hard and spurting his hot seed deep inside me with a loud groan. As my orgasm reaches its climax, he tightens his hold on my hips and lets his forehead fall to my shoulder in a struggle to catch his breath.

We both come down from our high, completely shattered and gasping for air. We don't dare move, and I find myself still physically unable to tear my gaze away from the sight of his thick, burly cock buried deep inside my cunt. It's the most stunning sight I've ever seen. "You can fuck me like that any time you want," I breathe, my pants coming in hard and fast.

Levi relaxes his hold on my hip and slowly trails his arm around my waist, holding me to him as I can barely keep myself up. His fingers trail soft patterns over my skin, and he meets my gaze through the mirror before dropping a feather soft kiss to my shoulder. "You see now why I like to watch?"

Biting down on my lip, I slowly nod, my eyelids dropping to a lustful stare. "I do," I tell him as a shy smile twists across my lips. "Could we … do it again?"

Levi's eyes blaze like molten lava and the responding grin that tears across his face is like waking up on Christmas morning. "For you," he tells me. "Anything."

CHAPTER SIXTEEN

The big SUV pulls to a stop outside of the dodgy, boarded-up house, and a shiver runs down my spine. The last time I was here, it went pretty smoothly, but I didn't like it. The boys threw me in the deep end when dealing with their newest dealer. He was like a teacher's pet, striving for a gold star, but despite what he allowed us to see on the surface, he was still shady as fuck. The home was a cloud of smoke and the all too familiar stench of a decaying body was coming from somewhere deep inside the house. Though, at the time I didn't recognize the smell, now … things are different.

I find myself hanging back, watching as Levi and Marcus both slip out of the car, but when Roman goes to make his move, I reach through to the front and take his elbow. "Wait," I rush out, meeting his eyes as he turns back to look at me.

His brows furrow, watching me with caution, and I know that this isn't going to go as planned. Hell, there is no plan. I'm making it up as I go, but I've come to learn that where Roman DeAngelis is concerned, you can't have a plan because he will usually shit all over it.

He holds my stare for a moment and my heart breaks, just like every other time he's looked upon me over the last few days. Before he can decide that he doesn't want to be here, I climb into the front and straddle his waist, placing my knees on either side of his strong thighs and try not to be so obvious about the excitement I feel when he places his hands at my hips.

"What do you want, Empress?" he says, his tone flat and impatient, though I've been around long enough to learn that he only calls me that when he's feeling particularly fond of me.

Leaning into him, I curl my arm around his neck and hold him to me, loving the way he reciprocates and holds me close to his chest, his arms circling my back as his fingers weave up into my hair. "Are you okay?" I murmur, turning my face in toward his, though this angle makes it far too hard to see his eyes.

His body goes taut beneath me, and I know what's coming before the words have even left his mouth. "What are you doing?" he growls, knowing damn well that I will push and push until I break through his walls, tearing him down bit by bit each day.

"I'm checking in, Roman," I whisper, all too aware of his brothers standing outside the car, wondering what the fuck is keeping us. "That visit from your uncle … it's been weighing on your mind, and don't try to tell me it hasn't. You haven't said anything since he left two days ago. You spent most of yesterday drunk and in a rage, and today … I don't know. Today you're off, and I hate seeing you like this."

Roman shakes his head and drops his hands to my waist, forcing me back to meet my eyes. "You don't know what you're talking about," he says, his eyes hardening.

"Don't," I growl, my hand moving to cup the side of his face, forcing him to keep holding my stare. "Don't shut me out. You're hurting and I want to help you."

"That's just the thing, Shayne. There is no helping me."

Leaning into him again, I brush my lips over his, melting at the way his move against mine. "You're wrong about that," I murmur. "You just need to let me in."

Feeling his body tense beneath me again, I pull back and go to push my way out of the car before he gets the chance to tell me exactly what he thinks, but he catches my arm and holds me back. "You don't know what you're asking of me," he finally tells me as I settle back onto his lap. "I'm not like my brothers. I don't easily forgive, and I sure as fuck don't forget. I live in a much darker world than they do, and to let you in would be to end you. You're too good for this, Shayne. You may think you can handle these bullshit drug deals and the occasional bullet through the head, but this world will wear you down and kill you. If you were smart, you'd cut and run at the first chance you got. Stop trying to force this."

I shake my head. "I can't do that," I tell him, placing my hand on his chest to feel the rapid beat of his heart beneath. "Not when you've already forced your way in."

He swallows hard and I see the pain in his eyes. "That was a mistake."

Gently pressing my lips to his again, I kiss him deeper, feeling something so damn right settling inside of me. His tongue moves with mine as his fingers soften on my waist, both of us finally coming home.

Not wanting to push my luck, I pull back from him, hating the feel of my lips being away from his. "You may be able to lie to yourself, Roman DeAngelis," I murmur, curling my fingers around the door handle and gently pulling the lever. "But you can't lie to me."

With that, I push my way out of the car and come face to face with Marcus and Levi, who both watch me through narrowed gazes. "What was that all about?" Marcus questions, the jealousy sneaking up on him despite already knowing damn well how I feel about his brother. He already gave me the green light to pursue something with Roman if it felt right, and I'm in too deep to reconsider.

I push past them and make my way to the dilapidated fence surrounding the property, pulling the rusty gate open and following the sidewalk to the front door.

There are brown stains coating the concrete that look a lot like dried blood, and I shake my head dismissively. I'm no stranger to bloodshed, at least not anymore.

If I've learned anything from the boys, it's that there is always someone watching, someone waiting for you to fuck up. Dried blood on your doorstep is an amateur move.

I hear Roman getting out of the car behind us and quickly making his way through the gate. I don't bother looking back because I don't know if I'll be able to handle the rejection I see in his eyes.

He's definitely not ready to explore whatever this thing is between us, though I know he wants to. That's not what that was all about anyway. He's hurting in a way that none of us can relate to. His son is missing and that's bound to play on his mind every moment of every day, and I hate that for him. He's sinking further and further into the darkness, and I want nothing more than to pull him back out. He's reckless and emotional, and that kind of mix isn't going to get us anywhere.

Coming to a stop at the door, I glance back at Marcus and Levi, making sure they're ready, and with a firm nod from Levi, I reach for the door handle and twist.

I expect to see a cloud of smoke and a bunch of losers high on the couch, but the place is clear. Hell, it even looks as though someone hit it with a spit shine. There's no rotting flesh stench, no blood splatters across the wall, not even the loud metal music we'd heard the first time we came through here.

My brows furrow, and as I slowly creep into the boarded-up home, I see Marcus from the corner of my eye, slipping his gun from the waistband of his pants.

"I don't like this," I murmur, my eyes scanning the room, searching for some kind of threat. I mean, damn. If Marcus feels that something is off, then I should be running for the fucking hills.

My heart thuds wildly in my chest, feeling way out of my league. It's one thing to see my target in front of me and have time to come up with a plan, but these spontaneous moments where I have to be completely ready scare the shit out of me. No amount of training could help me to keep up with the boys during a shootout. I'd be the first casualty.

Without another word, Levi pushes himself in front of me, taking the lead as he makes his way through the property. We go room by room, listening intently. The boys don't make a damn sound on the old rickety floorboards, and it has chills sailing down my spine. They really are the boogeymen sneaking around your home at night.

We come out into the main living room and kitchen, right where we'd been last time, and it's a stark contrast to the rest of the house. It's a fucking mess. There are scuff marks across the floor, pills spread far and wide, and piles of scattered money as though someone could only carry so much as they desperately tried to flee.

"Fuck," Marcus spits, shoving his gun back into his pants and looking around. "The place has been cleared out. The fucker is gone."

Roman slowly turns, surveying the room with a trained eye. "No," he says, "It's been ransacked. Our dealer didn't do this, though I bet he bitched out, too fucking scared to face us. He'd rather cut and run," Roman adds, turning his gaze toward me with a meaningful stare. "Guess he knows what's good for him."

Narrowing my gaze on the asshole, I avoid flipping him off before I circle the room and pick up a discarded pill. "Do you think he's dead?" I ask.

Levi shakes his head. "No, but he sure as fuck won't be coming back here any time soon."

"Shit," I mutter, tossing the pill back to the ground and turning toward the boys. "So, what do we do now?"

"Now," Marcus says, a grin splitting his face in two as Roman's phone chimes with an incoming text. "We get to have a little fun."

Amusement brews deep in my chest as I stride toward him, my eyes glistening with silent laughter as Roman digs his phone out of his pocket. "Why do I get the feeling that this is going to be the best game of hide and seek that I've ever had?"

"Just you wait," Marcus says, wrapping his arms around me and pulling me in before dropping his lips to mine. "You're on our team now and we play by our own rules."

I can't help but laugh as he adjusts his hold on me, slinging his arm over my shoulder as we make our way back out of the empty property. Levi follows us out and we get a few steps before I look back over my shoulder and find Roman hanging back in the kitchen, his fist clenching so tightly around his phone that I fear for its glass screen.

"Wait," I murmur, pulling out from under Marcus' arm before doubling back.

The boys stare after me as I rush back toward Roman, our earlier conversation completely pushed aside. Seeing the look on their eldest brother's face, Levi and Marcus trail back as well. Soon enough, I'm standing before him, my hand on his arm as I meet his horrified stare. "What is it?" I question in desperation, my gaze dropping to his screen to catch the end of a video that gives me absolutely nothing.

Marcus presses his wide chest behind my shoulder, reaching around me and taking the phone out of Roman's hand. Turning it around to face us better, his thumb pushes the scrollbar of the video back to the beginning and he hits play. I immediately suck in a loud gasp, my hand gripping Roman's and squeezing it tight.

"Fucking hell," Levi mutters, watching over Marcus' shoulder to see the video of Roman's newborn son sleeping peacefully in his bassinet.

Horror washes over me as the video plays. At first, it seems innocent until a knife cuts into the image, dropping down beside the baby's face and plunging deep into the soft mattress. He sleeps on, completely unaware of the horrors happening around him, and just how much danger he is in.

Tears spring to my eyes as Marcus' hand drops to my shoulder, squeezing it tight, silently letting me know that it's going to be okay.

The camera turns, and in the very next frame, Giovanni's face appears. A sick grin pulls at his lips and as bile rises in my throat, the screen goes black.

"No," I rush out, grabbing the phone out of Marcus' hand and playing it back again, Roman silently watching it over my shoulder as the deepest kind of rage builds within him. "What … what … NO!"

My tears fall, splashing against the phone. I hastily wipe them away as my desperation gets the best of me. Glancing up at Roman, I see the same fears reflected in his eyes that resonates deep inside my chest. "What are we supposed to do?" I cry. "He's going to hurt him. He's too little for this, too innocent. We have to get him back."

Roman swallows, silently holding my terrified gaze, at a complete loss, just like me. He's spent days on end searching out his father and has gotten absolutely nowhere. The man is a ghost and not one of us has any idea how to draw him out and put an end to this nightmare.

Levi takes the phone out of my hand, his brows furrowed as he starts the video again. "Look here," he says, pausing the video on the baby's face and pointing to the side of the screen where the bassinet ends. "There's something familiar about those floors."

Marcus tears the phone out of his hand and zooms in, his brows furrowed as he looks over the image. "It could be anything. A million homes would have polished floors like that."

"It's too dark," I tell them, trying to see what they're seeing and getting nothing. "It's impossible to make it out."

"But look," Levi insists, snatching the phone and shoving it into Roman's face, his determination sending a wave of hope coursing through me. "They're *your* fucking floors. That polished marble with the light gray vein." Levi cuts himself off, flipping the phone around and fast forwarding the shot to where the knife is plunging deep into the mattress. "Look at the reflection in the blade. The window finishes, the fucking high ceilings and shelving. That's the home you built, Roman. Father has him at Victor's place."

A deep, guttural growl rumbles through Roman's chest as he takes the phone and looks it over again, his jaw clenching as he looks over the frame. "Are you fucking sure?" he asks, though I see the positivity in his eyes. He fucking knows where his son is, and nothing will stop him now.

"Positive," Levi demands.

And without another word, the four of us storm out through the boarded-up home, the shit-scared drug dealer the least of our worries.

CHAPTER SEVENTEEN

Silence surrounds us as we pull up outside the mansion that Roman built. It was a long drive here, but not nearly as long as the first time we made the trip. Roman drove like a fucking maniac, breaking every traffic law known to man, though it's not like he ever abides by those laws anyway.

It's well after three in the morning and the heaviness that's sat on my heart for the past few hours has been enough to nearly kill me. I've never panicked like this, never felt this overwhelming fear, not even when I was locked in Giovanni's basement cells.

This is an innocent child's life hanging in the balance, and I don't trust Giovanni for a damn second to not hurt that sweet baby.

I made a promise to Felicity as she died before me that I would take care of her baby, that I would keep him safe, and damn it, I plan on keeping that promise, even if it's the last thing I do.

The SUV sits idle in the massive driveway. There isn't a light on in the house and I have absolutely no idea how we plan to do this. The long drive here was silent. We didn't discuss a plan and we sure as hell didn't stop to load up on weapons. We're unprepared, though something tells me that's when the boys are at their best. Tonight will be about acting on instinct, and if someone gets in their way, they better hope that the brothers are in a merciful mood, though the odds aren't stacked in their favor.

Levi opens the glove box and pulls out a gun before handing it back to me. "Point. Shoot," he warns me. "Do not hesitate."

I swallow hard and take the gun, feeling the familiar weight in the palm of my hand. "I won't," I tell him, the anxiety rising high in my chest, though I won't dare tell them that. They'll most likely bench me, and I'm not down for that shit, especially not when people like Victor and Giovanni could be running around. I need to play my cards carefully. Getting that baby back is the main focus here, and it doesn't matter who or what they need to sacrifice to make that happen.

Roman pushes his door wide and the boys follow his lead. I scramble after them, their long strides making them almost float across the massive driveway. "What's the plan?" Marcus questions, checking over his gun before tucking it back into the waistband of his pants. The set of his jaw makes him look like the devil rising straight out of hell.

"Don't have one," Roman spits, his gaze shifting to the massive mansion and lingering on a window at the far east side. "We go in and take out every last fucker who stands in our way. Do not stop until you have my son."

Levi nods and takes off to the left while Marcus goes to the right, leaving me flanking Roman with a ball of nerves resting heavily in my chest. We skip up the front steps and come to a stop at the very top, looking over the massive front door that's been recently replaced.

He tries the handle and I'm not surprised when it doesn't budge. "Fuck," he murmurs, not wanting to cause any kind of scene that would have the occupants waking up. If we're going to get the drop on them, then we're going to make it count.

With a raised brow, I watch Roman pull something from his pocket and twist it onto the front of his gun. My knowledge on guns is as shit as it comes, but judging by all the movies I've watched, this is some kind of silencer. Roman takes a step back and I do the same, keeping my wide eyes on him.

He takes the shot and his aim is perfect, just as I knew it would be. Without skipping a beat, he steps into the door and slowly pushes it open, pausing to wait for any type of alarm.

The house remains silent, but that doesn't mean that a silent alarm hasn't been tripped.

His sharp, skilled gaze scans the darkened foyer, and I can't help but keep my stare on him, using him as my guiding light in this uncertainty. "We good?" I murmur, keeping my tone as low as possible, terrified that anybody could jump out at me at a moment's notice.

His gaze narrows before he nods to me and slowly creeps deeper into the mansion. "Follow me," he finally mutters, his tone curt and sharp, the seriousness of the situation dripping from his voice.

Roman takes off, and I grip my gun tighter as I trail after him. I can't see shit and have absolutely no idea where we're going. I've been through here once before, but we beelined straight for the expansive formal living area and never ventured any deeper. This place is a mystery to me, filled with all kinds of secrets that I'm certain I don't want to uncover, but I trust Roman to lead me through it. He knows this place better than he knows the ins and outs of the castle he was kept prisoner in for ten years.

He leads me to the grand staircase and a part of me dies, hating this for him. This was supposed to be his, this was the home he was supposed to raise a family in, and now we're breaking into it for the second time.

We take the stairs two at a time and I struggle to keep up with his speed. He gets to the top and glances back at me before reaching back and gripping my hand. He pulls me along, his determination to get to his son like nothing I've ever experienced from him before.

He leads me right through the mansion, beelining straight for the east wing to the room he'd been staring at from the driveway. Reaching the last door in the long hallway, he stops and silently presses his back to the wall before seeking out my stare. Roman's brow arches high. "You ready?" he questions. His silent warning is loud and clear; do not fuck this up.

I swallow hard and nod as my hand tightens on the gun. We have no idea what we might find in that room ... or who for that matter. "You go for the baby," he instructs. "And I'll take care of anything else. You save my child and leave, even if it means leaving without me. Is that clear?"

The heaviness I'd felt earlier returns two-fold and I nod, knowing that no matter what, I will come through for him, even if he's bleeding out on the ground. If I don't, he'll kill me himself.

"Clear," I tell him, letting him see the conviction in my eyes.

Approving of what he sees, his gaze drops to his gun, and he quickly checks it before stepping away from the wall and positioning himself in front of the bedroom door. Nerves flicker through me and he spares me one last glance before his heavy booted foot slams against the wooden door and splinters it into a million pieces.

Roman barges through the broken door, gun held up as I race in behind him. He quickly scans the room, searching out whatever threats are hidden within. Seeing the crib in the far corner, I sprint like a motherfucker racing from the cops, trusting that Roman will have my back.

Four steps. Three steps.

Two.

Dread sinks heavily into my chest the closer I get. The room is nearly pitch black but there's no mistaking the empty crib in front of me.

I pull up short, my momentum sending me right into the side of the crib as I grip onto it with everything I've got. "Fuck," I breathe, spinning around to find Roman standing in the center of an empty room, watching me with wide, hopeful eyes. I shake my head, my heart splitting right through the center as the fear of the unknown washes over me. "He's not here."

Roman's face falls and he drops to his knees, the overwhelming grief and terror for his lost child tearing up everything inside of him. It's the most gut-wrenching thing I've ever seen, but now isn't the time to break. That baby needs us now more than ever and falling to pieces on the ground isn't helping him.

I race to Roman and grip his arm, trying to pull him up. "Come on," I urge him, the desperation clear in my voice. "We can break down once we have him back. We need to go. We can't stay here."

Roman looks up at me with dead eyes and a tear falls down my cheek. He doesn't move and I find myself moving closer to him, giving him this moment to come to terms with our failure tonight. "We're too late," he mutters, gripping my waist and dropping his forehead to my stomach. "He's gone."

My fingers curl into the back of his thick hair, and putting aside my own fears and haunting thoughts, I tear his head back, forcing his stare to mine. "Don't you dare give up on your son," I seethe, spitting the words through my clenched jaw. "This isn't over yet. Felicity's dying wish was for that baby to be kept safe. I gave her my word. Don't you dare make me a liar, Roman DeAngelis. Setbacks happen, but breaking down on the floor while your son is still out there is unacceptable. Now get the fuck up and be the man I know you to be. We are not out of options yet. Victor is still in this house somewhere and we won't be leaving until we get the answers we need."

Roman meets my stare and I watch the determination and fight come storming back into his eyes like molten lava destroying everything in its path. He gets to his feet and stands right in front of me, gripping my chin and tearing it up. He crushes a bruising kiss to my lips and before a gasp can even escape from deep in my chest, he's gone, racing out the door.

I stumble back on my feet, trying to find a grip on reality before rushing out of the room after him. I break into the hallway to find him almost at the grand stairs, and I hurry after him, not wanting to be left alone up here with who knows how many hidden threats lying in wait behind each of these doors.

Roman pauses at the top of the steps and I come to a stop behind him, my hand slamming up against his back to keep me from falling into him. His hand shoots out, stopping me before I tumble straight down the steps, and as he does, I find Marcus waiting at the bottom. "The baby?" he questions.

I shake my head and Marcus cringes, his jaw clenching as fire tears through his dark eyes. "Fuck," he says, shifting his hard stare to Roman. "We've got Victor down here. The rest of the house is cleared."

Roman nods and grips my hand before making his way down the stairs. I follow behind him as a wave of unease settles into my chest. I don't know how this is going to go down or just how far the boys will go, but every cell inside my body is warning me to prepare myself. This is going to be brutal.

We reach the bottom of the stairs and I hate the way Roman releases my hand. He steps out in front of me and Marcus immediately takes his place, dropping his hand to my lower back as he leads me through the big property.

We step into a sitting room at the front of the house, the floor-to-ceiling windows looking out over the big circle driveway with the perfect view of the water fountain in the center and the gardens off to the right. If the sun were up, I'm sure it'd be an impressive sight, but right now, all I can seem to focus on is the man tied to a chair in the center of the room.

Victor pulls and tugs against his binds, but Levi and Marcus are skilled men. I don't know which one of them tied him up, but they did a spectacular job. This motherfucker won't be going anywhere.

Levi stands by the far wall, leaning against it to give him the perfect vantage point of the room, what's beyond the window, and the exit. His gaze sweeps across to me, and without a word passing between us, he knows that Roman and I have failed. Pain flickers through his deep eyes and I want nothing more than to run across the sitting room and fall into his strong arms, telling him that everything is going to be alright. But for now, the main focus is Victor.

Marcus shuffles around the room, putting himself directly behind Victor while I trail to the front of the room with Roman, wanting to see Victor's face.

My heart races.

Victor pulls against his binds, growling as his eyes flick between the three brothers. He knows what kind of shit he's in and it leaves me wondering if he truly thought that he'd get away with it. Did he really think that the boys wouldn't track Giovanni here? That they wouldn't hold him personally responsible for allowing Giovanni to take off with Roman's newborn son.

Shit, this motherfucker is done for.

A smirk pulls at my lips, and I hate myself for how obvious I am about his downfall. I can't pretend to know all about the ins and outs of the DeAngelis Mafia, but this man has spent who knows how many years standing at Giovanni's side. He carries out the jobs that Giovanni is too fucking pussy to do himself. This man is nothing but a swine, taking up too much space on this planet. I can only imagine the shit he's done to the boys over the years, and today, they get vengeance.

I can only imagine what they have in store for him, and damn it, it shouldn't excite me the way it does, but what can I say? The boys have well and truly dragged me kicking and screaming over to the dark side, and I'm not gonna lie, I kinda like it over here.

Victor's darkened gaze sweeps by me and he pauses for a moment, probably having assumed that I was dead. I can only imagine Victor and Giovanni sitting up into the early hours of the morning, sipping on expensive whiskey while laughing about the way Giovanni kidnapped me and shoved me in a cell beside a laboring Felicity and his cheating wife.

Not seeing me as a threat, his gaze quickly shoots back to Roman's, seeing that the floor is all his tonight.

Roman takes his time, but every second he doesn't make his move, the anguish and rage only builds within him. He places himself directly in front of the large window and stares back at his uncle, his body like a silhouette in front of the big glass pane. "Where are they?" Roman's voice finally rumbles through the room, his tone daring his uncle to challenge him, so Roman has an excuse to slit his throat.

Victor roars, pulling against his binds. "Release me," he spits, "and

I might allow you to live."

Roman laughs and I can't help the grin that cuts across my face. Who does this guy think he is? Does he not know what his nephews are capable of, or does he assume that using a stern tone with them is going to have them shitting their pants and turning into yes men?

Roman scoffs. "You are in no position to be making demands. Now I will ask you again, where is my father and my baby?" he demands, quickly shooting his gaze toward Marcus at the back of the room and nodding.

Victor keeps his stare on Roman, knowing he's the one pulling the strings, but I can't help glancing over his head to watch the way Marcus subtly shuffles around and steps in closer. My brows arch high as I spy the familiar red container filled with gasoline and my eyes only widen as he hoists it up and starts to pour it over his uncle's head.

Victor spits and flinches under the flammable liquid, and when Marcus finally eases up, he shakes his head, sending droplets of gasoline far and wide through the room. The smell hits my nostrils and I do what I can to not hold my hand to my nose to block it out.

A deep rumbling growl tears from Victor, and something tells me that he's clearly worked out how tonight is going to go for him. "You think I'm going to tell you now?" Victor laughs manically. "You've got no fucking hope."

The rage is too much and Roman races in toward his uncle, gripping him under the chin. "WHERE ARE THEY?"

Victor continues to laugh. "Your father should have slaughtered you when he had the chance."

Levi pushes off the wall and steps closer while still giving Roman his space to run the show. "That's really how you want to play this, Uncle? Come on, I thought you were a smart man."

Victor spits as gasoline drips from his hair. "Oh, I am, Nephew," he says. "Which is exactly why I won't speak. Your father will rise up, and when he does, this bullshit war that you've fabricated would look like nothing but a joke. He's got you right where he wants you, always five steps behind. You three are a joke, now hurry up and do it," he growls, sharpening his deadly glare back on Roman. "Send me off in a blaze of glory."

Roman glances at Marcus again and not a second later, Marcus tears Victor's head back as Roman reaches out and forces his jaw apart, most likely breaking it in the process. Marcus pours the gasoline down his throat, and he has no choice but to swallow it to avoid drowning.

Gasoline splashes all over the sitting room and I find myself backing up, seeing only one outcome here and being smart enough to know that I don't want to be anywhere near him when he goes up in a ball of explosive flames.

Marcus stops pouring, only to start splashing the gasoline around the room. He walks out and leaves a trail behind him, spreading it far and wide.

Roman releases Victor's jaw and he immediately starts to cough and splutter, looking like complete shit. I don't doubt that he'll be hurling all over the room soon enough.

I don't know shit about gasoline poisoning, but I know it can be lethal, though something tells me that he'll be dead long before the gasoline gets a chance to shut down his system.

Levi moves in next to me and presses his hand to my lower back before leading me out of the room. Just as I look back over my shoulder, I see Roman leaning into his uncle. "You're a fool, Victor. Always have been. Giovanni DeAngelis will never rise. His empire is mine."

Levi pulls me from the room and all but races to the front door. Marcus is there and the three of us run down the front steps, my hands clenched tightly in both of theirs.

My foot hits the hard pavement of the circle driveway, and just as I look back over my shoulder to search for Roman, a loud explosion tears through the property, sending a bright orange glow soaring through the front sitting room window. The glass shatters with the force of the blow, and I drop to the ground as I stare up at the massive home, watching in horror as the flames quickly take over.

"NO," I scream, scrambling to my feet. Both Levi and Marcus hold me back. "ROMAN IS IN THERE."

"He knows what he's doing," Marcus tells me, pulling me hard into his chest, caging me in with his strong arms.

I claw at his skin, the desperation ripping through me like a fucking chainsaw tearing through flesh. The panic sets in, and though it's barely been a second, it feels like a goddamn lifetime.

My panicked stare scans over the property, watching the way the flames quickly trail from room to room, destroying everything in their path. Just when I think there's absolutely no hope, a dark silhouette appears in the open doorway, the flames lighting up the foyer behind him like an inferno leading straight to hell.

CHAPTER EIGHTEEN

Roman storms down the stairs as the home he built goes up in flames behind him. His face is marred with soot, and he doesn't dare look up at his brothers as he passes.

My heart breaks for him. All he wanted out of this was to get his son home and safe, and once again, we came up empty handed. It's like running headfirst into a wall over and over again, hoping for a different outcome. But this … the home he built for his future, the home he always planned to raise his children in, where he wanted to give them the life he never had, it's gone.

Marcus' hold eases on my waist as I turn and watch the eldest DeAngelis brother walk away. He strides across the big driveway, the glow from the burning mansion shining down upon him and showing off the tight way he holds his shoulders. He's been standing on edge since the moment he found out his son was alive, and losing him again tonight was exactly what he didn't need.

"Fuck," Levi mutters, watching his brother with the deepest sorrow in his eyes. "What the hell are we going to do? That baby is as good as gone."

Marcus shakes his head, his hand dropping to my lower back. "I've got no fucking idea," he says, his tone low and filled with an ache that tears at my chest. "This is going to destroy him."

"Father is going to retaliate when he finds out what we've done to Victor."

Marcus nods, more than aware of the consequences he just walked straight into. "It's not going to be pretty," he comments as his hands find my wrists and slide up to my upper arms, holding me at his chest as I struggle to peel my eyes off Roman.

He reaches the black SUV and braces his hands wide against the hood as his head hangs forward. The muscles in his back are tight, and I can only imagine what kind of fresh hell is going through his head right now. Either way, he looks about ready to raise hell … or drown in it.

My hand falls against Marcus' chest as I look up to meet his dark eyes, but the overwhelming grief that is staring back nearly knocks me right off my feet. "Give us a minute," I tell him.

Marcus' grip on my arms tightens. "That's not a good idea, babe. There's no telling how he's going to react to this. Give him some time to cool down."

"I'm with Marc," Levi says, stepping a little closer and placing a hand on my hip. I glance back over my shoulder to meet his broken stare. "Roman … he feels things hard. He bottles it up until he can't take it any longer and then explodes. You don't want to be there when that happens."

I shake my head, my gaze settling back on the destroyed man across the driveway. "I can't," I murmur. "Look at him. He needs someone. I'm not just going to leave him there to let this eat at him. He needs to get it out. He needs to scream … or strangle something. I don't fucking know, but I'm not just going to stand by and let him bottle it all up. It will destroy him."

Levi grips my arm and tears me out of Marcus' grasp, spinning me around to face him front on. "I don't think you're hearing me," he warns. "If you push him to talk about it before he's ready, he *will* fucking strangle you."

My fingers curl around his tight grip and I rip them off my arm, my eyes narrowing as a silent, furious rage builds within me. "And you're not hearing me," I spit, hating how my stubborn nature always seems to clash with their need to rule over every aspect of my life. "Roman needs me, and whether you like it or not, I'm going over there to help him. He needs an outlet, and that outlet is me. You need to learn to trust me," I say, glancing back at Marcus. "Both of you do. I know what I'm doing."

Levi's gaze shifts up over my head to Marcus, caution deep in his obsidian eyes as they seem to have some kind of silent conversation. After a short beat, Levi lets out a defeated sigh and gives my arm a gentle squeeze. "Fine," he mutters. "You can go, but if he loses his shit, you get the fuck out of there."

I raise a brow, irritation burning deep within me. "Thanks," I murmur, resisting the urge to roll my eyes at the way these boys think they can confess their undying love and suddenly be rewarded with the ability to order me around. "But I wasn't asking permission."

Levi's gaze hardens and I don't doubt that he's fighting the need to whoop my ass, but I don't hang around to find out. Slipping out from between them, I make my way across the massive driveway toward Roman, determined to help him in what little way I can, though if I'm completely honest, I have absolutely no idea what I can offer him to make this any easier.

He stands with his back to me and gives no indication that he hears me coming, and as I get closer, I find myself glancing back over my shoulder. Marcus and Levi are nowhere to be seen, but I don't doubt that they're still close, ready to jump in and save me if it comes down to it. But for the most part, they've offered me what little privacy they can manage, and for that, I'm grateful.

Moving in behind Roman, I gently place my hand in the center of his back, feeling the taut muscles beneath. His body shakes with rage and it tears at something within me. Roman and I have always had a strained relationship, right from the beginning. We butt heads at every turn, but that asshole has more than grown on me, and seeing him in this kind of distress hurts me in a way that I wasn't prepared for.

His body tightens under my touch and he becomes impossibly still.

Turning into him, I look up at the haunted man who stands before me, slowly trailing my hand from his back around to gently capture his bicep beneath my fingers. "Roman." His name comes out as the softest whisper that has his head slowly rising.

He turns his attention on me and a gasp pulls from the back of my throat as his dark, dead eyes land on mine. He looks like a complete stranger, completely lost to pain and grief causing havoc over his heart. I know with every beat of my heart that I would do or say absolutely anything it takes.

I step into him, my chest gently brushing up against his arm as the darkness surrounds us, leaving nothing but an orange glow coming from the inferno behind us, heating my skin and raging loudly into the silent night. "Let me take your pain."

Roman holds my stare for a long moment, his desperation like two deep, hollow pits of helplessness looking back at me. Then as if flipping some kind of switch deep inside of him, the pain and grief flooding his dark gaze turns to rage. "There is no taking my pain," he growls, his low tone vibrating right through my chest and eating at me.

His hand snaps out and circles my throat, and with a hard yank, he throws me down against the hood of the SUV. A pained gasp tears from my throat as he keeps me pinned under his strong hold, his body pressing against mine as he leans over me to get right in my face.

My hands grip his on my throat as the darkness swirling in his eyes bear down on me. "Don't you fucking get it?" he growls, his face just inches from mine. "It's fucking over. He's gone. MY SON IS GONE."

I shake my head, pulling at his hands just to get a breath in. "I don't believe that," I tell him, sucking in low, shallow gasps. "We will find him. This is just a setback."

He leans in a little closer so his nose brushes up against mine. "We won't. Victor was right. My father is always five steps ahead of us. I will never get to see my son. I'm going to have to spend every day of the rest of my fucking miserable life knowing what kind of hell my father is putting my son through, and there's not a damn thing I can do about it."

Releasing one of my hands from his on my throat, I loop it around his neck and thread my fingers up into his hair, trailing my nails over his scalp. "You're going to be okay, Roman," I breathe. "I know you don't have faith that we can find him, but I have enough for the both of us."

Roman closes his eyes, the pain tearing through him at speeds he simply can't keep up with. When he opens them again, they're impossibly darker and filled with the most intense desperation I've ever seen. He lets out a heavy breath and the conflict tearing through him blasts into me as though I can feel every little fucked-up emotion he does.

His hand eases on my throat, allowing me the chance to suck in a deep breath as his thumb trails back and forth over my skin, then just when I think he's going to pull back and take a moment to breathe, his lips crush down on mine in a bruising, angry kiss.

My eyes widen in surprise, but as his kiss grows more impatient, more desperate, I let him take what he needs, kissing him back with the same ferocity. Our lips clash, and our tongues fight for dominance as his other hand grasps my waist, squeezing tight.

A low growl tears from deep in his chest and I feel it vibrating straight through to mine. There's absolutely nothing erotic about it, and I quickly realize that this isn't about finally giving in to his most basic urges but needing an escape from the tortured thoughts haunting his mind, and damn it, whatever he needs, I will give him. I'm his outlet. My body is his salvation and my heart is his escape.

His body pins me to the hood of the car and I wiggle my legs free to wrap them around his waist and his responding groan is all the approval I need to keep going. My fingers tighten in his hair, gripping tightly as his fingers dig into my skin.

I don't bother stopping him to ask if he's sure because he's not going to give me an answer. And though he might regret it later, at this very moment, this is exactly what he needs.

It's going to be hard, fast, and angry. This won't be about pleasure. It won't be about coming, and hell, it'll probably even hurt, but I welcome it. Maybe a part of me even needs this just as bad as he does. His need comes from a place of desperation where mine is pure lust for the man who has tormented me for months. How fucking sick am I to want this with him?

All I know is that the moment he is done with me, it will be over. He's not going to cuddle, and he's sure as fuck not going to offer me a warm towel to clean up. It'll be raw and ugly and leave a gaping hole in my chest, but I'm here for whatever he needs.

My legs tighten around his waist as he grinds against me, his massive cock straining through the front of his jeans, desperate for more. A needy groan escapes through my lips and his hungry kiss swallows the sound. Then all too soon, Roman releases my throat and tears himself away, forcing me to release my hold in his hair. He pants heavily, a crazed expression in his eyes, and for a moment, I wonder if he will walk away, but he just stares at me with the deepest need in his eyes.

The silence kills me, and as I watch him, I see the indecision creeping into his stare. He knows this is wrong, that he's taking advantage, using me for his sick need to get off just to feel something other than the grief for his lost son and the anger that plagues him. But I don't allow him the chance to question it further as I nod, letting him know this is okay. "Whatever you need, Roman. I can handle it."

His eyes blaze with something I've never seen before, something I don't quite understand, and as my chest rises with a sharp breath, his hands fall to the waistband of my pants, tearing them down my legs. My underwear goes down with my pants and he quickly discards them on the ground behind him, then before he can give himself a moment to change his mind, he reaches for the front of his jeans and releases his cock.

It springs free from the confines of his pants, and I hate that from this position, I don't get to feast my eyes upon it, but the way it brushes up against my inner thigh tells me exactly what I need to know. He's a fucking big boy. Though I already knew that from the rooftop of the high-rise, only now, I actually get to see what's going down.

He doesn't tear my shirt off like his brothers would have, and he doesn't waste time removing his jeans. This isn't about that. This is about getting in and getting out. Hard, fast, and raw.

Roman barely gives me a chance to prepare myself before he grips my thighs and yanks me toward him, dangling my ass right off the hood of the SUV. My legs curl around his waist, and before I can even get a good grip on him, he slams his thick cock deep inside my cunt, not even waiting to check that I'm wet.

I cry out, his intrusion stretching me wide as his fingers dig into my hips, holding me still. He pulls back, his cock coated with my arousal, and I tilt my hips into a better position to take him deeper. He thrusts again and a groan tears from the back of my throat as I slam my hand down, searching for something to grip onto to keep from falling off the hood.

"Fuck," I grunt, tipping my head back as the sheer satisfaction of having Roman deep inside me slams through my chest.

He takes me again, harder and faster. My chest rises and falls quickly, matching his speed and I can't help but watch the way he clenches his jaw, the sharp lines telling me so much more than he says out loud. A low rumble sounds through my chest and he holds me tighter, pain flaring in his eyes, making me realize that he's holding back in fear of hurting me.

My hand falls to his on my hip and I squeeze it tight, my nails digging into his flesh. "I can take it, Roman," I grunt through a clenched jaw as he thrusts into me again, stretching my walls and sending a wave of pure pleasure pulsing through me. "Give it to me. Take it out on my body."

The fiercest desire comes over him, and without a second more of hesitation, he pulls his hand out from under mine and places it on top before interlocking our fingers. He squeezes hard and slips his other hand under my ass, holding me up, and with that, he gives in to his most basic, animal urges and fucks me like he'll never fuck again.

His thrusts are wild and raw, hard and deep, hitting me in all the right places. If he hadn't been holding onto me so tight, he sure as fuck would have sent me straight through the front of the windshield. I scream out, my pussy clenching around him, instantly accepting his brutal need as I release the hood with my other hand and press my fingers to my clit.

He watches me, rubbing furiously at my clit as he fucks me hard, panting and groaning with every wild thrust. His balls slap against my ass over and over and I moan, that familiar burn growing deep inside of me. "Fuck, I'm going to come," I pant.

He doesn't respond, simply adjusts his stance to come at me from a new angle that sends my eyes rolling into the back of my head. I'm left desperate to roll over and have him hit it from behind bending me over as he brutally fucks me into submission … but that will have to wait.

My pussy clenches and I cry out. "FUCK, YES."

A needy grunt pulls from the back of Roman's throat, and as my eyes come back to his, feeling the way his hand tightens in mine, I realize just how fucking close he is. "Give it to me, Roman," I demand as my pussy reaches its limits and turns into a spasming wreck. "Let me have it."

Roman's jaw clenches, and as he takes me one last time, he comes hard, shooting his hot load deep into my cunt with a loud groan. "FUCK," he roars, breathing heavily as my walls clench around his thick cock, violently coming undone around him.

His hold eases and he pushes me further up the hood of the SUV so that he can release me without dropping me in the process, but damn it, he doesn't dare let go of his hold on my hand. He takes slow deep breaths as I come down from my high, trying to figure out how the hell I was able to handle that.

He meets my eyes and there's a strange hesitation there that has my chest constricting with pain. He carefully pulls out of me, knowing I'm bound to be sore, and I try not to react. I'm definitely going to be feeling that tomorrow. "Are you okay?" he questions as he meets my eyes.

I sit up on the hood, feeling his warm seed seeping out of me, but that's the least of my problems. Reaching up, I hook my arm around his neck and force him to hold my stare. "Are you?"

He swallows hard and a hint of darkness flashes in his eyes, but the strained anger seems to have subsided, allowing him to breathe easier. He gives a subtle nod, brushing his thumb over the top of my knuckles. "For now."

Relief settles into my chest as I tilt my head forward, meeting my forehead with his. "Then I'm okay," I tell him, catching sight of the burning mansion from the corner of my eye and knowing it's bound to draw the attention of the authorities, especially with them already watching the DeAngelis family closely after both Antonio and Ronaldo's murders. "I know you were hoping to get more out of being here, but we need to go."

He nods and releases my hand before tucking himself back into his jeans. He helps me down and hands me my pants. As I take them from him, Marcus and Levi appear from around the corner of the burning mansion, both of their dark eyes coming straight to mine. Levi's strained gaze is filled with anger, and he looks as though he could tear his brother apart for being so rough with me, while Marcus looks like he just came to the realization of what it truly means to share.

My stare drops away as a sliver of guilt tears through me, and without another word, the four of us get back into the SUV and leave the burning mansion behind, knowing that what just happened here will never be spoken of again.

CHAPTER NINETEEN

The sun is just peeking over the mountains far in the distance when Levi's voice sounds through the silent SUV. "Phillip's vineyard is only thirty minutes south of here," he says. "It couldn't hurt to stop by and see what he knows."

Roman keeps his eyes on the road as Marcus' gaze swivels from out the window to the front seat. It's been a long drive, and while long drives are becoming more frequent in my life, the silence in the car has made the past two hours seem like a lifetime. The tension in the car is thick. I mean, the boys knew that eventually Roman and I would seal the deal, but perhaps they were hoping it wouldn't have been quite so soon. Though they don't need to panic, despite how good and raw it was, I doubt Roman will slip up and allow himself to indulge in me again, because for that to happen, the two of us would have to put our differences aside and allow the other in, which isn't as easy as it sounds.

A minute passes before Roman finally nods and veers into the outside lane, preparing to pull off at the next exit, unknowingly sending a wave of panic soaring through my chest. The last time I saw Phillip, I was playing dead on the dirty ground while listening to the sickening sound of him assaulting Ariana in the worst possible way. The last thing I want to do is see his face again, but I can't possibly skip the opportunity to save her from the fresh hell that he no doubt rains down on her night after night.

"Ariana is there," I remind them, though something tells me that they're not the kind of guys who would simply forget something like that. "She saved me from him. We're taking her home."

Roman's gaze meets mine through the rearview mirror and I see the indecision in his eyes, wanting to keep focused on finding his son. In the big scheme of things, Ariana is nothing but scum on the bottom of his shoe after her betrayal. She was once his rock, but that's all in the past now.

"You know it's the right thing to do," I state, just in case he surprises me for the millionth time and decides to leave her ass there.

He rolls his eyes as the softest huff pulls from between his lips, warning me that he's really not in the mood to argue right now. Though there's no need, he'll do the right thing. He always does ... you know, when he's not doing things like murdering people and kidnapping innocent women from their shitty apartments.

The added half hour to our drive is painful and I silently wish for Marcus to snap out of his jealous fury and allow the tension to seep away, but he needs time to stew. He'll eventually come around ... I hope. Levi on the other hand just stares out the front windshield, and every now and then I catch him curling his hand into a tight fist as he side-eyes his eldest brother. But just like Marcus, he'll get over it.

We drive down a long, private road that gives Phillip plenty of warning that we're here, though with our tinted windows, I doubt he knows it's us. He probably assumes it's Giovanni coming to discuss business after everything that's been going down recently.

Roman slows as we approach the massive home, which was no doubt built with blood money and slave labor. It's just as beautiful as Roman's home was, and I can't help but wonder if this was originally intended for Marcus or Levi.

The SUV comes to a stop right outside the door, and as we pile out of the car, the massive front door peels back. Phillip stands in a black business suit, and judging by the disheveled state of it, along with the heavy bags under his eyes and the glass of whiskey in his hand, he's had a bit of a long night.

We walk toward the front door and as he gets a good look at his early morning visitors, suspicion creeps into his dark gaze. "Nephews," he says in greeting, his back straightening with unease as his gaze flicks to mine. Surprise flashes in his eyes but he does what he can to mask it. He holds my stare a moment longer, realizing that not only am I alive, but that I know his dark little secret.

Phillip's eyes narrow with a silent warning that I immediately disregard, and assuming he got his point across to keep my mouth shut, he turns his attention back to the boys, the clear threats that stand on his front doorstep. "What are you doing here?" he questions.

Roman eyes him cautiously before striding straight past and welcoming himself into Phillip's home. Levi follows and Marcus pauses a moment to allow me to go first. Not wanting to hold up this little pissing contest, I scurry along, unsure of how this is going to go.

Following Levi into the big house, a shiver trails down my spine. This isn't exactly a home that I want to be in, but we have a mission and I plan to see it through.

Despite Phillip's disheveled appearance, he clearly still has a little energy to cause shit as his lips twist into a wicked grin when I pass him. "Come to see what you missed out on, hey?" he murmurs, his deep, low tone sending shivers down my spine. "You're supposed to be dead."

"What's the matter?" I challenge, pausing to glare at him. "Disappointed that you never got a chance to fuck my dead corpse?"

His face drops and a flicker of anger appears in his eyes as his body goes still. "You don't know what you're talking about, girl."

A smirk pulls at my lips. Apparently, his little dead girl fetish is a bit of a secret. "Don't worry, pervert. You don't need to be shy. It's nothing that I haven't already told the boys all about."

Before he gets a chance to fire back some appalling comment, Marcus steps into my back and gently urges me to keep walking, not wanting to set him off before they get a chance to interrogate him. We walk in through the front foyer and the boys fan out in a way that puts Phillip directly in the center, leaving him no easy escape. "What is all of this about?" he questions, though I'm sure he already knows. "Where is your father? Has he sent you here?"

Marcus narrows his gaze. "Tell us what we need to know, and we will leave peacefully."

"Why don't you tell me what I need to know," he starts, way too confident in his current company, proving that it's definitely in the genes. "I find it peculiar that just two hours after a blaze tore through my brother's home, you three show up on my doorstep."

"What are you suggesting?" Marcus questions.

Phillip's gaze narrows and slowly glances from brother to brother, skipping by me as though I couldn't possibly know what the hell is going on. "Don't play coy with me, boy, I am not in the mood. You know exactly what I am suggesting. You killed my brother and that poses an issue for me."

Roman raises his chin. "How so?"

Phillip's voice lowers and the tone that sounds through the large foyer sends a chilling shiver through my veins. "That kill was mine," he growls. "I've stood in Victor's shadow my whole life. I had big plans for him."

Marcus shrugs his shoulders. "Snooze, you lose, old man," he says, provoking Phillip and making Levi's face twist into a cringe. "Victor had many enemies, and if you wished to end his life, then you should have moved a little faster."

"What was your grievance with my brother?" Phillip spits. "He did not owe you anything."

"On the contrary," Roman says, stepping forward. "He had information that I needed and his failure to share earned him a one-way ticket to hell. So I will warn you now, if you don't tell me what I need to know, then you will be meeting with your late brother sooner than you had anticipated, and I promise you will not enjoy it."

Phillip narrows his gaze, looking over the brothers in a new light. "It is true, isn't it? You're taking over the family business."

Levi's lips pull into a wicked smirk and a darkness settles over his gaze that has me oddly turned on despite the dull ache that's been pulsing between my legs with every step that I take. "It was about time, don't you think?"

Interest sweeps over Phillip's face, and I see the exact moment he decides that this new turn of events could work in his favor. "Where is your father now?" he questions, his eyes going far away as the wheels start turning inside his head, probably trying to figure out how he can gain from this.

"That's what we've come to ask you," Roman says, his tone a subtle warning not to fuck with him. "Up until last night, my father was staying in Victor's home, yet when we arrived … poof," he says, blowing his fingers out in front of him. "Gone."

Phillip laughs. "And you think he would come to me?"

"If we thought he had come here," Marcus says with a sick grin. "You would be dead on your doorstep by now."

Phillip eyes him cautiously before turning his gaze back to Roman. "So if you do not think he is here, then why come here at all?"

"Because apart from the fact that you have something that belongs to me," he says, referring to Ariana and making my heart bleed when he says he still considers her his. "You're one of the last people to have been in contact with him, and I need to know what you know."

A noise sounds on the stairs behind us and I flick my gaze around just in time to see a little girl dressed in her nightgown. Realizing something is going on at the bottom of the stairs, her head shoots up and a soft gasp pulls from between her lips. She looks to her father, and for a moment, I want to hate the boys for not having checked if anyone else was in the house, but then that's on my shoulders as well.

"Daddy," the little girl says, her wide eyes terrified as she takes in her eldest cousin who she no doubt had been trained to be fearful of. "What's going on?"

Phillip swallows hard. "Nothing, honey. Your cousins are just here for an early morning business meeting," he says, making my stomach churn with how sweet he is to his daughter while another woman rots away, most likely in some dungeon cell beneath the foundation of this home. "Go and watch your shows. Mommy will make you breakfast soon."

The little girl, who must only be four or five, glances at the three boys again, and I have to commend her for the caution that spreads over her face. Assuming she somehow gets away from her father, she might even grow into a really smart girl who can save herself from this messed up world, something I should have done before I allowed it to corrupt my soul to the point of no return.

The girl scurries away and all eyes turn back to Phillip. "You need to leave," he says. "You never should have come here where my children sleep."

"The ball is in your court, Phillip," Roman says as though this is some kind of hostage negotiation. "Tell me what I want to know and handover Ariana. No one needs to get hurt, but fail to give me what I've come for and well …"

Roman's sentence trails off as his gaze sweeps back to the stairs, letting Phillip know exactly what he would do. My stomach twists at just the thought, but a part of me has to believe that Roman is just bluffing. He would never hurt that little girl, but Phillip doesn't need to know that.

Rage burns in Phillip's gaze before he finally nods. "False wall in the east wing office. She's down there."

Roman nods before glancing at Marcus. "Go. Take Shayne with you."

Marcus silently walks away and my eyes widen, realizing this is really happening. I scurry after him, not wanting to be left behind as I hear Roman going on. "And my father?"

We disappear around a corner before I get to hear Phillip's response and I keep myself right behind Marcus, not wanting to get separated from him in this big home. Who knows what other dirty secrets are buried here.

We find the office a short moment later, and Marcus pushes through the locked door with ease and we step into a massive room. It's bigger than my whole fucking apartment, but I'm not surprised. Everything in this world is big and coated in luxury. It's ridiculous and most likely funded by drug money.

Despite it being just past six in the morning and the likelihood of someone walking these halls are about the same as the likelihood of me spreading my legs willingly for Giovanni, I close the door behind us.

Phillip said something about a false wall, but I don't see a damn thing. Marcus moves across the room, searching for what's hidden in plain sight as my hands skim over the walls. This isn't exactly something that I have experience with, but I'm not going to lie, it's sending adrenaline through my veins like a wildfire.

Not finding anything on the side wall, I step in front of a massive floor-to-ceiling bookshelf and scan over everything. It's packed with books that I'm sure Phillip has never read. There are fancy bookends, limited edition books, and gold trimmed photo frames. Ornaments and fancy sculptures fill every available space and I stare in wonder. Now, if only the books had titles like 'The Hornets Slutty Hornbag' then I'd really be impressed. Hell, I might even believe that Phillip had read them.

Reaching through the bookshelf, I gently tap on the expensive wooden backing and listen to its sound. It's definitely hollow on the opposite side, and just like in the movies, I start pulling on the ornaments and sculptures until I can finally figure it out. "Here," I tell Marcus as he stands across the big office, searching behind the mahogany desk. "It's behind here. I just can't work out how to open it."

Marcus rushes over and examines the bookshelf with a trained eye, but a gold skull catches mine. Everything else on the shelf is old school, but this is new and shiny, and it definitely doesn't fit with the rest of the office. Reaching through, I curl my fingers around the skull and try to move it. It's stuck to the shelf, so instead of tearing the fucker right off, I try twisting, and after turning it just enough that the skull faces the massive window overlooking the manicured gardens, the whole bookshelf falls back.

"What the fuck?" I breathe, my eyes wide as I look over it.

"Took the words right out of my mouth," Marcus says, quickly glancing my way with an arched brow, most likely wondering what hidden rooms have been waiting to be discovered in his family home all these years.

Not wasting any more time, Marcus grips the heavy wooden shelf and pushes it back inside the wall. A loud click sounds through the office, and I hear the faint echo on the other side. With the shelf clicked back into place, it slides effortlessly, and a small walkway appears before us.

As if knowing that there's no way in hell that I'll be going first, Marcus steps into the dark walkway and I follow closely behind him, not liking the look of this at all.

A set of stairs leads down into the darkness and everything inside of me screams for me to not go down there. I've done the whole dungeon cell thing before and it's really not my jam. There's only a sliver of light shining past the bookshelf, but beyond that, there's nothing.

Going against every cell in my body, I move forward, following Marcus into the unknown, and letting my fingers drag along the wall to guide me down the concrete stairs. It smells, but it doesn't hold the same pungent stench as Giovanni's basement. This is more like a damp room that hasn't seen the light of day for years, plus there's a heavy scent of sex in the air that has my chest tightening with unease.

My fingers brush over something on the wall and I double back, making Marcus pause to watch me over his shoulder. Feeling a switch beneath my fingertip, uncertainty settles through me. This switch could be for anything, but there's also a good chance that it's a light.

My face twists with a cringe but the chances of finding Ariana down here without a light is next to none. Letting out a shaky breath, I flip the switch and a dull light spreads through the underground cell and settles the unease pulsing through my stomach.

Marcus sails down the rest of the steps and I quickly follow behind. We hit the bottom, and just as we turn a corner into a wide concrete cell, a metal pole comes hurtling toward Marcus' head. His hand snaps up with quick reflexes and catches the pole just moments before it would've cracked his skull.

"Marc?" Ariana breathes, her eyes wide as her chest rises and falls with quick, panicked movements, assuming we had been Phillip coming back for more.

"Fuck," Marcus says, throwing the metal pole aside as Ariana drops to the dirty ground, grazing her knees as she begins to sob into her hands, the relief overwhelming her system.

"What in the ever-loving fuck is this?" I ask, glancing past her into the fucked-up little room where Phillip has been keeping her. It's set up like an old home from the seventies. An old metal frame bed with a flower duvet. There's even an old-fashioned nightstand with a lamp, which I'm assuming doesn't work. A small bathroom that offers no privacy and no shower. There's even a fully stocked dresser with old brushes, hair curlers, and makeup.

Marcus scoffs, kicking the metal pole and sending it halfway across the room. "Apparently, Phillip has some mommy issues," he mutters as Ariana takes a deep breath and tries to pull herself together.

"Yeah, they're not his only issues," I tell him, reaching down to Ariana and grabbing her arm, trying to be gentle, but it's not like we have all day. "Come on. We need to go."

I tug hard and am met with resistance as Ariana cries out. "Fucking hell. Stop. Do you think I'm just sitting down here like some fucking damsel waiting for some bitch to come and save me?" she spits, reminding me that she's not just the woman who saved me from Phillip, but also the woman who set me up with Lucas Miller to be tortured and murdered. "I'm chained."

My gaze drops and I cringe, finding the ankle cuff and heavy chain that's bolted to the wall by her bed, giving her just enough space to get around her room, but not giving her the chance to get anywhere near the stairs. "Shit," I grunt, looking around the room for some kind of way to free her. I should have noticed the chain before, but I was too distracted by the hell hole she's been living in.

I'm busy searching when Marcus pulls the gun from the waistband of his jeans. "Do you trust me?" he asks Ariana.

Her eyes bug out of her head, reading his intentions and gaping at him as though he's lost his fucking mind. "Do I trust you?" she shrieks, panic taking over as she holds up her hand that has the angry scarring from when Marcus pinned her to her front door with a knife. "That's a joke, right?"

Marcus rolls his eyes, not really down for her dramatics after the day he's had. "What else do you suggest?" he demands, arching a brow at her. "I can either shoot the chains off and hope to fucking God that the bullet doesn't ricochet and kill me, or I can fucking leave you here. Worst case scenario, I miss and you get a fucking hole in your foot, best case, you get to see the fucking light of day and walk free. Take your pick."

Ariana quickly shoots her gaze toward me, silently questioning if she should trust him, and I shrug my shoulders. "He managed to pin your hand to the door with that knife from thirty feet away without skipping a damn beat. He's your best option ... *your only option.*"

"Fuck, fuck, fuck," she mutters before bringing her foot forward and looking away.

BANG!

Marcus shoots before Ariana's head has even completely turned away, and I stare in shock. I'd expected a countdown or something like that, but no, he didn't even give her the consideration of aiming first. Just shot like there were absolutely no consequences. But when it comes to Marcus DeAngelis, there rarely are, and that's proven a moment later when the chain snaps under the bullet's pressure and falls aside.

I suck in a loud gasp as Ariana screams. Her head instantly whips down to her ankle, finding the cuff still tight around her skin but free of her chain. "Fuck," she breathes wide-eyed.

"Let's go," he snaps, not giving her a moment to catch her breath.

He grips my hand and drags me back to the stairs, not giving a shit if she follows or not, but she's not stupid. She knows an opportunity like this will never come again. She trails behind us, sticking right on my heels in her desperation to get out.

As we reach the top of the stairs and walk back out into the big office, I find myself pulling back on his hand. "Hey," I say, stopping him in his tracks as Ariana steps around us, hovering close. Marcus looks back at me, his dark eyes meeting mine with hurt. "Are we okay?"

He watches me a moment longer before a softness creeps into his hard exterior, breaking him down. He steps back into me, resting his hand at my waist. "Yeah," he finally says. "It's one thing seeing you with Levi. That started off slowly and I had time to prepare, but Roman. He went balls to the fucking wall and claimed you in a way that Levi and I just can't seem to do."

My brows furrow and I shake my head. "What are you talking about? It was just sex. There's nothing more there."

He shakes his head. "I ain't talking about the sex, babe. The fact that you got through to him like that, made him see reason and calm down when his whole fucking world is caving in on him. He's going to try and take you for himself, and you'll be so fucking blinded by it that you'll go willingly."

I push up onto my tippy toes and rest my hand against his warm cheek, hating that my actions today have made him doubt the way I feel for him. "That will never happen," I murmur, brushing my lips against his. "It's not possible because a life without you by my side isn't a life worth living."

He pulls back to look directly into my eyes. "Promise?"

I nod as a smile tears across my face. "Cross my heart and hope to die."

Marcus grips my chin and draws me back in to kiss me deeply, making butterflies swarm through my stomach. "And don't you fucking forget it."

CHAPTER TWENTY

*B*ANG! BANG! BANG!

"FUCK," I screech, throwing myself out of bed, wide-eyed and panting. My heart races as I peer around, trying to find the threat. My frantic glare lands on the big asshole sitting across the room, looking guilty as shit with his hands paused mid-air over his drum set.

"Shit, did I wake you?" Levi questions as the single light from his private bathroom sets a spotlight over him and his drum set.

"Did you wake me?" I shriek, the sarcasm thick in my tone. "Yes, you freaking woke me. What the hell are you doing? It's …" I lean across his massive, super-king mattress and hit the home button on his phone, lighting it up to check the time. "It's 3:00 am! What the ever-loving fuck, Levi?"

Levi cringes and his whole face scrunches, making him appear like a guilty little kid who just got caught with his fingers in the cookie jar. "Sorry, little one," he says. "I was trying to be quiet."

"Trying to be quiet," I huff under my breath as I rub at my tired, sleep deprived eyes. "They're drums. They don't come equipped with a silent mode. You bang them, and they go BOOM! Every time."

He tilts his head forward and looks up at me through his thick row of long lashes and gives me the most innocent, but guilty expression that has me immediately cursing myself for bitching him out. "Whoops," he says, putting the drum sticks together and gently placing them down. "I'll stop. I just couldn't sleep and my hands were twitching to play. Honestly, I didn't mean to wake you. I've played a few times through the night and you've just slept through it. I figured tonight would have been the same."

"You play while I sleep and I just lay there?"

A wicked grin pulls at the corner of his warm lips, and as his eyes sparkle, I prepare myself for whatever's about to come out of his mouth. "Damn straight I do," he says, "that cute little heavy breathing thing you do works as the perfect beat for a count of eight."

My eyes bug out of my head. "You're lying."

He shakes his head and my cheeks flame with embarrassment. "Wish I was."

Levi moves to come back to bed and I shake my head. "No," I say. "Stay and play. I'm awake now. It's not like I'm going to get back to sleep anyway. I was having shitty dreams about being locked up in your father's dungeon cells again."

"Fuck," he mutters under his breath, his eyes softening and filling with pain, hating the shit I've been through at his father's hands. "Did you want me to come and hold you?"

My heart warms, loving how much he cares for me. It's a complete contrast to the man I met when I first got here. I never would have thought this kind-hearted, caring man was buried deep inside of him, but I'm so glad that it was, because now he's someone I could never imagine my life without. What's with these DeAngelis men ruining me for other men? I'll never be able to go back to the life I had before them. "Nah," I tell him, a soft smile pulling at my lips. "I kinda just want to lay here and watch you play. You always look so at peace when it's just you and your music."

"Sure?"

I nod and he hesitates for a moment before finally scooping up his drumsticks and holding them down against the drum. He moves them slowly on the kit, dragging the tip across the top of it and creating the softest hum throughout the room. "Have I told you how fucking gorgeous you are when you're sleeping?"

"Should I be creeped out about the serial killer watching me while I sleep?"

He brings the tip of the stick out and taps it gently against the drum. "Always," he says, his eyes hooded as his heavy stare lingers on me.

He starts a slow beat and I push myself up against the headboard, leaning back against its soft cushioning. "Was something on your mind?" I ask him, hating that he's having trouble sleeping.

He shakes his head. "It's nothing important," he says. "Just picturing the way Roman fucked you today. I didn't like it."

"Why's that?"

"Because you're the most precious thing to me," he says over the sound of his drums, "and you should be treated as such."

A grin pulls at my lips and he rolls his eyes before the words have even come out of my mouth. "I seem to recall more than a few times where you've fucked me just as hard. I probably still have bruises in the shape of your fingers littered across my skin. I might be precious to you, but that doesn't mean I'm fragile, and you know it."

"I know," he grumbles.

"You're not … jealous, are you? Seeing me with Roman …"

Levi scrunches up his face and shakes his head. "Nah, I've told you before that I'm cool with it. I just don't like seeing him take advantage of you like that."

"And if I told you that I encouraged it, and that while he was using me to forget the monsters inside his head, I was also using him right back."

A grin cuts across his lips as he picks up the beat on his drums, his foot gently bouncing with the bass. "Then I'd say that I should have known better."

I relax into the cushioned headboard and let the conversation fall silent between us, wanting nothing more than to zone out and listen to his sweet music, only watching the way his muscles flex and bulge with each hit of the drum has me paying far more attention than I intended. Everything about him draws me in—the body, the tattoos, the deep, growly tone, and that fucking smirk that makes everything clench deep inside of me. Levi DeAngelis is something special. He's like a drug that I simply can't get enough of.

I watch him a moment longer, my greedy eyes sailing over his strong body, and the longer I watch him, the hotter I get. My bottom lip catches between my teeth as he increases the tempo of his beat, and his eyes … goddamn it! His eyes are full of fire, watching the way that I watch him. It's the most erotic thing I've ever seen. I don't know how he does it. Have I always been attracted to drummers or is it just Levi?

My hand falls to my collarbone, trailing little circles over my skin, and hell, I don't even realize I'm doing it. My hand slowly trails down my body, between my tits, and over my stomach. I suck in a breath as the soft brush of my nails send a wave of tingles sailing over my skin, and before I know it, my hand slips below the blanket and slowly brushes over my clit.

A breathy groan pulls from between my lips as I circle my clit, my eyes becoming hooded as I watch the erotic sight before me. My hand sinks lower and I push two fingers into my cunt, instantly feeling that soft ache, reminding me exactly where Roman had been only twenty-four hours ago. My fingers move in and out, matching the beat of Levi's drums and feeling just how wet and ready I am for him, but judging by the dark, intense look in his eyes, he'll be staying right where he is, more than intent on watching the show.

My lip comes free from the confines of my teeth, and Levi shakes his head as a low growl tears from deep in his chest. "Bite that fucking lip again," he scolds me, his tone deeper than I've ever heard it.

I obey right away, biting my bottom lip as my fingers brush past my clit again and force another soft moan out of me. "Shit, Levi," I breathe, my body already so worked up by just the mere sight of him playing his drums.

"Pull those blankets back, Shayne," he murmurs, the sound of his voice sailing right through my chest and making my pussy clench. "Let me see you."

Wanting him to appreciate the moment just as much as I am, I peel the blanket back and a cold rush of air brushes against my soaking cunt, making me jump as a soft gasp slips through my lips. My fingers keep moving, slipping in and out, and just to make sure he gets the full X-rated version, I spread my legs even wider and adjust my hips to show him absolutely everything.

He picks up the beat of his drums and I follow suit, knowing all too well that despite him being across the room, he controls my every move.

"Take my glass from the bedside table," he instructs.

My brows pinch together as I quickly glance to his side table to find a half empty glass of something, and not wanting to disappoint, I reach across and curl my fingers around the cool glass. I watch him expectantly, more than ready to play along with whatever game he's wanting to play.

"Drink it."

Swallowing hard, I bring the glass to my lips while keeping my fingers slowly moving in and out of me while my thumb moves up to circle my clit. I breathe in the brown liquid and decide that it's bourbon as I tip it up, the condensation from the bottom of the glass dripping onto my bare tits and slowly trailing down my body, catching every little bit of Levi's attention.

Drinking what's left of the bourbon, I lower the glass and meet his heated stare once again. "Take an ice cube," he tells me.

Fire burns through me in the most delicious way, remembering the first time he'd touched me. He'd teased me with an ice cube until finally pushing it inside of me, and damn it, I'm so here for round two.

A grin pulls at my lips as my gaze darkens, loving the way he watches me. "Now what?" I purr, holding the ice cube between my fingers and letting the chilled water drip over my body.

"Play."

One word is all he needs.

I bring the ice down to my body, slowly trailing it over my collar bone and down to my breast. The ice melts quickly beneath the warmth of my skin, and as I circle my nipple, it quickly pebbles, desperate for Levi's touch. When my skin starts to burn beneath its cold touch, I trail it down further, groaning as the water pools and runs, messing the sheets beneath me.

I suck in a gasp as I trail the ice over my stomach and jolt the further I go, making my pussy clench around my fingers. I try to keep to Levi's beat on the drums, but the ice is distracting me in a way that I wasn't prepared for.

I push it further down, squirming under the chill, and as it finally makes contact with my clit, I suck in a deep gasp, briefly closing my eyes and tipping my head back. "Oh fuck," I whisper, sliding it over my clit in tight little circles.

Needing something more, I lower the ice further until I can finally push it into my pussy, gasping as the ice moves inside of me. I slowly push my fingers back in, nudging it further and groaning with delight. I can't help but squirm as Levi watches me, determined to come before the ice completely melts.

My fingers keep the ice moving within me and my other hand comes back to my clit, teasing it with quick little circles until my body can't possibly take anymore.

Levi's tongue rolls over his bottom lip, and the hunger in his eyes is enough to push me right over the edge. I come hard, crying out Levi's name as my pussy clenches around my fingers, melting the last of the ice. My walls spasm wildly as my orgasm pulses right through my body. My toes curl and I groan low, biting down on my lip once again.

Too intense to keep going, my fingers pause inside of me, needing to come down from my high. I take a few deep breaths as my body finally begins to relax, and just when I think it's over, Levi stands from his drum, throwing his sticks down.

He strides toward me, palming his massive cock through his shorts as a grin tears across his face, his eyes warning me that the ice was only a warmup. "Spread those fucking legs, baby," he murmurs. "I'm hungry."

Sneaking through the halls of a massive mansion is a lot harder than it sounds, especially when you have hot cum leaking out of you and trailing down the side of your leg. I duck into the nearest bathroom, grumbling to myself as a soft hue rests against the massive window, telling me the sun is just about to make an appearance.

I can't say that a night of sex was really on the agenda when I went to bed last night, but I'm not going to complain … well, only about the cum dripping down my leg. That's unfortunate, but to be fair, Levi offered to help clean me up as I scooted out of bed, but I insisted that he get some sleep. Hell, I even switched off his bathroom light and slipped out of his room just to give him the silence he needs.

Getting myself cleaned up, I tiptoe back toward my room, not wanting to wake anyone, but as I pass the massive stairs that lead down to the foyer, Ariana's familiar tone breaks through the silence. "I swear," she murmurs, trying to keep her voice low, but in such a big open space, concealing a tone like hers is nearly impossible. "I just want to get out of here."

My brows furrow and I creep toward the edge of the stairs and peer down into the foyer below, finding Ariana with a Louis Vuitton suitcase and a passport in her hands. Roman stands in front of her, his jaw clenched and betrayal deep in his eyes. "You fucking hear me, Ariana," he says. "If you ever come back here, I will destroy you. That's a promise."

She shakes her head. "Come with me," she says. "It was always supposed to be just you and me. We can get far away from all of this shit and start fresh. That girl isn't good enough for you. She's just a little bitch who likes getting off. She's a whore, and you know it. Just come with me. We can make it work."

I clench my jaw. She was so close to earning just a little bit of respect from me until she had to go and ruin it. Even after everything she's been through, she still can't figure out where she's going wrong.

I roll my eyes. I had started to feel sorry for her. It was a long drive back here and she spent most of it curled in a ball. Roman even sat in the back and allowed her the smallest comfort of sitting by her as she sobbed, mentally replaying everything she'd been through since Giovanni first took her. So yeah, I felt for her. I even considered sitting her down and offering her a tea or coffee and a chance to talk it all out to help move past the haunting memories, but to hell with it now. If she wants to keep being a back-stabbing bitch, then that's on her.

Roman laughs, the amusement crossing his face until he realizes that she's serious. His smile fades away and he pulls back from her. "You're fucking kidding, right? I would rather dig my own eyes out with a rusty switchblade than let you claw your way back into my life. You're leaving right fucking now and never coming back. Forget you ever knew me."

"Roman, no," she says, panic thick in her tone. "Don't do this to us. We have so much history. How can you just throw that away? You were the first man I ever loved. *The only man.* Please."

Feeling as though this is getting far too personal, I go to walk away, but the slight movement has Roman's gaze shifting to me. He holds my stare for a moment before dropping it back to Ariana's, and for one blazing second, a rush of memories come flooding back, each of them forcing me to clench my thighs.

"I wouldn't go back to you if you were the last woman on earth, not even for a quick fuck. I've moved on," he says, his gaze quickly sailing up to mine again before dropping back to the woman who stabbed the knife straight through his chest. "You and I were over a long time ago. Get the fuck out and don't come back."

Roman steps toward the door, gripping the handle and tearing it wide, allowing the cool morning breeze to violently slam upon her, blowing her hair back off her face. Roman doesn't say another word as she tries to capture his stare, but he refuses and allows a bored expression to rest over his face.

The seconds tick by and being completely out of options, she lets out a pained cry and walks out the door, dragging her Louis Vuitton behind her. The moment she clears the threshold, Roman slams the door with a loud *BANG* and steps aside to watch her from the window, making sure she goes.

Minutes tick by until I hear the subtle sound of a car, and not a moment later, Ariana hits the gas and takes off, hopefully to never return again.

Certain that she's out of our lives forever, Roman turns back to face me, his deep stare lingering on my blue eyes, then all too soon, he tears his gaze away, turns on his heel, and walks away.

CHAPTER TWENTY ONE

My mouth barely fits around my burger as I struggle to take a bite. I don't know why I made it this freaking big, but there were just too many options. What can I say? I'm a girl who likes a little bit of everything … or maybe a lot.

Sauce dribbles out the bottom and I try to catch it before it can make a mess all over the marble floors, but naturally, coordinating myself, a burger, and a spill at the same time is like building a rocket ship and learning how to fly the stupid thing.

Juice spills right down the front of my cropped tank, and as I try to avoid fucking it up even more, the essence of the burger falls straight out the bottom. "No, no, no, no, no," I shriek, as the meat patty splatters on the ground in a mix of tomato, lettuce, and cucumber, leaving me holding nothing but the empty burger bun.

My heart aches as I stare down at what was supposed to be the burger of a lifetime. I even drizzled the sauce just right. "Clean up on aisle twelve," I call. "Dill? Doe? Where are you big bastards?"

At the sound of their names, the enormous jet-black wolves barrel through the mansion, the clicking of their claws on the marble floor sounds through the house, telling me exactly where they are. Their big wolfy asses come hurtling around the corner and bounding toward me.

Seeing the mess of food on the ground, their pace picks up and my eyes bug out of my head. They're going too fast. "Fuck," I panic, not even allowing myself the chance to fuss over the way Dill is running at full speed, despite the fact that he's still supposed to be taking it easy. "Slow down. SLOW DOWN!"

Dill's tongue lolls out of his mouth and I remember who the fuck I'm yelling at. There's no slowing these big bastards down. It's either get out of their way or risk being trampled.

Getting closer to the mess of burger, the wolves hit the brakes, underestimating their speed, and sliding right along the polished marble, barreling straight past the burger and into my legs before I can make a full escape. A piercing shriek tears out of me as we turn into a mess of limbs on the ground. I narrowly miss slamming into the opposite wall as the wolves immediately get back up and pounce on the burger as though they didn't even realize that my life just flashed before my eyes.

I flip both of them off before crawling across to the massive window and reaching up to grip the small ledge so that I can haul myself up, only as I reach the window and stretch up, a flash of movement catches my attention. My head whips around, gaping out at the long driveway to where three big black vans are pulling up.

Panic tears through me as my eyes widen with fear. "UMMMMM, GUYS," I holler through the big house, yanking myself up off the ground and racing through the house to where I'd last seen Marcus. "WE HAVE VISITORS."

I get as far as the front foyer when I find all three of the boys barreling toward me, their sharp gazes sailing over me before landing on the front entryway windows. They peer out to see the black vans while I silently panic.

"Fuck," Roman grunts under his breath, probably irritated with himself that all four of us had missed the vans coming through the front gates, but the only way they could have gotten in was if they knew the code.

"Who is it?" I rush out as Marcus doubles back to grip my hand, pulling me away in some ridiculous bid to keep me safe from whatever threat is about to come barging through the door.

He shakes his head. "I've got no fucking idea, but from my experience, a van ain't good. Bringing three of them … now that's just showing off."

"What?" I breathe, my eyes bulging out of my head as Levi settles into the corner of the big floor-to-ceiling window and pulls the gun from the back of his pants, giving him the perfect vantage point to take out any threats.

He watches them for a moment, his back straightening as the drivers get out of the vans and make their way to the back. Levi's brows furrow, watching them carefully as Roman prepares an onslaught of weapons. "Something doesn't feel right," Levi mutters, "I don't think this is an ambush."

Roman scoffs, still preparing the weapons. "You really want to take that risk?" he questions, giving his younger brother a hard stare.

Levi shakes his head. "I'm ready to go either way. I just don't think it is what we're all thinking," he comments, turning his gaze back to the window. "They're opening the back of the first van."

A silence fills the foyer and Marcus immediately pushes me out of the room again, but there's no way in hell that I'm going anywhere. I'm staying with the boys, right where I can see them at all times. I've had way too much bad luck on my own. "Would you stop fighting me?" Marcus spits.

"Then stop pushing me," I fire back at him. "I'm not going anywhere."

His jaw clenches, the sharp set of his cheekbones only making him look like a fucking demon right out of a nightmare. "I'm not fucking around, Shayne."

"Neither am I."

"Wait …" Levi says slowly, his brows drawn as his tone has Roman easing up on the weapon. Hell, he even stops what he's doing to glance up at his brother. "It looks like some kind of delivery."

"Delivery?" Roman grunts, before turning a glaring gaze on Marcus. "What the fuck did you order?"

Marcus' hands fly up, his instincts to defend himself freeing me from being pushed into some small, dirty hallway cupboard. "I didn't order anything," he shoots back at Roman, his tone filled with offense at being blamed for whatever the fuck is going on here. "It was probably Ariana weeks ago before she got ran out. You know how she liked to indulge in her credit cards."

Roman watches Marcus for a long moment before finally glancing back at Levi. "What is it?"

Levi's stare remains out the window, his brows furrowing further by the second. "I ... I think they're decorations."

"Decorations?" Marcus questions, his hand curling around mine and keeping me close as he trails closer to the nearest window to get a quick look. We peer out into the driveway to find the back of all three vans wide open and a total of six men in matching uniforms hauling shit out of the vans. "The fuck is going on?"

Roman creeps in closer, moving in behind me and peering out over my head, his brows drawn with a fierce suspicion as he shoves the gun in his hand back into the waistband of his jeans. "I have no fucking idea."

Marcus turns to glance at his brothers, a stupid grin pulling at the corners of his lips. "Not it," he says in a chirpy singsong tone making Levi rush in just a moment later. "Yeah, I'm out too," he says, meeting Roman's hard stare. "This one is all yours, brother."

Roman sighs and takes another look out the window. "As if I'd trust you assholes to take care of this in the first place." And with that, he walks across the foyer and tears open the front door, his back taut and still prepared for a threat.

I find myself creeping closer and closer to the door until I eventually stand right at Roman's side, all to his dismay. He subtly reaches out and pushes my body half behind his before shooting me an irritated glare, but hell, after I allowed him to use and abuse my body like his own personal play toy the other day, I have got a newfound ability to get away with whatever the hell I want. Though, I don't doubt it comes with an expiration date.

Realizing that I'm not about to scurry away, Roman turns his attention back to the six men at the bottom of the stairs. "Can I help you?" he says, his tone sailing right down to them as clearly as if he'd been standing right behind them.

One guy stops what he's doing and turns to glance up at Roman, shielding his eyes from the hot afternoon sun. "Where do you want this stuff?"

"I don't fucking want it," Roman shoots back. "What's going on here? We didn't order any of this."

The guy stares at him blankly, his brows drawing down before he glances at some other dude stacking a bunch of chairs onto a wide trolley. "Aye, he says he didn't order this shit."

The trolley guy pauses and glances up at Roman before letting out a frustrated sigh and digging papers out of his pocket. He glances over them. "Are you Giovanni DeAngelis?" he questions, blocking out the sun just as his colleague had. "It says something about an annual party. We have ongoing instructions to be here on this date every year."

A moment passes before Roman's murmured "Ah, fuck," fills the airs around us.

Marcus and Levi appear in the doorway as the delivery guys stare up at us, impatiently waiting to be told what to do. "The fuck is going on?" Marcus questions as Roman turns to meet his brother's confused stare.

"It's that stupid DeAngelis annual ball Ariana had Father start a few years back. That was supposed to be tonight," he says, clearly having figured out what the fuck this is all about.

Marcus scoffs. "Like fuck we're going ahead with that shit," he says, looking down at the delivery men and indicating to the piles of shit they've started unloading. "Pack it all up. We don't need it. The only balls I'll be showing up for are the ones between my legs."

A laugh catches in my throat and I immediately choke on my own air while Marcus slaps a helpful hand into the center of my back. "You good, babe?"

"Hold up. Don't pack up anything just yet," Levi says, holding his hands out and stopping the delivery guys before anyone can make any hasty decisions. He glances at his brothers. "Everyone comes to this fucking ball. All the cousins and their wives. It'd be the perfect opportunity to stake our claim as the new leaders of this family."

Roman looks thoughtful for a moment before turning his gaze to Marcus. "Plus, it's a good chance to figure out what's being said, see where loyalties lie."

"Not to mention," Levi throws in. "Tensions are riding high. Someone is bound to break and send someone else to an early grave. We couldn't possibly skip out on prime-time entertainment like that."

Marcus sighs. "Seriously? You know how those fucking suits make my balls sweat."

I look up at Marcus. "Twice. That's twice! How does someone

bring up their balls twice in such a short time?"

Levi's brows arch in consideration. "It's really not that hard," he tells me. "Now talking about someone else's balls in such a short time without coming across as batting for the other side is where it gets a little tricky."

"You talk about other men's balls often?"

Levi laughs, his lips kicking up into a ridiculous smirk. "You'd be shocked at how often the topic comes up."

Roman shakes his head, irritation flaring in his obsidian eyes. "Can we get back to the fucking ball?" he demands. "Are we doing it or not?"

Marcus shrugs his shoulders and lets out a heavy sigh just as another van pulls into the top of the driveway that says something about 'Delight Catering' on the side. "Are either of you going to spend the next few hours calling everyone to let them know it's canceled? Because I'm not," he says, knowing damn well that they won't be doing it either. "People are going to show up whether we want them to or not. We might as well go ahead with it and use it to our advantage."

Roman nods in complete agreement. "Then it's settled," he says, glancing down at the delivery drivers. "Start unloading and make it quick. I don't want anyone in my house any longer than necessary."

They immediately get to work and the four of us trail back inside, leaving the front door wide open while the catering company has the brains to drive right around back to the staff kitchen entrance. They let themselves in and get busy while I gape at the boys. "A ball?" I question. "What the hell am I supposed to wear to a ball?"

Marcus grins. "You've seen that massive collection Ariana has upstairs, right?" he says before pulling out a black AMEX card and handing it over. "But if none of them are doing it for you, buy one of your own and have it delivered."

I stare at the gold card, never having seen one of these in the flesh. I gape up at him, knowing damn well that every dress in Ariana's collection is more than my style, but the thought of getting something specifically for me is already making my dark heart brighten with excitement. Besides, Ariana's collection is just that. They're her dresses and I'll never feel comfortable wearing them. "Do I … do I have a limit?" I ask, the excitement bubbling up in my stomach and making it impossible to stand still.

Marcus laughs and shakes his head. "You've seen the weapons collection we have, right?" he smirks. "Do we really look like the type of guys who worry about budgeting? Get what you want, babe. This ball is about showing off our new queen, not just getting intel. Make a fucking lasting impression."

When Roman or Levi don't bother to rein in Marcus' wild suggestion, I grip onto the card just a little tighter and run for my fucking life before they have the brains to reel me in.

The soft, shimmering moonlight shines in through my bedroom window, hitting my back as I watch myself through the big floor-to-ceiling mirror. It creates a glow around me like some kind of halo that makes me feel even more incredible than

I already do.

The boys agreed to let me hire a hair stylist and makeup artist for the day and even went as far as hiring a masseur to pamper me. It has literally been the best day of my life, but when my gown was hand delivered in a big white box with a big gold bow, my world imploded in the best possible way.

I've never been treated like this in my whole life. I feel like a princess, and a part of me still struggles to believe that this is my new reality. Fuck spending my day working behind a dirty bar for shitty tips. I don't ever want to go back to that old life.

My gaze travels down my gold, beaded Versace gown in awe. I spent two hours scouring every corner of the internet for the perfect dress when I finally came upon Kate Hudson's 2003 red carpet Versace gown, and I had to have it … or at least something similar. It's so simple and elegant, perfect for tonight. When I first started looking at gowns, I wanted something dark and edgy, something to draw from that dark corrupted part of my soul, but this gown ultimately won out. The second I laid my eyes on it, I knew it was right.

Naturally, apart from spilling out credit card numbers, I had no idea how to pull the type of strings to get the gown I wanted, but Levi stepped in and proved that he was so much more than just a devil between the sheets, and three hours later, it's here.

The gown flows down into a small train, and I'm surprised to see just how heavy it is. I can't say that I've ever worn a proper gown before. I had that silk gown the boys put me in when I arrived and another dress I wore here to a business meeting. They were gorgeous dresses, but this isn't anything like those occasions. This shit here is the real deal.

My hair is up off my back in gorgeous curls that have been arranged into the most stunning up-do that had me in tears. My makeup has been crafted to perfection with smokey eyes and just a hint of gold, and God, the lashes. I've never worn false lashes but now they're my obsession.

I kept a natural lip with just a hint of gloss, not wanting to go overboard with the makeup to keep the attention on the gown, and damn it, it's everything I hoped it would be.

Nerves settle in the pit of my stomach. I haven't eaten anything since my burger went splat on the marble floors, but now I'm thinking that I should have made time to eat … or maybe I just need a drink. There are going to be a lot of people here tonight, all of the boys' extended family, all of whom I couldn't care if they lived or died, but I still want to make a good impression. The boys are in the middle of claiming the DeAngelis Mafia Family as their own, and they need to make tonight count. A single hint of weakness and they'll have the masses coming for them with pitchforks and fires.

A light rap sounds at the door before Marcus pushes his way into my room. "Babe, you ready?" he questions, raising his head and stopping dead in his tracks as his dark gaze trails over me. "Holy fuck," he breathes as my gaze trails over the way he wears his suit, looking like he just stepped straight out of Serial Killers United Magazine. He's in all black, but I didn't expect anything different, and despite knowing exactly what he was going to wear, it still doesn't fail to take my breath away. He's absolutely perfect.

A soft blush creeps over my cheeks as I look up at him through my long, thick lashes. "Do you like it?" I question nervously, the moonlight shining through the window going a long way to making this moment feel even more magical.

"Do I like it?" he scoffs, offended by the question. He slinks through my room slowly, each step making my heart race just a little bit faster until he moves right in front of me and brushes the backs of his knuckles down the length of my arm, his tone softening to a light whisper. "You look like a fucking angel here to steal the hearts out of every man you come across. You're a fucking goddess."

I step into him, placing my hand against his chest as the moment wraps around me. Immediately getting lost in his dark eyes, I brush my glossy lips over his. "I love you, Marcus DeAngelis."

His hand falls to my waist, holding me tighter. "Damn right, you do," he murmurs against my lips. "Now let me show you off to the fucking world before I change my mind and keep you locked in here for myself."

"Well then," I murmur, a smile resting on my lips as my hand falls into his. "Who am I to deprive the masses of my beauty? Let's go."

CHAPTER TWENTY TWO

My six-inch stiletto heels click against the expensive marble floors as Marcus leads me out of my room and through the mansion fit for a queen. Soft music fills the property and a wave of murmured chatter comes from the level below.

People started showing up half an hour ago, and while a good host would be there to welcome guests at the door, I couldn't quite bring myself to be the first at the party. Besides, if I intend to do this right, then I need to make my grand entrance count, and what better way to do that than by walking in with Marcus DeAngelis on my arm.

It's a perfect night as we walk toward the massive staircase. I glance out through the windows at the front of the house. The place is lit up like a damn Christmas tree and has butterflies emerging deep in my stomach. Cars litter the property, waiting in long lines and pulling up at the top of the circle drive. Guests pour out in dazzling suits and gowns that take my breath away. They make their way up the grand staircase and their cars are driven away by the valet service that I'm sure Giovanni paid handsomely for.

Marcus guides me to the top step, and as my heel touches down and I gaze over the lingering guests making their way through the foyer, already with champagne flutes in their hands, my brows begin to pinch together. "I thought this was the annual DeAngelis Family Ball," I murmur, holding onto Marcus' strong arm to keep from tumbling down the stairs. "Who are all these people?"

"Would you believe it if I told you they were all here because DeAngelis blood runs through their veins?" he questions, his gaze sweeping across to mine with a mischievous sparkle that has me doubting every last word that comes out of his mouth.

"That's impossible," I say, keeping my low tone. "There must be hundreds of people here."

"Correct," he says, his hand dropping to my lower back. "My guess would be this party is pushing four hundred guests, each one of them an integral member of this family. Cousins, their children, uncles, wives, grandparents—every version of extended family you can think of, and I can guarantee they are all here tonight. Apart from my father, of course. Though, he will hear all about whatever happens within these walls, I have no doubt."

My gaze narrows and I slow my stride. "Your grandparents? Like the very people who raised your father? You're lying."

"Cross my heart and hope to die," he says, pulling me along. "There are generations of DeAngelis men and women here tonight.

Generations past, present, and future. It's the FBI's version of a wet dream."

"Well, shit."

We hit the bottom step and a waiter immediately offers us a drink off a silver platter and Marcus scoops it up without hesitation and throws back every last drop. "Too fucking right," he says, his actions speaking much louder than his words. He places the empty glass back down and replaces it with two new ones, handing me one before taking a sip of his own.

Marcus leads me through the massive property, and as we get closer to the wide entrance, the chatter from within seems to get louder. The music drowns out most of it, but as more and more guests begin arriving, I can only imagine just how loud and eventful tonight will be.

We reach the main doors as a giddy nervousness settles into my veins, forcing me to grip Marcus just a little tighter. The impulsive need to kick off these ridiculous shoes and sprint back to my room slams through me, and as if reading me like a fucking book, Marcus drags me through the doors and I'm immediately overcome with awe.

The room dazzles me with a crystal chandelier framed by gorgeous silk drapes, becoming the masterpiece of the night. I've only been in this room once or twice and only because I was lost, but I could have sworn that the chandelier wasn't here before. I can only imagine how much that big bastard must have cost, but apparently, money isn't an issue when you're the most feared man in the country.

Tall pillars surround the room and are frosted with the most delicate lights that make the room glow. Hell, it looks freaking heavenly in here, but the men that fill the room are anything but.

Stealing my gaze from the impressive decorations and forcing myself not to ask how the hell this was all pulled together so quickly, I focus on the guests, unnerved by the way each and every eye seems to flicker my way. Before I get a chance to question Marcus, he finishes what's left in his glass, making it two in a matter of minutes. Placing the glass down on the waiter's tray by the door, he drops his hand over mine at his elbow and pulls me along. I lower my gaze from all the guests who watch me like a hawk, wondering how the hell a nobody like me could be so special to gain the attention of all three of the famous DeAngelis brothers.

My gaze sweeps lower, needing to have drunk a little more to brave meeting their eyes. So instead, I take in their gowns, and it takes me only a second to realize that every last gown in this ballroom is as black as Marcus' soul.

My eyes widen and I pull back on his arm, a soft gasp pulling from between my lips. "They're all in black," I shriek quietly. "What the fuck, Marc? Is there a dress code?"

"Damn fucking straight there is," he tells me, his gaze dropping down the gorgeous gold gown perfectly draped over my body, hugging it like a second skin. "You wanted to make an impression, didn't you?"

A wicked grin tears across my lips and I realize that I'm going to need a shit load more than just a glass of champagne to get me through the night. Taking a page out of Marcus' book, I bring the champagne flute to my glossy lips and tip it back, downing every last drop before handing off the glass. "That was a risky move," I warn him. "Each one of the women in this room are currently painting a target on my back, and I can guarantee you that every last one of them thinks I'm an arrogant bitch with an ego too big for my own good."

"And I hope they do," he tells me. "These women are the ones keeping their husbands' beds warm, and they're going to be the ones whispering in their ears telling their sorry husbands exactly what they think of you, and even though their words will be spiteful and full of hate, their husbands will come away with one thing."

Marcus pauses and gives me a hard stare, making me want to wring his neck for stopping there. "Seriously?" I grumble. "Is this supposed to be some kind of dramatic pause?"

Marc grins, his eyes lighting with excitement. "They'll come away knowing that you're dangerous. Any woman who can ruffle the feathers of a Mafia wife, is a woman to watch out for."

I'm just about to tell him how stupid a move like that was when a dark gaze meets mine across the room and the breath is knocked right out of my chest. Levi stands with his big frame directly in front of one of the many floor-to-ceiling windows, the soft glow from the moonlight casting a halo around him. He talks with a man in a suit that looks like it cost more than I made in a year, but Levi completely zones out, watching me as though I'm every single one of his dreams.

A flush spreads over my cheeks, and as his gaze sweeps over my body, I'm hit with the overwhelming need to run to him. My thighs clench and I want to hate myself for being so obvious. He has such a profound effect on me, it's too much. I hate it, but at the same time, I absolutely love it.

The man beside him continues to speak animatedly about who the fuck knows what, and it's clear from the way I hold every ounce of Levi's attention that he has absolutely no idea either.

A smile tugs at my lips and a shyness comes over me, one that I shouldn't have considering the filthy things that man has watched me do. His intensity becomes too much, and I drop my gaze away, only to find Marcus' heated stare. "He's right, you know. You look like a fucking wet dream."

Pressing into Marcus, I drop my hand to his wide chest and glance over my shoulder at Levi, knowing he's watching my lips and reading every last word that comes spilling from them. "Then the second this party is over, the two of you better show me how much you appreciate this dress."

Levi's eyes flash with desire as a soft growl vibrates through Marcus' chest, rumbling against my fingers. "Consider it done."

A thrill fires through me, but it's short-lived as guests stop to greet Marcus, each one of them approaching cautiously. His reputation in this world goes far and wide. I don't miss the way he positions me slightly ahead of him, forcing me to take the brunt of the attention, which inadvertently means the kind of leering I don't want. I meet great uncles, cousins that I never knew existed, cousins of those cousins, and aunties. Hell, I'm almost positive that Marcus doesn't know who most of these people are, but there's no doubt that they're all family. The DeAngelis genes are strong here. Dark hair and dark eyes, except all the wives who seem to be at least twenty years younger with fake tits, manicured nails, and hair so full of bleach, it could start a fire.

Fights break out and everyone goes on about their night as though they don't even see it. The music subtly gets louder as Marcus presses another drink into my hand before he swooshes me around the room to show me off like a fucking star.

At least an hour passes before we've done the rounds, and I'm positive that after meeting at least a hundred different people, I don't remember a single name.

Roman breaks away from an older gentleman who looks an awful lot like an older version of Giovanni, and I can't help but wonder if that's Grandpa DeAngelis. Roman's eyes are hard and cautious, watching every last person in the room with suspicion, and I can't help but wonder what they all think of us. Are we some kind of sideshow, thinking we can slip straight into Giovanni's position without consequences?

Grandpa DeAngelis keeps his back to us as he swirls the brown liquid in the middle of his glass and finishes it before slamming it down on a nearby table. He holds his head up and hightails it straight for the exit. "What the fuck was that about?" Marcus questions as we all meet in the middle, hovering over a table.

Roman clenches his jaw, glancing at the exit to make sure he's going. "He had a few things to say and let it be known that he didn't appreciate us running Father out like that. So I told him he can either get on board or fuck off. I'd be more than happy to put his body in the ground."

"Shit," Levi says, making me jump as he moves in from behind me with a drink in hand. He places it down on the table and a ring of condensation instantly forms around it. "He's not going to appreciate that."

"He can suck my dick," Roman mutters. "He's been in Father's ear for far too long, pulling his strings like a goddamn puppeteer, but not anymore. Both of them can go to hell."

I pick up Levi's drink and take a sip before putting it straight back down, the foul taste practically burning a hole through my tongue. "You guys aren't a big fan of your grandfather?"

"Hell no," Marcus says, his tone darkening and sending a wave of unease over me. "The old fuck was the one to give me my first black eye. I was only five."

I gape up at him, anger swirling deep in my stomach as the need to race after the bastard and gouge his eyes out slams through me like hot acid. Only, I don't get a chance to even whine about it before a wicked grin settles over Roman's lips. "Well I'll be fucking damned," he says, amusement thick in his tone as he watches the door. "The asshole found a set of balls after all."

My brows furrow as I turn to look at the door and find Louis standing at the entrance, one hand on his wife's lower back, the other reaching for a drink. He doesn't bother getting a drink for his wife, and as he strides deeper into the room, I feel a sickening tension thickening in the air. "This isn't good."

"Nah," Marcus laughs, watching the way Victor's remaining four sons seem to pause and watch him like a hawk, their hands slowly reaching for their guns as every last guest in the room discreetly moves aside, determined not to be collateral damage if this turns ugly. "This is what I call entertainment."

I roll my eyes and watch closely. Victor was only killed a few nights ago, and from the soft whispers I've heard throughout the night, all fingers are pointing to Louis, assuming it was payback for murdering his only son, and damn it, the hard set of his jaw proves it. If only these fuckers knew that both Antonio's and Victor's blood is on our hands … hell, Ronaldo's technically is too. Though we weren't the ones to pull the trigger there. Though, I have to give it to Louis, he hasn't lashed out yet. He's been cool, calm, and collected as he bides his time. Though I'm sure he's upset that someone else got to Victor before he got the chance.

"Do you think something is going to happen?" I ask, my gaze flicking from one side of the room to the other, watching Victor's remaining sons closely.

Levi shrugs his shoulders. "Hard to tell," he says. "Louis is lethal. He'll even give us a run for our money, but they'd be foolish to do something here with so many witnesses. Everybody knows that they'll eventually go after him, but it's bad taste to spill blood at a family event."

I scoff. "I didn't realize you guys actually had morals. That's cute."

Roman shoots me a hard glare and I don't doubt that I'm going to get bitched out later for referring to anything that has to do with them as cute. "You want to see cute?" he tells me, grabbing what's left of Levi's drink on the table and throwing it back. "I'll show you fucking cute."

My brows furrow and I watch as Roman turns his back and starts walking toward the top of the room where the live band is vibing. Seeing Roman approaching, they put their instruments down and give him the floor.

"Ahh, shit," Marcus mutters. "So, we're doing this now."

Roman stands front and center, but with the guests' attention still waiting for a shootout between Louis and Victor's sons, Roman pulls his own gun and lets off two perfect shots. One bullet sails past Louis' wife and shatters the glass in his hand, while the other skims right over the top of Phillip's head, making his wife drop to the ground and scream until her lungs give out, and his two young daughters turn into sobbing messes on the floor beside their mother.

All eyes snap to Roman while my gaze lingers on Phillip. He should have been killed during our little visit the other day. He's a vile man and should be offered the most brutal ending, one that I would be more than happy to give. He gave us absolutely nothing in our quest to find Giovanni, though a part of me believed that he truly didn't know. But what he did tell us sent a wave of nausea and terror through my veins—Giovanni is recruiting an army to force his way back in, or at least that's what Phillip heard, and if it's true … shit. The very thought has haunted me night after night, but I trust the boys. If they didn't think they could handle it, they would have made the necessary arrangements.

Roman's deep, booming tone fills the air and my gaze snaps back to him. He stands tall and with the eye of every man, woman, and child in the room on him. Half of them watch him with respect, knowing he is a leader among men, while the others watch him with fear, concerned about why he's here addressing the family and not his father.

"My brothers and sisters," he says, spreading his arms wide in a welcoming gesture. "Welcome to our home. My brothers and I duly welcome you to the annual DeAngelis Family Ball. It is an honor to host you, and an even greater honor to stand before such an impressive show of blood."

The room cheers and I watch as Roman's eyes darken with a sinister excitement, loving the way the crowd eats into his bullshit. "I must thank you all for making the trip out here. We all grieve for Victor DeAngelis. His death, among others, has saddened our hearts, but I believe that he would have wanted tonight to go ahead. So it is in his honor that we celebrate tonight."

The room erupts again, and I don't miss the way that Roman's gaze quickly flickers back toward mine as though proving some kind of imaginary point. He turns back to his doting crowd and holds his hands out, settling them all down as a pained expression forces its way across his face. "However," he continues. "News of Victor's untimely passing is not the only devastation I must share with you tonight."

A hushed silence falls over the crowd, and as if sensing that something big is about to go down, a thick tension spreads over the room, making chills run down my spine. "I am sure by now, you have all noticed my father's absence tonight, along with his new wife, Ariana. My father is a complicated man, and his wife nothing but a whore who lives off the desire to betray those around her. My brothers and I have suffered at our father's hands for too many years, and I feel that it is my duty to share with you all that from here on out, the three men you have all feared for so many years have officially inherited our rightful positions at the head of this family. Giovanni DeAngelis no longer rules over you …" he says, watching the horror, shock, and fear washing over the faces of the men, women, and children in the crowd. "We do."

CHAPTER TWENTY THREE

Three. Two. One.

Booming voices erupt from every corner of the ballroom as Roman stands before them, acting as though he didn't just drop the biggest bomb that ever existed. Because this chance doesn't just affect the people in this room, it will rock the whole fucking world. Hell, nobody gives a shit about the tension between Victor's sons and Louis anymore. That shit is old news compared to this.

A tall man hovering in the shadows of the room steps out and pushes his way through the crowd, staring up at Roman as the people around us warily watch Levi and Marcus. "Are you saying you and your sick brothers murdered the head of our family?" the man demands, his voice sailing over all the gasps of horror.

"No," Roman says, the people in the room quickly shutting up so they don't miss what's being said. "My father is very much alive and will stay that way if he has anything to do with it. I'm sure many of you have seen the way he cowers when in our presence. My father is weak, and has officially lost control. Giovanni DeAngelis has betrayed you all. He kidnapped my newborn son and ran away, and I urge anyone who may know of his whereabouts to come forward, otherwise you will suffer his same consequences."

"You and your brothers are children," the man spits. "What the hell do you know about leading this family? You will turn us into a laughingstock. We'll all be cuffed and jailed under your command."

Roman laughs. "How lost you are, Uncle," he says in a mocking tone, making my brows pinch together. Uncle? Is this Giovanni's other brother who I haven't met yet? What was his name? Shit ... Joseph, maybe? "My father was already in bed with the FBI. Who do you think gave up the location of your country manor last year? That place was raided, right? You lost over four million in cash then came running to my father for help, and he sat there and promised you that he would find the fucker who did it and punish them. Who's the fucking laughingstock now?"

Roman's gaze lifts to the crowd as Levi and Marcus watch the room with trained gazes. "My brothers and I are no fools," he says slowly. "We know that loyalties are not easily won in this world. Loyalty is earned, not expected, so we will allow you the opportunity to decide for yourself. Will you follow us and remain an integral member of our family, or will you disgrace your family name, your blood, to back my father?"

Roman pauses for a brief second before going on. "We do not expect an answer now. We understand that options must be weighed.

So, we will allow three days, and in three days' time, the most senior members of our family will come to me with their families' response."

With that, Roman stalks off the stage leaving everyone in stunned silence.

He starts making his way back to us when he's pulled away by the same man who questioned him. "Who is that?" I ask, glancing up at Levi.

"Joseph," he says, confirming my earlier thoughts. "He's my father's younger brother. Fucking bastard if you ask me. He keeps to himself but when he wants to make a splash, he makes it count."

Unease rocks through my chest. "Is he going to be a problem?"

Levi's lips press into a hard line. "It's hard to tell," he says as I notice people in the crowd discreetly moving for the exit, terrified what a reign of the famous DeAngelis brothers could truly mean. "Roman will make an offer that will sway him to our side. He's a smart man. He doesn't do anything for nothing."

Roman finishes whatever hushed argument he's having with Joseph, and with a twisted smirk settling over his warm lips, he makes his way back toward us. "Everything cool?" Marcus questions, his gaze sweeping the room to see men watching us closely, deep in thought, while others look as though they're trying to figure out how to play the cards that they were dealt.

Roman shrugs his shoulders as a waitress in a plunging black top comes past with a silver tray of drinks, each of them looking like something that would have my stomach turning. He gingerly takes a few before handing them out to his brothers and grabbing a glass of champagne for me. I take it with a subtle nod and immediately look away. The air between us has been strained ever since the whole fucking on the SUV thing, and honestly, I'm just about ready for him to pull the stick out of his ass and actually acknowledge that it happened, or at the very least give me a high five for a job well done.

He looks back to his brothers and holds his glass up between them, and they respond by raising their own drinks. "Nothing has ever been better," he announces with a sick, sadistic kind of pride. "We're finally getting everything we're owed."

Levi smirks back at Roman and clinks his glass against his brother's. "About fucking time."

A low, rumbling laugh vibrates through Marcus' chest and he throws back his drink before glancing between his brothers. "So, now that's over. Do I need to be here?"

Roman scoffs. "No, but you have to wonder if separating yourself from us is a good idea right now. Every one of the men in this room want to take what we've just stolen. You turn your back now and it's bound to get stabbed."

Marc winks and curls his arm around mine. "I'll take my chances."

Before I even know what's going on, he pulls me away, and I stumble over my six-inch heels before gripping onto him tighter. He holds me steady, and as I glance up at him, I find a deep hunger growing in his eyes.

Oh, my!

"I hope you're not dragging me away to have your wicked way with me, Marcus DeAngelis," I tease, knowing damn well that's exactly what he intends to do. "We're in the middle of a party with a bunch of men who would love nothing more than to catch you with your pants around your ankles."

"I hope they do," he warns me, the darkness pulsing out of him and making my thighs clench. "Then that way they'll know that not only can I achieve the impossible, but I can do it while fucking my girl like a goddamn rockstar. Besides, what kind of leader would I be if I didn't thrust the gift of my perfect bare ass upon my men?"

A laugh bubbles up my throat and I choke it down, not wanting to bark out an obnoxious laugh while surrounded by a group like this—a group who could break out into a war at a second's notice and turn the formal ballroom into a bloodbath. "I don't know about thrusting the gift of your ass upon your men," I tell him, his darkness and hunger slamming into my chest and claiming me all the same. "But I sure as fuck know something else you could thrust into."

A wicked grin stretches across his face as we slip out the back entrance of the ballroom. He leads me up a narrow hall, following behind an older couple who try to make a hasty escape, the idea of Giovanni's sons taking point terrifying them. They scurry along and Marcus watches them closely, probably wondering how he can fuck with them one last time before they disappear for good, only their conversation has me coming up short. "Those boys are kidding themselves," the gruff old man murmurs to his wife, having absolutely no idea who stalks him through the long hall. "Giovanni will not stand for this. He will come back with a vengeance, and I do not want to be here when that happens. It will be a massacre."

"Oh, honey," his wife says, putting her hand to his arm. "What shall we do? They're going to demand our loyalty, and if we deny them, they will come for us. We will never be safe again."

The old man scoffs. "Nothing," he says. "We allow nature to take its course."

"What do you mean?" she questions as they reach the end of the hallway.

The old man reaches for the door that leads out through the staff kitchen. "Gia Moretti," he states bluntly. "She won't stand back and allow them to rise up. She knows how ruthless their reign will be. They will destroy everything that stands in their way, and if she's a smart woman, she'll take them out before they get the chance to rise."

With that, the old couple disappear through the door, leaving me slowing my pace at Marcus' side, gaping up at him in horror. "What he said," I breathe, my hands shaking with fear. "Is he right? Will Gia come for you?"

Marcus pauses outside a small closet and peers after the couple, despite them being long gone. "Nothing is ever considered a sure thing in this world," he reminds me, knowing I've already learned that the hard way. "But he's right. If she's a smart woman with her family's best interest at heart, she'll make a move against us before we get the chance to rise. I wouldn't be surprised if she's already heard whispers and has a plan in place."

My eyes bug out of my head. "Are you kidding me?" I gape, the idea of such a dangerous woman coming for my boys is absolutely terrifying.

Marcus nods, the seriousness in his eyes sending a chill over my body. Marcus is rarely serious, so when he is, it means something big. "Don't you worry about Gia Moretti," he tells me. "We'll be ready for her whether she comes tomorrow, or a year from now. We have something she needs, and she won't fuck with that."

My eyes bug out of my head. "Tell me you didn't steal something from Gia Moretti?"

Marcus laughs, his eyes flashing with amusement as his hands fall to my waist. "Trust me," he says, his smirk stretching wider. "You're not ready for that conversation. Now, that's enough talk about Gia Moretti and her plan to destroy us. I've been needing to tear this fucking dress off you and sink my cock into your tight little cunt since the moment I walked into your bedroom, and not even Gia can stop me now."

His eyes flash with that familiar, dark hunger that has my pussy aching with need. "Who the hell am I to stop you?" I murmur, leaning into him and pushing him back toward the door of the small closet. "Make me scream until my throat bleeds."

I reach around Marcus and turn the handle of the door, and before I know it, I'm pressed up against the other side of it with Marcus' lips at my throat, my legs wrapped around his waist, and his thick, needy cock buried deep inside me.

"Ugh," I groan, scrunching my face in discomfort as Marcus' warm seed leaks out of me, slowly smearing between my legs. I pause outside the bathroom door as Marcus walks on by, continuing back to the party with a more than satisfied smirk playing on his warm lips.

The door is locked, and I lean up against the wall, waiting for my turn. I can't help but watch after Marcus, and as if feeling my stare on his back, he glances over his shoulder, eating me up with those dark, knowing eyes. They sparkle with a deadly secret and a thrill shoots through me as what we just did replays over in my head. My cheeks flush with a hot blush and he winks, sending a wave of need shooting over me all over again. Just when I think he couldn't possibly work me up anymore, he makes a show of wiping his thumb across his delicious lips, reminding me exactly where those lips have been.

"Oh, good God," I groan, squirming under his intense gaze.

Seeing the desire sweeping through me, Marcus laughs, the soft sound rumbling right down the long hall. All too soon, he's pushing back through to the party, leaving me to deal with the mess spreading between my legs.

The woman before me finishes up, and I don't miss the way she pauses as she exits, eyeing me up and down with a cautious stare, clearly not sure how I fit into this little DeAngelis brother combo. A grin pulls at my lips, and seeing the darkness filling my eyes, she quickly huffs and scurries away as though the idea of what I could be capable of doesn't scare the shit out of her.

Laughing to myself, I push my way through to the small, private bathroom, and quickly clean myself up. I don't know how Marcus does it. One second, we're talking about our imminent death at the hands of the Moretti Mafia Family, and the next thing I know, Marcus is making me scream so fucking loud that we sure as hell would have raised the dead.

He came hard, and damn it, I'm positive that I came even harder. Nothing could have possibly made it any better … except for Roman and Levi joining the party. We only got to experience the four of us that one time on top of the high-rise building, but I was blindfolded. That night was all about me feeling their pleasure, but if roles were reversed and it was all about their pleasure … well fuck. Butterflies swirl through my stomach at just the thought of what I could do to them. Just to hear that soft growl coming from between Roman's lips and knowing that it was all because of me would be like all of my Christmases coming at once.

Hearing voices at the door, I quickly focus on what I'm doing, more than aware that I'm getting distracted by just the mere thought of spreading my legs for those devious men.

The voices get louder as they make their way down the hallway. I don't recognize them, but the harsh, whispered tones have my back stiffening with unease. I quickly wash my hands and move to the bathroom door, pressing my ear right up against it to hear the men standing on the opposite side, clearly unaware of me standing so close.

"We move tonight," one of the voices says, the dark whispered tone putting me on edge. "We meet back here after the party and finally put an end to this shit."

"This is our last shot," another voice says. "If we're going to make a move, it has to be now. I want blood. I won't wait any longer."

Oh, fuck.

My heart races as fear pulses through me. Whoever these men are, they're planning some kind of attack after the party, and something tells me the boys are their target.

I have to get out of here. I have to warn them, but more than that, I have to figure out who these bastards are.

They speak for a minute longer, giving absolutely nothing else away, and as their voices begin trailing down the hallway, I let out a shaky breath. If I wait a moment longer, they'll disappear around the corner and any chance of figuring out who they are goes right out the window, but if I walk out of here now, I risk one of them seeing me. And though nobody is as dangerous as the three DeAngelis brothers, the men at this ball can be just as unpredictable and vile. Getting caught could cost me my life, but not taking the risk could mean theirs.

Fuck.

My hands shake as I curl my fingers around the handle and slowly peel the door open. Pushing my way out into the deserted hallway, I make a break for it, keeping my pace calm as the loud clicking on my heels against the marble is bound to give me away.

I glance back over my shoulder and finally find them. The four remaining sons of Victor DeAngelis.

My heart sinks. They've worked it out. They know it was us who killed not only their father, but their brother, Antonio, and now they want to make us bleed.

Shit.

They're right down the opposite end of the long hallway, and just as they go to move around the corner, one of the brother's peers back up the hall and his eyes come straight to mine, widening with the realization that I was in the bathroom, overhearing their conversation. "Hey," he calls up the hallway, his brothers immediately looking back at what's caught his attention.

He turns back to face me and instantly starts making his way back up the hall. I pick up my pace, my heart pounding with fear. "Hey, get back here."

Oh, fuck, fuck, fuck.

I bolt like a fucking line-backer, my heels slamming down on the hard marble.

"I just want to talk," the guy calls after me, his brothers barreling down the hall after him. "She fucking heard us," he says back to his brothers.

He quickly gains on me, and I curse myself for wearing a dress. When the fuck will I learn my lesson? From here on out, I wear tights and runners wherever I go, because apparently having one night free of this bullshit isn't possible.

"Fuck, fuck, fuck, fuck." My chants match the speed of the irritating clicking coming from the bottom of my heels, and I push myself faster, gripping the hem of my gold dress and yanking it up. Knowing my luck, I'll probably trip over the expensive material and face plant right into the floor, and while my nose has always had a slight angle to it, I really don't have the time for a nose job right now.

The man's long strides are twice as big as mine, and by the time I reach the entrance of the massive ballroom, the fucker is right on my heels.

I barge in through the throng of people, my eyes bouncing around the room in a panic, desperately searching for those three familiar faces. I don't look back as bumping into someone could put me right into his murderous hands, so instead, I slip and weave through the crowded bodies, ignoring the gasps and grunts from the people I piss off on the way.

My gaze sweeps the room for the third time, and just as I go to take another step, the desperation begins to get the best of me. A rock-hard arm shoots out and captures my waist. My back slams up against a hard chest, and before a scream can tear out of me, Levi's lips are at my ear. "What happened?" he growls, knowing all too well that only a massive threat could have me running like that.

My gaze snaps back to the entrance of the big room, finding Victor's son staring after me, watching through a narrowed, pissed-off gaze. I blink, and as if I'd imagined him there, he's gone.

Roman moves in beside me and I look back just as Marcus moves in front of me, the three of them boxing me in. "I won't ask you again," Levi spits, more than able to feel the rush of my pulse beneath his hold. "What happened?"

"Victor's sons," I tell them, panting as I try to catch my breath. "They're planning an attack after the party. They want you all dead."

CHAPTER TWENTY FOUR

The last of the wait staff disappears into the night and I stare after them, knowing what this means. The party is officially over and now we're on watch, waiting for Victor's sons to return.

My nerves have been on edge since the fucker chased me into the ballroom. His eyes were filled with such a dark hatred and anger that it's had a wave of chills sweeping through me ever since.

It's been hours since the four brothers left, but every cell in my body tells me that they're still here, still lingering and waiting for their chance to take out their cousins, just as the boys took out their brother.

My heels are long gone, but as we stand at the top of the grand stairs watching the headlights of the last wait staff disappearing down the long drive, I allow the bottom of my dress to trail across the ground. I couldn't find it in myself to go take it off, separating me from the boys. I've stuck right by them all night, and while the boys carried on throughout the party as though there wasn't a threat coming their way, I sure as fuck couldn't.

My panic and nerves have more than gotten the best of me.

Roman steps forward, putting him right at the edge of the top step before opening his arms wide. "Come out, come out, wherever you are," he calls into the night. "Let's get this over and done with. I know you're out there. My yard reeks of your foul stench."

My eyes bug out of my head and I gape at Roman. "The fuck is wrong with you?" I spit under my breath, trying to keep my comments discreet. "What are you doing?"

"I'm tired," he snaps back at me. "It's been a long day. We might as well get it over and done with. Besides, they're a bunch of fucking pussies. They don't stand a chance against us. If they wanted us dead, they would have hired a trained assassin who would have demanded more than they could afford. This is nothing but a meeting."

"A meeting?" I question, my brows furrowed as I watch the four brothers step out from different dark shadows of the yard, their hands up to show they hold no weapons. "No, it's more than that. I heard them say they're out for blood. This is an attack and you're all but cheering them on."

"Look at them," he scoffs, his gaze traveling over his cousins as though dealing with their bullshit is beneath him. "Does it look like anything more than some fucked-up meeting trying to get in our back pocket? I wouldn't be surprised if they offered to suck dick just to get whatever the fuck it is they want."

"A meeting?" I confirm, glancing over the cousins. "That's it? Just a meeting and you decided to keep it to yourself all night while I've been in a panic, thinking you're all going to die."

Roman glances back at me with a bored expression. "I'm not your man, Empress. It's not my job to cater to your erratic emotions. You've got my brothers for that. Take it up with them."

Anger bubbles through me and I narrow my gaze, reaching back to Marcus. My hand instantly comes in contact with his cock, and I palm him through his pants, not missing the way Roman's gaze watches my every move. Anger and jealousy flash through his dark eyes, sending a wave of sick satisfaction crashing through me. "You're right," I tell him, copying his same bored tone. "You're not my man. You're a scared little boy who refuses to take what he wants because his own fucked-up emotions and daddy issues have left him shaking in his boots."

Knowing Roman's inability to control himself, Marcus reaches out and takes my waist before gently pulling me back out of Roman's reach. My hand falls away from his junk as I feel his lips by my ear. "Point proven," he mutters, nodding down to the four men creeping closer to the mansion. "Can we focus on that, before you give my brother a reason to tear my dick straight off my body?"

My hard glare never leaves Roman's, holding it with the same intensity in which he holds mine, only forced to look away when the four cousins reach the bottom step and refuse to go any further.

Roman lets out a sigh and the four of us move toward them, not in the mood to have this conversation yelling back and forth up the stairs.

We get three quarters of the way down the stairs when Roman

decides that we've gone far enough. He comes to a stop and his brothers meet him on the same step while I hover a few steps back, not willing to get quite so close, especially as the brother who'd chased me down the long hallway seems to do nothing but glare at me.

"There are more conventional ways to arrange a meeting with us," Levi comments, already seeming bored with the conversation.

The oldest-looking brother stands in the center of the four and raises his chin, trying to appear as though he's not shitting himself, but I see the fear deep in his eyes, even in the darkness that surrounds the mansion. "We were left with no choice," he says. "Our father was killed three nights ago, and our brother only weeks before that. We are getting desperate."

Marcus moves just an inch, and it's enough to put the four brothers on edge, more than aware of just how unhinged their cousin can be. "Desperate men make desperate mistakes."

The guy who'd chased me snarls at Marcus, his filthy glare looking over him like shit under his shoe. "We don't make mistakes."

Marcus scoffs. "Standing outside a closed bathroom door while having a conversation about your plan to meet here after the party isn't considered a secret? Because it sure fucking sounds like one. You gave yourself away the moment you opened your mouth. Now, what's this about?"

The older brother glares at the chaser and draws the attention back to himself, the other two silently standing by, too afraid to even open their mouths. "Louis killed our father," he states, making it clear that they're not as clever as they think. "He came into our family home, tied him to a fucking chair, and burned the property to the ground. I want his blood."

A twisted grin pulls at Roman's lips, and while I see the raw truth of him laughing at these fools for not having figured out what's really going on here, they see nothing but a deranged, twisted man that's excited over the idea of spilling blood. "Then take it. What are you waiting for? He was here tonight. You could have ended him at any point, and yet you're standing here at the bottom of our stairs with your tails between your legs. You're weak. All of you are."

The brother presses his lips into a hard line, his jaw clenched as anger swirls through him. "We are not weak," he spits. "There is a difference between weakness and restraint. We are smart men and know when we are out of our league."

"Is that what you tell yourselves?" Marcus questions with an amused grin.

All four of the brothers glare at him, and I hold back a grin of my own. He has a point. It's clear they're here to ask a favor, but in this world, smart men know that favors don't get you anywhere. They are nothing but foolish.

Roman watches them through a narrowed, suspicious gaze, and I can practically see the wheels spinning in his head. "What's in it for us?" he questions, already seeing their request before it's even been spoken out loud. "If we take out Louis and end this war once and for all, then what do we get in return?"

"Our loyalty," the main dude spits, clearly not thrilled about it.

Roman laughs. "Your loyalty ain't worth shit to me," he says.

"Words are nothing but words. Victor was so far up my father's ass that he would have taken his own sons' lives at the very thought of them pledging their loyalty to us. You're telling me that you're willing to stand against your father's life work just to see us slit Louis' throat? I don't fucking buy it."

"What fucking choice do we have?" he demands. "We need Louis gone, and you three are the only ones fucked enough in the head to make it happen. Whether we like it or not, you're here for the long haul, and when it comes to self-preservation, we'll do whatever the fuck it takes. Too many lives have already been lost, and after our brother's role in getting you locked in that fucking castle, we owe it to you. We will vow our loyalty under the condition that Louis dies."

Roman watches them cautiously, studying each and every one of them. "You'll back us against our enemies? Against your own fucking blood?" he questions. "You know this move has already ruffled feathers. The family is divided, and a war is imminent. It's knocking on our door just waiting for us to let it in. Are you prepared for what being loyal to us truly means?"

Each of them swallows hard, quickly glancing at one another before finally nodding. "Yes, cousins," the front and center dude says. "We're prepared."

Roman glances to each of his brothers and the blank stare on each of their faces gives absolutely nothing away, yet somehow, they read each other's minds perfectly. "Okay," Roman finally says, his expression darkening more by the second. "Consider it a deal. Louis' head for a lifetime of loyalty," he says, slowly scanning his gaze over each of his cousins. "I do not need to remind you what happens to men who cross me and my brothers."

"We swore our loyalty," the chaser cuts in, not liking being questioned. "We stand by our word."

"Very well," Roman says. "We'll let you know once the job is done."

"Good," main dude says. "We look forward to it."

And just like that, the four cousins slink away into the shadows, and the boys turn to make their way back up the stairs, acting as though they didn't just get hired to complete a hit that they were responsible for in the first place. "Uhhhhhh," I say, following them up the stairs and back into the big house. "You guys realize that you're killing a man, to get payback for the other man that you killed?"

Marcus looks back at me, a wide grin stretching across his handsome face. "Poetic, isn't it?"

I shake my head and grumble under my breath. "Fucking insane is what it is."

We all make our way into the informal lounge room and the boys drop down onto the couches, instantly throwing ideas off each other for how they intend to take out yet another uncle. I shake my head as I cross the room and reach up over the fireplace, pulling down a fancy as fuck sword that's been wasted as decoration. "Aren't you guys tired?" I complain, striding across the room and laying the sword down on the ground before searching around the room and finding the long fire poker beside the fireplace.

I go to grab it as Marcus leans back in the couch. "Fucking dead tired," he mutters. "But there's too much to go over from that party.

We need to work out where our enemies lie."

I drop the fire poker down by the sword and scan the room again. "Shit, where am I going to find three more long pointy things?"

Levi grins. "I've got a long pointy thing for ya."

I choke on my own spit as Roman glares, cutting off whatever bullshit Marcus was going to follow that one up with. "What the fuck are you doing?"

"Trying to make a pentagram," I murmur as I realize that I can use the sheath from the sword. "Figured I'd try and summon the devil so he can take you assholes right back where you belong."

Marcus laughs and gets up from the couch before grabbing hold of me and dragging me back. "Fucking hell, babe," he says, dropping back onto the couch and pulling me down with him. "If we're going to the deepest pits of hell, then you better fucking believe that we're dragging you right along with us."

A grin plasters across my face and I turn into him, pressing my lips to his as his fingers lock onto the small zipper on my back. "I wouldn't have it any other way."

CHAPTER TWENTY FIVE

The moon hovers high in the sky as we barrel down the road, speeding through the twisty streets of the dodgiest area in town. My gaze lingers on the dark sky, watching the way the moon seems to travel with us, though I seem to get stalked by everything else, why not get stalked by the big old cheese ball in the sky?

"Why do we always have to do this shit in the middle of the night?" I question, my gaze flicking back to the guys.

Levi glances at me as Marcus silently sleeps like the living dead on my right. "You're kidding, right?" he questions. "You're not seriously asking us why we do shit at night."

My eyes roll so hard that I fear they might roll straight out of my eye sockets. "Of course I know why you have to do this at night, I'm just over it. I don't think I've had a proper night's sleep since meeting you guys. Like, can't you just wear a disguise? Grow a mustache or something?"

Roman's irritated huff from the front seat has me wanting to reach through the front and nut punch the bastard, but when he turns off into an area that has every single streetlight shot out, I forget what the hell we were talking about. "Well, this ain't shady at all," I murmur, my eyes wide as the need to lock the door slams through my chest. "Where are we?"

Roman drives toward a big warehouse and pulls up around back, keeping the SUV hidden in the shadows. "This is my father's warehouse," Roman says as Levi reaches back and gives Marcus a shove to wake him. "Anything you need in this world, I can guarantee you'll find it here. Drugs, guns, dirty money. This is the heart and soul of my father's operation. Sure, he has other warehouses in case this one gets raided, but without this, he's got nothing."

Levi's eyes flash with something dark as he slowly turns to meet my stare, and I see the twisted need to destroy his father glowing deep in his gaze. "And now, it's all ours."

Damn fucking straight!

The four of us pile out of the car and the boys fall in around me as though this is somewhere I need to be protected. The warehouse looks as though a good huff and puff could blow the fucker down, but something tells me that looks are deceiving. Giovanni DeAngelis is a smart businessman, and he's not going to allow his whole operation to come undone with a simple storm. There's more to the picture here, I'm just not seeing it yet.

The boys look left to right as though they're expecting someone to jump out at them, but after Roman's announcement during the party and the whole family divided, I wouldn't be surprised. Feathers are ruffled, people are on edge and want to align themselves with who they think will come out on top, and everyone who chooses wrong will be punished. The boys were lenient, giving the family a few days to think it over and make the right decision, because in the end, anyone who stands against these three assholes is already considered dead.

We approach a back door and my gaze scans over it. At first glimpse, it looks just like any shitty old back door on an abandoned warehouse, but looking closer, it's hard metal with an advanced tech locking system that my brain can't even begin to work out. "What the hell?" I breathe, taking a step back to get a wider view, realizing that the whole building is made out of this stuff, but to the naked eye, it appears as anything but.

Levi scoffs and steps in front of a keypad before entering a code and leaning down. My mouth drops open as it scans his eyes and I gape in wonder. "That did not just scan his eye," I say, unable to wrap my head around all of this. I mean, fuck! It looks like the kind of shit you see in a James Bond movie.

Marcus grins as the door unlocks and automatically slides back, allowing us entry. "The retinal scanner was my idea," he says proudly. "Pretty fucking cool, right?"

"Super cool, and not over the top at all," I smirk, following the boys inside.

"You do what you gotta do," Levi says, walking out in front of us as though he knows the place like the back of his hand. "People like Gia Moretti would do anything to find a place like this. We have to keep it protected."

My brows shoot up. "Then why would your father allow you access? Wouldn't he have scrubbed your eyeballs from the system to keep you out?"

Roman shrugs his shoulders. "If the old bastard could, he would have."

We walk into a dark room and go through a second security check before another big door slides open, spilling light out into the dark space. My eyes bug out of my head seeing the insanity before me. It's like a shopping mall at Christmas time. People working like slaves with stacks upon stacks of product.

"What the ever-loving fuck is this?" I breathe, following the boys lead as they walk into the clinical space. I can't help but notice just how cold it is, and as I glance around, I realize that all I see is products perfectly stacked and ready to go, each one of them labeled with Giovanni's mark. "How does all of this stuff get here?" I ask, unable to tear my gaze away from everything as I slink after the boys.

Marcus glances back at me. "It doesn't. Everything is manufactured right here."

"What?" I grunt, pausing as I scan the giant room again. Maybe I missed something. "Where?"

"Downstairs," Marcus says. "This fucker is three levels deep. We keep everything stacked up here for easy distribution."

"No shit."

A cocky grin pulls at his lips as I roll my eyes, realizing that these guys are so much deeper into their father's business than I originally thought. Hell, they even seem like the brains of the operation.

We stop in front of a big metal door and Roman enters a code into a keypad. A little light flicks red three times before turning green. We hear big metal locks unlatching, and with that, Roman pushes against the door and walks in.

I follow with wide eyes as we step through to a computer tech's holy trinity. Computers line every desk, big, small, even ones with rounded screens. There are things I've never even seen before or know what they do, but damn, they look expensive. I doubt even the FBI or CIA have this kind of technology. No wonder the boys have gotten away with the type of shit they do for so long.

"Hey, Mick," Roman says, walking up to the guy running the world's most elaborate computer lab. "How's it going?"

The guy, Mick, pushes back from his desk chair, and as he turns to face us, his eyes come straight to mine. He clearly wasn't expecting a tag along. He eyes me warily but quickly decides that if I'd been welcomed in by the boys, all is good. "Hey man," he says, leaning into Roman and doing that weird hand thing that guys do before reaching around and clapping him on the back. He gives Levi and Marcus a welcoming nod before turning and facing a big, frosted glass wall.

I watch him with a curious stare as he steps around his impressive desk and moves toward the wall, pressing a button that has my mouth dropping open again. The frost on the glass fades away, showing off the massive warehouse with the best vantage point to see every angle of the room.

The workers all go about their jobs and I inch closer to the glass wall. "Nobody even blinked," I mutter, knowing damn well that had I been on the other side of the glass and the boss' three sons just walked in, I'd at least risk a sneaky glance. "Are they just that disciplined, or do they not give a shit?"

Mick smirks with a proud sparkle in his eye. "We're completely concealed in here. It's like the two-way glass you see in those interrogation rooms in cop shows. We see them, but they can't see us."

"No shit," I breathe, completely impressed.

"Yeah," he says. "Not gonna lie, I was impressed by it when I first started here, but the amount of wedgies being plucked, ball grabs, and dumb shit I've witnessed because they don't know I'm watching makes it a little less cool."

"Can we get back on track?" Roman says, looking bored. "We don't have all night."

Mick clears his throat, and his eyes widen just a fraction, proving that while he may be on friendly terms with Roman, he's still shit scared of him, and I don't blame the guy. He's probably the guy Giovanni hired to scrub clean every surveillance camera in town whenever the boys decide to sneak out at night.

"Right," Mick says, nodding and shuffling over so that the boys each get an equal view of the warehouse floor. "Everything is right on schedule. We have deliveries going out tomorrow night and a few local guys making collections over the next few hours. The shipment set for Mexico is experiencing a few hold ups though."

"Why?" Roman growls, his sharp stare slicing back to Mick's.

"We've heard some whispers about a raid. They're expecting us to make a move tomorrow, so we thought we would hold off for a few days. I haven't been able to get a hold of your father, which is why I called you down here. Figured you'd have a little insight on that."

"Who tipped them off?" Levi questions, stepping closer to the glass wall and slowly scanning over each of the workers.

Mick shakes his head. "I've checked over everyone, gone through their phone records and traced their movements. Our guys are clean. This came from somewhere else."

"Fuck," Marcus says, his gaze falling back to Roman's. "After the ball last night, it could be anyone."

Roman nods, deep in thought, his lips pressing into a tight line. "Keep tracing it," he tells the guy. "As for the shipment, I want you to handle it. Personally set it up with the client, don't even tell the driver where he is going or what he's carrying until after he's left my warehouse."

Mick's brows furrow and something flashes in his eyes. "Your warehouse?" he questions. "Is something going on that I need to know about?"

Roman glances at his brothers before turning back to Mick. "Changes are coming," he says. "Keep your head down, and everything will be fine. I like you Mick. I don't want you to give me a reason to have to replace you. Is that understood?"

"Crystal clear," he says, nervously glancing my way before returning back to Roman. "Now as for your ... personal stock?"

Roman's lips twist into an amused grin as my brows shoot up, realizing that this is the inside guy who's been switching out all of Giovanni's labeling for the boys'. "It's fine, she knows all about it," Roman explains. "But these are some of the changes we were referring to. We're running our father out, so we're going to need every last one of these products rebranded as our own."

Mick's eyes widen and seeing the high racks stacked to the brim with product, I can only imagine just how big of a task they're asking of him.

"You … you want me to rebrand *all of it?*" he questions, watching the boys cautiously, making sure he heard Roman right.

"That's exactly what we're asking of you," he says. "No more hiding. Every client now belongs to us, every dealer and run will have our names on it. I want every account payable to us. Hell, I want the fucking factory transferred into our names. Can you do that?"

Mick nods and it's clear from the hesitation in his eyes that he knows just how dangerous a move like this could be for him.

"You now work for me and my brothers," Roman tells him. "Look out for us just as you've always done, have our back and I swear to you, we will have yours."

"You know I've got you covered," Mick says. "But your father—"

"My father can't do shit," Levi says, stepping back from the glass and crossing his strong arms over his chest. "Though I suggest you watch your back for a while. There's only so much we can do to help you, but he will know it was you, and while we can update the security and lock him out, there's no stopping him from getting vengeance some other way. Don't assume that we can always be there to save your ass, keep your eyes open."

Sweat coats his forehead as he moves back around to his desk and drops down into his seat. "Alright," he says, pulling up some kind of fancy system that I can't even begin to understand. "Let's make this happen."

He starts madly typing away at his keyboard, and I can't help but watch over his shoulder as he pulls up the boys' branding and sends it directly to the printer. All shipments are put on hold, and I don't doubt the second we leave, a shitload of workers are going to be called in to get everything ready and rebranded.

The order goes out and I watch through the glass as the workers look over their new instructions and immediately get to work, tearing off the old branding with their brows pinched in confusion. "I hope these guys are going to get some kind of bonus for this," I mutter under my breath, imagining just how pissed I'd be if I'd learned that I had to rebrand millions of little pills, baggies, and who the hell knows what else, after spending countless hours doing the job in the first place.

The boys awkwardly look between each other before Roman rolls his eyes. "Fine," he grunts, clearly not thrilled about it. "The workers can get double time as long as it is completed by this time next week."

Mick's eyes widen with surprise and he nods, more than down with this plan, though it's clear by the look on his face that he hadn't expected this, not in a million years. He gets busy, and as I watch the warehouse workers kick into gear, my brows furrow. "Wait," I rush out. "If you rebrand everything, your father is going to know that you guys were the new dealer stealing his clients all along. I thought you wanted to pin it on Antonio."

Levi shrugs his shoulders. "Plans change, babe," he says. "The fallout from Antonio's death is too good to change the story now. All eyes are on Louis, and I don't intend on bringing the attention back to us. With any luck, they'll all be dead before they can put the pieces together and realize it was a perfectly planned series of executions."

"And as for the branding?" I question, pointedly glancing toward the glass wall.

Marcus steps in behind me, his arms curling around my waist. "Rebranding everything was going to happen at some point, so why wait? Our original plan has already gone to shit and our father was going to figure out it was us eventually. Plus, he's not exactly in a position to stop us. Now's the time to make our move. Besides, don't you think it's a little thrilling, knowing he's about to feel the sting of our knife in his back?"

I scoff and a grin pulls at my lips. "I think he's already feeling it," I laugh. "But as long as you're sure, then I'm down."

Marcus grinds against my ass. "You're always down."

I roll my eyes and once the boys have finished their business, we make our way back out of the impressive tech room, leaving Mick to get busy calling in all his workers.

Marcus drops his heavy arm over my shoulder and leads me back out the way we came, keeping us concealed from all of the night shift workers. Levi stops to haul a big bag of pills over his shoulder and grabs a few stacks of dirty cash.

We reach the first exit, and as Marcus stops to hash in the code that Roman had only used twenty minutes ago, I hear the telltale sound of a big roller door opening and can't resist turning back.

A black Mercedes pulls to a stop outside the roller door and the boys slow, turning back to see who's coming. Roman's shoulders tighten and for a brief second, I wonder if it's Giovanni. Hope surges through me, and as much as I never want to see that man again, if it is him, it gives us a way to locate Roman's son.

The four of us pause and Marcus discreetly pulls me behind a big stack of dirty cash that's wrapped in plastic, keeping us hidden and out of sight. Though if someone were really looking, they'd be able to find us.

Roman and Levi move in front of the stack while keeping themselves discreetly tucked away. I can only see the top of Levi's head but there's a morphed reflection of Roman in the plastic wrap and I'm able to make out the way he slowly pulls a gun from the back of his pants.

All eyes remain locked on the black Mercedes, and as the door opens, I hold my breath. If it's Giovanni, there might even be a chance that the baby is tucked away in the back seat.

My heart races. I've never wanted to see that asshole more in my life.

A pair of expensive black shoes hit the ground and I lean out from behind the stack of cash, needing a clearer look. Marcus' hand curls around my elbow, ready and waiting to yank me back if need be, but when the man steps out of the car and his familiar head appears over the top of the open door, my chest sinks.

It's not Giovanni, but hell, I wasn't expecting this guy.

My brows shoot up and I gape up at Marcus. "Is that our dealer?" I question, my voice hitching a little too high for someone who's supposed to be hiding.

Marcus scoffs, equally as stunned. We were expecting to see a lot of things here tonight, but not him, and certainly not in an expensive suit worth more than he could possibly afford and a car that looks as though it gets valet parked every night. "It sure fucking is," Marcus says as Levi and Roman discreetly return to us.

"The fuck is going on here?" Levi questions, keeping his gaze locked on our dealer, the guy who is supposed to be shit broke, living in the worst part of town in a home that's falling apart.

"I smell a fucking rat," Roman says, anger sweeping over his sharp features.

The last time we paid a visit to our dealer, his home looked ransacked. Broken glass and drugs littered the floors, and it looked like someone had made a run for it with as much cash as they could carry. And while it's definitely possible to get robbed in that neighborhood, it didn't feel right. Roman thought it was a setup, especially considering the dealer never called to beg for his life.

We watch him a moment, watch how familiar he is with the workers loading up his car with product, and how seamless the transaction is. A lowly local drug dealer wouldn't be pulling up like this, and the boys sure as fuck wouldn't risk someone so disposable and unreliable to know the location of the heart and soul of their business. No, this guy is a fucking rat. He's far too comfortable here.

"He's been working for our father this whole fucking time," Levi comments, seeing exactly what I see. "He was planted into our lives. I knew that asshole was too quick to offer his services after we shot his boss. Father's got the little bitch spying on us."

"He knew," Roman murmurs, shaking his head as he lets out a heavy sigh and moves back to the electronic keypad. "All this fucking time. Our father knew the competitor was us. That old bastard. He's always five steps ahead of us."

We push out through the door and Levi quickly gets to work on the next one. "So, what do we do about it?" I question, not having dealt with a rat quite like this before.

Roman draws his phone out of his pocket and catches the door behind us before it can close all the way. "The only thing we can do," he says, hitting a button on his phone and listening to the shrill ring of the dealer's phone across the warehouse. "We invite him for dinner."

CHAPTER TWENTY SIX

Leaning over the top of the bar, I fill myself a glass of something smooth, needing the little hit to help me relax. It's been a long as fuck day, and with the dealer due to arrive in the next hour, I need to be prepared.

It's well after nine and I'm not going to lie, when Roman suggested that we were going to have him over for dinner, I kinda figured he meant a normal dinner time like seven or eight, but nooooooo, not these assholes. Apparently when you invite someone over for dinner, what they really mean is *'why don't you come over for a midnight snack?'* I was even stupid enough not to snack so that I didn't spoil my meal, but now my stomach is fucking pissed.

I knew I should have snuck into the dining room and stolen a juicy piece of steak a few hours ago. My hunger has turned me into a raging bitch, and when I'm like this, not even serial killers would want to stand in my way.

White rum fills my glass, and just to be fancy, I drop a few perfectly round ice cubes into my glass. I take a sip and my eyes flutter in delight, but the way the cool liquid drops right to the bottom of my empty stomach only serves to remind me that I'M FUCKING STARVING!

Straightening up from the bar, I place the cool glass down on the polished wood and go to drop my ass down on the stool, only the intense feeling of someone watching me brings me up short. I suck in a breath as my heart leaps into my throat.

I flip around, my sharp gaze sailing straight to the shadows of the darkened room, just as the boys had trained me. My gaze sweeps from left to right and back again. Coming up blank, I try to convince myself that it was all in my head, until three, looming figures step out from each of the remaining corners of the room.

Black ski masks cover their faces and my hand curls around my glass, ready to launch it at one of the fuckers' heads, only as they move a little closer into the dull light of the bar, my grip loosens.

The three tall men slowly move toward me, each of them shirtless with nothing but a pair of black pants, their faces completely covered by the masks, showing nothing but their dark, obsidian eyes.

They don't make a sound, and if it weren't for their familiar tattoos, I'd have absolutely no idea who was who. Marcus stands front and center, the tattoo of Felicity staring back at me, but it's the hunger in his eyes that has me slowly pulling myself up from the stool.

Levi is at my right, the intricate, dark lines of his tattoo peeking out from under the base of his ski mask and trailing right over his chest and down his right arm. Roman silently comes at me from the left, and I have to slightly turn my head to see him fully. His body is so tight and it's clear that he holds a shitload of tension in his muscles. He's never fully able to relax, but hell, for some reason, he decided to participate in whatever the hell this is, and I'm so down with that.

They all slowly move toward me, and my heart rate picks up as my eyes move from left to right, wanting to watch them all. My core clenches as a deep dark thrill shoots through me. If this isn't what I hope it is, then I'll never forgive them for working me up like this.

They're still halfway across the room but I'm already panting, the anticipation enough to bring me to my knees, and hell, if that's where they want me, that's exactly where I'll be.

My throat gets dry and I reach back, curling my fingers around the cool glass, and with one smooth motion, I bring the rim to my bottom lip and throw back the white rum, indulging in the sweet burn as it sails down my throat.

Their gazes darken by the second, and I see each of them straining through their pants, the desperate need to have them sending me into a flurry of desperation.

Holy hell. What have I gotten myself into?

They creep closer and closer, and my panting becomes too much. I need to have them now. I need to feel their hands on my body, filling every fucking crevice and making me scream like never before.

My body grows hotter by the second and the anticipation is almost too much to bear. If this is some sick, twisted joke and they're going to turn and walk away, then I'm going to be pissed.

Their eyes are like hot lasers upon my skin as they step into me, standing so close I can feel the warmth radiating off their skin, I could just die.

Levi meets my stare as the desire reflected in his eyes is enough to have me melting right here on the spot. "Fuck me," I murmur under my breath. His eyes sparkle, and though I can't see his lips beneath the mask, I know he's grinning at the way the three of them have me all wound up.

He drops to his knees, and as I glance down at him, I can't help but notice the way his tight abs roll and bunch with his movements. He tilts his chin up, holding my heated stare as his hands gently curl around the back of my leg.

He pulls on it, forcing my foot off the ground before gently placing it down on his strong thigh and sliding his hands up the back of my leg until he reaches the top of my thigh-high boot. It's a subtle movement, but the way he grips the small zipper between his fingers and slowly drags it down my leg is one of the most sensual things I've ever experienced. Perhaps it's his eyes on mine as he does it, or maybe it's just the idea of what they plan on doing to me once the boots are stripped from my body.

He pulls the boot free, tossing it aside, and I groan as Levi places my foot back down and switches it for the next, repeating the same agonizingly slow and sensual movements. I'm completely mesmerized by him. He has my complete attention, that is until Marcus' warm hands brush over my exposed waist.

My eyes snap toward his and the fire within them makes my

stomach clench. They're so dark and deadly, and just the knowledge of a man like him wanting me has me soaking wet with need. His fingers trail down my waist, capturing the front of my jeans.

Marcus pulls against my jeans and I fumble forward a step, as my other boot is completely pulled from my foot and tossed aside. Levi releases his hold on my foot, and I quickly catch myself before tumbling straight into Marcus. His fingers are rough on the front of my jeans and he pops the button with quick, skilled fingers. A soft gasp tears from my throat as he holds my gaze, refusing to release me.

The zipper slides down, and just the thought of his hands being so close to my almost exposed pussy has me panting with desperation.

With me now a step closer to Marcus, Roman slips in behind me, his wide, strong chest pressed right up against my back. I know we have a bit of a strained relationship, but holy mother of all things sweet and holy, I'm more than willing to put it all aside for just a few hours with him.

Desperate to feel his warm skin beneath my fingers, I slip my hand behind my back and feel the sharp ridges of his abs. A soft escape of needy breath hits my ear, and my eyes immediately flutter with the sweetest satisfaction. It's one thing knowing that Roman has it bad for me and refuses to acknowledge it, but it's a whole different situation when he physically can't resist the temptation and his lack of control gets the best of him. Knowing that my touch alone could bring him to his knees makes me feel more powerful than any woman should ever have the right to feel.

He moves in tighter behind me, plastering himself to my back as his fingers move up over my body. They get higher and higher, and for a moment, I wonder if he's planning on gripping my throat, but his movements pause at the collar of my cropped tank.

His hands fist into the material and swiftly tear it straight off my body. A gasp pulls from the back of my throat and my body stiffens and jolts with the raw intensity flowing through my veins. Roman's hands instantly return to my skin, brushing over it with need, and my body trembles beneath his touch.

Marcus pushes my jeans down over my hips, taking my thong right along with it and the desperation is too much. I turn back and meet Roman's heated gaze over my shoulder and the fire pulsing between us is stronger than it's ever been. I don't know if it's the ski mask or because we're not one on one, but something has him willing to let go of all the tension and just relax. It's almost as though he's trying to hide his real emotions, to allow himself to be in the moment, but not today. If he wants to indulge in me, then he's going to do it completely.

Reaching back, my fingers slip under the fabric of his ski mask, and I pull it up just enough to expose his inviting lips. My hand curls around the back of his head, and not being able to help myself, I push up onto my tippy toes and fuse our lips together.

His body stiffens at first. He hadn't been expecting this. Hell, it's probably one of the reasons he was so down to wear the ski mask, but it's not like I was expecting this either.

My lips move gently over his, allowing him the chance to pull back or take control, and as his body slowly begins to relax into my touch, he kisses me back, reminding me just how good it really is.

My pants are pulled right off my feet and Marcus throws them aside with my boots and the shredded scraps of my tank, and as Roman's hands continue exploring my skin, Levi moves in closer on his knees. He pushes my legs apart and Marcus steps to my side, allowing Levi the space he needs to work his magic.

His warm lips brush along my inner thigh and a soft groan bubbles through my chest, the anticipation of what's about to happen almost too much to bear. I'm left wondering if he pulled off his mask or just raised it the same way I'd done to Roman, but it's not important enough to tear my lips away to look.

He slowly kisses his way higher, teasing and taunting my body with what's about to come, and my knees quickly grow weak, but Roman's strong hold keeps me upright.

Butterflies storm through my stomach, and with every touch of their hands, their tiny little wings seem to flutter faster until Levi's lips finally close over my clit, his tongue gently flicking that sensitive bundle of nerves. My body jolts with electricity and I gasp into Roman's mouth before feeling the smile pulling at his warm lips.

Levi doesn't dare ease up, teasing me with his skilled tongue, sucking and nipping as he pushes two thick fingers deep inside of me. My fingers knot into Roman's hair and I pull back from his kiss, needing a chance to catch my breath, but the DeAngelis brothers are not patient men.

Marcus moves in closer, his fingers skimming across my ribs and up over my bare breast as his lips press down on my shoulder. His fingers trail soft circles around my nipples, pebbling beneath his touch, and when his fingers close over it and give it a gentle pinch, my body flinches. "Ohhh, fuck," I moan, melting back into Roman's kiss as Levi worships my cunt as though it's the only thing keeping him breathing.

The familiar sound of a zipper is heard through the room, and considering both Marcus and Roman's hands are on my body and only one of Levi's hands is buried deep inside of me, I have to assume it's him freeing his big monster cock.

A thrill shoots through me, imagining the way he's working it up and down with a tight fist, and I can't resist reaching for both of his brothers. My fingers skim over the top of Marcus' black jeans, and I make quick work of freeing him, groaning as his velvety cock hangs low and hard. This thing should come with a warning.

My fingers brush up and down his impressive length as I pull the zipper down on Roman's jeans, the desperation to feel them both rocking through me. His cock springs free and I waste no time closing my fists around them both, slowly working up and down, matching the rhythm of Levi's tongue flicking against my clit.

My body quivers and shakes as Marcus' soft groan fills the air. I find myself pulling free of Roman's kiss, only to turn toward Marcus. He releases my tit and curls his hand around the back of my neck, forcing me closer before crushing his lips to mine in a bruising, dominant kiss, a low growl rumbling through his wide chest.

Levi curls his fingers deep inside of me and I gasp into Marcus' mouth, my knees shaking and getting weaker by the second. Liking the way my body responds, Levi goes again, rubbing his fingers over the same spot deep inside my cunt over and over, making my eyes roll in the back of my head. He sucks my clit into his mouth and flicks it with his tongue before doing it again and making me groan.

My knees buckle, and if it weren't for Roman's strong hold around my waist, I'd already be a puddle on the ground. "Oh, God," I pant, pulling free from Marcus' lips as I tighten my hold on both of their cocks, picking up my pace and rolling my thumb over their tips. "I'm gonna come."

Levi's wicked grin against my clit is everything, and with one more swipe of his curled fingers deep inside of me, I come hard. A loud cry tears from the back of my throat as my pussy convulses, turning into a shattered mess. Levi doesn't ease up on his tongue or fingers and I ride it out, practically fucking his face as Roman's excited breath brushes over my shoulder. "Oh, God," I cry a little louder, my knees buckling and my fists tightening around them.

My orgasm tears through my veins, every nerve ending set on fire, and I throw my head back to Roman's shoulder, clenching my eyes as the high rocks through my body. "Fuuuuuck," I groan low, letting it overtake me until it finally begins to ease.

My eyes open and I breathe hard, dropping my gaze to Levi's and watching the way he slowly strokes his thick cock. I get the briefest glimpse of him licking his lips before he pulls his mask back down into place, and though I don't see either Marcus or Roman do the same, I sense it as the atmosphere in the room morphs into something much darker and more intense.

Roman adjusts his hold at my waist and pushes me down to my knees, forcing me to release both him and Marcus as I crash down directly in front of Levi. He stabilizes me with a hand on my hip, and as I catch my breath and look him in the eye, I find nothing but intense hunger. I have no idea how they intend to do this. Well, I have a slight idea, but either way, I'm down for whatever they want.

Roman comes down behind me, his hand falling to my ass and giving it a firm squeeze as Marcus remains on his feet, slowly stroking his long, thick cock.

My mouth waters for him, but there's too much jostling coming from Levi to risk taking Marcus just yet. Turning my gaze back to Levi, I find him resting back, ready and waiting for me to ride him until the sun comes up.

Roman lifts me from behind, placing me on top of his brother and I immediately take him, my already needy cunt stretching as I'm lowered down on top of him. The boys don't make a sound, but the way Levi takes my hips and digs his fingers into my flesh tells me exactly what I need to know.

I slowly move, taking it easy to get my body prepared for more as I feel Roman moving in closer to my ass. His fingers curl over my shoulder and he pushes me down until my chest is flat against Levi's, leaving my ass up in the air, ready for him to take whatever he needs.

I bite down on my lip and push back as his tip nears my entrance, more than eager to feel him stretching me wide. Roman takes my hip with one hand to steady me and holds his cock in the other, slowly guiding himself in.

My ass burns for just a moment, and he strokes his thumb over my hips, letting me know that he'll be gentle and give me the time I need to get comfortable.

Letting out a strained breath, I lift slightly off Levi's chest and pull at his mask until his inviting lips are staring back at me, and without wasting a goddamn second, I press my lips to his, letting his intoxicating kiss distract me from the pain.

My body relaxes and I quickly get used to the feel of them both buried deep inside me, and only when I'm ready do I push back against Roman, silently letting him know he's good to do his thing, though I just hope he doesn't fuck me like he did on the hood of the SUV. It's one thing to have a man slamming into your pussy like that, but my ass has given strict instructions that whoever shall pass, shall do so with the utmost respect.

Catching my drift, Roman starts to move, going slow and steady while also fucking me deep. He moves back then thrusts his hips forward as I come up slightly on my knees, giving Levi space to move up into me. They match each other's thrusts, one pushing in while the other pulls back. It's the most erotic kind of dance. I fucking love it.

Roman pulls me up off Levi's chest and curls his hands around my body, holding me tight to him. He grips my right tit with one hand as his other trails down my body, only stopping when his fingertips brush over my clit.

A sharp gasp tears out of me, and as he starts rubbing tight little circles, just the way he knows I like it, my gasp turns into a needy moan.

Marcus moves into my side, his big cock proudly standing at attention, and I can't resist taking him into my mouth. My fingers curl around his base, gently squeezing as my mouth closes around him, and just because I like achieving a standing ovation from everything I do, I look up at him with my big blue eyes as I flick my tongue over his tip.

I work up and down his long cock until I feel him at the back of my throat, using both hands wherever needed. The boys hold onto me tighter, and while they still remain silent, their short hisses of breath lets me know that I'm giving them more than what they bargained for.

Roman and Levi pick up their pace, fucking me harder until I'm groaning around Marcus' cock. My eyes roll back in my head, and despite only coming a moment ago, I can already feel my body reaching its limit.

Hands roam over my body. Teasing. Grabbing. Pinching. Flicking. And I cry out, the sound muffled by the bulging cock halfway down my throat.

Each stroke, each touch, each thrust, pushes me closer and closer to the edge, and just as Roman's fingers close around my clit and give a gentle pinch, my body completely comes undone.

My orgasm rocks through me and everything clenches. I squeeze both Roman and Levi as the walls of my pussy begin to spasm and my brows pull together, concentrating hard on not biting down on Marcus' cock. The high explodes through me and it's so intense that tears spring to my eyes.

My body instantly goes weak and Roman holds me up, refusing to let me give up now. The boys keep moving and the high only gets wilder and more intense, then just as I reach my absolute peak, all three of the brothers come hard.

I taste Marcus in my mouth, feeling him spurting his hot seed right into the back of my throat as Levi grips low on my hip, his whole body flinching as he pours himself deep into my cunt.

Roman thrusts hard and stills behind me, his fingers digging into my hip as his others keep circling my clit. As they all slow their movements, I swallow down everything Marcus has on offer before finally pulling back and releasing him.

Heavy pants tear from my chest as I try to catch my breath, and as Roman releases my hip, I fall forward, barely catching myself before slamming heavily into Levi's chest. Roman's hand splays on my lower back as he gently pulls from within me, being careful not to hurt me, and as he moves away, I'm left with just Levi. "What the ever-loving fuck just happened?" I breathe, dropping my hand on his chest beside my face.

Levi's heart races under my ear as he simply stands and cradles me in his arms. Marcus and Roman are nowhere to be seen, but something tells me they still have their eyes on me. Levi goes to make a move and I raise my head off his chest. "Wait," I call out.

He pauses and I reach for the bar, nearly falling out of his arms as I curl my fingers around the white rum, pulling it into the safety of my arms. "Alright," I say, glancing up at Levi with his mask still firmly in place as I uncap the rum and bring it to my lips, needing all the help I can get to bring me down from such a wicked high. "March on, soldier. There's still two hours before your dealer is supposed to show up and I wanna do it again."

CHAPTER TWENTY SEVEN

A loud buzzer sails through the mansion as I walk in through the living room to find the three boys. A devilish grin settles over Marcus' face as he glances back at Roman, who couldn't look more bored if he tried. He quickly looks my way, and before my heart even gets the chance to clench, his dark eyes are gone again.

"Is that the dealer?" I ask, pausing in the doorway, trying to convince myself that his silent rejection doesn't sting, especially after he spent twenty minutes buried in my ass.

Levi glances back at me, his eyes sparkling with the knowledge of what we've spent the last few hours doing, and damn it, I'm lucky I can even walk. "Sure is," he says, pushing up off the couch and holding out a hand.

Reaching out, I gingerly take his hand as Marcus pulls out a phone and presses a button that I'm sure has something to do with the front gate. We all walk out to the massive foyer and a soft groan slips through my lips at the dull ache between my legs.

It's only been a few hours since the boys surprised me in the bar, and I can't even believe it happened. It was everything and more. The way they touched me and had my heart racing. I couldn't get enough. Having just one of them to myself is incredible, but getting all three at the same time? God, no woman on earth could possibly be this lucky.

I can't help but watch through the side window as the dealer speeds down the long driveway in a beat-up piece of shit car. A laugh bubbles up through my chest. "Wow, he came prepared for a show," I tell the boys, more than amused by the shitty car he probably just stole off the street, though I'm not going to lie, I prefer the black Mercedes he was hauling drugs around in last night.

The shit box pulls to a stop and Roman reaches for the door, pulling it open and sending a cool breeze blasting through the foyer. We step out into the night and watch the dealer from the top of the stairs.

He gets out of the car and looks up at the massive home with apprehension. He's nervous and he should be. The boys have never invited him anywhere, let alone a private dinner at their family home. It's not normal protocol for a dealer and his suppliers, it's so abnormal that just the thought of stepping inside this property should have him shitting his pants.

The dude puts on a brave face and looks up at the boys with a tight smile before reaching into the back and grabbing a bag, most likely filled with the cash he owes them. Assuming he doesn't know what's been going on with Giovanni and his sons, he probably thinks this is their way of sending a message about the missed meet a few weeks ago. He probably assumes that if he gives the boys what he owes them and more, he'll get knocked around a bit and then sent on his way.

If only he were smart enough to know what happens when you cross one of the DeAngelis brothers. The asshole probably assumes he'll be safe if he keeps kissing Giovanni's ass.

He throws the bag over his shoulder, and judging by the way Marcus' body stiffens, he doesn't trust this guy one bit. Who knows what the hell he's got hidden within that bag, though we'll know soon. There's no way the boys will let him get a foot inside their home without checking him first.

The dealer reaches the top step and gives the boys a tight smile. "This is about the money, isn't it?" he questions boldly before tossing the bag at Roman's feet, the light sheen of sweat across his forehead suggesting that he's just a tad nervous. "I swear, the other week was a complete shit show. I had the cops on my tail and had to clear out for a while. Everything I owe you is in there."

Roman watches him for a moment, completely ignoring the bag at his feet. The silence is loud and the boys allow it to go on just long enough for it to feel uncomfortable. "Why don't you come inside?" Roman suggests. "We've put out quite a spread."

My stomach growls at the thought of finally getting a meal, but something tells me the only thing getting roasted tonight is him.

He gives a tight smile but clearly seeing no way out, he nods and allows Roman to lead him through the door. The dealer walks by Marcus, Levi, and me, and we wait a moment before turning and following them through.

The big doors fall closed behind us, leaving the bag of cash out on the front steps, and as we walk back through the foyer, I glance up at Levi, my brows furrowed with frustration. "So ... when Roman said that we've put on a spread, did he actually mean that? Cause I'm starving," I murmur, keeping my tone low enough so that my whining doesn't ruin whatever stoic, tension-filled vibe Roman is going for.

Levi glances down at me, his brows pinched as he tries to figure out if I'm being serious or not. "You haven't eaten?" he questions. "It's almost the middle of the night."

I shake my head. "Why would I?" I question, confusion settling deep in my veins. "You guys invited this asshole for dinner. I didn't want to spoil a good meal, but now I'm kinda wondering if 'dinner' was a code word for something else."

A smirk pulls at his lips. "It's definitely something else," he says. "Why don't you go and eat. We'll handle this. Besides, what we have planned for this guy ... it's not exactly something you're going to want to see."

My brows arch high, and just like that I know that I'll be hanging around for as long as it takes. What's a little hunger in the middle of the night?

"So, uhhh, nice place you've got here," the dealer murmurs, trying to ease the tension in the room while effectively cutting off every thought of food sailing through my mind. "I bet it would have cost a pretty penny to build something like this."

"Wouldn't know," Roman says in a bored tone, not even bothering to look back as he continues leading the guy through the mansion. "It's my father's place."

My eyes all but roll right out of my head. If anyone knows anything about building mansions and the costs that go into it, it's Roman, but apparently that's not exactly a topic he feels the need to discuss, not tonight anyway.

"Your father's place?" the guy stammers out, his eyes widening just a fraction, his first real hint that things aren't quite what they seem, though he should have figured that out the moment Roman called and invited him here. "Are you guys … uhh … house sitting or something like that?"

"Something like that," Roman mutters darkly, his tone taking on a subtle hint of excitement, one that only people who have been around him for a while would be able to point out. "He's on an extended vacation."

"Oh, umm … cool," he says, trying to shake off his unease.

Silence fills the mansion once again, but the second Roman leads us out the back and into the cool night's breeze, the odd tension seems to fade away. We walk for another minute, and I do all that I can not to wrap my arms around myself and start shivering. This is definitely a blanket and warm fire kind of night, but I'm not about to destroy whatever vibe the boys are going for by having my teeth chattering in the background.

Roman leads us out to the massive courtyard that overlooks the most stunning, modern pool I've ever seen. There's a light layer of fog resting on top of the water, and the expensive lights built into it make it appear as though it's glowing. A small fire pit has been set up, and I try not to be so obvious about my relief.

Roman finally stops walking and indicates to one of the many chairs around the fire. "Why don't you take a seat," he offers as his brother drops down next to the warm fire. I do the same and immediately lean forward in my chair, not bothering to scoot all the way back into it as I feel the warmth brushing across my skin.

The dealer hesitantly takes a seat, and I don't miss the way he cautiously watches Roman. I don't doubt that he's heard everything he needs to know about the men sitting around him. He would have done his homework, and considering he's been working for Giovanni long enough to be in his top ranks, he'd know more than the average shit-kicker dealer found out on the streets.

Roman walks back toward a fully stocked bar and glances toward our guest. "What's your poison?" he questions, grabbing a few glasses, presumably for his brothers.

"I'll take whatever you're having," he says, his gaze flicking around the small group as he tries to make a show of relaxing, but to be completely honest, he looks anything but relaxed. In fact, he's doing nothing but making himself appear constipated.

Roman goes about his business pouring drinks, and I try not to smile at the way he pulls out a bottle of white rum and fills it just enough before adding a few cubes of ice, just the way I like it. I've got to give it to him, the asshole certainly pays attention.

Marcus and Levi rest back in their chairs, both of them keeping their heavy gazes on the dealer, undoubtedly making him even more uncomfortable as they wait for Roman. Their twisted little moves have me pressing my lips into a hard line, desperate to focus on anything to keep me from laughing.

Roman finishes what he's doing and piles up the drinks on a silver tray before setting it down on a table and handing them out, leaving me for last. As Roman hands me the cool glass, our fingers brush and his sharp gaze holds mine for just a moment, kicking my heart into gear.

I swallow hard as I take it from him, but when his expression hardens and he snatches his gaze away, anger pours through my veins like molten lava scorching everything in its path. The fuck does he think he's doing looking at me like that? It was only a few short hours ago that his thick cock was buried deep in my ass. The least he could do is offer me a smile. For fuck's sake.

Trying to ignore his usual asshole tendencies, I focus on the game at hand.

The dealer is offered a drink and as he takes a long, needy sip, I realize that after all this time, we've never even asked him his name, but then, I guess it no longer matters. When the cops come knocking on the door, questioning if we know a man by the name of *blah, blah, blah,* we can honestly say that we don't, which is nice in this world. Honesty is rare around here and it goes a long way.

Finding a pair of balls, the dealer drops the glass to his thigh and glances up at the boys, skimming his gaze around the circle, bypassing me, and coming back to Roman, who's obviously taking the lead on this one. "So, what's this all about?" he questions. "I assume that it's not often you invite your dealers for a late drink."

Roman lets out a breath and leans back in his chair. "You're right," he says, his gaze dropping to the contents of his glass as I notice Dill and Doe prancing across the yard as though only just realizing that we're out here. "We don't like to bring people into our lives. We've always been private men; however, your sales skills have managed to catch our attention, and because of that, we have a proposition for you."

His brows fly up into his hairline and he gapes at Roman as though he can't believe what he's hearing. "A proposition?" he questions, a sigh of relief in his tone. "I thought this was about missing our meet the other week."

"We'll get to that," Roman says, a dark hint in his tone. "For now, let's discuss what you can do for us."

A grin pulls at his lips as he leans forward in his seat, the flames from the fire sending flickering beams of light across his face. "I'm listening."

Roman pauses a moment as Dill and Doe come to sit by us, casually watching the fire all to the dealer's horror. His eyes widen with fear at the massive wolves, but he keeps his mouth shut, waiting to hear whatever the fuck Roman has to offer him. "You strike me as a smart man," Roman starts, bullshitting his way through this by starting with a compliment. "So I am sure that you would have heard whispers that my father is being run out."

His brows shoot up again. "I, ahhh, no. I hadn't heard that."

Roman nods. "Well, consider yourself now in the know," he says before continuing. "My brothers and I will be taking over the family business, which means there will be some changes."

"How am I supposed to fit into these changes?" he questions. "I'm just a street dealer."

"You've shown promise," Roman admits. "Your ability to sell products is like none other that we have seen … at least not for a while. Taking over our father's business means that we will be taking over his stock, and we're going to need someone to move it for us."

The dealer watches Roman through narrowed eyes, and I can see the gears ticking inside his head. "How much product are we talking?" the dealer questions. "There's only so many connections that I have in this industry. I'm not sure how much more I could move."

"Not even for a handsome bonus?"

Interest sparkles in his eyes and he takes a moment, throwing back what's left in his glass. "I mean, that's a full-time job right there. What you're asking of me, I'm going to need access to planes, cars, shipping containers."

Roman nods, understanding how smuggling drugs works. "That's no problem," he says. "Perhaps you could use the same ones that you've been using while working for my father."

His eyes bulge just a fraction before trying to school his features. "I, uhmm. I'm sorry? Your father? I've never met your father."

Roman scoffs and stands, swirling the contents of his glass again. He begins pacing behind the chair and I watch how the dealer focuses on every last step. "You know what really gets to me?" he questions, pausing to meet the dealer's terrified gaze. "Snakes. Liars. Scumbag dealers who were placed into my life by my father with the intention to fuck with me."

The guy stands, violently shaking his head as he holds his hands up, feigning innocence. "I swear, I don't know what you're talking about. I'm just a dealer. Nothing more."

Roman's eyes sparkle. "And I'm just a businessman, nothing more."

The dealer pales, knowing all too well that Roman is so much more than just a businessman—they all are. "Look," he starts. "I don't know where you would have heard something like that. Someone clearly has a vendetta against me and wants to see me slaughtered, maybe a competitor. I know Gia Moretti's dealers are feeling the sting since I've been taking their customers."

Roman laughs. "You think Gia is threatened by a dealer making a measly ten, maybe twenty grand a week in stolen product? You're a bigger fool than I thought." Roman leans against the backrest of his vacated chair and focuses his hard stare on the dealer as the wolves stand beside him. "We were at the warehouse last night. We saw you with our own fucking eyes. You signed your own death sentence."

The glass drops straight out of his hand as his whole fucking life flashes before his eyes, finally realizing that fucking with Giovanni is one thing, but fucking with his sons is an entirely different game.

Roman steps around his chair as Marcus and Levi both stand, blocking his escape, though with Dill and Doe standing by, he won't even get a step before they're on him.

Marcus steps around the back of my seat and leans forward,

curling his hand around my throat as his lips skim over the sensitive skin on my neck. His thumb moves in a gentle circle, skimming right over the artery in my throat. "When in doubt," he tells me, a deep, wicked excitement building in his tone. "Always go for an artery."

A thrill shoots through me and I sit up a little straighter, my eyes wide.

Roman moves in front of the dealer, his eyes deadlier than I've ever seen them. "Do you know what happens to men who try to fool us? Men who plot and plan for our destruction?" he pauses, letting his words sink in. "They die by our hands, their throats torn right out of their bodies."

The man gapes at him and in a last-ditch effort to try and save himself, his fist rears back and he throws a punch right at Roman's face, but there's nothing quite like Roman's reflexes. He catches the man's fist in his hand, mere inches from connecting with his jaw.

The dealer gasps, fear rattling him as he holds Roman's hard stare. "Doe," Roman demands.

And just as Roman releases the guy's fist and turns his back, Doe bounds past the small fire and launches herself at the dealer, giving him only the slightest warning before slamming into his chest. The dealer screams as Doe effortlessly takes him down.

Savage growls tear through the night as her teeth gnash against his skin, going straight for his throat. She grabs hold of him, her head violently whipping from left to right as blood spurts up around her in a horrendous wave. I gape at the wolf. My precious, sweet Doe who rests her giant head in my lap, who cries for her brother when he's injured. I knew she was capable of wicked things, but I never thought she could do something like this.

Blood sprays across the pool, splattering in the water as a chilling scream tears from the dealer. He fights against her hold, desperate to get her off him, but she's far too heavy. Not even one of the boys could force her off, not now. This sweet girl is in the zone and there's no stopping her until her job is complete.

She keeps at him, the growls and scuffles in the night like nothing I've ever seen. Perhaps this is the scene the boys envisioned for me when they told the rest of the world that I'd been mauled by a bear … though perhaps I don't want to know.

Marcus' lips move over my skin. "Are you ready?" he breathes. "Any second now."

And not a moment later, Doe tears the dealer's throat right out of his body, sending a spray of blood far and wide. She shakes her head, flicking his throat around like a toy before looking back at Roman with a proud stare. Roman nods to her, and with that, she struts away and plops down beside Dill, dropping the throat in front of him like a gift as the dealer's body convulses and shakes.

CHAPTER TWENTY EIGHT

A heavy pang of regret settles into my chest as I curl my hand into Levi's, threading my fingers through his. "Are you ready for this?" I murmur, hating how heavy today is going to be.

We stand outside the castle the boys had called not only home for so many years, but their own personal prison. I knew today would come eventually, but nothing can prepare somebody for this, nothing will ever make it okay.

Levi shakes his head. "No, but it has to be done. She's been suffering up there for too many years. Her body should have been put to rest a long time ago. We owe her this."

I nod before glancing up at him. He's been taking it the hardest. He's always blamed himself for his mother's death, but he couldn't be more wrong. Roman and Marcus got more time with her, and have more vivid memories, but Levi was too young and doesn't get to remember her in the same way that his brothers do.

"Come on," Marcus murmurs, his tone heavy and filled with a deep kind of pain that tears at my chest. "Standing out here and staring at the castle isn't going to help put her to rest."

Roman lets out a heavy sigh and makes his way toward the front door as the early morning sun begins to peek out over the mountains, sending a ray of light shining down over the castle. I'm not into spiritual things or believing in some kind of ultimate power, but if that ray of sunlight shining down on us isn't some kind of sign, I don't know what is.

The rest of us follow Roman with heavy hearts right up to the very top of the castle. Memories of my time here assault my thoughts. Some were good, hell some were incredible, but others were so horrendous that just the thought of ever reliving them has me in a ball of sweat. I can't even imagine how it must feel for the boys having to come back here. Hell, they still have a whole lot of shit they need to move out. Those few loads they took a few weeks ago didn't even make a dent in the piles of shit they've accumulated over the years.

It takes a lifetime to reach the top room of the castle, and as we push our way through, the heaviness hits me in a whole new way. The boys were only kids when she passed, and they never got their chance to say goodbye. Sure, it's heavy and my heart is plagued with grief, but this is their mom. Whatever I'm feeling right now, they're feeling it so much harder, and because of that, I need to do everything in my power to be strong for them—even Roman who couldn't possibly allow himself a moment of weakness.

The room looks just as we left it—creepy as fuck.

Snow White lays in her frozen coffin, her face barely visible through the frosted-covered glass. I hated coming in here the first time, and I hate coming in here now. I've only just been able to stomach the fucked-up things the boys like to do in their spare time, but this is a whole new level of fucked up. I don't know what the hell Giovanni was thinking putting her away in here, but I don't doubt for one second that the boys will do whatever it takes to make this right.

Marcus lets out a heavy sigh, his heart out on his sleeve for the world to see. His gaze lingers on the coffin and the brave man I'd seen downstairs is a complete stranger to the man I see now. "Sorry, Mom," he murmurs. "It's time."

He spreads a blanket out on the floor as Roman steps around him, moving toward the side of the coffin. All three of them look sick with what they have to do, but without them, their mom would be doomed to rot in this frozen casket until the end of time.

Levi steps around the opposite side of the blanket before moving into Roman's side, and I keep out of their way, wanting to give them the privacy to do this themselves. I'd offered to stay down in the car or chill out in the living room while they took care of business, but Levi wanted me here.

Roman's fingers curl around the side of the frozen casket and linger on the hinges for a short moment, knowing that once they crack that seal, there's no turning back. He mutters something to Levi, so quiet that I don't hear them from across the room, but whatever it is has Levi letting out a pained breath before finally nodding.

Roman pulls on the hinges and strains against them, the frozen glass working against him as Marcus moves into his other side. The hinges finally come free with a deep crack and the glass top of the casket slowly begins to rise.

Marcus puts his hand on the lid, helping it along, and when it finally opens all the way, the three of them just stare. "She looks just as I remembered," Roman murmurs, a soft smile playing on his warm lips. "A little rough around the edges, but she still holds that subtle softness."

Marcus scoffs. "You'd be a little rough around the edges if you were frozen solid too."

Roman gapes at his younger brother as Levi's eyes bulge out of his head, struggling to hold onto a laugh. His lips press down into a tight line, but the laugh is too strong and comes tearing out of him. Levi tries to choke it back down, desperately trying to swallow the booming roar but there's absolutely no hope.

A grin pulls at the corners of my lips as Marcus smirks at his brother, pleased to have at least one person find humor in this dark moment.

As Roman stares at Levi struggling to control himself, his lips strain against his will, pulling at the corners. "Do you find this funny?" he demands.

"No, no," Levi says, shaking his hands while trying to rein it all in. "Not at all, but apparently you do."

Roman glares at his brother, his lips instantly settling back into their usual tight line, not pleased to have been called out for almost breaking down his carefully structured walls. "Let's just get this done."

A newfound seriousness comes over them as Roman reaches down to his dead mother's decaying body. Marcus hovers close by as Levi seems to take a hesitant step back, horror deep in his eyes. The boys have lugged a million dead bodies around the streets of the city and have never had an issue, but this one is different. This one hits home.

Roman's arms slip under her body, and as he goes to lift her out of the coffin, Marcus scoops in beneath him. "Careful of her head," he rushes out, cradling her head as though it's the most precious jewel in the world. His hands become knotted into her matted hair as Roman holds her close to his chest.

The two of them carefully step back together, terrified of disturbing her fragile body before slowly lowering her down to the blanket. Roman gets down on his knees, his heavy eyes expressing everything he refuses to say out loud.

Once she's safely on the ground, Roman moves back and Levi hesitantly takes the edge of the blanket and drapes it over her body. Tears well in my eyes. For so long, I thought the boys were incapable of feeling this deeply. I thought they were monsters, unable to recognize basic human emotion, but every single day they continue to surprise me. They continuously force me to reconsider every judgmental thought I ever had about them.

They're deep, honest men with hearts bigger than anyone I've ever met, but they've been broken and shattered over and over again. They've been forced to build cement walls around their hearts to not only protect themselves, but to protect their brothers. They're stronger than I could have ever known, and it makes me hate their father more. He turned them into these beasts, stripped them of their innocence, and forced them into a world where they were corrupted and destroyed. He deserves the most brutal death, and I can't wait to give it to him.

The boys' mother disappears beneath the blanket and my brows furrow, not understanding why they need it. They could have just carried her out to the car like they usually do, but I guess maybe they want to do this with a little more respect. Besides, she's been dead for twenty-something years, and I doubt they've ever had experience with a corpse like this. There's no telling what could happen once her body begins to thaw.

They secure her in the blanket, and before I know it, Roman is scooping her into his arms again. He holds her bridal style instead of the over-the-shoulder bullshit the boys generally reserve for me.

Everybody stands back, allowing Roman to walk out first, and the somber look in his eyes is enough to bring me to my knees. He refuses to meet my stare, and I don't blame him. I've been pushing him too far, forcing him to feel things that he's probably not ready to admit, but now isn't the time to push. If he needs to talk, I need to trust that he'll come to me.

We follow Roman back out of the massive castle, and I hope to God that this is the last time I'll have to be here, despite how this place still somehow feels like home to the boys. Once everything is said and done, I'm sure we'll build a place of our own. Hell, maybe we'll even get a kick out of knocking down Giovanni's family home just to build our own in the boys' image, a home where Roman can raise his son and have a family. I don't know if I'll fit into that, but the idea of not being a part of that new life darkens something deep in my soul.

We step out through the main door and it's still crazy to me that the door opens and closes just as it was always intended. The keypad is fucked and there's no way to keep anyone locked inside. We've come so far in such a little time, but the war on the horizon still terrifies me.

Snow White is placed gently into the trunk of the big SUV, and within moments, we're sailing out through the massive iron gates and through the rolling hills. The drive is silent, each of us staring out the windshield with heavy hearts.

My fingers curl through Levi's and I hold onto him with everything I've got, wishing that I could somehow take his pain. He loops our joined hands over my shoulder and pulls me into his side, needing me close, and that's exactly how we stay until Roman brings the SUV to a stop four hours later.

Climbing out of the SUV, I glance out at the rolling, grassy hill that overlooks the sandy, crystal-clear beach below. "It's beautiful," I breathe, not intending to have said the words out loud.

Roman steps past me, moving toward the trunk. "It is," he says. "I think she'll like it here."

Glancing back at him over my shoulder, he meets my heavy stare and I nod. "You're right. It's perfect." Roman holds my stare for a moment, and as something softens in his eyes, I know that he's going to be alright, but that doesn't take away from just how hard this will be.

Reaching into the trunk, Roman scoops his mother into his capable arms as Marcus grabs the three shovels stashed in the back. Together, we walk as one to the very top of the green hill, and I smile as I find the grass littered with little white and yellow flowers.

Looking out from the top of the hill is a scene that takes my breath away. The sky is a rich blue with not a cloud in sight, and the late morning sun shines down upon us. The breeze flowing in from the ocean brushes against my skin, blowing my hair back off my face. I can only imagine just how beautiful the horizon would be at sunset. The boys really have chosen an amazing resting place for their mother. She'll be happy here.

The boys get busy digging a deep hole as I drop down in the long grass beside their mother. "I'm sorry you didn't get the chance to see the incredible men your three boys have turned into," I tell her as I straighten her dress and fix her hair, making sure it's perfect, the way any Mafia wife would have wanted to be presented. "You would have been so proud of them. Though perhaps you've been watching over them all this time and already know just how amazing they are."

I like to think that on some level, she can hear me, but I'm not completely insane. Not yet at least.

Glancing down at her one last time, I fix the blanket around her before stepping away.

One by one, the boys take a break from digging and sit with their mother, telling her about their life, telling her the things that no mother should ever have to be burdened with, telling her how desperately they wish she had been able to stick around, how badly they needed her.

Each word that tears out of their souls kills me, but I keep my gaze on the water below, offering them what little privacy I can, until finally, the hole is as deep as it's going to get and the boys are ready to say their last goodbye.

Marcus and Roman jump down into the bottom of the deep grave as Levi crouches beside his mother. "I'm sorry," he murmurs, his eyes softening with pain as he scoops her into his strong arms. "We should have done better by you. We'll see you again Mother. I swear, we'll make you proud."

And with that, he lowers her body into his brothers' arms to be laid into her final resting place. She's covered up with the blanket, protecting her body the best way they can before Levi offers them a hand and pulls each of his brothers out of their mother's grave.

A heavy silence settles over the hill, and even the soft whistle of the breeze seems to fade as the boys fill the grave one shovelful at a time. We each sit at the top of the hill, looking over the ocean as the sun sinks lower and lower until finally, it kisses the horizon, plunging the earth into vibrant shades of pink, orange, red, and yellow.

CHAPTER TWENTY NINE

ROMAN

My hand balls into a fist as it hovers by Shayne's bedroom door. I've come past here four fucking times already, and each time I've walked straight by, too fucking pussy to stop and say what I've been meaning to say for so damn long. Once those words come out of my mouth, there's no taking them back.

Shayne has been a rock to me, though she wouldn't know it. She's kept me grounded and focused through all of this. She keeps me breathing. Without her, I would have gone off the rails. I owe my life to her. I would have run full steam ahead into a shitty situation and lost everything, but she helps me see the clear picture ahead. She's been forcing me to live, not just sail on by without a fucking care in the world. I don't know how, but she's breathing life back into me, and in return, I've been a fucking prick.

I can't handle it. Once I tell her that she's somehow become my whole fucking world, she becomes an even bigger target with an even bigger chunk of my soul to destroy if she were to be taken away from me, just like every other woman I've allowed into my world.

It's fucked up. Loving her means to keep her at an arm's distance, but a woman like Shayne would never accept that. She'd tell me to shove my fucked-up need to keep her away straight up my ass and fuck off with it. What can I say? The girl has a way with words.

My hand falls away and I mentally berate myself for being such a soft cunt. Shayne would never back down like that. She'd grab the fucking bull by the horns and force him to listen to her. She's a stubborn spitfire like that.

Soft murmurs come from within the room, and instead of pulling away, I find my hand coming straight back up. The door isn't closed properly so I give it a gentle push, sending it gliding across the top of the plush carpet.

My brothers lounge back in her bed, Levi sprawled across the end while Marcus lays on the opposite side, his hand braced behind his head. Shayne sits cross-legged beside him, and her gaze immediately snaps up to mine. Suspicion rises in my chest, but as I take in the scene a second longer, I realize that no one's been getting their rocks off in here, at least, not yet. There's no telling with Shayne. My brothers are hornbags and she's generally down for anything they throw out there.

Not going to lie, I've never been so fucking jealous. Every night I hear them fucking her like they can't breathe without her, but little do they know, the sound of her whimpers, gasps, and pleasured groans have me crippled, gasping for air. Every. Fucking. Night.

I've been lucky enough that she's allowed me close, allowed me to touch her just long enough to keep the blood pumping through my veins, but I can't do it anymore. I can't be without her any longer.

It's been a few days since we sat up on that hill, saying our final goodbyes to our mother, and there's been a big gaping hole in my chest ever since, and while my brothers see straight past it, Shayne hasn't. She sees me like no one ever has before.

Her eyes linger on mine and without a single word spoken between us, she knows why I'm here. She scoots across her bed moving closer to Marcus, placing her hand down in her vacated space and silently inviting me over.

I can't fucking resist.

I push in past her bedroom door and my brother's murmured scoff sounds through the room. "Look who finally made it past the door," Levi grumbles, not bothering to look back over his shoulder.

Irritation stirs in me as I keep walking, but when Marcus' gaze lifts to mine, my hand immediately begins reaching for the switchblade in my pocket. "What was that?" he questions, a smirk resting on his lips. "Your fifth attempt?"

The blade flies from my fingers, plunging deep into the pillow beside his face, making Shayne gasp in surprise. "Come and say that to my face," I warn him.

Marcus goes to make a move, not one to back down from a fight, but Shayne puts her hand on his hip, keeping him grounded. "Knock it off," she mutters, slicing a hard stare toward Marcus. "This is my safe space. There's none of that bullshit going down here. Is that understood?"

Marcus rolls his eyes and settles back into his position beside her as he yanks my knife out of the soft pillow and makes a show of sliding it into his pocket, warning me that I'll never see that particular blade again, but as Shayne's eyes come back to mine, I couldn't care less.

My brothers talk quietly between themselves, but it's clear that Shayne has absolutely no interest in whatever the hell they're talking about, her attention is all mine. I stride up toward the side of her bed, and don't fucking hold back. I'm done with that shit. What's the point of denying what's so clearly in front of my face?

Dropping down onto the side of her bed, I curl my arm around her side and pull her down to me. She catches herself against my chest, her soft fingers splaying against my shirt and no doubt feeling the rapid beat of my heart beneath.

Her curious eyes linger on mine as I look up at her. "You okay?" she murmurs so softly that I doubt my brothers can hear her. "Do you need to talk about the baby?"

I shake my head. "As much as it kills me to admit, I think he's perfectly safe with my father. He won't physically hurt him, not while he's still so young. The abuse didn't start for us until we were able to understand what the fuck was going on."

"Are you sure?"

"Positive. He's a cruel man, but he understands that children are born innocent. He'll have some poor woman working night and day to care for the baby, only checking in every now and then to ensure that he remembers his face. Then when he's a few months old, he'll start to nurture him just enough to make him love, just so when the time comes to destroy him, it'll hurt that much more."

Shayne closes her eyes, the reality of my father's plan for my son darkening a piece of her corrupted soul, but as she opens her eyes again and looks deep into mine, her brows furrow. "That's not what you're here to talk about, is it?"

I don't respond, but I don't need to. She knows me on a deeper level than I even know myself, and I don't know how the fuck that happened while I was busy pushing her away, but she gets it. She always has.

My hand falls to Shayne's on my chest, and I curl my fingers around the soft skin of her wrist, feeling the steady beat of her pulse below and watching the way her eyes widen with understanding. "We don't have to do this," she whispers, giving me the out she's so used to me needing.

My hand curls up around the back of her neck and I pull her down to me, feeling her breath across my lips. "It's time, Empress." The softest whisper escapes her lips before she closes the gap and brushes her lips over mine. She kisses me softly, too scared to push for what she really wants, knowing how quickly just a bit of pressure could have me backing right out of her room.

Shayne pulls back and her gorgeous blue eyes meet mine, seeing just how serious I am about this.

"Out," she demands, her chest rising and falling with rapid movements as she holds my stare.

"Huh?" Levi grunts, his head snapping up to try and steal her gaze away from mine.

Shayne kicks her foot out, connecting with his hip and sending him sprawling back on the bed, and if she'd kicked him any harder, the fucker would have gone flying right onto the floor. "You heard me," she says, reaching behind her to pinch Marcus under the arm. "That goes for you too. Both of you, out."

Marcus jumps away from her as he whines. "What, why?"

A grin pulls at my lips. He makes it too easy to mess with him. "Because I'm going to fuck your girl until she forgets who you are," I taunt him, knowing she'll never go for the idea of just being mine, especially not now that she's head over heels in love with my two asshole brothers, though I don't know if she actually realizes it yet.

Shayne groans and shoves me in the ribs before glancing back over her shoulder to Marcus. "We just need to … talk," she tells him.

"Right," he scoffs.

"Go now, Marcus," she warns him. "Before I tell him how you told me about the time you shot him in the ass when you were kids."

Betrayal tears through me as I gape at my brother. "We made a pact," I spit. "Where's your sense of loyalty?"

Marcus shoves Levi in the back before glancing down at his nonexistent watch. "Oh, shit. Is that the time? We better get going."

The boys disappear through the door and I don't miss the way

Marcus pulls the door shut behind him, going the extra mile not to click it into place, but in all honesty, an easy escape is probably in both of our best interests, seeing as though the two of us have rarely had a single conversation that didn't include trying to tear each other's head off.

Shayne's soft gaze falls back to mine. I swallow hard as I scoot up on her bed, leaning my back against the headboard so I can meet her eye to eye. Wanting to be right in front of me, she moves over me, straddling my lap before nervously gripping the hem of my shirt and playing with the material between her fingers.

Her gaze drops, and I catch her chin before she can lower it. "Don't," I rush out. "Don't look away from me."

Her brows furrow and she watches me for a moment, the silence growing louder between us. "Why now?" she whispers.

"You know why," I tell her. "It's been there since the very beginning, and I know you feel it too. I can't deny it anymore, Shayne. I can't keep pushing you away."

"I don't want you to."

My gaze drops to my arm where the tattoo of her bite stares up at me and a hollowness spreads through my chest. "I've put you through the worst kind of hell," I remind her. "I've done terrible things. I've denied you over and over again, pushing you away like you mean nothing to me. I've hurt you, Shayne. I didn't trust you when it mattered the most. You should still be pushing me away. You deserve so much better than me."

"You're right," she murmurs, her fingers brushing over the tattoo.

"I've spent months trying to tell myself that what I feel for you isn't real. Especially after what happened when Marcus got shot. I wanted to hate you so much, but you just kept showing up for me, you always have. You've protected me the only way you knew how, right from the very start. You made it impossible for me to hate you, and I don't want to keep trying. I want to be with you, Roman. I'm not scared of this."

My dark gaze bores into her innocent eyes. "You should be."

Shayne shakes her head and hesitantly brings her hand up before brushing her fingers over the side of my face. I can't help but lean into her touch, letting it soften something deep inside my chest, something I've never quite felt before. "When will you finally realize that denying yourself happiness and love isn't living at all? Everything has always been taken from you, and I don't know how he's done it, but at some point in your life, your father has made you believe that to fall for someone is to be weak, and I don't believe that for one second. I think being vulnerable and opening yourself up to someone else, to let them in, shows that you're stronger than he could ever be."

"You're making me question everything I've ever known, Shayne, and that scares me more than the thought of losing you."

She shakes her head. "You're never going to lose me," she murmurs. "Don't you see? You've had me since day one. I've always been yours."

A grin pulls at my lips as the seriousness in her eyes begins to fade. "I don't suppose you mean *just* mine?"

Shayne's lips twist into a crooked grin that has something fluttering deep inside me, something I've never experienced before. Is this what that weird butterfly thing is that chicks are always talking about? "No chance in hell," she tells me. "Me and your brothers are a package deal. If you want me, then you need to accept that I'm wholeheartedly theirs, just as I am yours."

Her fingers twist into the back of my hair, and I can't help but notice how the tension seeps out of her shoulders. "I just have one question," she says, her eyes locked onto mine. "Why now? You've always been so adamant that we would never happen. You've been pushing me away every chance you got. I just … I don't understand."

Silence consumes me as I try to figure out my response. "To be honest, I'm not entirely sure. I think it was burying Mom. She was barely my age when my father took her life, and it got me thinking just how short life can really be. What if that was you? My father could have easily ended your life when he took you to those cells in the desert, and I can't stop thinking about how I never would have gotten the chance to tell you how fucking badly I have craved your touch since the second I laid eyes on you. Life is too fucking short for me to keep pushing you away. We could all be dead next week, and I want to live knowing that if I were to get a bullet through the head, I had everything I needed."

"You're really sure about this?"

I nod, hating that I've pushed her away so much that she barely believes me now. "I'm sure, Empress. I won't push you away anymore. I can't promise that it's always going to be easy. You've got three assholes who fight, argue, and get jealous over the stupidest shit. We have short tempers and throw fucking switchblades when challenged. But bear with us. I call you Empress for a fucking reason."

"Really?" she murmurs, her brows arching with interest. "And why's that?"

"Because I've always known that you would rule over us. It was inevitable."

Her eyes sparkle with the sweetest warmth, and it's almost as though I can feel the heat spreading through her veins. She adjusts herself on my lap, moving in closer, still hesitating as she doesn't know how to be with me yet, what boundaries she can push and where she needs to hold back. She leans into me, her eyes hooded as I feel her soft breath brushing over my lips. "Are you in love with me, Roman DeAngelis?"

My voice drops to a soft whisper as my lips move over hers. "Like you wouldn't fucking believe."

Shayne sinks into me and captures my lips in a deep kiss, a soft moan rumbling deep in her chest. Satisfaction and pleasure roll through me and hope surges through my veins. Fuck, I think I even feel a shred of happiness for the first time in my life. A weight lifts off my shoulders and is replaced with a fiery freedom that crashes through my chest, and for the first fucking time in my life, I feel as though I could do anything, and it's all because of her.

My hands curl around her waist as my lips pull into a smile. Is this what I've been missing this whole time?

Holy fuck. I feel invincible.

A laugh bubbles up my throat and my arms curl tighter around her waist, pulling her in hard to my chest. A breath escapes her and she laughs as the hunger takes over. A needy groan vibrates through her chest as she reaches for my shirt, quickly bunching up the fabric and tearing it over my head. Her hands instantly come back to my body, roaming all over my skin as though she can't quite get close enough.

Her desperation to have me spurs me on, and while I want to take my time, the need to be inside her pushes me on. I've only felt those tight walls of her sweet cunt around my cock twice, once on the hood of the SUV and once on the rooftop, and hell, I doubt she even knows that was me, but I've craved it every moment of every day since.

Our teeth gnash together, desperate and wild as my hands fist into the back of her tank. I tear it clean off her body, pleased to find no bra standing in my way. The fabric falls between us and she pulls back, breaking our kiss as she pants to catch her breath. My lips drop straight to her neck, exploring every inch of creamy skin that I've dreamed of tasting for the longest time, and she's so much more than I bargained for. Her taste, her feel, her touch.

Fuck, I'm a goner.

She grinds on top of me, and even through her tiny shorts, I feel the heat coming off her. She's ready and nothing is standing in our way, not now. My cock strains against my sweatpants and a groan pulls from deep within my chest. I have to have her now.

My arm curls around her waist and I go to throw her down, more than ready to worship every inch of her body, but more than that, I need to taste that sweet cunt on my tongue. I need to watch her come undone under my touch. I need to make her scream, but apparently, I'm not the one running this show. "No," she growls, her hand snapping out and catching the headboard before I get a chance to throw her down into the soft blankets.

My brows furrow as I meet her heated stare and she shakes her head. "You'll get your turn," she pants, tightening her grip on the headboard. "But I've been waiting too fucking long to slide down over your thick cock and ride you, and nothing is going to stop me."

Well, fuck. How could I deny a woman who speaks such sweet words?

I ease up on her waist, letting her know that the floor is all hers. Whatever she wants, she's going to get. Hell, even if that means I get to fuck her a million times before I get the chance to finally taste her. It'll all be worth it. Gripping her hair, I pull her head back, forcing her eyes to mine. Her lips hover so close that I can feel her heated breath mixing with mine. "Do your fucking worst."

A devilish, dark sparkle hits her eyes, and a grin stretches across my face. I think I just unleashed a beast, and holy fuck, I'm so down for it. And to think she was the one trying to send me and my brothers back down to hell, but I'm starting to wonder if she's more devil than angel.

She reaches down between us and slips her hand inside my sweatpants, her tight little fist curling around my straining cock. Satisfaction rocks through me. I've jerked off a million times since meeting this little she-devil, and nothing can compare to the feel of her fist squeezing my cock.

With my sweatpants restricting her movement, I lift my hips, raising us both off the mattress before yanking my pants down, giving her free rein to do whatever the hell she wants. "Holy shit," she breathes, her forehead dropping to mine as she tries to catch her breath. "How are you all so big?"

A wicked grin pulls at my lips, and sure, hearing her referring to the size of my brothers' cocks ain't really the best thing for a man's ego in this position, but considering our fucked-up little relationship, I'll have to let that one slide.

Sensing her desperate need to be touched, I pull her up off my lap just enough to tear her shorts down her gorgeous thighs, and damn it, she's not wearing any panties. She kicks them off the second she can, and I don't waste any time lowering her back down, feeling just how ready she is for me.

Shayne grinds against me as she pumps her fist up and down, roaming her thumb over my tip and grinning with excitement flashing in her bright blue eyes.

She's fucking gorgeous, but when she looks at me with that devilish little smirk in her eyes warning me that she's about to fuck me like a goddamn boss, it's all I can do not to come right there in her hand.

Shayne presses up onto her knees, and not being able to wait a second longer, she positions my cock right by her entrance and slowly lowers herself back down, her heat consuming me like never before. She groans and gasps the lower she gets, gripping my arms and digging her nails into my skin as she adjusts to my size.

She goes balls deep and I suck in a hiss of breath through my teeth. "Fuck," I growl, the rumble vibrating through my chest as she gasps and rocks her hips, adjusting herself. "I've missed this sweet cunt."

My hand curls around her body, traveling down until I can grab a handful of her perfect ass. I squeeze tight and she rocks her hips again, making us both flinch with undeniable pleasure. She eases up on my arm and settles her arms around my neck, balancing herself before she truly starts to move. "Oh, fuck," she moans before a sharp grunt and gasp sail through her lips.

She bounces on top of me, her slick pussy moving up and down my cock, coating it in her arousal. Her head tips back and I capture her bouncing nipple in my mouth, flicking my tongue over the tight bud. "YES, ROMAN!" she cries out, a light sheen of sweat coating her body as she gets worked up.

She slams down over me and my cock flinches, her tight pussy effortlessly gliding up and down my length like a fucking glove made just for me, proving just how amazing she is. I always knew she'd fuck like a goddamn pornstar.

She squeezes me tight, and I release my grip on her ass cheek, slipping my hand down further and feeling where we meet. My fingers mix with her arousal, and I pull back just an inch, slipping them up higher to her ass and pressing against it. She gasps and then groans. "Oh, God, yes," she says, breathing heavily as I apply a little more pressure to her ass.

She pushes back against me and I grin. "Fuck, you're a greedy little thing."

"Don't fucking deny me, Roman DeAngelis. Give me exactly what I want."

I push deeper into her ass and love the way she comes alive under my touch. Hell, I didn't think any woman was capable of giving more energy than what she was already giving, but Shayne continues to surprise me. She goes off like a fucking rocket, squeezing my cock tighter as she moves up and down.

She rocks forward, grazing her clit against me. "Oh, fuck," she cries out, throwing her head back and groaning low. I'm desperate to shoot my load deep inside her needy cunt, but there's no way I'm about to spoil the show. I'll hold out as long as she needs, even if it kills me.

She takes me deeper, harder, and faster, and my fingers bite into her creamy skin. "Shit, Roman," she cries out. "I'm going to come."

Damn fucking straight. I can't wait to feel her come undone around me.

I thrust up into her, taking her even deeper before flicking my tongue over her nipple. She groans, her eyes clenching as she pushes herself just a little bit further, wanting everything she can get, and fuck, I don't blame her. I've made her hold out for so damn long.

Her arm tightens around my neck as I pull her in closer, our bodies grinding against one another while she moves, then as she rocks her hips forward and her sweet little clit rubs against me, her body breaks into a wild spasm.

"Shiiiiit," she moans, her cunt squeezing and convulsing around me, shattering into a million exhausted little pieces. She throws her head back, her eyes clenched and her grip tightening on me, and fuck, I let myself go, coming hard into her tight cunt, pouring every last drop deep inside her.

"Holy fuck, Empress," I breathe, straining to catch my breath. I've been fucked by all sorts of women in a million different positions, but nothing even comes close to the way she just made me come.

Her body slowly begins to relax as she collapses into me, panting to catch her breath as her pussy continues to spasm. "Oh my God," she mutters, her lips moving over my shoulder as I curl my arm around her body again, holding her close and keeping her from falling into an exhausted heap on the mattress. "That ... fuck."

She trails off, not having the energy to complete her sentence, and I smile, knowing I just found my forever.

Shayne takes a moment, slowly regaining her energy, and only when she starts to wriggle on top of me do I raise her chin off my shoulder and catch her lips in mine. "I hope you weren't finished," I tell her, pulling back from our gentle kiss before lowering her down to the mattress and hovering over her spent body. "Because I'm hungry for dessert."

She sucks in a breath as I lick my lips, and without wasting another goddamn second, I slide down her body, spread those beautiful thighs, and finally close my lips over her sweet little cunt.

CHAPTER THIRTY

My knees shake as I make my way to my private bathroom in disbelief. Surely I'm imagining the last two hours. That had to have all been in my head.

Roman. Fucking. DeAngelis.

Hooooly shit.

I knew it would be good, but goddamn, he had a lot of time and effort to make up for and make up for it he did! I've been with him a handful of times, but it's either been as a group or a thorough pounding with the sole intention of clearing his head. The emotion was always taken out of it, but what we just did … that was different. It meant something and it was everything I'd hoped it would be.

Roman DeAngelis has finally cracked and admitted what we both have known from the very start, he's wickedly in love with me, and I wouldn't have it any other way. He's been pushing me away since day one, but every single time, it's only made the connection between us stronger. Now, the only problem is getting me to admit the same.

I know the feelings are there, same with both Levi and Marcus, but actually saying them out loud is terrifying. Maybe the boys are much stronger than I am, after all. But to be fair, those three little words may have slipped out with Marcus, but I was in the moment, my back slammed up against a small closet door during a ball, and I can't be blamed for the word vomit that tore out of me after such a thorough fucking.

Closing the bathroom door behind me, I prance to the shower, leaning in and turning the spray on full blast as I allow myself only a moment to come to terms with everything that's just happened.

Does this mean that Roman and I are together now? I'm almost certain it does, but when a man like Roman DeAngelis is making the rules, one can never be too sure. All I know is that the moment he stepped into my room and looked deep into my eyes, I knew it was time. And hell, it's been a long time coming.

A soft gasp slips through my lips as I step directly under the water, far too distracted by Roman to have checked the temperature first. The water quickly warms and I ease back into it, tipping my head under the hot spray. I'm covered in a sheer layer of sweat, and after two hours of hot, needy fuckery, this shower is like a sparkly, bright red cherry on top.

After rinsing shampoo from my hair, I grab the soap and lather it between my hands, and just as I'm about to spread it over my body, a soft rap sounds at the door before it's pushed open. "I'm gonna figure out something for dinner," he says. "Are you all good in here?"

His eyes darken as he watches my hands roam over my body, spreading the soap over every inch of skin. "I'm more than good," I tell him, my tone dropping at the sheer memory of his thick cock pushing deep inside of me as his lips claimed my throat, but today, his tongue was definitely the MVP. This man has skills that most could only dream of. "Perfectly alright, unless there's something you needed …"

A low groan tears from deep in his chest as my soapy hand travels lower and lower down my body. "Fuck," he murmurs, swallowing hard, mesmerized by my movements. He adjusts his cock in his pants and if it weren't for the fact that he has one hell of an important business meeting to prepare for after dinner, he'd probably already be in here with me on my knees and his thick cock hitting the back of my throat. "Don't fucking tempt me."

My hand dips between my legs and a soft gasp slips between my lips as my thumb brushes past my clit. My eyes flutter at the sudden onslaught of pleasure, but as I focus on Roman again, his eyes are flaming with a wild need. "What a shame you're busy," I taunt. "I'll have to call one of your brothers up here."

His eyes blaze and I laugh, pulling my hand back. I'm more than happy to go again, but I'd be lying if I said that I wasn't a little worn out. I've been dicked high and low, left and fucking right. One dick, two dicks, three. This pussy needs a break, if only for a night. "Go," I laugh. "I'll be out in a minute."

His dark gaze narrows as he watches me a moment longer, but

after a short pause, he finally nods. "Okay, just call out if you need anything."

A warm smile spreads over my face, and as the strain from his need seeps away and he's left with nothing but adoration, I'm once again reminded of just how fucked up this is. It's going to take some getting used to. Hell, what are we supposed to say to each other now that I don't need to argue with everything he says? I'm sure we'll find that common ground eventually and everything will just fall into place, but it'll definitely be an adjustment.

Roman goes to walk away, and as his gaze drops, it immediately becomes plagued with deep thought. The door closes between us and I let out a heavy breath. He's nervous about tonight's meeting with the family, all three of the boys are, but I believe in them. They're going to gain the family's loyalty and Giovanni will have no choice but to bow out.

Not wanting the boys to get lost in their thoughts for too long, I quickly finish in the shower and grab a towel. I dry off and get myself sorted out before stepping back out into my room and finding something to wear that demands respect but doesn't scream desperate. The options are endless, but at the same time, I also feel as though I have absolutely nothing to wear. After all, tonight's meeting is going to be monumental, and I want it to be perfect.

Fuck, it sucks being a woman.

After twenty minutes of back and forth, I settle with a pair of black pants, knee-high boots, and a crop. Fuck the whole trying to impress bullshit. It's too hard. I gave it a good try, but I can't keep changing my mind like this. It's driving me insane. Besides, if they don't like me the way I am, then fuck them.

Striding out of my room, I listen for the boys. I can faintly hear Roman down in the kitchen, and the soft thumping of Levi's drums sails through the air. A sweet peace settles through my chest. I could more than get used to a life with the boys. It's unconventional, but it's perfect.

My stomach growls and I start making my way down to Roman when goosebumps spread over my skin and an unsettled feeling fills my stomach. My back stiffens and my gaze shifts through the hallway as the odd sensation of being watched nags at me.

I narrow my gaze and take a slow breath, turning and looking up and down the hall to find it completely empty. "Marcus?" I question, my tone dropping with suspicion. I've had this strange feeling once before, and it came just moments before the three DeAngelis asshats stalked me through the castle with the murder puppies. It was one of the most terrifying experiences of my life, but the assholes won't be getting the best of me like that again.

Marcus doesn't step out of the shadows, and I let out a frustrated groan before turning back and continuing down the hall. "I know you're there, Marc," I mutter, knowing damn well he hears me. I keep moving but guilt slams through me, and I find myself pausing to look back at the shadows. "I know I told you that Roman and I were just going to talk, and well, I think the neighbors even know how that turned out, but I swear, this doesn't change the way I feel about you."

Silence. Complete fucking silence.

I roll my eyes and turn back. I guess tonight we're playing games. Marcus has been possessive since the very start of our twisted little relationship, so I'm really not surprised. Though, it would be a shitload easier on everybody if we just sat down and talked it through like normal people do.

I pick up my pace and grin to myself as I feel him keeping up with me. He can be an asshole at the best of times, but sometimes, his assholery is just the right kind of twisted that sends the best kind of thrill soaring through my veins. Now, if he wants to stalk me right through the property and into a dark room, I'd be down for that.

The dirty little thought pulls my grin wider and I pick up my pace, seeing just how ready he is to play, and as I glance back over my shoulder, I see the slightest glimpse of his black hoodie disappearing into an open doorway, I laugh.

"Well, well," I tease, stopping and turning back. "Isn't it funny how the tables have turned?"

I start heading back toward the room, ready to catch him in the act in the most twisted game of hide and seek, and just as I reach the open doorway that looks into the darkened room, Roman's voice comes trailing up from the kitchen. "Dinner, fuckwits."

The soft thumping of the drums stops before Levi's deep tone bounces through the mansion. "Yeah, yeah," he grumbles, irritated about having to stop. "Coming."

I take a step into the dark room just as another voice cuts through the silence. "Only fuckwit around here is you," Marcus calls through the house, his deep tone coming from downstairs.

My eyes widen with fear as my heart leaps out of my fucking chest.

Oh, fuck.

A petrified scream rises in my throat but before the sound can come tearing from between my lips, a dark figure comes bounding out of the shadow, his dark eyes locked right on mine. His hand slams over my mouth as his tight grip curls around my waist.

My heart's rapid beat is almost painful, and I struggle to catch a breath, my pulse deafening in my ears. The stranger pushes me back against the wall, shining just a ray of light on his face, and proving once and for all just how wrong I'd been.

The man is all versions of tall, dark, and handsome with one hell of a strong grip, but one thing is for sure, I have no fucking idea who he is. Short, black dreadlocks frame his sculptured face as black eyes stare back at me. "We can do this the easy way, or the hard way," he warns me. "Scream, and I'll kill your little fuck toys downstairs, is that clear?"

Panic surges through my chest as I try to figure out a game plan. The man is far too strong for me to try and get away, but there's no way in hell he'll be able to take out the guys. There's one of him and three of them.

I slowly nod, and the man hesitantly releases his hand from my mouth, allowing me to suck in a deep breath. "What do you want?" I spit, fixing him with a lethal stare.

"Tell them you need a minute," he demands, his tone fierce and full of authority, yet there's something there that tells me he's not about to pull a knife and slaughter me, so there's that. But then, can I really trust that?

I swallow hard, not sure what to do, but he's not exactly giving me a choice. If I scream, I'll most likely be dead before the boys can even get up here, but if I don't, I'll have to find out the hard way what he wants.

Sucking in a breath, I prepare to scream for my fucking life when he leans into me, his wide chest pressing against mine like a lead weight. "Don't even fucking think about it," he warns. "I have six men downstairs with three bombs set and ready. The DeAngelis brothers are surrounded and they have no fucking idea. Now, I warned you that we could do this the easy way or the hard way. What's it going to be?"

Fuck.

There's no way in hell I'm about to risk their lives like that, and with no sane choice left, I let out a sigh and glare at the asshole in front of me as I call out to the boys below. "Just need a minute."

"Smart move," the guy warns. "Now, you're going to come with me, and you're going to do it without making a goddamn sound."

CHAPTER THIRTY ONE

Twigs and low-lying branches dig into my skin as the too confident for his own damn good dread wearing psychopath leads me through the woods behind the DeAngelis mansion with two of his men following behind. His grip on my arm is tight, but he doesn't hold me with the same crippling fist like others have in the past, and I have to wonder if maybe he's not as bad as I think he is. Stupid, but maybe not all bad.

"They're going to kill you," I warn him as we break through the opposite side of the woods and out to an empty street. Two black SUVs sit up on the curb and we storm toward them, my feet barely able to keep up with their ridiculous pace.

"Let them try," the man grumbles. "If they know what's good for them, they'll keep the fuck away."

An unladylike snort comes tearing out of me as I glare up at the man. "You have no idea who you're dealing with, do you?"

He glares right back. "And apparently, neither do you," he says as we reach the first SUV. He stops by the back door and reaches around me to pull it open before making a point of staring inside the cab. "Get in."

Everything screams at me not to get in the car, but I won't get even a foot away before they're on me, and I don't want to see what happens if I try something they won't appreciate. Besides, I have the GPS tracker in my arm now, and while I never actually checked with the boys that it's working, I have to trust that they know what they're doing. They'll come for me, the only question is, how long will it take for them to realize I'm gone?

I scoot along in the backseat of the car, less than impressed to find another man already waiting inside. I try to stick to the side, but finding the dreadlock asshole moving in beside me, I have no choice but to scoot along to the center.

Dread blooms in my chest as I watch the two other men climb into the front seats of the car, and before I know it, the driver is taking off at a million miles per hour. The other SUV follows, and my brows raise. I hadn't realized there was anyone in there. I figured it was for the other men still left inside the mansion.

We turn down a few side streets before finally pulling out onto the main highway, and I don't miss the way the driver puts his foot to the floor, giving the SUV as much gas as it can possibly handle and shooting down the road like a fucking jet.

Three other black SUVs fall in line, and my back stiffens looking all around us as we turn into some kind of convoy. "What the hell is this?" I demand, despite knowing that I'm in absolutely no position to be asking questions.

No one answers me, but I didn't expect them to. So instead, I sit in silence, taking note of every turn and every small detail that I wish I was privy to every other time I'd been taken against my will. Though, I have to be honest, these guys haven't cuffed me or shoved a bag over my head, and that's either really nice of them, or really fucking stupid. I haven't decided yet. Either way, kidnapping 101 would highly suggest that these assholes are amateurs. The boys would never make such a foolish mistake … unless they weren't planning on keeping this little meeting private … or maybe they weren't planning on keeping me alive long enough for it to matter.

Fuck.

We drive for an hour before the car pulls off onto an abandoned dirt road and nerves shoot through my veins. We've got to be close to wherever the hell we're going. Another fifteen minutes pass and I start to get agitated. If they're taking me somewhere to lure the boys out, then what's the point of hiding so far away? They're only making it harder on themselves.

My hands ball in and out of fists on my lap and the dreadlock dude watches me, taking note of every weird little quirk and reaction as though he's trying to make sense of me. I tune him out and after another ten minutes that seems to go on for a lifetime, the dirt road gets an upgrade and turns to gravel.

The SUV slows and I peer out the window, trying to see through the fog of dust kicking up under the tires of the cars in front. Old, rickety buildings begin to appear on either side of the road and my brows furrow, realizing this is some kind of abandoned town. There's an old gas station, an old grocery store, and what looks like a dance studio. These places appear as though they haven't seen the light of day for over a hundred years, and I can't help but wonder what happened to this small town that forced everybody out, but more so, only an hour away from civilization. Why hasn't this been bought by some big developer and turned into a mall or gated estate? It definitely has the potential and the space. Personally, I'd be happy with an epic water park, but that's just me.

We drive deeper into this strange, abandoned town until the convoy finally begins to slow. We pull into an old factory that looks as though it might have printed millions of newspapers in a past life but now it's just sitting here waiting to crumble.

"Out," dreadlock guy says, his fingers curling around the door handle.

He steps out into the dusty factory, and I follow behind, squinting into the late afternoon sun that shines in through the broken windows. The dust particles catch in the light, and as a group of men form around me, I find myself looking around. I don't see anyone else in the big factory, but that doesn't mean that we're alone.

What the hell do they want with me?

The men bring me to a stop in the center of the factory building and my chest tightens, realizing that I'm only moments away from finding out the reason why they've brought me here. Silence surrounds us, and as the seconds tick by, it only seems to get louder. I could hear a pin drop.

The familiar clicking of heels against the dirty concrete sounds from deep in the factory. The sound gets louder with every click and my heart pounds faster. It's definitely a woman, but who? And what does she want with me?

I follow the sound of the heels, squinting into the shadows, and after three more steps, I finally see her.

A beautiful woman struts toward me in a strappy, black cocktail dress that fits her subtle curves perfectly. She's older than me, maybe in her mid-forties, but she doesn't look a day over thirty. Her dark hair is twisted up into a neat up-do as her soft, natural makeup gives off the fiercest don't fuck with me vibe.

This woman is a badass, and though I've never met her before, I have a nagging feeling that I know who this is.

Gia Moretti.

"You're a hard woman to get a hold of," she says, her gaze sweeping over every inch of my body and shamelessly judging me. Her lips press into a flat line as her gaze narrows, and when she finally nods and a flash of approval flickers in her eyes, the nerves settle in my stomach. "Do you know who I am?"

My gaze narrows, certain that she has some bullshit elaborate plan to use me against the boys. "I know who you are," I tell her, trying to appear as though the idea of being in this woman's presence doesn't scare the shit out of me. "I don't know what you want with me though, but I do know that you must have an epic sized pair of balls to take me right out of the DeAngelis mansion. A feat like that doesn't come without consequences."

Gia watches me for a moment, her gaze narrowed. "Is that a threat or a compliment?"

My lips press into a line as I shrug my shoulders. "I have no idea. Take it how you like," I tell her before indicating to my wrists. "I'm assuming that since I'm not bound or blindfolded, that I'm not here as a prisoner."

"No," she finally says. "You're not a prisoner. Simply a guest."

Testing her words, I hesitantly step forward, taking me out of the center of the circle created by her henchmen, and I'm not surprised to find them stepping with me. "Ahhh," I say, arching a brow. "So, I may not be a prisoner, but I'm no guest."

"Can you blame my men for being wary around you?" she questions. "We have been watching you for a very long time. Any woman who could have Giovanni DeAngelis shaking in his boots and gain the attention of all three of his sons is a woman who I need to know."

Uncertainty flutters through my chest. "What do you mean you've been watching me? How do you even know who I am?"

She takes a step toward me, her chin raised with authority. "I know a lot of things, Miss Mariano, just as I know that you murdered your father in cold blood and slaughtered one of my men with a chainsaw."

I shake my head as the memory of what I did to James comes crashing through my head. It was brutal and cold-hearted. It was like a wakeup call, telling me just how far I've fallen, but it was also done in the privacy of the boys castle playground. There's no way she should know about that. "How … how do you know about that?"

"When you are in my position, you'll find that people like to offer up information in exchange for—"

"Life?" I scoff, cutting her off.

"Precisely," she says. "Now, tell me why you thought it was necessary to slaughter one of my men?"

Panic surges through me and I swallow hard, fearing that one wrong word out of my mouth could see a bullet straight through my head. "He was a nobody, just some rich asshole who thought he could get away with horrible things," I explain. "He kidnapped a woman from her home and raped her countless times. I rescued her from him, and when he thought he could come for me instead, we casually let him know that type of behavior wouldn't be tolerated. It was a simple misunderstanding."

Her gaze narrows but the hard set of her jaw gives nothing away. "And what happened to the woman?"

I shake my head. There's no way in hell I'm about to give up any information on Jasmine. "The woman is none of your concern. She's been through hell and deserves to live in peace," I say, fixing her with a hard stare, warning her to back off. "Now, please tell me what this is about."

"You're defiant," she muses. "I like that."

Not knowing how to respond to that, I ignore her comment and try to move her along. "You and I both know that you're on a clock here. The DeAngelis brothers track my every move, and they will no doubt be here any minute. So, I suggest that you say what needs to be said before they arrive and rain hell over this place."

A fond smile pulls at her lips and she nods. "You're a clever girl, Shayne. Stubbornly stupid, but clever. You've figured out this world quickly and adapted to survive. Many other women before you haven't made it this far. But you are right, the infamous DeAngelis brothers will be here shortly, and I'm sure they'll have plenty to say when they arrive."

"Why do I get the feeling that this is so much more than seeking revenge for killing one of your men?"

She steps toward me before slowly circling. "Because it is, dear," she murmurs, leaning in to whisper in my ear. She completes her circle, walking right around until she meets my eye again. "James was a problem since the day he joined my ranks. You did me a favor by taking his life."

"Then I suppose you owe me one."

Gia laughs and shakes her head. "Let's get one thing straight," she starts. "I do not owe anybody anything. You took James' life for your own satisfaction. The fact that it benefits me is purely coincidental."

I let out a sigh. I could have seen that coming a mile away. "He was in business with Giovanni."

"I am well aware of his indiscretions," Gia says, her eyes darkening with anger. "However, I did not drag you all the way out here to talk about James. We're here for you."

My brows furrow. "Me?"

"Indeed," she says, stepping into me again. "Why do you think

Giovanni took you in the first place?"

I pull back, uncomfortable with just how close she stands. "Because my father owed him a gambling debt. I was his payment."

Gia scoffs. "Is that the bullshit they fed you?" she demands, shaking her head and rolling her eyes in exasperation. "What a joke. Giovanni targeted you because he discovered that you are my biological daughter, the sole heir to the Moretti fortune, and you are set to inherit my position at the top of the Moretti family. He intended to marry you off to his eldest son to gain access to me and my family."

I gape at her, my jaw dropping to the floor.

What the ever-loving fuck?

CHAPTER THIRTY TWO

She's insane, well and truly fucked in the head. "Umm … what?" I say, a laugh bubbling up my throat. My mother? The fuck is this bitch on? "Come again?"

"You heard me, child," she says, unimpressed by my response. "I am your mother. I gave birth to you in a small hotel, deep in the heart of Seattle, twenty-two years ago. No one was to know of your existence. The Moretti family was rising in power and had many enemies. It was not a good time to be raising a child, you would have been targeted, and I could not accept that. This life is no life for a child."

I swallow hard, trying to come to terms with everything. I never knew who my mother was. My father never spoke of her, but I learned at a young age not to ask him questions, especially ones that he didn't believe were any of my business. "You're my mother?" I repeat.

She nods, holding my stare. "I am."

My heart races just a little bit faster, trying to comprehend what being the daughter of Gia Moretti truly means. "You're my mother, and you thought shipping me off to live with my father was the best thing for me?"

She nods again. "Yes, your father was a respectable man. He had a nice home and had his finances in line, plus I supplied him with enough cash to keep you well and truly looked after. You had everything you needed. Private schools, nice clothes, a car. How dare you insinuate that I didn't have your best interest at heart."

A booming laugh tears from deep in my belly as I become overwhelmed by every last ridiculous comment that comes flying out of her mouth. "My father was a violent drunk," I tell her. "He gambled every last cent we had. I didn't go to private schools or have any fancy cars or clothes. I hid in my room at night to avoid getting beat and would eat my breakfast out of the closest trash can to avoid starvation. By the time I was a teenager, I was locking my door because I was too fucking scared that he was going to welcome himself in. You didn't supply me anything. I suffered every fucking day and have the scars to prove it."

Gia steps into me, gripping my chin to tear my gaze up to hers. Anger swirls deep in her eyes, though something tells me she won't hurt me. "What the hell are you talking about?"

I pull out of her grip, that same fiery anger burning in my veins. "You've got the wrong kid, lady. I ain't no private school, Mafia princess."

I go to turn when I hear the sound of tires skidding along the gravel road and relief pours through me. Whatever the hell this is can be over. The boys can take me back home, and I can pretend that I didn't hear a damn word, or that her eyes aren't scarily similar to mine.

Gia's guards flinch as the boys barrel out of the car and make their way toward me, their eyes quickly scanning over mine to make sure I haven't been harmed. "Don't do anything stupid," she warns them as they move closer. "You've got a lot of nerve coming here."

Roman's stare shoots to Gia and my brows furrow noticing how casually they move. Why aren't they storming in like usual? Why aren't their guns already in their hands? "You had a lot of nerve coming into my home and taking what's ours."

"Yours?" She laughs as all three of the boys step straight through the circle of guards, not one of them trying to stop them. "You kidnap my daughter and expect me to stand back and watch you corrupt her?"

Marcus steps into my side and curls his hand around mine, silently letting me know I'm safe, but I turn to face them, my gaze shifting over each of their guilty expressions. "You knew about this, didn't you?" I demand, spitting my words at each of them and tearing my hand from Marcus' as the fiercest wave of betrayal crashes through me, destroying the trust I have for the boys in one fell swoop. "How could you not tell me something like this?"

Levi clenches his jaw, his gaze snapping back to Gia's before returning to mine. "It was part of the deal. We keep you safe from Giovanni, and she allows you to stay with us."

I laugh, my hand curling around my stomach. "Allow me?" I scoff, turning my furious gaze on the woman who's supposedly my mother.

"You don't have the right to allow me to do anything. Your blood may run in my veins, but you are no mother to me."

"How dare you," she spits. "I checked in on you every month. I paid your way through life."

"Well, you did a fantastic job," I scoff, turning back to the boys. "Get the fuck in the car. We apparently have a few things to discuss."

Guilt crosses their gazes again and I shove my hand into Marcus' side to get him moving, but Gia strides forward, halting our escape. "You are not going anywhere until I am done with you."

I glance back over my shoulder, my irritation making me stupidly brave. "You were done with me the second you shipped me off to live with my father. You said so yourself, you were rising in power. You had the funds and the resources to raise me in an appropriate setting and keep me safe. Hell, ever heard of boarding school? Instead, you chose to send me away to a man you barely knew. Admit it, you just didn't want to be my mother. You wanted to ship off your mistake and live your life at the top of the world."

Gia shakes her head and something breaks deep in her eyes. "I did not know your father was abusing you. Had I known, I would have stepped in. One of my men would meet with your father once a month and return with a full report. Clearly, someone has betrayed my trust, and I will look into it." She moves toward me and takes my hand, warmth filling her eyes. "I know you don't want to believe me, but you are wrong. I would give it all up to go back and be the mother you always deserved."

Sincerity pours out of her and my eyes well with tears. "What would have been so horrible about raising me by your side?" I whisper over the lump in my throat.

Gia glances at the boys by my side and shakes her head. "Look at them," she says. "Look at the life they've been raised in. They learned to slaughter men before they learned to drive. How could I inflict that same life on my only daughter?"

I swallow hard and glance at the boys, a part of me knowing that she's right, while the other part of me desperately wishes I had the life I was always meant to have. "I don't know about you," I murmur. "But when I look at them, I see three incredibly strong men who've overcome all odds. They're not weak for being raised with their father, they just had to learn the true meaning of what it takes to survive much earlier than anyone else, and because of that, they're stronger than anyone I've ever known."

Gia watches me through a curious gaze and her intense stare has me ready to crumble. "You're in love with these three men, aren't you?"

I nod, knowing she sees it just as clearly as I feel it.

She lets out a sigh before quickly glancing toward the dreadlock henchman. "That's going to be a problem."

The guard nods back to her and she returns her gaze to me. Then without a moment of warning, the dreadlock guard raises his gun and lets off five perfect rounds in the space of two seconds, each bullet spearing right through the eyes of the remaining guards in the room.

They drop to the ground and my eyes bug out of my head. "What the hell?" I screech as Marcus grabs me and yanks me behind him, all three of the boys with their guns out, two trained on Gia while the third is aimed at the sole remaining guard.

"I am sorry you had to witness that," Gia says, not disturbed by the boys' guns on her in the slightest. She takes a heavy breath and focuses her hard stare on me. "I'm sick, Shayne," she finally says, telling me what it is she's dragged me all this way to say. The boys stiffen beside me and my brows furrow, not understanding what's going on. "I have a year, maybe two left, and when that happens, it will be expected of you to step into my position."

Horror tears through me, but before I get a chance to tell her how sorry I am for her illness, while also telling her that she's insane if she thinks I'm going to step into her position as head of the Moretti family, she continues. "The DeAngelis family is our greatest enemy and has been for generations. It's taking me great restraint not to pull my gun on them now and end their miserable lives, however out of respect for you, I will not. But the issue at hand is that the moment you step into my position at the head of the family, every one of your dirty little secrets will be exposed, and the moment they discover your romantic connection to these men, you will be slaughtered like an animal."

My gaze shifts to the dead men around us. "That's why they're dead?" I question.

Gia nods. "I cannot risk word of this getting out."

"Well, fuck."

"Exactly."

Silence rests between us as a heaviness rests over my shoulders. I still don't know how I feel about the most dangerous woman on the planet being my mother, and I sure as hell don't know how I feel about her being sick and dying within the next two years and forcing me to take a long as hell walk in her shoes. It's clear that's why she's come to me now, but the whole thing has my chest constricting and struggling to breathe.

Not sure where to go from here, I'm thankful when Levi steps up and asks the one question we all want to know. "So, what now?" he questions. "We're sure as hell not giving her up."

Gia shakes her head, her eyes constantly coming back to mine. "I don't want you to give her up," she tells the boys. "I want you to continue to keep her safe, keep loving her, keep giving her the life she was always meant to have." She pauses as she steps toward me again. "Just know that I will always be watching, always lurking, and when it's time, I will find you again."

With that, she nods to her guard and the two of them start walking out of the old factory, but just as they go to step out through the big doors, I race after her. "Wait," I call out, bringing them both to a stop. Gia looks back with hopeful eyes and something breaks within me. "Earlier when you said that I was hard to get a hold of. What did you mean by that? Have you tried to reach out before?"

A fond smile pulls at her lips as she nods. "I have," she says. "However, your boys have erected quite the walls around you."

"How do you mean?"

She shrugs her shoulders, trying to think of an example. "Ahh, most recently, my men broke that pregnant woman out of Giovanni's cells."

"What?" Roman rushes out, his eyes wide as he steps forward

beside me, his hand coming out and pressing against my stomach as though he needs my physical touch to keep himself grounded. "You had Felicity?"

"Was she yours?" Gia questions, her eyes hardening at being interrupted by none other than a DeAngelis. "I figured that baby belonged to one of you."

"What did you do to her?" Roman demands.

Gia shrugs her shoulders, not at all concerned by Roman's relationship with Felicity. "The usual. She knew the castle and we figured she'd be our best shot at gaining access to Shayne. We freed her from your father's cell and told her that if she could get Shayne out, that she could keep on running with her own life. We gave her the gun, the passport, and the getaway car. She had everything she needed to succeed, but she still failed. She was weak."

Roman steps forward and the guard flinches. "She was captured and put back in a cell to rot. You could have saved her."

Fury rises in Gia's eyes, and she moves right into Roman, his height dramatically towering over her just as it does me, but yet she manages to appear so much taller. "I let her go, even after failing her only task. I released her. My men didn't pursue her in the woods. It is not my fault that she was captured again, and it's certainly not my fault that you three were too daft to go after her."

"What did you just say?"

"You heard me," she snaps. "It wasn't just your father's men in the woods that night. You slaughtered my family right along with his, something I will not forget."

"Don't act as though I'm the villain here," he warns her. "You brought your men onto my turf. It's not my fault they got slaughtered, that's on your shoulders. You know the rules."

Pushing Roman's hand down from my stomach, I force my way between them, giving Roman a hard shove back, as let's face it, I don't have big enough balls to shove Gia as well. "Okay, I think everything has been said that needed to be said," I tell them, nodding to Marcus and Levi to take their brother off my hands before he barges right past me and starts another war that we're not in the position to fight.

They step in and pull Roman back and Gia does the same, giving me space before turning her heated gaze on me and visibly trying to calm herself. "It would be wise to keep this knowledge of your lineage to yourself," she warns me. "It would not be good for anyone if word got out that I had a daughter. There are a lot of wicked men gunning to step into my position, but the only person I see strong enough to lead a family like mine, is you."

I nod and she takes another step back. "You best get out of here," she says. "Don't you have an important meeting to get to?"

Marcus stiffens along with the other two and shoulders in front of Roman. "How the fuck do you know about our meeting?"

She gives him a thumbs up. "Good job on plausible deniability," she taunts. "Gold star for you." Meeting his blank expression, she rolls her eyes. "I am Gia Moretti of the Moretti family. It is my job to know when my enemies are falling, and you three, are most definitely falling. It was a brave move, I have to give you credit for that, but I have stood against your father for too many years. He will rise again, and when he does, you three better watch your backs … that is, if I haven't beaten him to the punch."

Gia grins at the boys, the insinuation thick in the air that at least one of the men in the DeAngelis family is feeding her information, and fuck, the boys don't like it one bit.

Without another word, Gia promptly disappears with her dreadlocked guard, leaving me with only one thing to do—curse these three motherfuckers out until my throat bleeds.

I slowly turn, the rage boiling inside me, and as I meet their heavy stares and watch the guilt pour across their handsome features, I take a deep breath, knowing damn well that there's about to be some long as fuck sentences tearing from deep inside me, and this bitch is gonna need all the help I can get. "WHAT THE FUCK IS WRONG WITH YOU ASSHOLES?" I demand. "YOU KNEW THAT GIA FUCKING MORETTI WAS MY FUCKING BIOLOGICAL MOTHER AND YOU DIDN'T SAY A GODDAMN WORD? FUCK!"

Roman lets out a heavy sigh and steps between his brothers, putting himself right in front of me. His fingers brush over my arm and I flinch away from him, the betrayal stinging me like never before. "Come on," he murmurs, his brothers hesitantly moving in behind him, more than ready for me to whoop their bitch asses. "You can curse us out in the car, but Gia is right. We need to get back home before we miss this meeting, otherwise we'll lose them for good, and everything we've worked for will be all for nothing."

I glare up at him, my sharp stare boring into his liquid lasers. "Fine," I tell him. "But I'm driving, and you better believe that I'm going to take it out on the car, and don't think for one second that you will get a fucking word in. The three of you are going to sit in the back in complete silence and I'm going to curse your bitch asses until my throat is raw. Got it?"

They all nod and I turn on my heel, stalking back toward the black SUV only to see Gia's car escaping from the back of the property. "Hurry the fuck up," I tell the assholes at my back. "Get in before I leave you here."

And just like that, I storm around the car and get in the driver's seat, having to slide the chair forward just to be able to reach the pedals. My fingers slam against the automatic start and the engine roars to life as the three sorry fuckers who thought it was a good idea to betray my trust slide across the backseat. The door has barely closed behind Marcus when I hit the gas, and without skipping a beat, I let them have it.

CHAPTER THIRTY THREE

Expensive Lamborghinis and Ferraris litter the front drive as I bring the SUV to a stop outside the DeAngelis family mansion. "Fuck," Marcus mutters, the first word he's said the whole way back. "Can't you park around the side or something? All these motherfuckers are going to see us climbing out of the back together like a bunch of delinquent school kids."

"Get the fuck out before I cause a scene," I tell him, my throat scratchy from yelling at them for the last hour.

The boys groan and slide out of the car as I cut the engine. Family members who look just like them watch from the top of the stairs and I smirk at the slight embarrassment filling their veins. Though, it won't last long. They're at the top of their game. They could be caught with their pants around their ankles, fucking a custard pie while singing *Mary Had a Little Lamb* and they'd still manage to look like the most lethal men on earth.

Small victories, right?

Roman and Marcus walk ahead as Levi waits for me, not wanting me to walk alone into a room full of DeAngelis Mafia killers with questionable morals. His hand presses against the small of my back and as he leads me up the grand stairs, I find myself falling closer into his side.

"Can we put everything aside and show a united front, just for the next few hours?" he questions, his tone low and private. "Then I swear, after that, you can go back to hating on us."

"Lucky for you," I mutter darkly, "my throat is too sore to keep cursing your bitch asses out."

"Good," he says, sending a tight smile to some dude lingering on the stairs. "After this meeting, I'll find something to ease your throat and we can explain how we found out about your … lineage."

I groan and pause, stopping him as I glance up into his addictive, dark eyes. "If anyone finds out in there—"

"They'll kill you," he says bluntly, finishing my sentence. "You cannot let it slip. These guys … they put on a brave front, but when it comes to Gia Moretti, they're shit scared. She's not someone our people want to fuck with, and until now, we've happily lived side by side. While our family is significantly bigger, hers is a new brand of brutal, and that's saying a lot coming from me. She's not a forgiving woman, and the fact that she stood back and allowed Roman to mouth off to her like that speaks volumes. She has big plans and for whatever reason, she needs me and my brothers alive for it."

Panic flutters through my chest as I glance up to the top of the steps to find Marcus and Roman watching us, making sure we're alright. "Is she going to come for us?"

Levi presses his lips into a tight line and slowly shakes his head. "No, I don't believe so. I haven't had much experience with the woman, but I do believe that she is genuine in her feelings toward you, and I don't think she will do anything to jeopardize that relationship, at least, not yet."

Fuck.

I swallow hard and nod before continuing up the stairs. Roman and Marcus wait for us, and as one, we push through the doors to find the foyer flooded with bodies. I suck in a breath. I expected a lot of things when walking in here, yet for some ridiculous reason, I hadn't expected them to bombard us at the front door.

"Shit," I breathe, scanning over all the faces that turn our way, annoyed to have been held up. "Would it have killed you guys to lock the door before coming after me?"

"They would have found a way inside whether the door was locked or not," Roman murmurs, handing out fake smiles and curious glances, wondering which of these assholes will finish their night by stabbing them in the back. I have a few guesses, but one can never be too sure.

Nerves bloom deep in my stomach as we make our way through the formal dining room, and I can't help but notice a few familiar faces from the ball a few nights ago. But unlike the ball, those faces are now filled with apprehension, pinched brows, and frowns.

Tension fills the room, but that tension is nothing compared to the feeling of stepping through to the empty dining room to find the boys' grandfather sitting at the head of the table as though that's where he belongs.

Roman sighs deeply, and I follow the boys as they make their way through the extravagant room, all eyes focused on their grandfather. I don't miss the way that each of their shoulders pull back and the tight muscles beneath become rigid and hard.

"Grandfather," Roman mutters in welcome, clearly not too thrilled to see him so soon again after the ball, but it's not as though this meeting was avoidable.

The old man leans back in his seat, his thumb twisting over the heavy gold rings lining his fingers as he places a glass tumbler down on the table. "What is the girl doing here?" he demands, his deadly stare trailing over me with distaste, reminding me so much of Giovanni. "These meetings are not open for women, and especially not the current whore of the month. Do away with her."

Marcus laughs. "That's not going to happen," he says as we reach their grandfather. The three boys step around him, surrounding his chair and making his eyes nervously flicker toward them. I hang back, not wanting to be in the way of this particular pissing contest.

Marcus leans down, hovering by his grandfather's side. "Shayne stays, but you on the other hand … you're in our seat."

Their grandfather scoffs and pushes back in the chair before standing and turning to face them, not daring to step out from the prime position in the room. "You three are a joke, children merely playing dress up," he spits, the insult bouncing straight off them. "You are not ready to lead this family. Now where is your father? What have you done with him?"

Levi grins and tilts his head in that creepy way that has shivers trailing down my spine. "Come on, old man," he murmurs. "You've been trying to get rid of our father since the day he ran you out, but I have to be honest, it was ballsy of you to make an appearance at the ball. Tell me, did you show only because you knew he wouldn't be there? Sounds like a cowardly move to me."

The old man's eyes flash with fury as he steps out from behind the chair to shove his fingers into Levi's chest. "Don't you forget who founded this family," he growls. "Without me, you three would have nothing. I built this family; I was the one who rose in power. I put in the work, and your father took it straight out of my hands as though he was entitled to it. He doesn't know what it means to run an empire, and nor do you three smug brats. You think you can waltz in here and claim a seat at the head of my table, well think again. This is my home, my family, my blood, and you're stepping down before you embarrass yourselves. You'll get my family once I'm in the ground, and even then, you'll have to pry it from my cold, dead hands."

A smirk pulls at Levi's lips and I can only imagine what bullshit is about to come flying out of his mouth. His grandfather's eyes tighten, realizing just how easily the boys will follow through on his threat, and just as he clenches his jaw and his hand slips back for a weapon, a voice sails through the dining room. "Really, Father?" Louis says, striding toward the table and pulling out a seat. "You're going to shoot your grandson with the whole family just outside these doors? Bold move, no matter how foolish it may be."

My brow arches, and as if on cue, the rest of the family spills into the dining room and takes their seats around the grand table. With so many eyes on his back, the old man stands down, reaching for his glass tumbler and moving to the side. He takes a seat, directly beside the head of the table as the three brothers step into the prime position, watching in silence as their family gathers around them.

There's no elaborate meal or fancy waiters walking around in penguin suits like the last time I sat through a business dinner, tonight is simply business. They're here to say what needs to be said and then they'll be ushered straight out the door, hopefully with their lives intact.

I keep myself away from the table, not wanting to stand with the boys in case it causes some kind of stir within the family, more so than what it already has. But I don't think anybody, apart from their grandfather, has the balls to comment on it.

My gaze sails over the men surrounding the table, and I recognize a few of their faces from the ball. The boys' cousins are here, and the way they take the chairs furthest away from Louis speaks volumes. Joseph is here, sitting away from everyone like the lone wolf that he is, and I can't help but feel like this is some bullshit kind of high school cafeteria seating plan. Everybody sits away from their greatest threat while trying to keep a position that gives them an advantage. It's high school politics in the flesh.

Roman stands in the center of his brothers, all three of them taking up the space at the head of the table and looking over the nervous men before them.

"Thank you all for making the trip out here tonight," Roman starts, taking the lead as usual. "I know you've all had a long drive here, only to be kept waiting, and we apologize for that. However, we had urgent matters to attend to."

Their grandfather scoffs, his tone sailing right down the length of the long table. "What could have been so important that you kept my family waiting on a day like this?"

Roman arches a brow, intrigued by his grandfather's audacity. "If you must know, this afternoon, the love of my life, Shayne Mariano, was kidnapped and held hostage by the Moretti family."

Gasps and roars of outrage tear through the room as eyes fall to me, each one of them probably wondering how the hell I'm still alive.

Louis stands, his hand slamming down on the table. "What is the meaning of this?" he demands. He's certainly no fan of mine, but an attack against me is classified as an attack against the whole family, and for that, they would be outraged on my behalf.

Roman holds his hands up, indicating for the room to shut the fuck up, and that's exactly what they do. "It has come to our attention that our father has been making plans to move against Gia Moretti and her family, and as a warning, they came into this house, *our home*, and took Shayne right out of her bedroom. Now clearly, we were able to retrieve her without casualty, but this is a direct hit on us because of my father's stupidity."

"Why would he do that?" Louis questions, his brows furrowed. "We had peace with the Morettis. Starting another war with them now would be catastrophic."

"You tell me, Uncle," Roman fires back at him. "I know you don't have the greatest fondness for my father, but you're able to read him like a book. You declared only a few nights ago that you would remain loyal to him. So, you tell me why he would make such a foolish decision that would impact the whole family?"

Louis shakes his head, pressing his lips into a tight line, lost for words. "I ... I do not know. There must be some kind of misunderstanding. Giovanni wouldn't do that."

Roman leans forward on the table, his gaze sweeping across the room, "From the mouth of Gia Moretti herself—Giovanni has been attempting to infiltrate her family. He plans on taking her out and gaining control of the Moretti fortune. I don't know how he intends to do that, but it is a foolish game."

Roman skips right over the part where his father intended to marry his eldest son off to Gia's daughter, and I'm grateful. That little piece of information can remain private for now. Hell, maybe it should stay buried until the end of time. Nobody needs to know.

"Is this the man you trust to rule over our family?" Roman continues. "Is this what you want for your future? To be at war with Gia Moretti? You know what she is capable of. She holds no boundaries, no morals. Not one of us is safe. Our children, our friends, family. Standing with my father now, is welcoming Gia Moretti into your homes, into your bed. She is a leech who will suck the blood right out of us until there is nothing left. So, what's it going to be? Wait for my father to rise up and destroy us from the inside out, or stand with us and be the future of this family, stronger and more powerful than ever before?"

Uneasy murmurs erupt through the room as men turn to their neighbor to question what the fuck to do. From the looks of it, most of these men were planning to stand by Giovanni, trusting he will rise up and overpower his sons. But learning of his plan to stand against Gia has changed everything except how terrified the men are of the brothers before them. They're unhinged, lethal, and reckless, and they make no secret of that. Following them could mean a world of torment, a life in chains, but following Giovanni into a war with Gia would mean certain death.

My gaze settles on the boys' grandfather, and I watch as his smug expression slowly hardens, realizing what everyone else in the room is quickly figuring out too—the boys are going to win this. They're going to officially gain power over the family, just as it should have always been.

A chair scraping against the marble floor sends everyone's sharp gazes to the back of the dining room to find Victor's eldest son. "My brothers and I have spoken at great lengths over the past few days, figuring out our next steps, and we declare here tonight, that we will support Roman, Marcus, and Levi in their rise to power. They may be brutal, cold, and heartless killers, but they are the future of this family. No leader would be stronger. They have our loyalty."

Shocked murmurs tear through the room as wide eyes gape at the four brothers, every last person knowing that their father would be rolling in his grave right now. Though, we know something they don't. Their loyalty doesn't come free. The boys have to earn it, and I'm sure they'll do so with pride.

His declaration sets off a chain reaction. One by one, men stand and declare their loyalty to the boys while their grandfather acts as though every single declaration is a personal attack against him.

Everybody has their turn, but when Louis stands and focuses his hard stare on his nephews, the tension rises in the room. "Every single man in this room is foolish to believe these three children are capable of ruling over our organization. Giovanni is not here to defend his actions. Who knows if this bullshit with the Moretti family is even true. However, my fellow family members have already made their declarations and therefore leave me with no choice but to fall in line or risk my life by walking away. Do I believe that Giovanni will return to claim what's rightfully his? Yes I do. And because of this meeting, when that happens, every last one of us is fucked."

Louis drops down as an amused smirk plays on Marcus' lips. "Feel free to walk out," Marcus tells him, his tone filled with a deadly warning, the unspoken truth about what will happen to him the second he gets up floating in the air.

A heavy silence fills the room as Louis' hard stare remains locked on Marcus. "Wouldn't dream of it," he finally says, grabbing his glass off the table and throwing back what's left of it.

Marcus laughs, and I can only imagine how much his uncle's resistance is sweetening their cousins' deal. The boys are going to take great pleasure in ending Louis' life, but Marcus will relish in it. He's a special brand of crazy.

Roman slices his lethal glare to his uncle, something sinister playing in his eyes. "We won't forget what happened here tonight," he tells him, his lips pulling into a twisted grin and forcing a light sweat to appear on Louis' forehead. Perhaps he forgot who he was dealing with.

Roman turns back to the rest of the table, raising his chin and the pride shining through his eyes warms something deep inside of me. The boys have wanted this for so long, and after the abuse they've suffered at their father's hands, they deserve everything and more. Finally, it's right there in the palm of their hands. Now all they need to do is hold onto it, because in a world like this, it could easily slip between their fingers. "Alright, if everyone has spoken their piece, then I say we call it a night."

"What about your second in command?" A voice comes from across the table.

I have to step to my right to see the person's face, and my brow arches finding Joseph, the boys' final uncle who rarely has anything to say, nor wants anything to do with any of this. Hell, I'm surprised he's even here. Though I have a feeling it's out of obligation.

Roman indicates to his brothers at his side. "Do you believe between the three of us, that we really need a second in command?"

"Yes," he says, bluntly, not trying to offend, simply just stating a fact. "Every leader who has stood at the head of that table has had a second in command. Who do we fall back on if you three were indisposed? Who will lead us then?"

Roman glances at his brothers and as one, all three of their dark gazes fall on me. "Oh, hell no," I say, my hands flying up in defense as an eruption of rejection fills the room.

Roman's hand slams down on the table, silencing his family once again. "ENOUGH," he roars. "It is done. Shayne Mariano is our second, and in the event that we cannot lead, she will step into our place. Anyone who has an issue with that is invited to come and speak with us privately." His stare meets every eye in the room, and sensing the unspoken threat, they all wisely keep their mouths shut, and with that, he indicates to the door. "We're done here, you may all leave to spend the night with your families. As of tomorrow, we will start the search for my father, and it will not stop until he has been put down and my child safely returned to my arms."

No one hangs around.

The room clears in a matter of seconds, and I'm not surprised when Louis is the first one out the door. The boys turn to me, and Levi indicates to the back of the room, silently telling me to follow. They make their move, big, long strides that I have to struggle to keep up with.

Marcus pulls back, waiting for me to pass before following behind me, pressing his hand against the small of my back to lead me through a hidden door in the back of the formal dining room. My brows furrow as I look up ahead of us through a dark passageway. I've never been through here before. I didn't even realize there were passageways through here. It's creepy, and chilling, and absolutely everything I expect out of the DeAngelis family home. They probably use these secret passageways to escape when bombarded with raids and enemies. Knowing the boys, I'd be stupid not to assume they haven't hidden out in here a time or two just to overhear conversations that weren't meant for their ears.

We rush through the dark passageway, and a shiver sails down my spine. "What are we doing?" I mutter, reaching out for Levi in front of me to avoid tripping over his feet.

"Coming through on our end of the deal," Roman says from up ahead. "Now hurry up, we don't have time to fuck around."

My brows furrow and the boys pick up their pace. I try to keep up with them and Marcus scoops me up so I don't get left behind. Then all too soon, they come to a stop outside an old door. Roman glances back at his brothers. "We get the drop on him. Make it fast."

They nod and I swallow hard. "And me?" I breathe.

"Stay the fuck out of the way."

That I can do. In fact, that I am very good at.

The door is opened just a sliver and the boys slip out the small opening as I follow behind them. We come out at the side of the property into the dark night, and I hear the hushed conversations of the boys' family making their hasty escapes.

"There," Levi says, nodding up ahead.

I follow his gaze to where Louis scurries away from the mansion, practically bolting to his car in order to get out of here with his life. Beyond him are Victor's four remaining sons, waiting in anticipation. What better opportunity to take him out than now?

Roman grins and pulls his gun before twisting the silencer onto the top, not wanting to alert the other scattering family members. He holds up the gun, and without skipping a beat, takes a clear shot straight through the back of Louis' hand as he reaches for his car door.

He cries out, roaring in pain as his head whips around, searching for the threat. His eyes are wide and fearful but there's a dark edge hidden beneath the surface, reminding me of what the boys said months ago—Louis DeAngelis is just like them. He's a fighter, he's wild and unpredictable. Lethal. He needs to be pushed to the breaking point, and when he is, he turns as easily as if someone had flipped a switch.

If anyone hears his cry, they don't look this way, trusting their basic instincts to keep moving.

The boys spring into action racing in after him as he's blinded by the pain. They're on him in seconds, and even with his hand out of action, he's still able to fight back. He's weak, and as he gets in a few punches, I realize the boys are only playing with him. I've seen them fight more than I care to admit, and this here is about proving a point.

Levi cuts in front of his brothers, grabbing Louis by his bad hand and twisting it behind his back. He screams out as his nephew plasters himself to his back, leaving his body exposed to Roman and Marcus. "You won't get away with this," Louis spits, seeing they're clearly done playing with him.

Nobody moves, but Louis screams out again, and I can only assume that Levi tightened his grip on his hand. "We already are, Uncle," Marcus purrs. "Look around. No one is coming for you. They all want you dead just as much as we do. Where's your precious leader now?"

Louis smirks, a secret playing in his eyes. "Yours is going to be the shortest reign ever lived," he taunts them, groaning as Levi tears his arm further behind his back. "Turn around, assholes."

My head whips around just as the brothers do, and I suck in a terrified gasp, seeing Giovanni standing at the top of the property, his eyes cast down on us with a fucking wall of soldiers at his back.

Terror flies through me as the boys stiffen, furious anger streaming through our veins. Roman roars, his hand flinching at his side before lashing out like lightning, a blade slicing straight through Louis' throat.

Time slows as Levi releases his uncle, letting his body fall heavily to the ground. Someone races toward me as shouts are heard across the property, and I'm distantly aware of them coming from Victor's sons. Something curls around my wrist and I'm tugged back inside the secret door before feet pound against the hard ground.

My pulse thunders heavily in my ears and as I try to keep up with the boys, I realize that tonight is the night I've feared for so long.

Tonight is war.

CHAPTER THIRTY FOUR

"**F**uck, fuck, fuck, fuck, fuck, fuck," I chant, racing after the boys in a complete daze, my head whirling with the unknown while fear pulses heavily through my veins. We run back in through the dining room and past the foyer where Marcus pauses for a brief second, peering out through the window to check just how long we have.

"Two minutes tops," he curses, pushing off the wall to propel himself back to his brother. "It's gonna be fucking close."

"Did anyone see my baby?" Roman throws over his shoulder as Levi barges past him to tear open the internal garage door.

Levi shakes his head as I try to think back to the image of his father standing over the hill. "I … I don't know," I rush out, storming into the garage behind the boys, unsure where to go or how I'm supposed to be helping them. "I only looked for a second. I … I don't—"

"DID ANYBODY SEE MY FUCKING BABY?" Roman roars, cutting me off in his desperation.

"Didn't see him, bro," Marcus says, reaching a big metal door in the back of the garage as Levi slams his hand against a scanner. "But that doesn't mean he's not here."

A green laser scans Levi's fingerprints before I hear the heavy bolts clanking open and allowing them access. Roman reaches past Levi and grips the metal door before pulling it back to display rows upon rows of weapons. The boys don't waste a second, barging into the armory and loading up with everything they can get their hands on. Automatic weapons hang over their shoulders as they shove handguns in the back of their pants. With pockets full of loaded magazines and long daggers protruding from their combat belts, they seem ready for anything.

I gape at the sight, disgustingly out of my league, but what choice do I have? It's either fight or die running. There is no hiding out or cowering in a corner. It's time to put everything the boys have taught me into practice and hope that the assholes Giovanni hired to fight his war are as stupid as they look, because the element of surprise is the only thing I've got going for me, and that surprise is going to expire quickly.

Having wasted too many precious seconds gaping at the armory, I race in after the boys and grab a belt, hastily fastening it around my hips. I grab guns and shove them deep into my belt before taking every knife I can find. I strap them to my thighs and even shove a few down the inside of my boots.

Weapons dangle off me like some kind of arms dealer, and I glance up at one of the many automatic guns hanging high on the shelf. I could cause a lot of damage with a gun like that, but I haven't had any practice, and knowing my luck, I'd accidentally shoot the boys before I could even get a clear round off toward Giovanni and his men.

I let out a shaky breath. "Fuck, fuck, fuck, fuck, fuck."

What the hell have I gotten myself into?

Footsteps pound against the marble floor in the foyer, and my heart kicks up a gear. My eyes widen, listening to the sound of feet storming toward the garage. "Roman?" a voice calls out. "The fuck you at?"

Roman's brows furrow for a moment before stepping out of the armory and looking back toward the internal door. "Back here," he calls out. "Load up."

It's only moments before the boys' four cousins come bolting into the armory and I gape at them in surprise. I would have thought they'd have taken off at the first sign of Giovanni like the rest of this family. They quickly scan the room, seeing what they want before diving straight in.

"How long?" Levi grunts, grabbing a grenade and looking it over.

"He's close," the eldest cousin says. "Maybe a minute. Two if we're lucky."

Marcus shakes his head. "Thirty seconds."

My eyes bug out of my head and a cold sweat settles over my skin. "Fuck."

Roman and Levi both look my way, and I don't miss the strain within their obsidian gazes. They don't want me here just as badly as I don't want to be here, but it's in my blood. Gia Moretti is my mother and I'm apparently some kind of heir to her fortune. Backing out now would make me a coward. Besides, where the boys go, I go. They were the assholes who decided to make me their second in command, so I have no choice but to forge full steam ahead into battle.

Seeing the resolve in my eyes, the boys get back to loading up what they need, and as Roman slips a final knife into his belt, he looks back at his cousins. "You don't have to do this," he tells them, knowing what the odds are of each of them surviving. "There's still time to slip out the back door."

The eldest cousin checks over a gun and snaps his gaze to Roman's. "We pledged our loyalty," he mutters, his voice dark and rich with determination. "What would that make of us if we were to turn our backs now?"

Roman scans his gaze over the four boys before coming back to the eldest. "The likelihood of you all surviving this…"

His words trail off and all four of his cousins nod. "We know," the eldest says. "Now, where is the rest of your fucking army?"

Marcus grins, and throws his gun up over his shoulder, a dark sparkle in his eyes. "You're fighting with us now," he says, a wicked smirk pulling at his lips, reminding me just how fucking lethal these guys are. "We don't need a fucking army."

We hear the shouts of Giovanni's men outside and Roman glances over his brothers. "This is it, boys. The moment we've been waiting for. Remember, my son is our priority. We get him first, and then we get to play."

Darkness swirls in all of their eyes, and I see nothing but bloodlust. They're savages, complete psychotic heathens with the most sinister craving for blood. They're brutal, lethal, and violent, and I fucking love it.

"Let's go," Roman calls.

Our group pours out of the armory, and rather than wasting precious minutes going back in through the foyer and down the massive stairs, Roman slams his fist down over the button for the automatic garage door, keeping us on ground level.

They're going to expect us to come through the front, so whatever edge we can get, we'll take.

We stand in front of the massive garage door as it slowly rises, and with every inch, my stomach swirls. Marcus moves in closer to grab my waist and turns me into his chest. His hand falls to my chin and he yanks my head up, forcing my eyes to his. "I'd tell you to go and hide, but I don't think you're going to do that. So, whatever the fuck happens out there, stay behind one of us. We won't be able to protect you every fucking second, so you're going to have to come to the party and do your part, but if you keep behind us, then those fuckers will literally have to go through us first to get to you." I nod as he pauses, his dark eyes boring into mine. "Don't try to be a fucking hero. If someone slips past us and they're coming for you, call for us. Someone will help you. Is that understood?"

I nod again. "Got it."

His lips crush down on mine in a quick bruising kiss that takes my breath away, and as he pulls back from me and we find the garage door high enough to slip under, my nerves start to get the best of me.

"Marc, go." Roman demands.

Marcus doesn't hesitate, slipping under the open garage door and taking off like a fucking rocket toward the thick brush around the property. "Where's he going?" I rush out as Levi takes my hand and pulls me toward the garage door.

We all slip under it, the boys' cousins sticking to us like glue. "Marc has sniper training," Levi explains as we rush around the side of the property, far out of view of Giovanni and his men. "He's got the best shot out of all of us. He'll be able to take out a few of them before they even reach us."

"Shit, but wouldn't your father have men hidden out in the woods? You could be sending him right into a trap."

Roman glances back at me, his eyes softening just a touch. "Marcus can handle himself," he explains. "I don't want you going into this worrying about us. We'll be fine. You need to be thinking about yourself."

Levi nods as we slam our backs up against the side of the house, lying in wait. "If things get dicey," he says, "if something happens and we can't save you, then I want you to find an out. Take off into the woods. Call for Dill and Doe and run for your fucking life. They'll guide you out of the woods and to safety. Just know, whatever happens, we will find you."

I let out a shaky breath. The thought of having to cut and run makes me sick, but if I hang around waiting for death, that makes everything we've been through all for nothing. "Promise me, Shayne," Levi continues, his voice taking on a strained, hard edge. "Promise that you'll run if it comes to it."

I swallow hard and nod, tears filling my eyes. I hastily wipe them away, trying to gain control of my emotions. This is certainly no time to turn into a babbling, whiny bitch. "I promise," I tell him. "But I swear to God, if you assholes die, I'll kill you myself."

Roman scoffs. "Nothing can kill us, Shayne. We're the motherfucking grim reapers."

And with that, we take off into the night.

Levi pushes me toward Roman, and I hurry after him, keeping right on

Roman's heels as he bounds through bushes and toward the very front of Giovanni's army, ready to take them face on. I'm not going to lie, standing right at the front of the pack isn't exactly the position I want going into this, but I trust the boys to keep me safe. Marcus is out there somewhere keeping watch over us, and I need to believe that he's got my back.

Levi and the cousins rush off in different directions, and I quickly realize that we're surrounding Giovanni's army from all angles. A grin pulls at my lips. They'll never see us coming.

Roman pulls me down into a bush that looks over the front of the property, right to where we see Giovanni strutting down the long driveway as though he's some kind of god. His men stand at his back, not one of them holding Roman's baby. "Fuck," he says, his gaze scanning over each of them. "He's left my son somewhere."

"He's got to be somewhere close," I murmur. "Your father wouldn't let him out of his sight for long. He'll want him somewhere he could easily get to him if his plan turns to shit."

Roman nods, agreeing with me, but the only problem is that none of us know where the fuck that could be. "Come on," he says, his hand falling back into mine.

I follow him out of the bush, keeping in the shadows of the night. "There's got to be at least eighty men," I say. "I know you guys are good, but there's no way we can take on all of them by ourselves."

"Have faith, Empress. We've faced worse odds," he says, pausing to wait for his father to get just a little closer. "Just a little bit longer."

A few seconds tick by, and the moment Giovanni steps into the very center of the circle drive, preparing to take the stairs, a shot rings out.

One of Giovanni's men falls with a loud cry, the bullet piercing right through the center of his head. A spray of blood decorates the man beside him, and I cringe in disgust as the blood catches in the faint moonlight.

Giovanni holds up his hand, bringing his men to a stop as they frantically search around, desperate to find the shooter, but they'll never find him. Marcus is too good.

Another shot rings out, and a man on the opposite side of the pack drops like a sack of potatoes, the bullet piercing through his chest. He cries out in agony, and I watch as men duck down in fear. "They didn't know," I breathe as Roman's hand squeezes in mine. "Your father's brought them here to be slaughtered, and they had no fucking idea."

"None," Roman says. "He would have told them it was just a show of force to get us to kneel to his demands. They're not prepared for this. They're just random men off the fucking street. It's a shame really, but it's either them or us, and I choose you every fucking time."

Another shot goes off and another before Giovanni holds out his hands. "ENOUGH," he roars through the night, his face reddening as his gaze flicks from left to right, trying to pinpoint his sons. "SHOW YOURSELVES AT ONCE."

Roman laughs and tugs on my hand. "Show time."

And with that, everybody steps out, creating a barrier around Giovanni and his army.

A grin pulls at my lips, seeing Levi directly to our left and Marcus stepping from the woods on our right. Giovanni glances around, knowing just how much of a threat the boys would be coming at him from three different directions. He looks nervous, but his determination soars above that.

"Really now?" he says, holding his hands out. "You think you're a match for me? I have a hundred men here tonight and you stand before me with nothing but yourselves and your cousins? I came for a fight, but this will be a slaughter."

"Don't fool yourself, Father. You've never fought a day in your life," Roman laughs, mocking him like any emotionally abused son should. "What are you hoping to achieve here? We've already won your seat at the head of the table. The family has sworn loyalty to us. You've lost. You've got nothing left."

Giovanni scoffs. "You threatened the family into pledging their loyalty," he laughs, shaking his head. "But where are they now? It's just words, Roman. If they are not standing at your back, ready to end my life, then you don't truly have their loyalty. The family is still mine. It's always been mine, and you are nothing but a moronic child who thinks he's ready to play in the big leagues. Give it up, son. You can still walk away. This is your final warning. I would hate to have to end you like I did your mother, but I will."

Roman slips one of his many guns from the combat belt at his side and in a rapid flash of lightning, two perfect rounds ring loudly through the night. The two soldiers at Giovanni's side go down and Giovanni barely even flinches. "Too fucking late to come begging for forgiveness now," Roman calls. "Tonight, you die."

As if someone flipped a switch, the army roars at Giovanni's back and comes storming toward us like a stampede, bounding around Giovanni in their desperation to take us out. Roman fires off a few more shots, effortlessly taking out soldiers as Marcus and Levi join the fray. Their cousins hit the soldiers from the back and it turns into an all-out war, the army evenly spread around Giovanni like some kind of protective shield.

There's no way to get to him unless we take out the army first.

"Grab a knife," Roman throws over his shoulder, preparing himself for the fight of a lifetime. "Preferably a big one."

Fuck.

I swallow hard and grip the handle at my thigh before pulling the long dagger out of its sheath, and just to be prepared, I grab a gun in my other hand as well.

Shots ring out through the expansive property like thunder, and a bullet whizzes past my face as a shriek tears from the back of my throat. "You ready?" Roman demands as the army grows closer, his voice traveling over the roaring sound.

I swallow down my fears. I promised Felicity that I would care for her baby, and if this is what I have to do to ensure I keep that promise and get that baby into the safety of his father's arms, then that's what I'm going to do. "Born ready."

Roman scoffs, seeing through my bullshit, but he nods, appreciating that I'm with him no matter what. "Let's do this."

We forge forward toward the army, and Roman lets off a few more shots, getting a few easy kills out of the way before focusing on the fight. He jumps straight into action, pushing himself in front of me and keeping me protected at his back, but there are too many men to hold back.

My eyes are wide and terrified as I watch men pour around Roman, each one going for him with fury, but he holds his own, far too skilled and full of power than any of them could have possibly seen coming. He's superhuman, that's the only way to describe it.

He slams his gun right up into a guy's gut and pulls the trigger, effortlessly taking him down while his other hand shoots out, knocking out another soldier. Men drop as quickly as they can come, and it's clear that these soldiers Giovanni recruited are nobodies with absolutely no formal training. Roman was right, it is a shame that we have to kill them, but they got themselves involved in this mess and now they have to suffer the consequences.

Two men get around Roman and my heart races as they come for me. Nerves pulse heavily through my veins. It's one thing to kill a man who's already down or chained to the fucking metal beams holding up the ceiling, but having them actively fighting and probably a shitload stronger than me, now that's something new.

They bear down on me, and instead of bitching out or shitting my pants, I pull on my game face. I can do this. I was fucking born ... well, no. I certainly wasn't born for this, but I was trained a little bit and have a big enough chip on my shoulder that I can maybe make a good go of it.

With determination in my veins and fury in my chest, I storm toward them, meeting them before they have a chance to meet me. My dagger swings through the air and I spin widely, a battle cry tearing from between my lips. The blade sails straight through the first guy's waist, and his eyes widen like saucers, looking at me in disbelief. His hand drops to his waist just in time to catch the contents spilling out of it, and I gasp at the sight.

"CRY ABOUT IT LATER," Roman grunts. "FOCUS."

Fuck.

I blink, only now realizing there are tears in my eyes and slam my hand out again, thrusting the dagger toward the second guy. He skirts out of the way and looks at me as though I'm the vilest little bitch he's ever laid eyes on. He shoots forward, his fists come out at me, and I quickly stumble back a step, raising my other hand and pulling the trigger.

My arm jerks back with the momentum of the shot as the bullet sails toward his head, going so damn fast that I barely see the moment it tears off half his face. A scream tears from the back of my throat as he drops down, but I push my fear aside and forge forward. There are too many men crowding Roman, and I refuse to let him go down with me cowering behind him.

We fight side by side, and when things get a little shady for me, he sweeps out with a knife, amputating an arm or two. We quickly cull the soldiers, and with Levi and Marcus working their way from the side and the cousins at the back, it's not long before I can start to see through the throng of people.

An explosion rocks through the ground as bodies are hit with the blast, flying across the property. The blast sends me back onto my ass, and just as I scramble to get back up, a heavy boot presses against my chest, slamming me back to the ground. I scream out, but all is lost as I look up and meet Giovanni's dark stare as he presses the tip of a blade against my throat.

I suck in a breath, my body going still as I stare up into the face of pure evil. He smirks down at me, knowing the boys would move mountains just to see me smile, and with a victorious smirk, he turns his ferocious stare on Roman.

"STOP THIS NOW OR I END HER MISERABLE LIFE."

Giovanni's voice soars over the sound of the battle, and Roman's head whips around. His eyes go wide and I see his whole fucking world flashing before his eyes.

My heart breaks and without a moment of hesitation, he steps back from the army of men, drops his weapons, and falls to his knees before his father.

CHAPTER THIRTY FIVE

The battle ground turns to silence.

Giovanni's soldiers step away from the boys, panting and gasping, half of them slowly bleeding out on the ground. They quickly gather in the center of the massive circle drive, leaving Marcus and Levi wondering what the fuck is going on. They raise their gazes and the moment they see their father standing over me with a knife, barely a flick of the wrist away from taking my life, they stumble back, the worst kind of fear flashing in their eyes.

Roman's knee rests next to my hand and I stretch my fingers out, desperate for his touch and he quickly reaches down, grasping my hand in his. "You're going to be okay," he tells me.

"Now, now, Roman," Giovanni says, tsking his son. "What have I taught you about telling lies?"

Tears spill from my eyes as I remain impossibly still, taking shallow breaths to avoid pressing up against the tip of Giovanni's blade. My life is over tonight and I know it with complete certainty. This is the last time I will ever see the boys again. There's no way in hell Giovanni is going to allow us to walk away from this. He will take my life to punish the boys, and they will forever be forced to live under his rule.

Roman's heavy eyes linger on mine, and I see nothing but pained guilt and devastation. He knows it too. This is the end. I'm just another girl, in a long line of women who have been destroyed by his father.

Marcus and Levi are stripped of their weapons and shoved by the soldiers until they stand before their father, but their eyes are only for me. "On your knees," Giovanni demands, spitting each word like they're poison in his mouth.

They resist their father's demands until the soldiers kick their legs out from under them, dropping them onto the bloodied grass. Marcus groans as the soldier leans over him and nails him in the ribs, and I cry out, hearing the distinct sound of his bones breaking.

Giovanni's gaze flickers back down to me as though he'd forgotten I was here, and he looks across at one of his soldiers. "Take her," he spits.

His heavy boot comes off my chest, and I suck in a breath as the knife backs off my throat. My grip remains locked in Roman's, and I try to scurry away as Giovanni steps back to make room for the guard, but it's no use. My body is weak and the more I resist, the worse my death is going to be.

The soldier pulls me off the ground, tearing my hand out of Roman's as a pained cry pulls from deep in my chest. He drags me away, stopping only a few feet from where the brothers watch me over their father's shoulder, each one of them staring at me as though I'm their final hope.

My arms are yanked viciously behind my back to the point where I fear my shoulders will pop out of their sockets, and as I sob in pain and fear, the soldier slams his knee up into my back. His hand circles my throat and squeezes hard. "If you don't shut the fuck up, I'll slit your goddamn throat and fuck you in front of your boyfriends while you bleed out under me."

I swallow hard, not doubting for one second that he'll try it, though one of the boys will fuck him up before he gets the chance, only that will prompt Giovanni to have to punish them, and I can't fathom what else he could possibly do.

My heart breaks and I try to force the fear down, trying to be strong for them and figure out some kind of way out of here, but I'm way out of my league. We're fucked with no way out.

"What about them?" one of his soldiers questions, turning back to glance at the four cousins who look much worse for wear, though the fact that they're still alive speaks volumes. Soldiers stand at their backs, keeping them from making any kind of escape.

Giovanni's lips press into a tight line and it's clear that he's conflicted with this one. Victor was his closest brother. He confided in him, and these are his only remaining sons, but apparently that doesn't count for much in this world. "Kill them," he says, shrugging his shoulders. "Make it quick."

The cousins pull against the soldiers, grunting in agony, and before they even get a step away, they're executed like animals. Their bodies fall to the ground and a pained gasp escapes through my lips, horrified by Giovanni's cruelty. These were boys that he helped raise into men, he watched them grow, cared for them, and shared in their life as their most fearless uncle. They gave their loyalty to the brothers, but their hearts were with Giovanni, and yet he betrayed them like they were dirt under his feet.

The guards step over their fallen bodies and I tear my gaze away, unable to wrap my head around the disgusting display of betrayal. When the brothers kill, it's necessary, it's because someone has fucked up and they have a wrong to right. Sure, they do it in wild, absurd ways that get them all kinds of hot and bothered, but what they don't do is betray those who trust them. They are cruel men, but they have kind hearts, despite what they say.

Giovanni, he's something different. He cares for himself and himself alone, and he doesn't give a shit who he has to step on to get to the top. He is a vile monster with absolutely no moral compass, and I hate that I won't be offered the opportunity to tear his throat out through his ass.

Levi's eyes linger on mine and my heart breaks. A fat tear rolls down my cheek, and as it drops to my collar, his gaze hardens, darkening with desperation. He turns a furious glare to his father and I swallow hard, already hating what's next. "What do you want?" Levi spits, done with his bullshit games. "Name it and we'll fucking do it, just leave her out of this. She's already suffered enough."

Giovanni laughs, his gaze coming back to mine. "We've been here before, haven't we?" he says, his lips kicking up in a twisted smirk, referring to the night his guards pulled me out of my bed and he forced me to choose which of his sons should die. They were on their knees just like this, shock collars locked around their throats. He glances up and down the row of his sons and sings to himself. *"Eeny, meeny, miny, moe, which of my sons has got to go."*

On some level, I know he's just fucking with me, but the thought of him taking any of them to the grave has tears streaming down my face. "Fuck you," I spit, my words struggling through the soldier's tight grip on my throat as I do whatever I can to take his attention off his sons. "Where's the baby?"

"The baby?" he laughs, pulling a phone from his pocket and holding it up to the boys. "Oh, you mean this one?"

Roman's face pales and I strain against my captor's hold, unable to see the screen, but whatever it is, I know it must be bad. "I press one button on this phone, and it goes off."

Fuck no.

My heart sinks when Roman's hand cuts out toward his father, taking the knife right out of his grip, and effortlessly slicing the mens' throats at his brother's back before stepping into his father and holding the dripping blade to his throat. "Call it off," he growls, his tone so low that it vibrates right through to my chest. Levi and Marcus begin getting to their feet as Roman continues. "If you hurt one fucking hair on his head, I swear, I will make you regret it."

Giovanni stands eye to eye with his son, the blade at his throat all but forgotten as his lips pull into a wicked grin. "Stand down, Roman.

Submit to me and the child is yours."

A soft exhale pulls from Marcus as he steps in behind Roman, his hand pressing against his back. "Come on, brother. Let us live to fight another day. I'm not ready to lose this yet."

Roman doesn't budge, holding his father's gaze as he silently shakes with rage. "Roman," I whimper, swallowing hard. "Please. Give him what he wants, and your son is yours."

Roman scoffs, breaking his father's stare as he turns his broken gaze toward me. He steps back, watching me as though I have all the answers, but I've got nothing but pain and fears. There's not a damn thing I can offer to make this okay, and looking deep into his eyes now, it's clear he thinks this is a trap, but it's a risk that he has no choice but to make.

His son's life hangs in the balance and there's not a damn thing he wouldn't do to save him.

Three soldiers step in behind the brothers, dropping them to their knees before binding their wrists with tape, taking the knife out of Roman's hands, and tossing it back toward Giovanni. I clench my jaw watching my men fall from the highest pedestal, and without warning, my knees are kicked from behind and I fall into the bloodied grass.

Giovanni laughs and steps toward his sons before turning the phone in his hand. He looks down at the baby adoringly before something sinister twists across his face. He does something on his phone and then glances up to meet Roman's stare just as a booming explosion sounds in the distance, the blast lighting up the sky for only a moment.

My breath catches in my throat before an agonizing scream tears out of me, blinded by rage. Tears blur my vision, and I don't see anything, only hear the sound of Giovanni's howling laugh. I blink the tears away to find Roman breathing heavily, soldiers desperately holding the three brothers back until Giovanni throws the phone down in front of them. "Relax," Giovanni scoffs. "You make it so easy. Your brother is fine."

Roman just stares at the image of the baby, his chest rising and falling with violent gasps as Levi pulls against the soldier's hold. "Brother?" he spits. "You mean *his* son. Your grandson."

Giovanni slowly paces before them. *"Eeny, meeny, miny, moe,"* he sings, the words so low I barely hear them. A chill sails over my body and I shake my head, my heart racing a million miles an hour.

"Did I say brother?" he questions, stopping in front of Roman and meeting him dead in the eye. He leans down, smirking right at him. "That's exactly what I mean. That child you've fought so hard for, he's mine. Your little girlfriend was nothing but a cheap, used up whore."

No. No, this can't be right.

My chest sinks, my heart stopping in its tracks as I look to Roman to see nothing but devastation torn across his stunning face, his heart breaking right before my very eyes. I pull against the soldier's hold on my body, trying to push him off me. I'd give anything to run into his warm arms and tell him that everything is going to be okay, but how the hell is he ever going to go on from this, from believing all this time that he's had a son, only for him to be ripped out from under him.

Giovanni laughs to himself, pulling back as Roman pulls against his binds. "That's right, son. She was a tight little bitch with a nasty bite. Ariana couldn't give me what I wanted. She was a washed-up whore, so I took what I needed from Felicity. She was able to carry a son, one that I will raise in my image, one that will be everything you three could never be."

Fucking hell.

Pride surges across Giovanni's face as he watches his son fall to pieces at his feet.

There's no doubt that he could be lying, that he could be making this up just to fuck with Roman's head, but the pride in his tone, the joy at finally getting to tell his son what he's done is just too real. The baby really is Giovanni's son.

"Weak," Giovanni spits, looking over the three of them before turning to me. "This is what you've done to them. They were strong, fearless. They would have been gods among mere men, but you made them weak."

I shake my head, knowing just how wrong he is. "No," I tell him. "They're not weak. They're the strongest men I know, and you're just scared because you've realized that they're so much more than you will ever be, and without you, they will rise up to create an empire you could only ever dream of. You're the only weak bastard I see, and it's about time someone put a fucking bullet right through your head."

"My, oh my, Miss Moretti. You've got a nasty little mouth on you," he says. "If my sons were half as strong as you thought they were, they would have knocked that shit right out of you, brought you in line to be a good little whore, but you're wild and reckless, which is exactly why I need you."

Giovanni meets the eyes of his soldier. "Pull her to her feet."

He does exactly as he's been asked, yanking me up by the throat until my feet are firmly planted beneath me. Giovanni strides across the blood-soaked lawn, looking over me with interest. "You know, I think there's going to be a change of plans," he announces, his voice dropping low as his tongue rolls over his bottom lip. "I had hoped to marry you off to Roman to gain access to the Moretti fortune, but now that Ariana is nowhere to be seen, I think I might take you for myself."

Horror tears at me as I suck in a gasp, my eyes flicking straight to the boys to see the same disgust reflected in their eyes. Marcus shakes his head, the idea of losing me to his father tearing at his soul, while Levi clenches his jaw, looking as though he's about ready to break free of his binds and tear his father's heart out of his body with his bare hand. But Roman, he simply looks broken. His father took Ariana from him as a young man, and while that was no great loss in the end, it has still scarred him, and he always believed that Giovanni killed Felicity, the woman he wanted to marry. Learning that she was alive and pregnant this whole time, only now to realize that child wasn't his … fuck.

And now they could be losing me too.

No fucking way. I'll never let it happen.

I spit at Giovanni, hating myself for the atrocious act, but feeling it's necessary seeing as though my hands are pulled behind my back, making it impossible to gouge his eyes right out of his face. "Over my dead fucking body," I growl, watching as he retrieves a handkerchief from his pocket and wipes his face. "I would rather swim in a pool of acid and feel my eyeballs explode inside my body than become your wife."

"Careful now," he mutters darkly. "You're tempting me, but don't worry. I'll be sure to use you for everything you're worth before letting you drown in acid."

Bile rises in my throat as my chest heaves with heavy breaths. "I wonder what my mother would say if she heard this," I tell him, trying to be brave though I know he sees right through me. "In fact, her men only stormed through here this afternoon. I wouldn't put it past her to keep eyes and ears in this place."

His eyes flash with a hint of nervousness, and as his nostrils flare, he quickly pulls himself together before leaning into me. "I hope she's watching and listening to every little thing," he murmurs. "Because then she'll get to see exactly what I do to her precious daughter and hear her blood-curdling screams as I take her life from this world. Now, be a good little wifey and play a game with me."

Giovanni turns his back and strides toward his sons, his shoulders softly bouncing as though he's laughing. He reaches Roman, the furthest from me before turning to meet my stare, my stomach sinking with dread.

I slowly shake my head, knowing exactly what game he intends to play. "Tell me, wife. Which of my sons will die today?"

I don't say a word, remembering exactly what happened last time. He didn't have the balls to kill his sons, but that doesn't mean he didn't end that night with a brutal murder.

"Eeny, meeny, miny, moe," he sings almost like a chant, and then in a flash of lightning, he grips Roman's shoulder as his hand whips toward him, the long, delicate blade sparkling in the dim moonlight.

It pierces right through his stomach and a wailing scream tears out of me. The soldier holds me down as Roman's eyes widen in agony. His head whips toward me, his broken stare boring into mine as Marcus and Levi are held back by the guards.

Giovanni grins as the long blade is yanked back, sending a spray of blood across the lawn. He steps back from Roman, and the guard releases him, letting his heavy body fall to the ground and slowly bleed out.

Giovanni laughs as the screams continue to pull from deep within me, my throat burning from the piercing sound, but Giovanni is just as ruthless as his sons have always warned. He takes a step, his eyes sparkling with laughter, and without remorse, he looks me dead in the eye, grabs Marcus by the shoulder, and plunges the dripping blade deep into his stomach.

My body goes numb as Marcus lets out a pained cry, and my screaming turns into a horrendous wail. He grunts and the sound kills what little is left of my heart. "No," I whimper as Marcus' face turns a ghostly shade of white.

Levi pulls hard, fighting with everything he's got knowing what's coming next, and I cry out for all three of them.

The knife is pulled free from Marcus' stomach, creating the same sickening splash against the grass and just like Roman, he's pushed down into the hard ground to bleed out, his sad eyes pinned to mine, begging me to run.

I pull against the man at my back, my efforts weak and useless as I watch with a heavy heart. Levi's eyes are on mine, giving the soldiers hell as he tries with every last ounce of energy he has to try and free himself and get to me, but we're out of time. "Don't look," he begs me, trying to save me from my own demons. "Don't look."

A heaving sob tears from my chest as Giovanni steps up to his last son and I shake my head. "No, don't," I cry, the sound broken over the building lump in my throat. "Don't do it. You've proved your point. Let him go."

"And only do two thirds of a job?" he howls with laughter. "I hardly think so."

And just like that, the knife sinks deep into Levi's gut as the final part of my world is shattered.

Levi cries out, his head falling forward as the soldier releases him, letting his body fall into Giovanni, sinking the knife deep into his stomach. He groans, the sound sending a wave of agony soaring over me as I watch my worst nightmare come true.

Giovanni pushes back against his son's shoulder and yanks the long, thin blade out of him before dropping it into the grass and wiping his hand on his black suit. He releases Levi and I watch as he crumbles into the grass with his dying brothers, all three of their dark, obsidian eyes locked on mine, Roman looking as though he almost welcomes death.

Tears fall from my eyes, my whole world crumbling around me with absolutely no hope. Giovanni strides toward me, and I don't even bother to look up. "Come now, Miss Moretti," he tells me, stepping into me and curling his blood-stained hand around my arms. "Let's make this official. You will become my bride."

Giovanni pulls at my arm, and as the soldier releases me, I take my shot. I rip my arm out of his tight grip and race toward the boys, dropping down to my knees and grabbing at their hands, desperate to pull them up. "Come on," I cry, tugging at Marcus' hand, flicking my gaze back to Giovanni to see him coming closer. "Now. Come on. We have to go. Get up. You're not dying here. Not today."

Marcus squeezes my hand as Levi's fingers brush over my blood-soaked knee. "Run," he grunts, the words getting caught in his throat. "Run. Now."

I shake my head, not wanting to leave them here. "No," I rush out, Giovanni bearing down on me. "Not without you."

I tug on their arms, reaching for Roman but he pulls back. "LEAVE US AND FUCKING RUN."

Giovanni grips my arm, and as he yanks me up, desperation catches hold of me and my hand scoops through the grass, my fingers curling around the gold handle of the long, thin knife he used to stab all three of his sons.

I slam it up and the blade pierces through his shoulder. He cries out in agony, his grip loosening on my arm, giving me just a moment to break free. I take off at a sprint, tears staining my eyes as I run out toward the thick woods surrounding the property, soldiers racing after me.

Bullets whiz past my face and I scream out, slamming one foot down after another as bright beams of light flash toward me. I risk glancing back over my shoulder to find five black SUVs racing down the long drive with a man on a motorbike, three of the SUVs heading for me, while the other two storm toward Giovanni and his soldiers.

Gunshots ring out and my hands fly up over my head, not sure where the fuck they're coming from or who they're even aiming at.

The SUVs cut in behind me, circling me and forcing me to change direction as the move separates me from the soldiers. The black SUV speeds up, driving right alongside me, and I glance across to the driver as the window rolls down, the man on the motorbike pulling up right beside me.

Gia Moretti stares back at me through the driver's window, an automatic gun held tightly in her hand. She nods to the man on the motorbike, the wind whipping her hair all around her face. "Get on," she calls through the night, her voice barely a whisper as it gets lost in the breeze.

My head whips across to the man on the motorbike, and as he flips his visor up, I recognize the dark, mysterious man who'd kidnapped me only a few short hours ago. Before I even get a chance to ask what the fuck is going on, his arm snaps out, curling around my waist and hauling me up onto his lap.

He takes off like a rocket, shooting out in front of the SUVs, his long, dark dreadlocks flying in the wind behind him. I hold on for dear life, my body plastered to his as I stare back over his shoulder, watching Giovanni in the distance, his soldiers helping him to his feet as the two remaining SUVs back off.

He stares after us, his hand gripping his shoulder as he watches me leave, and as the motorbike hits the front gates and tears out onto the main road, I watch as he slowly turns toward his dying sons.

Three booming gunshots sound through the night and are the last thing I hear as I leave the DeAngelis family mansion for good, tears streaming down my face.

THANKS FOR READING

If you enjoyed reading this book as much as I enjoyed writing it, please leave an Amazon review to let me know.

https://www.amazon.com/dp/B09MVXT445

CONTINUE THE SERIES

MANIACS - Depraved Sinners (Book 4)
https://www.amazon.com/dp/B09R4NS8NG

It's raining, it's pouring.
My three kings I'm mourning.
Devil to wed. I think they're dead.
This phoenix will rise come morning.

They're dead.
I feel it right down in the bottom of my soul.

They were snatched away like trophies in the night and slaughtered before my very eyes.

Those three gunshots will forever ring through my mind, tormenting every waking minute of my life.

BANG! BANG! BANG!

Roman. Levi. Marcus.
The true leaders of the DeAngelis family and the rulers of my heart.

I will avenge them.
I will tear Giovanni limb from limb if that's what it takes.
All I know is that I won't stop until it's done.

Giovanni DeAngelis will die, and when he does, it'll be me who claims his throne.

STALK ME!

For more information on the Depraved Sinners series
join me online with the rest of the stalkers!!
I swear, I don't bite. Not unless you say please!

Website

Facebook Group

Facebook Page

Instagram

TikTok

Threads

Spotify

Pinterest

Bookbub

Goodreads

Newsletter

MORE BY SHERIDAN ANNE

www.amazon.com/Sheridan-Anne/e/B079TLXN6K

DARK ROMANCE STANDALONES

Pretty Monster | Haunted Love | Darkest Sin

Midnight Stage | War Games

DARK CONTEMPORARY ROMANCE SERIES - M/F

Broken Hill High | Haven Falls | Broken Hill Boys |

Aston Creek High | Rejects Paradise | Bradford Bastard

DARK CONTEMPORARY ROMANCE - RH

Boys of Winter | Depraved Sinners | Empire

NEW ADULT SPORTS ROMANCE

Kings of Denver | Denver Royalty | Rebels Advocate

CONTEMPORARY ROMANCE

Play With Fire | Until Autumn | Remember Us This Way

HOLIDAY ROMANCE

The Naughty List | Santa's Dark Secret